A PLU

SURVIV

A. AMERICAN is the national bestselling author of the Survivalist series. He has been involved in prepping and survival
communities since the early 1990s. An avid outdoorsman, he
has spent considerable time learning edible and medicinal
plants and their uses as well as primitive survival skills. He
currently resides in Florida with his wife of more than
twenty years and their three daughters. He is the author of
*Going Home, Escaping Home, Forsaking Home, and Resurrecting
Home.*

ALSO BY A. AMERICAN

SURVIVING HOME

Book 2 of the Survivalist Series

A. American

A PLUME BOOK

PLUME
Published by the Penguin Group
Penguin Group (USA), 375 Hudson Street,
New York, New York 10014, USA

USA | Canada | UK | Ireland | Australia | New Zealand | India | South Africa | China

Penguin Books Ltd, Registered Offices: 80 Strand, London WC2R 0RL, England
For more information about the Penguin Group visit penguin.com

Published by Plume, a member of Penguin Group (USA), 2013
Previously published in digital format by the author.

 REGISTERED TRADEMARK—MARCA REGISTRADA

ISBN 978-0-14-218128-7

Printed in the United States of America

SURVIVING HOME

Prologue

When it all went wrong, I was two hundred miles from home. I traveled a lot for my job, and I always had my get-home bag in my car. It wasn't that I expected things to fall apart, by nature I'm an optimist. But it always seemed to be the worst kind of irresponsibility to not be prepared. And it was that Boy Scout philosophy that saved my life.

The car quit, my phone was dead, and pretty soon I knew it wasn't just me. Everyone on the road was stuck and looking for a way home. I had known for a long time that if things ever went to shit, the average person was screwed: no power, no water, no food, no way to communicate with the government that was supposed to be running the show. And I knew that in that situation, my fellow citizens would quickly become the biggest danger. What wouldn't you do if you couldn't feed your family?

But what I wasn't prepared for was how quickly things would get bad. And in the weeks it took me to hoof it home, things got very bad indeed. The average person without food or water or hope would rob you for a meal. The average person in the same situation, but with kids to feed, might kill you.

I had thought about it a lot before the event, and I had tried to prepare. I didn't worry too much about my wife and three girls. My house was off the grid; we had food stored, solar power, and an independent water system. More important, I had good friends and neighbors. I knew people like my buddy Danny would look out for Mel and the girls. All I had to do was get home to them and everything would be fine. That's what I thought, at least.

Getting there wasn't easy. I got real lucky: I hooked up with Thad and Jess, and we looked out for each other. When I got shot, they saved my life and we were luckier still: we met Linus Mitchell—Sarge—a retired soldier, and some of his army buddies. They got me back on my feet and made it possible for Jess, Thad and I to make it home to our families.

Coming home was the single best moment of my life. Things in my neighborhood were under control, and despite that the world had gone to hell, for a little while, it seemed like it was all going to be okay. We had a cookout the night I came home, and it wasn't very different from other gatherings like we had had a hundred times before: family, friends and hope.

I know myself pretty well, and sometimes I can be kind of harsh about how people are adjusting to the world we live in now. It's a new world with new rules, and everybody has to make do for themselves. You have to make sure your family gets fed and make sure they're safe. There are too many people waiting for Uncle Sugar to fix things, people who thought at the beginning that if they just waited, things would go back to normal. But if I'm honest, the first night I got home, I wasn't too different. I thought the hard part was behind me, and I had no idea how bad things were going to get. I figured if I took care of my own, the rest would sort itself out. But I was wrong.

Chapter 1

We went to bed early after the cookout. It was nice to sleep in my own bed with my wife beside me. Ashley—mostly we called her Little Bit—wanted to sleep with us and really put up a fight, but we wanted some time to ourselves; it had been a while since we'd been together, and we were going to make up for it. Afterward, Mel was asleep and I was lying there, staring at the ceiling. In the past I would have gotten up and gone online, but those days were over. No more Internet, no more laptop, no more of a lot of things. I got up and walked out to the living room and sat down in my chair. The room was dark and silent. There was no AC running, no fan, no nothing.

Light washed over the window, and I heard an ATV heading toward the roadblock. I stood and looked out the front window as it passed by, and then the darkness and the silence returned. I sat down again in my leather chair, but soon I was up again and returned to my bed, and Mel.

Morning came and I was up before the sun. Mel was still asleep, as were the girls. I put on a pot of water to boil. I stood there for a moment taking the scene in, looking around at the kitchen, the fluorescent light glowing against the ceiling, and looking forward to coffee. The three-burner Butterfly kerosene stove is a truly wonderful piece of equipment to have. Once the burner is lit and the catalytic converter heats up, it produces no smoke and can be used indoors.

While the water was heating, I went out to the shop to look at the food stores. I was surprised at what I saw. Mel said she hadn't been very careful in the beginning, but that she had soon changed her ways and had started to conserve. It looked like the kids had put a real dent in the canned fruit. The soups and stews were hit rather hard, but there was still a lot there, and if we were careful, we could stretch it out for some time. It felt good standing there in front of those shelves, knowing it wasn't all a waste of time and money.

I grabbed a can of SPAM and headed back inside. The water was boiling and I added it to the press. I let the coffee brew for a minute, set a skillet on the burner and poured myself a cup with sugar and some powdered creamer. While the skillet heated, I added a little olive oil and sliced the SPAM. From the fridge I grabbed a few eggs and set them aside while the meat in the pan heated.

Mel came into the kitchen and said, "I smell coffee and SPAM."

"Morning, Sunshine," I said.

She went to the cabinet and returned with a cup and poured it full of coffee. She doctored her cup while I was flipping the SPAM.

"When do the girls usually get up?" I asked as I took the meat from the pan and cracked an egg into it.

"They usually sleep late, no school and all. They couldn't be happier," she said, taking a sip from the cup.

"Well, can't blame 'em. I would if I could," I said.

We sat down at the table in the kitchen and ate breakfast together. The sun was starting to come up and it looked like it would be a nice day. After another cup of coffee, I got up and headed for the bedroom.

"Really? After last night I can't believe you have the energy," she said with a smirk on her face.

I paused at the door, "I have more energy than you can imagine." I put on my Carhartt pants and my Ariat boots, something other than those damn Bellevilles I had walked two hundred miles home in. I pulled my tac vest on and draped the sling of my assault rifle over my shoulders.

Mel looked up from the cup in her hands. "Where are you going?"

"I'm going to walk up to the end of the road and talk to Danny. I just want to see how things are around here."

After strapping on the XD I headed for the door and walked down the drive toward the gate in the early dawn. The dogs, Meathead and Little Girl, came running up and jumping all over me. I knew I wouldn't be able to keep them in the yard, so I just let them follow me. We went out onto the road and turned toward the roadblock. It wasn't long before the dogs went nuts, barking and raising hell. I looked back and saw what they were barking at.

Coming down the road on her bike, like she usually did in the mornings, was Pat. "Shit," I said as I turned around and kept on toward the roadblock. I could hear her bike closing on me, and it wasn't long before she came alongside.

"Hi, Morgan, I heard you were back," she said with a forced smile.

"Yeah, finally."

"How was it? Was it hard?" she asked.

I looked over at her. "More than you can imagine."

"I bet. We haven't been anywhere since all this happened.

Neither of our cars work, so we haven't gone out," Pat said as she pedaled her bike.

We were almost to the roadblock. I just wanted her to go the hell away. "How's your family? Are your girls getting enough to eat?" she asked.

I saw what she was after. Pat was always a busybody, and now she was snooping around to figure out who had food. I just looked over at her and smiled. We reached the roadblock and I waved at Danny, who was walking toward me. He gave me a wave back and we shook hands.

"Hey, man," Danny said.

Pat rolled off to the side of the road and pretended to fiddle with the chain on her bike, just close enough to get an earful.

Reggie was at the roadblock with Danny this morning. He looked over and gave me a nod, and Pat waved at him too. He waved back without a smile. Our little neighborhood had two basic groups. There was Pat and her group, mostly old biddies and the ones where the woman of the house pretty much ran things, plus a few others that had that holier-than-thou attitude. The second was the rest of us, the ones who minded their own business but were always ready to lend a hand.

"Nah, haven't seen a soul, just like most days," Reggie said.

"Yeah, early on there were several people heading for the forest. Loaded with packs, some old trucks, some bikes and carts and shit. Then it pretty much dried up, not too many people anymore," Danny said.

"Then why keep this up?" I asked.

"Because there are still some shifty-ass folks that come through here, plus some other shit," Reggie said.

"Like what?"

Danny and Reggie shared a glance, then Danny spoke. "There have been a few girls come up missing. They disappear from their homes or when out walking around. No one knows what's happening to them, they just disappear."

I looked down. I had forgotten about the bodies—I mean, it was in my head, I just hadn't said anything about it. What with coming home and seeing everyone and the cookout we had the night before, it had slipped my mind.

"I was going to talk to you about it. I just didn't want to last night with the girls there. The last thing in the world I can imagine is one of them disappearing," Danny said.

"It's not that. I mean, it is definitely that, but on my way back, not far from here, I found the bodies of three people. One of them looked familiar, but I couldn't place the face, or what was left of it." I looked up at Danny and Reggie.

"Where?" Reggie asked, an edge to his voice.

"Sorry, Reggie. Morg, Reggie's niece has been missing for about a week. She lived over in Altoona near the Kangaroo store, and just disappeared," Danny said.

"Reggie, man, I'm sorry. I didn't know. I found them out at Baptist Lake. Two of them had been there awhile. There wasn't much left, and it was hard to tell whether they were male or female," I said.

Reggie looked me in the eye. "You stay here with Danny. I'm going to get Rick and Mark and some ATVs. Then we're going to go look for her."

"Bring someone back to man the barricade, I'm going too. Morg can ride with me," Danny said.

Reggie nodded at Danny then looked back to me. "What color was the hair, Morgan?"

I looked at Danny and he looked back with no expression. "Blonde, long, past the shoulders," I said.

Reggie's jaw tightened and he nodded his head. He went over and climbed on his ATV and took off like his ass was on fire. Pat managed to "fix" her bike a moment after and headed down the road as fast as her pudgy legs would carry her. Danny looked over at me. I shrugged my shoulders. "I didn't know," I said.

"I know, but this has had people scared. The thought that with everything else that is going on, some sick fuck is going around snatching girls has really had an effect," Danny said.

I leaned over the barricade and Danny came up beside me and rested his elbows on it. We just stood there as the sun climbed higher. He asked about my trip home and I gave him some of the details. I told him about Sarge and the guys, about Thad and Jess and what we had gone through. I told him the story of our ambush in detail, all that I remembered, anyway. I told him about Sarge's place and my trip through the forest. He laughed when I told him about the hippies.

"Man, I wish we were on the Run today, just paddling down without a care in the world," he said, staring off across the road.

"Me too, man, me too," I replied.

It wasn't too long before we heard the ATVs coming up the road. We both looked back and saw two four-wheelers and one Kawasaki Mule coming down the road. Mark was in the Mule. He and Rick, another guy from the neighborhood, had their uniforms on, Mark's sheriff's star clearly visible even at this distance. Behind them, her legs pumping up and down, was Pat. The guys came up and stopped. Reggie asked me to tell Mark and Rick what I had told him. As I relayed the story, Pat rolled up. I stopped talking as everyone turned to look at her.

Breathlessly she climbed off her bike and put the kickstand down. Mark had his son Jeremy in the Mule with him, and Lance was on the back of Rick's ATV. Jeremy and Lance would man the barricade while we were gone. Pat looked at Jeremy and told him to watch her bike while she was gone. We all looked around at one another, wondering where she was going. Without saying a word to anyone, Pat walked over and climbed into the Mule. Mark looked over at her and said, "What are you doing, Pat?"

"I'm going with you. This is serious, and we need to find out what's going on," she said as she pulled on a pair of knit gloves.

"You're right, it is, but you aren't going anywhere. Now please get out of there," Mark said.

"I most certainly will not. I have as much right here as any of you do," she said.

"I am still a deputy sheriff, and this is police business. I asked you once to leave. Now I'm telling you," Mark said.

Pat shot him a look, then one to me and Danny. "If those two are going, I can. They aren't deputies."

Rick looked over to Danny and me and said, "You two want to be deputies?"

We looked at one another and shrugged. "Sure."

"You're deputized," Rick said.

"You're not the sheriff. You can't deputize anyone," she fired back.

"Pat, I've been nice," Mark said as he and Rick moved toward her.

Sensing what was coming, Pat leaned forward and wrapped her arms around the roll bar of the Mule. Rick and Mark pried her arms off as graciously as they could. Pat was screaming like she was being eaten by a gator.

"Stop the damn screeching, Pat! You're being fucking ridiculous," Mark said.

They finally got her out of the Mule and walked her over to her bike, and Rick handcuffed her right hand to the handlebar.

"What are you doing?" Pat yelled.

Rick walked over and handed a cuff key to Lance. "When we're gone, take 'em off her. Take it off the bike first, then her wrist. I want those back." Lance nodded and pocketed the key. Pat shot him a look.

With Pat finally out of the way, Mark looked at all of us and asked, "You guys ready?"

Everyone nodded and moved toward their machines. I was headed toward Danny's Polaris when Mark called out to me, "Ride with me, Morgan, I don't know where we're going."

Mark pulled a bag from the bed of the Mule and handed everyone a radio. There were also three body bags lying there. "Where did you get these?" I asked him.

"The sheriff's office had some stuff that still worked." After he handed them out, we did a quick radio check. I climbed into the Mule and we pulled though the barricade.

I said, "Head up toward the Pittman Center and take that trail just past it, to the left. Baptist Lake is back there." He was focused on the road ahead and seemed a little tense. I asked, "Has old Pat been that big a pain in the ass the whole time? I mean, she's always been a pain, but that seemed a little over-the-top."

"Yeah, she's been trying to *coordinate* everyone to work

together. She tells everyone what to do. She wants us all to throw everything in a big pile to share," he said.

"She must be about out of food, then."

Mark looked over at me and said, "That's what I think too."

I pointed out the trail shortly after we passed the visitor center in Pittman. We all turned off the road onto the trail. It didn't take long to get back to the lake. Winters were rather dry around there, and there weren't any real wet places to negotiate. We came at the lake from the north side, and the bodies I had seen were on the south side. I told Mark about where they were and pointed in the general direction. He stopped the Mule and waved the others forward. Reggie, Rick and Danny all came up alongside.

"Rick, you and Danny go around that side. Reggie, you follow us around this side. Keep an eye out, and when you get down there, no one go running off toward the area. Let's see if we can find anything that might tell us who's doing this. We don't have a forensic team, but let's see if there's anything that might help us."

Everyone nodded and we all headed off. Reggie was trailing behind us and Mark wasn't going very fast. I glanced over my shoulder at Reggie and he just looked pissed. Looking over at Mark, I said, "Good idea having him follow behind you; he looks like he's ready to kill someone right now."

"That's why he's back there. I wanted him to go slow, otherwise he would have hauled ass down there, and if there was anything that might help he'd probably fuck it up. I sure hope this isn't his niece," Mark said.

It didn't take long to make our way around the little lake. The water was low and a large part of the bottom was exposed. As we neared the area where I'd found the bodies, I told Mark, and he stopped the Mule as Reggie came up beside us. "Why are we stopping?" Reggie asked.

"They were right over there," I answered him, pointing off toward the near side of the lake where three or four buzzards were taking to the air.

Reggie squinted his eyes and looked out over the dry lake bed. Rick and Danny had come out of the tree line a couple hundred yards to our left and stopped. We all dismounted and walked toward the bottom end of the little lake. There wasn't anything that said *Body over here!* and I couldn't really remember exactly where they were, but it wasn't a large area to search. Just a minute later, Rick found a femur. It was lying in the dirt alone, no other bones around it. Out of habit more than anything else probably, Rick took a business card from his pocket, folded it in half and set the little paper tent on the ground beside the bone.

From where we were standing, two lumps were clearly visible.

A few moments later we were standing over what was left of two of the bodies I had found just a couple days back. The one that had looked the worse for wear that day was now nothing more than bones held together by connective tissue. The one that had appeared to be freshly dumped was in pretty bad shape now; the various critters that feed on carrion had been hard at work. We stood in a semicircle around the bodies. Mark and Rick looked at the ground and the surrounding area for any sort of clue as to who had dumped them.

Reggie just stood there staring at the body with the matted blonde hair. Finally he looked over at Mark and said, "I want to check her and see if it's Christine."

Mark looked over at him and frowned. "From the condition of the body, how are you going to tell?"

"Looks like most of the back side is still there. She has a tattoo on her lower back, kind of a tribal thing with a butterfly in the middle. I want to know, now," Reggie said with a finality that Mark couldn't argue with.

Mark and Rick pulled black nitrile gloves from their pockets and put them on. Kneeling down, they turned the body over. While the animals hadn't been able to get at the back side of the body, the insects certainly had, but there was still enough of a tattoo visible to make it out. Reggie reached into his shirt pocket and pulled out a photo. It was of a blonde girl, probably eighteen or nineteen, with her shirt pulled up over her fresh tattoo. She was looking back over her shoulder at whoever took the picture with a huge smile on her face, her perfectly white teeth shining in the flash of the camera.

Reggie looked at the picture, then at the body, then at the photo. He handed the picture to Mark. "It's her. I have to take her home to her momma."

Mark took the photo and looked at it. He shook his head, looking at the once-beautiful young girl in the picture. Standing up, he handed it back to Reggie and walked over to the Mule and grabbed the body bags. "I don't see much here that would help us. We'll take the bindings and I'll make a sketch of these tire tracks; maybe they'll be handy later."

We spent about an hour collecting all the bodies. One of them was pretty scattered, and we tried to make sure we found all the bones, though I know we didn't. When we were done we loaded two bags into the Mule. Reggie insisted on taking the one with Christine in it on his four-wheeler. He laid the bag across the rear rack and strapped it with a couple of bungee cords. With the bodies loaded, we all climbed back on the various machines and headed back toward home.

When we came to our road, the four of us pulled off, but Reggie kept going toward Altoona. He didn't say anything as he passed. We pulled up to the barricade, where Lance and Jeremy were sitting. Rick went up to Lance and put his hand out. Lance dropped the cuffs into it. Rick put them on his belt then looked back at Lance. "The key too." Lance gave a sly little smile and reached into his pocket and pulled out the key, handing it over as well.

"Did she give you any trouble?" Mark asked.

"She was pissed. She cussed you for all you're worth, but no, she didn't give me any trouble. She told me I would regret it and that you had no right to lock her up like a dog," Lance said.

I stepped out of the Mule and went over to Danny's Polaris and climbed on. "Drop me off at the house," I said as my ass landed on the seat.

Danny pulled up to the front of the house. After I climbed off, he asked if I could come down to his place later and see if I could come up with some ideas to get some power going. We shook and I went up to the porch where Mel was sitting with a cup of coffee. She waved at Danny as he pulled away.

"Where'd you go? I saw all the four-wheelers go by—what's up?" she asked.

I told her about the bodies. It upset her, the thought of some sick bastard running around doing something like that,

14

at a time like this. She also worried for our girls, and I assured her that they weren't going anywhere without us, except down to Danny and Bobbie's house. There was only one way onto our street and we had decent security, so I wasn't worried about them walking down the road.

Mel asked if I wanted a cup of coffee, and I said I would love one. She went inside and came back with another cup and hers refilled. We sat on the bench drinking our coffee when the door opened and Little Bit came out. She was dragging a giant tawny-colored teddy bear, Peanut Butter. She looked so cute in her little footie PJs. Rubbing her eyes, she came over and climbed up in my lap and laid her head on the bear. It was wonderful beyond words to have that little girl in my lap, just to be sitting here with Mel and knowing all my girls were safe. After a moment she raised her little head and looked over the edge of my cup. "Can I have some coffee, Daddy? Can you move this?"

She was pointing at the AR lying my lap. I pulled the sling over my head and set the rifle aside. "Sure, baby," I said as she took the cup with her little hands.

She took a sip and hummed with pleasure. She looked up with a big smile. "It's good. Can I have the rest of it?"

This was the eternal question from her: can I have more? It didn't matter what it was, anything she had some of, she wanted the rest of. Maybe it came from having two older sisters, being the smallest: get what you can get, when you can get it. "Of course, drink it up. When you're done, go get dressed."

"Okay," she said and raised the cup again.

We sat on the porch and Little Bit finished her coffee. I tousled her long blonde hair, making her giggle. She finally finished her coffee and climbed off my lap and headed back into the house, the bear trailing behind her. Mel looked over at me and said, "You let her drink that, she's *your* problem for the rest of the day."

"No sweat. I have a lot to do today; she can follow along," I said and stood up. "I'm going to go out to the shop and check out the solar system and go through a few things."

"All right, I'm going to clean up the kitchen."

I headed out to the shop and was checking out the batteries, looking for any corrosion on the terminals, when I heard a high-pitched voice call, "Daddy?"

"In here."

Little Bit came through the door. "What'cha doin'?"

"Just checking a few things," I told her.

She helped me as I went over the batteries, cables and inverter. Then I went through the food stored there. It still looked like a lot of food, but when you thought of the fact that there was no way to run to the store, it wasn't. I was standing there looking over the stores when Little Bit asked, "What's wrong, Daddy?"

"Nothing, just looking at all the food we have." I chose the words carefully so as not to let her think I was worried; this wasn't her problem and her little mind didn't need to be troubled with it.

"Yeah, we have a lot, don't we?" she said.

"We have some." I looked down at her, she turned to look up at me. "But don't tell anyone about it, okay?" I said as I patted her head.

She leaned her head against my side, turning her face into me. "I won't. Someone might try and steal it. If anyone tries to steal it, I'll shoot them with my BB gun," she said.

"Don't go trying to shoot anyone. If you see anyone, you tell me," I told her.

"Okay, can I go get my BB gun?" she asked.

"Sure, just be careful with it." She was on her way before I even finished saying it.

After she was gone I pulled the twenty-millimeter ammo cans out from under the shelves and did a quick inventory of the ammo. I had about forty-seven hundred rounds for the AR and 1,250 for the .45s. There were also close to a thousand rounds of .22, 110 30-30 rounds and fifty twelve-gauge shells mixed between 00 buck and slugs, both high brass. I felt pretty good about the count. It wasn't an unlimited supply, but it was a substantial stockpile.

About then Little Bit came through the door with her Red Ryder in one hand, a length of 550 cord in the other. She said, "Daddy, can you put this rope on my gun so I can wear it like you do yours?"

I smiled at her and took a moment to fashion a sling for her little rifle. She stood there with a smile on her face, then put the sling over her shoulder when I was done and ran out of the shop. Going back inside, I found Taylor and Lee Ann awake. Lee Ann was standing in the kitchen looking in the fridge. "I'm hungry," she announced. "I want some eggs."

She took the bowl that had the fresh eggs in it from the fridge. "Dad, can you light the stove for me? I can't do it."

"Sure," I replied. I lit the stove and adjusted the knob for a low flame. She took a ten-inch skillet down and set it on the stove. I told her that was too big and I replaced it with an eight-inch. I showed her how to pour a little oil in the pan and keep the eggs moving so they wouldn't stick. Like any teenager, she told me, "I know," so I left her to her breakfast, telling her to clean up after herself and making sure she knew how to shut the stove off.

In short order there was a small argument over what she

and her sister thought they should make. I was in the bathroom when I heard the sliding glass door open and close. As I was coming back out of my room, Taylor came through the door again with a can of Red Feather cheddar cheese in her hand.

"What are you doing with that?" I asked her.

"I'm going to make a cheese omelet," she replied as she reached for a can opener.

I took the can from the counter. "You do not just go get what you want out of the shop. You have to ask before you get anything. We have to be careful with what we have. We only have twelve cans of this; you can't just use it for yourself. Do you two understand?"

Taylor looked dejected. "Yes, I just wanted something different."

Lee Ann was nodding her head. "I didn't want the cheese anyway," she said.

I put the can back on a shelf in the kitchen and went to find Mel. We needed to talk about the food situation.

Chapter 2

After a long day, Thad was sitting in his chair in front of a low fire in the fireplace. Anita was putting little Tony to bed. Thad looked across the room at his mother who sat in an old rocking chair, her hands folded in her lap. She had a smile on her face and was looking at Thad.

"What you smilin' at, Momma?" Thad asked.

"You, baby. You know how proud I am of you, you know how much I love you?" Then she slowly started to rock her chair.

Thad sat there looking back at her with a grin on his face. "I know. You gave me a lot of love over the years."

"I've always been proud of you. You is a good man, and don't let anyone ever tell you different," she said as she rocked.

"I tried to make you proud. It was important to me. You okay?"

"Oh, I'm fine. You came home," his mother replied and smiled.

She started to rise from the chair and Thad came over and helped her up. She said she was tired and ready for bed. Thad helped her down the hall, carrying a candle to light the way. He helped her onto the edge of her bed, where she pulled down the linens and made ready to get in. Thad set

19

the candle on the nightstand, and his mother asked him to hand her her Bible.

"You gonna be able to read with just this candle, Momma?" Thad asked.

"No, baby, I'm not gonna read. I just wants it by me is all."

Thad handed her the Bible and she swung her legs up and onto the bed. Thad helped her get the blankets arranged. After pulling the covers up, Thad leaned down and kissed her on the forehead. She placed her hands on either side of his face. "You a good man. I love you. You came home. You came home to me. And to Anita and Tony," she said with a smile.

Thad took her hands in his and squeezed them tight. "I love you too, Momma. And I have all I need now with you, Anita and Tony. If I didn't have anything else in the world, that's all that I would need."

She smiled at him. "Good night, son," she said.

She still had a smile on her face as Thad closed the door. He went out to the living room where Anita was sitting on the sofa. He sat down beside her.

"Momma seem like she actin' a little weird to you?" he asked.

"She sat on the porch looking down the road, waiting for you. She said all along that you would come home. She knew it. I knew it too, but she was so damn certain. She just seems so happy now, like she's finished something," Anita said.

Thad sat there for a minute thinking, but he said nothing more. He put his arm around Anita and pulled her close. She laid her head on his shoulder. They sat there a little longer before Thad got up and put two large logs on the fire before going to bed.

Thad woke before the sun came up, as was his habit now,

and dressed as quietly as he could. Anita stretched and sat up, sliding her feet into her slippers and reaching for her robe. They exchanged good mornings and a quick kiss as Thad headed for the living room. The fire was all but dead. There was just a slight glow coming from what was left of the bottom of one of the big logs he had put on before bed. Piling on some pine needles, he blew them into a flame and then added a small piece of lighter wood and some small sticks to get the fire going again. Giving the renewed flame time to take, he added some larger sticks. Satisfied the fire would sustain itself, he headed for the back door.

Thad pulled his coat on as he opened the door and stepped out; the cold seemed to wrap itself around him, and he quickly zipped up the coat. He walked out to the old barn to relieve himself. He had instituted this as a new rule in the house: he and little Tony would urinate outside. Hauling water into the house to flush the toilets was getting old. Little Tony thought it was fun to pee outside, and on those first times when he stood beside his father as they both did it, he would giggle and laugh. Thad couldn't help but laugh too, at the little boy finding humor in something as simple as peeing on the ground.

As he was answering the morning call he arched his shoulders against the cold. Going back inside, he found Anita at work in the kitchen on breakfast.

"Where's Momma?" he asked as he took off his coat.

"She ain't up yet."

Thad hung his coat on the hook by the door and headed down the hall. Opening his mother's door, he found her still in bed. He stood there for a minute looking at her, thinking she was asleep, but a strange feeling came over him. He went up to her and looked closer. She had her Bible on her chest with her arms crossed over it. She looked peaceful, too peaceful. Thad reached down and took her hand. It was cold, and when he felt her neck, it too was cold.

He stood there for another moment, allowing it to sink in, and then he slowly knelt down beside the bed. He wrapped his hands around hers and rested his forehead on them. She was gone. He didn't cry, but there was a hole in him now that he thought would never be filled. Slowly he laid her hand back on her Bible and stood up, and as he did he saw the dress on the foot of the bed. It hadn't been there last night. It was one of her church dresses, a simple black dress with a sewn-in white belt at the waist. A wide white collar was the only other adornment. Lying on top of it was a white hat with an upturned brim and a white net veil over it.

Thad slowly walked out to the kitchen. "Where's Tony?" he asked his wife.

"He still in bed." Then she looked up. "What's wrong, baby?" she asked as she came to him.

"Momma's gone," was all he said. Anita looked up at him and tears started to fill her eyes.

"Oh, baby, I'm so sorry. She waited for you. She knew it was coming, but she waited for you." She laid her head on his chest and sobbed quietly. Thad's mother had been as much of a mother to her as to Thad. She and Thad had met when they were in their late teens and she had practically grown up with his mother, calling her Momma all the while.

Thad quietly moved away from his wife toward the door. Anita looked up at him and asked, "Where you going?"

"Momma needs a coffin. I can't throw dirt in her face," he said, pulling the coat on for a second time.

"But where you going to get one?" she asked.

"Gotta build one, I guess." Thad stopped with his hand on the doorknob. "I hate to ask, but can you dress her?"

Anita paused a moment and then gave him a sad smile. "Sure," she said.

Thad walked out to the old barn made from rough-cut cypress log planks. He took a pry bar and hammer and began to pull the boards off the side of the barn.

Once he had what he thought was enough and had carried them to the workbench, he began to saw them into lengths, trimming the sides so they were straight. The work was slow with only hand tools, and around ten in the morning Anita came out with a cup of coffee for him. She looked at the box taking shape on the two sawhorses. She put an arm around her husband and stood there with him for a moment. Neither of them said a word. Thad looked at Anita and gave her a sad little smile, more of a crack in his face than a grin. She smiled back and nodded her head.

"It's a nice dress you laid out," she said to him.

"It *is* a nice dress, but I didn't lay it out. It was there when I went in this morning."

Anita thought about that for a moment. "She picked it out."

Thad didn't want to believe his mother knew she would pass, but then he thought of the things she had said to him the night before. He had thought they were weird then, even more so now.

Around one in the afternoon when old Mr. Jackson stopped by the house, he found Thad at work on the box.

"Sorry to hear about your mother, son," he said as he stood looking at the rough coffin taking shape.

"Thank you. I appreciate you looking out for mine while I was gone," Thad said, his hammer poised over a nail.

"That's what neighbors are fer. I'll go by an' get the

Brother. I'm sure you would like to have a little service for her," the old man said, running his hand over the rough boards.

"That would be nice. Momma would like it."

"Wood's a little rough, huh?"

"Well, it's all I got. I ain't throwing dirt in my momma's face, so this'll have ta do," Thad said, then hammered another nail in.

"Dug her grave yet?"

"Not yet. Soon as this is done I'll get to it."

"You need some help? When I get back with the Brother, I'll give you a hand."

"Thanks, but I planned on doing it alone. Little Tony wants to help, but I don't want him digging his grandma's grave."

"No different than a son diggin' his momma's grave. But I see what you mean. He is still a boy, but it's a different world now, Thad," Mr. Jackson said.

"I know. Some things I just want to keep from him a little longer. There'll be plenty of time for death yet," Thad said, picking up another nail.

"I'll be back. Y'all need anything?"

"No, sir, thanks for asking."

Mr. Jackson went back through the house to see Anita and make sure she was okay. He asked if Tony could go for a ride in the truck with him to get him out of the house for a while. Anita thought it was a good idea and allowed him to go. For Tony, a ride in anything was a rarity anymore, so he jumped at the chance.

When Thad finished the box, he took up a shovel and went to the rear of the backyard. His mother had a rosebush planted there. It had been there as long as Thad could remember, and he would bury her in front of it. Taking off his coat and hanging it on a fence post, Thad set the blade into the ground and placed his foot on it. He paused for a moment with his foot poised, saying a prayer for his mother, thanking God for her long life and for welcoming her into heaven. With that done, he thrust the blade into the ground. The dark loam gave way easily to the spade. The ground was not as hard as Thad had thought it would be, or maybe he was getting some help.

When Mr. Jackson returned with the Brother from the little Baptist church his mother attended without fail, Thad was waist-deep in a hole. The Brother and Mr. Jackson walked out to the grave and looked down at Thad.

"Sorry for your loss, Thad, but you know she is already with God," said the Brother.

"Thank you, Pastor Fish, and I know. Makes it easier."

The Brother was a black man in his fifties. He was wearing a black suit for the occasion. Taking off his coat, he unbuttoned his sleeves and rolled the cuffs up. "Step out of there, son."

Thad knew he wouldn't be able to argue with the man and did as he was told. "You go get yourself a drink. Have you had lunch today?" Pastor Fish asked.

"No, sir, but we're planning on having dinner after the service. You'll stay, won't you, and you, Mr. Jackson?"

"Thad, I am a Baptist preacher. I will not pass up a meal from one of the congregation. It's the eleventh commandment," the preacher said as he took up the spade and stepped into the hole.

Thad grinned and went to the house. Anita met him at the door with a glass of water. They talked for a moment about the dinner and that he had invited the Brother and Mr.

Jackson. She told him she'd figured they would stay and had already planned on it. The dinner would be simple: pork chops, collard greens, pinto beans and corn bread. Thad said that sounded fine to him, drained his glass, gave his wife a kiss and went back out to the gravesite.

The Brother was still there in the hole and told Thad that he and Mr. Jackson would finish the work; he needed to get cleaned up for the service. Thad turned back to the house. Anita led him to the bathroom, where he found an old washtub sitting on the toilet, steam rising from it. He looked over his shoulder at Anita, and she said, "I figured you'd need to clean up, and I didn't think them two would let you do any more work today."

When Thad finished washing, the house was empty. Looking out the kitchen window, he saw everyone outside by the grave. He had kept himself busy all day, not thinking about the fact that she was gone. Now with the coffin sitting beside the grave, the pile of fresh earth next to it, it was undeniable. As he came up to the group, Anita reached out and took one hand, little Tony the other.

Mr. Jackson took off his straw hat and the Brother opened his Bible.

"We are not here to mourn a death; we are here to celebrate a life. Beatrice was the kindest soul I ever knew, and I mean that. She never had a cross word for anyone."

Thad snickered, causing the Brother to pause and Anita to look up at him. Everyone looked at him expectantly. "'Cept my daddy when he was still with us," he said.

The Brother closed his Bible over a finger, holding it in one hand. "Well, you got me there, Thad. Let me rephrase that: she never had a cross word for anyone, 'cept Amos, when he was still with us, rest his soul. He was all the more reason the woman was a saint, to put up with him." The last part was said with the Brother's face raised toward the sky, his arms held slightly out and apart. Thad and Anita both gave a soft laugh, which changed the mood of the service— now it felt more like a celebration.

After a short sermon, it was time to lower the coffin into the grave. Thad hadn't thought of how to go about it, but was pleased to see that Mr. Jackson had. When it was time, he motioned Thad to the other side of the hole and told him to take up the ropes lying there. They each grabbed a rope in either hand and lowered the coffin.

When it was finally resting in the bottom of the grave, Pastor Fish took up the spade and a scoop of earth. He held it over the grave and said, "Ashes to ashes, dust to dust, from the earth we come, to the earth we shall return." With that he slowly shook the dirt out into the hole onto the box. When he was done he handed the shovel to Thad, and he too took up a scoop of earth. He held the shovel over the hole for a moment saying nothing. He just stood there looking down, and after a moment he slowly dumped the dark soil into the hole.

Anita took up the spade next and did as the others had, followed by Mr. Jackson. Little Tony reached down and took up a handful of dirt and dropped it into the grave. The little boy stood there for a moment looking down into the hole, then looked up at his dad and said, "Mema's in heaven now."

Thad looked down at the little boy and said, "She sure is, son. She sure is."

Anita and Tony went into the house to prepare dinner

while the men saw to the task of filling the grave. When the grave was covered, Mr. Jackson looked over at Thad. "Do you have a marker for her?"

Thad looked at the rosebush at the head of the grave. "That'll do. She tended that rosebush for years. It will live longer than any of us. I think it will make a fine marker for her."

Pastor Fish put an arm around Thad's shoulder. "I think it's a fine marker, son; no stone or piece of wood would be nearly as lovely." Thad looked at him and nodded his head with a little smile.

The men picked up their coats and headed for the house. On the back porch, they found a washtub full of water waiting on them, along with a bar of soap and hand towel. All the men washed their hands then went inside. Anita and Tony had set the table: a plate of thick chops in the center, a bowl of pinto beans and a large bowl of collard greens. Everyone took a seat and Pastor Fish said grace, thanking the Lord for a life well lived, for the continuing lives of those present and for keeping them all safe.

When the grace was said the plates were passed around the table where a chop, beans and greens were spooned onto each. Anita got up from the table and went to the stove; opening the oven, she took a cake of corn bread out and carried it over to the table. Seeing the corn bread, Mr. Jackson rose from the table, saying, "That reminds me." He went outside, returning with a paper bag under his arm. Sitting back down at the table, he pulled a quart jar of honey out of the bag. This brought a smile to everyone's face.

Talk around the dinner table was friendly, and nothing was said of death. The talk centered around fond memories and of things to come. A little fear was mixed with this. As everyone was finishing up, Pastor Fish said, "Miss Anita, thank you for a wonderful meal. I haven't had anything this good in a long time."

"It wasn't much, but thank you."

"It was lovely, Miss Anita, don't doubt it," Mr. Jackson added.

"That's why I married her; she a fine cook," Thad said as he put an arm around his wife. She shot him a look and pushed his arm off.

"Oh, really?" she said.

Thad faltered, and everyone let out a laugh. Anita smiled and Thad started to laugh too.

Chapter 3

Sarge was sitting on the deck in front of the shack. For a change he was relaxed and not cussing anyone, but that may have been because no one was around. He was leaned back in the chair with his feet up on an old cypress stump he had cut and used as a footstool or table, depending on the moment. His M4 was lying in his lap, and he was drinking coffee from one of the ridiculously stained 101st mugs.

He was sitting patiently and quietly waiting. He didn't have to wait long. From over his left shoulder came a stern command: "Do not move. Raise your hands where I can see them."

Sarge smiled and raised his cup to his lips, taking a sip of the black coffee. The voice came over his shoulder again. "I said raise your hands where I can see them or you're a dead man."

"You boys may as well come on out where I can see you before I kill all four of you," Sarge said as he lowered his cup.

A long pause followed, and Sarge just sat there with a grin. He had heard them long before they ever saw his place and had arranged a little welcoming party for them. Finally a voice he knew yelled out, "Linus, they made me bring 'em, don't kill me!" It was Don. Sarge hadn't seen him since the day he went to his store in Suwannee. Since what went down there—the gunfight with the Department of Homeland Security assholes—he hadn't even thought of him.

"All right, come on out before I kill the *three* of you, then," Sarge said, taking another sip of coffee.

After another short pause, the voice called out again. "Is Mike, Ted and Doc here?"

Sarge set his cup down on the deck. "Lay down your weapons and come on up here so we can talk like men. I'm gonna stand up now, and your hands better be empty when I do."

He stood up, flipping the safety off on his M4, and started toward the corner of the shack. Rounding the corner, he saw Don standing in front of three camoed men. They were wearing the same outfits that Mike and his crew wore, and all of them were soaking wet. "Where's all their guns, Don?" Sarge asked.

"They laid 'em all down back there," Don replied, jutting a thumb over his shoulder.

Sarge looked over Don's shoulder. "You three come on up here where I can see ya." The three men cautiously stepped forward with their hands half-raised. "You boys ain't real stealthy, are ya?" Sarge asked.

The three men looked at one another, then at Don. Don just shrugged his shoulders.

Sarge asked, "What are you guys doing here?" and lowered the M4 to waist level.

"We're looking for Mike and Ted," the one in the front of the trio answered.

"For what?" Sarge asked.

"We're friends of theirs. We need their help."

"We'll see about that. Mike, come out here and see if you know these dipshits!" Sarge called out.

Mike came out from under the deck. He had been standing in the water under the cabin, looking up through the cracks at the men as they stood there. Ted was out in the swamp, crouched behind an old cypress stump. He had zip-tied ferns to his boonie hat. That along with the camo paint on his face made him practically invisible. Doc was inside the cabin, lying under one of the cots.

As Mike came out from under the deck, he said, "Hey, Andy."

The one that had answered Sarge's questions looked down into the dark water at the camoed face looking up at him. "Mike?"

"Yep. Travis, Chris, what's up?" Mike said, wiping muddy water out of his eyes.

An hour later, Sarge stood up from the table, took off his hat and ran his hand through the gray stubble on his head. He let out a long breath and stood there with his hands on his hips. "You guys actually think this can be done?" he asked.

Don piped up. "I tole 'em they was fuckin' nuts," he said, then opened up another of Sarge's Sam Adams. Sarge glared at him, then looked back to Andy.

"It's still in the planning; we're waiting for confirmation from other unit commanders that they're on board. We can't use the usual comms, so it's going a little slow," Andy said.

"How far up does this little goat rope go?" Sarge asked.

"As far as we know, all the way to the commander in chief," Andy said.

"You realize what you're talking about is mutiny, pure and simple. Under the current circumstances, I don't think there will be any quarter for anyone involved; there's only success or death."

"Everyone involved is well aware of the circumstances," Andy said.

They discussed the details, Sarge asking questions the whole way. The plan was still in its infancy and was being developed on the fly. The gist of it was that the DHS was being used as a praetorian guard of sorts to carry out a "transformation of the country." With more than two hundred thousand people working for DHS directly and another sixty thousand working for the TSA, it was a substantial force. Granted, only a fraction were under arms, but that number was growing by the day.

Inside the Department of Defense, there were also rumors that foreign military contractors as well as domestic corporations were to be mobilized in the effort. The plan by the administration was bold, to say the least. It had a slim chance of success if everything went right, let alone amidst the eddies of chaos currently beginning to swirl across the nation. Dedicated patriots in the armed forces of the US had come to a decision early on to resist. That didn't mean that everyone in uniform was ready to defend the nation from threats within, but enough were.

"What do you need from us? You came out here, so what do you want?" Sarge asked.

Andy looked over at Mike and Ted; Doc was out on watch along with Chris. He said, "These guys are already on a termination list. DHS knows what they look like and is actively looking for them." He looked back at Sarge. "They know you're with them, but they don't really know who you are or what you look like. We need to use that to our advantage."

"Well, in the big scheme of things, we're pretty small fish, really," Sarge said.

"True, but we're responsible for the situation here in Florida. Well, my Commanding Officer is. What he wants from you guys is harassing actions. He wants you guys to conduct guerrilla assaults against them at any opportunity."

Sarge stood there for a minute thinking, taking it in. He looked at Mike and Ted. They met his eyes and nodded. "Your call, boss," Ted said. Mike gave a quick couple of nods of his head.

Sarge looked back at Andy. "Hell, I ain't even in the damn army anymore."

Andy smiled and said, "Then you can't be charged with mutiny, can you?"

Sarge laughed and said, "Not that it really matters."

Sarge asked Andy about support. If they were to conduct raids against the DHS, they would need more than a couple of carbines and one machine gun. Andy made Sarge's day when he told him that they had a care package for him. It consisted of some demo and incendiary goodies, ammo and another M249. What really brought a smile to Sarge's face was the four AT4s and the M203 and the 25 HE rounds for it.

"Well, where the hell is it?" Sarge exclaimed.

Andy said it was in the boat they had come in on and he told Chris and Travis to go bring it in. Sarge asked the others if they were hungry; he was always looking for a reason to cook.

Andy said, "Hell, Sarge, I'm in the army, I'm always hungry."

Sarge went to his little kitchen and began to whip up a lunch of fried catfish, pinto beans and corn bread. Andy looked over at Sarge in his apron and dish towel draped over his shoulder.

"Damn, Sarge, looks like you know your way around a kitchen."

Mike called out, "Yeah, he'll make someone a fine wife one of these days."

Sarge slowly turned around. Ted made for the door. Sarge thumbed open his holster and drew the 1911, the very distinct sound of the hammer rolling back sounded like thunder in the cabin.

Mike bolted upright and screamed, "Shit!" He shoved Andy ahead of him and ran like hell for the door. Ted was already outside on the deck. Doc had a "what the fuck?" look on his face as Mike and Andy nearly knocked him into the swamp. Clearing the door, Andy slammed it shut, leaning against it. His eyes were huge. "He wouldn't really shoot you, would he?" he asked.

"Probably not," Ted said, and then to Mike, "Why do you always have to wind him up like that?"

Mike grinned. "Think of it as a live-fire exercise."

Andy said, "I think DHS is gonna have more than it can handle."

"I shit you not," Mike said.

Chapter 4

I sat on the porch enjoying a cup of coffee and the quiet of early morning. I used to sleep in, and I really enjoyed it, but since getting home I couldn't seem to sleep past six. I was twirling the empty cup like a cowboy with a six-gun, one of the cups we had bought at Devils Tower, when I heard my gate rattle. I picked up the AR and walked down the steps.

Mark was walking up the drive.

"Morning, Mark, what's up?"

"Mornin', Morgan, how's it going?" he asked as he stuck out his hand.

"Pretty good, how 'bout you?"

"Good as can be expected I guess. I need a favor," he said with a dour face.

"What can I do?"

"I need your Suburban. I need to go to Tavares and see the sheriff. We need some help out here and some direction on what to do. I have a feeling things are about to go to shit in a big way," he said, his hands resting on his gun belt. He was wearing a pair of BDU pants and a sheriff's office polo shirt with an SO jacket over it, the big gold star embroidered on it.

"I'll be happy to drive you anywhere you need to go. You're the law and I'm glad you guys are out here, but I can't give you my truck," I said.

36

He didn't say anything, so I said, "If that's a problem, we can settle it right now. The law's confiscating vehicles in some of the places I been. You guys doing the same?" I unslung the carbine from my shoulder and flipped off the safety as I did.

Mark said, "Put the rifle down, Morgan. I didn't mean it that way. If you'll take me where I need to go, then that's fine. But you may be doing more running around than you plan on."

I flipped the safety on and slung the carbine. "I'm glad to help. You cover my back and I'll cover yours."

He stood there for a moment, then nodded his head, stuck out his hand and said, "Deal."

We shook hands again, and then I had to ask, "What makes you think things are about to go to shit?"

He went on to explain of the rumbling and grumblings coming from up and down the street. He had already had to get involved in a fistfight across the street from his house over a hen. Two men actually brawling in the yard over a chicken. Then there was the water issue. Without power, most folks couldn't pump water. Some of them had generators and were using them sparingly to pump water. A couple of the idiots had run their generators in the early days almost continuously and were out of gas. He had complaints about gas thefts, livestock thefts and suspicious people sneaking around at night.

"I haven't seen or heard anything," I said. I hadn't heard any of this and I was surprised, but not *too* surprised. I had seen plenty of what desperate people were capable of on my walk home.

"I need to talk to you about that too. You ain't heard none of this 'cause no one talks to you. There are a bunch of folks around here who think you got more than your fair share." He had a look of concern on his face.

"What? What the fuck do these idiots think they're going to do, try and take it?" I said.

"There's been talk," he said.

I looked at him and he just shrugged his shoulders. He told me that he had vetoed the idea, that he had told people we needed to work together and we couldn't take anything from anyone. It had to be a community effort. I told him that I wasn't going to give shit away unless I wanted to, and that no one except him and Danny had even talked to me about anything. I asked how he was doing food-wise.

"Starting to get a lil' thin at the house. That's part of the reason I want to go see the sheriff. I haven't asked for anything yet, and I want to see what they can help me out with. Anything I get, I will try and distribute fairly to as many as I can." I could tell by the look on his face it was more than "a little thin" at the house.

"Look, between you and me, and I mean that, I can help you a little," I said.

He gave me a quizzical look. "How?"

"Wait here," I told him and I went around back to my shop. Inside, I took a look at the buckets stacked against one wall. All of them were labeled on the outside in black Sharpie. I scanned the buckets and selected one from the stack. From the other side of the shop I took a package of five cans of Sam's Club canned chicken and headed back out front.

Mark was standing there when I returned. He looked at what I was carrying and asked, "What's that?"

"Well, the label on the outside pretty much tells you. In this little bucket you got ten pounds of rice, five pounds of beans and a few other goodies, plus the canned chicken here." I set the chicken down on the bucket when I finished.

He looked down at the bucket and the cans, and for a moment he didn't say anything. Then he looked up at me. "I can't take this. I mean, how much do you have?"

"You can take it. I have some, but not as much as you're thinking. Like I said before, you are the law, and I am willing to do anything I can to help you guys. But don't get the idea that I have some mountain of food back there. I don't, but I am willing to contribute to you. Take it," I replied.

Mark looked down at the bucket again. "I don't know what to say. Thanks," he said as he shook his head.

"When do you want to go to Tavares?" I asked.

"As soon as I can get Rick's ass going. We'll come down as soon as we are ready."

Mark picked up his bucket and cans and turned to walk out. After a couple of steps he stopped and looked back, shook his head, turned and started toward the gate. I went inside to find Mel in the kitchen. She was pouring herself a cup of coffee, a terrycloth robe tied tight around her waist and a pair of slippers on her feet. As she was about to take a sip of the coffee I came up behind her and wrapped my arms around her, slipping my right hand inside the robe.

"It's too early," she said taking a sip of the coffee. "Where have you been?"

"Mark came by. He wants me to take him to the sheriff's office in Tavares in a little while," I said.

"In the Suburban? I was wondering how long before people started asking us to give them rides," she said as she took another drink of her coffee.

"Yeah, well, he is the law around here. I'll help him out," I said.

Mark had parked his four-wheeler out at the gate. After closing it he put the bucket on the back and secured it with a bungee cord. He was holding the cans of chicken cradled against his chest as he backed the big Honda out onto the street. When he turned to head down the road, Pat came tooling up on her bike. He wasn't interested in wasting time with her, so he gave her a nod and headed down the road. All the while her eyes were glued to the cans in his arm and the bucket on the rear, the Sharpie writing clearly visible to her.

Mark and Rick came back about eight thirty. I had loaded the truck with some bottled water, some MREs and a first aid kit. I also threw some tools in the back. I was laying a come-along in the back when the guys pulled up on their ATVs. Mark looked into the rear of the old Chevy and asked, "What's all this for?"

"You guys haven't been out much since all this happened, have you?" I asked in return.

"The sheriff's office brought us home in a Humvee not long after, but no, not since then," Rick answered.

"I had a nice long walk to see how things are going. So forgive me if I am a little paranoid," I said.

"Whatever floats your boat," Mark said.

I went in the house and came out with a Mystery Ranch three-day assault pack, kissed Mel good-bye and told her I'd be back when I got back. As I was heading for the door, Taylor came running up and said, "Can I come, Dad?" She always wanted to come along, didn't matter where I was going. Kinda cool actually that my sixteen-year-old daughter wanted to hang out with me, but this wasn't a trip for her.

"Sorry, kiddo, not this time. We need to see how things

are going before I take you guys out," I said to her. She looked dejected, but she understood.

Back outside, Mark was in the passenger seat and Rick was in the back. I started up the old Suburban and put all the windows down, even the rear glass; if we need to shoot at anyone, I really didn't want to take out any glass. Mark had an AR and Rick had a Remington 870. Both of them wore the same uniform: tactical pants and SO polo shirt and coat. Looking over at Mark, I said, "Here goes nothing." He nodded and we headed out the drive. I stopped at the gate and Rick closed it, much to the disappointment of Meathead, who thought he was going for a ride.

I got around the roadblock and we waved to the two guys manning it. They waved back and I hung a left onto Highway 19, heading south. Having been on the barricade on our street several times, I was well aware of the level of traffic on the road. Lots of folks on foot, bikes, lawn tractors, big tractors, and my personal favorite, go-carts. Someone in the area was doing a booming business in old go-carts. There was the typical number of ATVs and dirt bikes. Passing through Altoona, the parking lot of the Kangaroo store was full of people. It had become a sort of market. If you had something to trade or needed something, it was the place you came to.

Passing through Umatilla, I noticed that the feed store was still doing a pretty good business, with a heavy security presence. I saw at least five men with long guns, one on the roof with a scoped rifle. It looked as though Howard, of Howard's Feed, wasn't taking any chances. At the intersection of highways 19 and 450, there was an Umatilla PD cop that waved me to a stop, using his shotgun to get the point across. I looked over at Mark, who said, "What a fucktard."

There was no real respect for the Umatilla PD. Several little scandals in the recent past had almost resulted in the disbanding of the department.

"I'll take care of this," Mark said.

Pat was pumping her legs for all they were worth. She knew what she had seen, and by God she was going to do something about it. If the sheriff's department had food to hand out, then she was going to get her fair share. *That damn Mark thinks he's all high and mighty now that things have gone to hell*, she thought. She was going to show him just how wrong he was. And that Morgan, she never liked that smartass anyway. Smartass and a hoarder to boot.

As I pulled up to the Umatilla officer, he lowered his shotgun a bit but still had it ready to bring up. He stepped up to my door and, seeing all the hardware in the truck, he jumped back and raised the shotgun again. "Let me see your hands, all of you!" he shouted.

"Dumbass," Mark said as he pulled his wallet out and flipped it open. He stuck the badge contained in it out in front of me so the officer could see it.

The officer lowered his riot gun. "Sorry, deputy, I didn't see you."

Mark got out and walked around to my side of the Suburban. He recognized the officer as the officer recognized him. "How's it going, Walt?" Mark said.

"Oh, pretty good. You know we're supposed to confiscate running vehicles?" Walt said.

Mark just looked over his shoulder. "Well, I beat you to this one."

Walt looked at the truck, then at me. "He one of yours, why ain't he in uniform?"

"You let me worry about him. We'll be on our way now. I have to go see the sheriff," Mark said.

"Oh, okay. Hey, if you get any news from up there, stop by and let me in on it, would ya?" Walt asked Mark as he headed around to the passenger side.

Mark winked at him and with a little nod added, "Count on it."

Once he was back in, we took off again. He wasn't impressed with the UPD, and as far as Mark was concerned, any info we got from the SO was privy to members of the department only. If someone wanted the UPD to know about it, then someone else could tell them.

We continued down 19 headed toward Eustis. I was interested in seeing what the guard armory there was up to. As 19 approaches Eustis city limits, the road splits into two one-way sections separated by about a block. We were on the southbound side heading into town. Right before the split, there is a lake on one side and a canal running to Lake Eustis on the other. It was a perfect bottleneck and the Eustis PD and the guard were using it to full effect.

We were waved to a stop at the business end of several weapons. There were two Humvees, one on either side of the road. The one on the east side had an MK19 mounted on it; the other had a Ma Deuce mounted on the turret. Mark opened the door and started to step out and he was greeted with a chorus of shouts and commands. With one leg on the ground and the other still inside, he opened his jacket to show the embroidered star on his shirt and shouted, "I'm with the sheriff's department!"

A couple of guys in full battle dress cautiously approached, weapons shouldered and at the ready. As they got closer, one of them shouted, "Everyone out! Hands where we can see 'em!"

Mark looked over at me and said, "Move slow." I nodded and opened my door.

Mark continued to step out with his hands up. I followed suit, as did Rick. One of the two men approaching us called out over his shoulder, "Weapons!"

We were ordered in no uncertain terms not to move a muscle or we would be shot. I looked over at Mark and said, "What the fuck did you get me into?" He just looked over at me.

As the two guys got close enough, Mark said again, "I'm a sergeant with the SO."

The one on his side of the truck asked for his ID, which he produced, then they asked for Rick's, which he produced, then they asked for mine, at which I handed him my driver's license. The guy took it and looked at it for a minute, then asked for my department ID.

"I don't have one," I replied.

"Only law enforcement is supposed to be armed. No civilians are to be armed. Keep your hands up," he said as if he were reciting it from a script.

Mark looked over and said that I had been deputized after things went to shit. This confused the two for a moment until a voice from behind them called out, "Hey, Morgan!"

I looked past him to see my friend Vance walking up. He looked so out of place amidst all the hardware around us. He was wearing a revolver in a nice leather holster and carrying a lever gun with a matching bandolier for the ammo for it.

He walked right up to me, past the guardsmen standing in front of me, and stuck out his hand. The guardsmen stepped aside and we shook.

"Holy shit, Vance, how the hell are ya?" I said.

"Doing all right," he said.

With his appearance, the tension died down somewhat. We walked up to the roadblock as we talked. I asked what he was doing in town as his place was a pretty good ways out. He told me that they had come to the Eustis PD, where his wife, Jenny, worked. They had run out of fuel for their generator, and water was an issue. Since the PD was right beside the armory, they figured it would be a better place to be. Turned out for him, he was right. The guard and the PD were working together to keep things peaceful in town and so far it was working out.

He asked how my family and I were and I gave him the CliffsNotes version of what had happened to me. He was a good friend and I was glad to know he was all right, not to mention that he was in with the guard unit here. He told me the guard muster had been less than 50 percent, but they were straggling in, usually after all their supplies at home ran out. Then they showed up with all their families and friends. The guard was only allowing immediate family into the armory and that had caused a little trouble but was being dealt with as it came up.

Mark and Rick went off to get with PD to see what was up while Vance and I talked. The Suburban was left sitting right where we had exited it. I asked about his kids and wife, and all were well. Then I asked about his livestock. He had quite the little farm going. He just laughed and said, "Follow me." We went around behind the armory to find a pen where his goats and pigs were, and even a chicken coop. He had managed to talk the guard into using one of their trucks to go out to his place and get everything. He had walked in by himself the first day, going to the PD to talk to them about some help. This was before the declaration of martial law. Now they had the protection of heavy firepower and a pretty good law enforcement presence.

Mark and Rick came down the sidewalk and said we needed to get moving. Vance and I said our good-byes with promises to try to get together later. Back in the Suburban, we were allowed to pass and continued on through town. It didn't take long to get to the SO. There was a significant security presence there too, but this time we didn't have any trouble.

Mark told me to stay with the truck and that they would be back as soon as possible. I asked him what they were going to do in there. He said he wanted to know what was going on, what the sheriff wanted him to do and if the SO could help out in any way. As the two of them headed into the offices, I went to the back of the truck and dropped the gate. Sitting down, I pulled out a canteen and took a drink and waited. There was a lot of activity. I saw some guys working on a couple of the newer Rhino ATVs and walked over to see what they were doing.

They told me they were trying to find a way to get it to run. The older versions ran fine, but they couldn't get the newer ones to, and they had a bunch of them. They were trying to find ways to remove or bypass all the electronics, but so far they weren't having any luck. Another one was being eviscerated, its engine and all the internal parts scattered all around it as they tried to install a different engine. I walked back to the truck as Rick came up.

"Let's go," he said as he climbed in.

"Where to?" I asked.

He guided me around to the back of the sheriff's department, where Mark was waiting. There was a stack of stuff beside him. We started loading it all up: MREs, bottled water, lifeboat-style ration bars and what I assumed to be some ammo from the weight of the boxes. There were also cases marked HUMANITARIAN AID in big letters. After we loaded all the stuff, it filled the entire rear of the Suburban as well as the rest of the back seat beside Rick.

Mark climbed into the passenger seat with a box in his lap. I asked what was in it, and he just looked over at me and wiggled his eyebrows and smiled. "Goodies," he said.

We didn't talk much on the way. Mark said he wanted to get some people together and have a meeting when we got back. It didn't take long to get there. I was genuinely surprised at the overall calm of the area; there wasn't the kind of trouble I had run across on my way home. I actually started to relax a little, and then we got back to our road. As we pulled off onto our little dirt road, the two guys at the barricade started to wave frantically at us.

Chapter 5

After dinner was done and all the guests had left, Thad settled down in his chair with Tony in his lap. Anita was on the couch and a fire burned in the fireplace. The only sound in the room was the old manual wind-up clock on the wall with its rhythmic click, clock, click, clock. Thad sat there with his son in his lap, his mind elsewhere. Anita looked over at him in time to see a tear run down his cheek. She got up and picked up the sleeping Tony and took him to bed. Once Tony was tucked in, Anita stopped in the hallway to the living room. Leaning against the corner, she looked out at her husband before she turned and went to their bedroom. Thad sat there, just staring into the fire.

In the morning, Anita found him on the couch, the quilt that was usually draped over the back of it pulled up around him. She went back to the bedroom and came out with the comforter off the bed and put it over him. Going into the kitchen, she started breakfast. She stoked a fire in the old stove, went outside to the back porch and took the slab of bacon kept in a cooler out there. While the weather was still cool, this worked fine, but when the seasons changed, it would be a useless way to keep their meat. While she was out there, she also grabbed a large piece of salt pork and brought it in.

With the stove heating, she set a skillet out, then a large

old pot. After laying the sliced bacon in the pan, she went outside and used the old pitcher pump to fill a bucket and carried it into the kitchen. Anita poured the beans into a pot and covered them with water, then dropped the piece of salt pork in, set the lid on and put it on the stove. Thad woke up as the bacon aroma started to fill the house.

They talked of the future over breakfast. Their food stores were running low and Anita wanted to know what they were going to do; as a mother and wife, she was afraid. Thad told her he just didn't know, and that he was going to go and see Mr. Jackson later that day and see what the two of them could come up with. Thad walked over to the sink and looked out the window into the backyard. There was frost on the ground and on the mound of earth that covered his mother.

Mr. Jackson had an old place in what was now the Big Cypress Swamp. His place there had been allowed to remain even though it was in what was now a state park. He kept a pigpen with around forty hogs in it, plus a real nice flock of chickens. In addition to the hogs and birds, he kept a couple of cows and had one bull. With the bull he was able to get one or two calves a year, plus he was able to milk the cows and keep some milk and farmer's cheese around.

Thad helped Mr. Jackson muck out the pigpen. It was cold, nasty work, but it needed to be done. Afterward, Thad cleaned out the coop while Mr. Jackson tossed some hay to the cows, leading one into the barn to milk her. He used a funnel to pour an old soda bottle full of milk.

"Here, Thad, take this home to your boy. Growin' boys need milk," Mr. Jackson said as he handed Thad the bottle.

"Thank ya, sir. I jus' don't know what we are going to do. Food's gonna run out soon," Thad said.

"Don't worry. You come around and help me from time to time and I'll keep y'all in groceries." As he said it, Mr. Jackson moved to a door in the kitchen, opening it. It was a pantry about eight feet long and four feet wide with shelves from top to bottom. The shelves were stacked with jars of home-canned food. Mr. Jackson pointed into the pantry and said, "Mary used to put up everything we didn't eat right away. I growed it and she canned it. I can still grow it; maybe you and Anita can help can it."

Thad stood there looking into the pantry. His eyes were wide. The old man went in and started putting cans into a cardboard box. Going over to the sink, he took down a piece of cheesecloth that was hanging from a cabinet knob and dropped it into the box. Thad took the box and the milk out to the truck and sat them on the seat. Mr. Jackson came out and set a bag into the bed of the truck.

"Thanks for the food, Mr. Jackson. I'll be back in a couple of days to help out. If you need something in the meantime, just come by," Thad said.

"Thanks for all the help, Thad, an I'll do it if'n I need anything. Next time you come by, bring your axe; we need to split some wood. We'll work together and you can take some home with you," the old man said, slapping the cab of the truck.

Thad went home with the load of food and Anita was thrilled beyond words. The sack the old man had put in the truck was full of cornmeal. Anita would be able to keep them in corn bread for a while. Tony got excited when he saw a jar of strawberry preserves. Since things had fallen apart, sweets had been hard come by, probably what it had been like two hundred years before. Dinner that night was rice with stewed tomatoes, the pinto beans started that morning and, of course, corn bread. It wasn't exactly gourmet dining, but a full meal these days was a kind of celebration no matter what ended up on the table.

Thad spent the next day at home with Tony, playing Battleship. They lay on the living room floor in front of the fireplace while Anita sat on the couch crocheting a sweater. It was one of the happiest days Thad could remember, even though Tony beat him more often than not. Anita came out with a special treat for the boys at lunchtime. Since she had the milk and rice, she made them some rice pudding. She served it hot to them with some cinnamon on top, and Tony licked the pot clean.

The next morning, Thad got up early to go help Mr. Jackson. He lit a candle and found his way into the kitchen, where he cut a piece of corn bread from the cake pan covered with a dishtowel. Jamming a piece of ham into it, he ate it as he was heading for the door. Little Tony came out of the hall rubbing his eyes and said, "Daddy, kin I come an' help?"

Thad said, "Not this time, little man. I'll be bringing a load of firewood home today and you need to stack that mess in the barn to make room. Can you do that for me?"

"Yes, sir," he answered, then yawned.

"Then go on back to bed. After your breakfast, you get started on that woodpile," Thad said and pulled on his coat.

Little Tony turned and padded back down the hall to his room. As was now Thad's habit, he picked up the double barrel, the Glock already on his belt, and headed out the door. The old truck was still running, and he had gotten a little gas from old man Jackson. Thad climbed into the truck and headed down to the farm. It was only a short drive and the heater was only just warming the cab when he pulled up. Looking up the drive to the old house, Thad thought he saw someone in the yard, just a fleeting glimpse. But these days a glimpse was enough for him to shut the truck down and walk up the long drive to the house.

Walking as quietly as he could, he kept his eyes fixed on the house. When the front of the house came into view, he stepped behind an old pine tree. Sitting in front of the house was an old Scout International. Thad saw a man come out with an armload of boxes and put them in the back of the Scout. He could hear talking inside the house, but not the old man's voice. After the man went back into the house, Thad made a quick dash to the back of the Scout. Looking in, he saw boxes full of the preserves from the pantry, as well as guns and other items he recognized as Mr. Jackson's. The bed of the old man's truck was likewise being filled with Mr. Jackson's things.

As Thad stood there looking into bed of the truck, he heard a voice scream, "Daddy!" Thad looked up to see a girl of fourteen or fifteen standing in the doorway holding a box. He looked at the girl, both of them frozen. A man appeared behind the girl, raised a pistol and fired a shot at Thad that hit the bed of the truck, a piece of the bullet entering Thad's left arm at his elbow. Thad dropped to the ground; he could hear the heavy sound of boots coming closer.

Thad rolled to his side and looked under the truck. The man and the girl were running toward the truck, and they were close. Thad stuck the old sawed-off under the truck and fired into their legs, both barrels. He heard screams and quickly reloaded the shotgun. He could see the man on the ground. He was holding his legs and screaming through gritted teeth. The girl likewise was holding what appeared to be a compound fracture of her lower left leg. A moment later he saw another set of legs appear in the doorway of the house, then heard a scream, and these legs ran toward the truck.

The woman fell to her knees between the man and the girl. Thad could see her hands and they were empty, so he stood up, shotgun raised. The woman looked up at him, tears in her eyes. Thad moved around the back of the truck and the woman began cursing him. The man reached for the pistol he had been carrying.

"Don't do it!" Thad shouted, and the woman leapt for the weapon. Thad fired and she fell face-first in the dirt. The girl let out a scream and the man tried for the pistol again. Thad fired the second barrel into him and he never moved again. He quickly drew his Glock and approached the three, picking up the pistol from the ground. Seeing the girl was in no condition to do anything, he went past her into the house. Thad found the old man in the living room. Kneeling down beside him, he raised the old man's head from the floor. He was still breathing, but blood was coming out of his mouth and nose.

"You hang on now, I'm gonna get you some help," Thad said through clenched teeth.

The old man raised a weak hand and put in on Thad's arm and shook his head. "No. I'm gonna die, Thad, an' I don't want to be alone. Stay here with me."

Thad sat there holding the old man in his lap. Mr. Jackson told him how the girl had come to the door asking for help. She looked hungry and afraid, so he had brought her in. As soon as he closed the door and turned around, she shot him twice. Both bullets entered his chest and he knew right then he was a dead man. He lay there and played dead, praying to God that Thad would come, not to help him but to avenge him. Thad told him that the man and woman were already dead, and the girl had some serious wounds.

Between coughs and in a raspy voice the old man said, "I've always been a Christian man, an' I've made peace with my maker, but do me a favor, Thad."

With tears in his eyes, Thad replied, "Anything, Mr. Jackson."

"Go outside and kill that bitch before I die. I want 'em all dead before I die," the old man said through clenched teeth.

Thad looked down at him, gently laid his head on the floor and stood up. Walking outside, he found the girl where he had left her. She was lying in a fetal position, crying. Thad walked up to her and shouted, "Why?"

The shout startled her and she looked up at him. Again he shouted at her: "Why?"

"We're starving. We needed food, and he had so much," she cried out.

"That old man would have given you anything you wanted. He didn't need to die," he said. "But you do."

The look of horror on her face lasted only a moment. Thad pulled the trigger and she was gone. Thad went back in the house. The old man was still alive. Thad knelt down beside him and said, "It's done."

A hint of a smile cut across the old man's lips. "You bring your family here; this place is yours now. You know how to take care of things. It'll keep you going." His eyes closed and he was gone.

Chapter 6

Andy and his boys left soon after lunch. They had handed over the party favors they told Sarge about and Ted was busy storing them away. Sarge was sitting at the table in the cabin looking at Don. He said, "What the fuck am I supposed to do with your ass?" Don was sitting across the table from him, sucking on the bones of a catfish, his hands covered in grease up to his wrists.

Don looked up at him and said, "I can't go back after what y'all did; they'll kill me for sure."

Sarge sat there looking at the fat man as he licked the grease off his fingers. He hadn't really known him much more than their conversations over the counter of the hardware store, and after Sarge and the guys had shot some DHS goons there, Don was a wanted man. Still, all he could think was that Don was a nasty bastard. His face was covered in grease and he had eaten more than anyone else. Don leaned back in his chair, wiping his face with a dish towel.

"Them was some fine vittles, Linus," he looked around the little cabin and said, "Say, you got any more beer around here?"

"Mike!" Sarge yelled.

"Out here, boss."

"Meet me out front, now," Sarge bellowed as he headed

out the door. Don just sat there sucking his teeth and picking at them with a bone.

Sarge almost ran into Mike when he came out the door. "What's up, boss?" Mike asked, seeing the look on the old first sergeant's face.

"I want that fatass out of here now," Sarge said as he spit into the tea-colored water of the swamp.

"Where do you want me to take him to? He knows where we are. Hell, he led Andy and his team right to us."

Sarge pondered the situation for a moment. "We can't just tell him to leave. The first time he gets hungry he'll lead whoever he finds right to us. We have to find a new place. This joint is hotter'n hell full of lawyers."

"Where we gonna go? From what Andy said, they're looking for us now," Mike said.

"Well, I figure they've had enough time to trash my place, probably been all through it. You an' me'll take a ride up there, set up on the other side of the river and watch it for a few days, see if anyone comes around."

"You gotta be fucking nuts. Go back to your house? That'll be the first place they'll be looking," Mike said.

"No, that's the last place they would expect us, and I don't want to move back into my house, dumbass, there's something there I want to get. They probably didn't mess with it because it looks like junk, but it ain't," Sarge said.

"What? We took everything worth taking."

"My old truck. It was under that cover in front of the shed out back. If they looked at it, it looks like an old junker, but it runs like a scalded dog. I had the starter took off and no plugs in it, but they're there. If we can get it, then we'll have wheels as well as a boat."

"Sounds like an awful big risk to me."

"What the hell you want to do, sit around here till they shove a Hellfire up our ass? They *will* find us, so we gotta move."

"What about Don?" Mike asked.

"We'll leave his ass here. There's enough food and stuff to keep him going. I ain't real worried about him, I'm worried about us."

The two guys manning the roadblock when we left were still there. They were two of the neighbors I'd see on the road, the kind I'd wave to all the time but never actually met. When we pulled up, one of the guys ran to the passenger side of the truck. Mark put down his window and said, "What's up, Billy?"

Billy's eyes were wide and he was half out of breath. "Mark, man, am I glad you're back. You need to get home fast, like now, go!"

"What's up?" Mark asked with a look of confusion.

"There's trouble at your house, go, go, go!" Billy said, backing away from the truck.

I didn't wait to hear any more. I took off down the road toward Mark's house. As his house came into view, we could see a crowd of people in front, and his wife (who I barely knew at all) was standing in the front door with a shotgun leveled at the people in her yard. She was shouting at someone in the front of the group. Some in the group heard the truck coming down the road and turned to look as I swung it through his gate. The truck hadn't even stopped when Mark jumped out, AR up and at the ready.

The crowd parted as he ran toward them. Rick was hot on his heels and both of them were screaming. I stepped out of the truck and stood beside it, waiting to see what was going to unfold. Most of the people did as they were told and moved out of the way of the two deputies as they ran forward, except for three. At the front of the crowd was Pat, with her husband and son. The two men both held rifles pointed at Mark's wife, who had scratches on her face and a bruise beginning under one eye. As Mark came running up, Pat turned to meet him. She looked like a wild animal. Her hair was sticking out all over, the hair bands doing shit to hold it together, her face was red and she was dirty. It was clear she and Mark's wife had been at each other.

Pat's eyes grew wide at Mark's approach. He was running for all he was worth. Without saying a word, he slammed the butt of the AR down onto the back of the husband's head, and before the son could react, Rick did likewise to him. Both men landed on the ground in a heap. Rick leaned down to grab their weapons, and when he did, Pat jumped on his back, screaming like a banshee. She wasn't there long, however; Rick brought his right elbow around and caught her in the jaw, knocking her out cold. She fell straight back onto the ground.

Some in the crowd started to shout and they closed in. Mark was trying to talk to his wife while keeping an eye on the crowd. She was shouting at him, and he back over his shoulder at her. With all the commotion, other folks from our little neighborhood were running up to see what was going on. It was getting out of hand damn fast. It wasn't long before Pat was on her feet, screeching at Mark. She was accusing him of hoarding food that the county was providing and not giving it out. He said he didn't know what she was talking about, to which she replied that she had seen the food this morning on his four-wheeler. What happened next wasn't really his fault, it was just reaction. He screamed back at her that I had given him the food, not the other way around.

This brought the argument to a halt. The group just looked at Mark, and he back at them. Then one of them turned and looked at me and the truck. Trying to bring down the tension, Mark then said we had picked up food today and everyone would get some. That's when they all turned. First one of them broke into a run, then the rest of them, all straight toward me.

At first I just stood there dumbfounded. Their mouths were agape, eyes wild, people that lived down the road from me looking at me like wild animals. My stupor didn't last long though, and I brought my rifle over the hood and flipped off the safety. A shot rang out. Everyone, including me, instinctively ducked, some diving for the ground. Two more shots quickly followed, and this stopped the stampede entirely.

"That's fucking enough!" Mark yelled, his rifle resting on the top of his shoulder pointing straight up. The crowd turned.

"What the hell is wrong with you people? I just told you we had food to distribute, and you think you're going to run over there and take it?" Mark screamed at the top of his lungs. His eyes now had a wild look too. His mouth was open, the corners pulled down, exposing his teeth.

"Any one of you try and take anything from that truck will be shot, do you understand me? I am the law here. The sheriff gave me the authority today to deal with things as I see fit, and I will be the final say, got it?"

Pat was sitting on the ground alongside her husband and son, but it didn't stop her mouth. "Oh, you're the law now, huh? You decide who gets what? What are you going to do, start shooting people?" Her husband, Leland, struggled to his feet. Rick stepped up behind him.

"I ain't going anywhere, *dip*uty," he sneered.

An ATV sounded behind me and Danny came riding up, his M4 over his shoulder.

"What the hell's going on?" he asked as he shut down the machine.

"Mark told them we got food from the county today, and they thought they would rush the truck and take it," I said, still lying over the hood with the rifle pointed at the crowd.

Leland said, "You folks know me, we're friends with almost all of you." He looked in my direction and continued. "All of you worth a damn, that is. If there's food around here, it needs to be shared out evenly amongst everyone here. Why in the hell do we need to take orders from some shithead with a tin star?"

The crowd muttered and looked at Mark and then at me.

Mark said, "Because I am the law around here. There *is* no more 911. No one is coming to help you out except Rick and me, that's it."

Leland shouted, "There ain't no more law!"

"You stupid fucking redneck, even if you took the food in that truck, where do you think you will get any more when it's gone? Can you go to Tavares and get more?" Mark asked.

"I ain't worried about that. I'm worried about what's in that truck, and who's gonna get it. I know you have your favorites around here," Leland spit, looking over at Danny and me.

"What in the hell did I ever do to those people?" I asked Danny.

"I don't know, I ain't never had any trouble out of them. Bobbie and Pat talk all the time," Danny said.

Leland said, "There's more of us than there are of them! He thinks he's going to run herd on us, tell us what to do, who gets what and when, but I ain't gonna be beholden to no man!"

The people in the yard began muttering again, but it seemed they were divided. Leland's son, Randal, finally got to his feet, standing behind his father. Randal had been in trouble with the law his whole life: drunken fights, theft, maybe even dealing drugs, but he had never been picked up for that. No one much cared for him, but his parents had always been happy to make excuses for him. To them, the law had it out for Randal and always had. Nothing was ever their fault, and someone was always keeping them from getting what they deserved.

"I guarantee you one thing, you will look over your shoulder for the rest of your days. You and anyone with you," Leland said.

I looked over at Danny and said, "I've had enough of this shit." I slung my AR and started walking toward Mark. That was a risk, but it looked like the crowd had calmed down, and I didn't want to get them riled up again. I was hoping Mark would take control of the situation, but he looked unsure of what his next move was.

Mark was stuck in the old days; he was a lawman. He was used to arresting people who got out of line and taking them to jail and let the judicial system sort them out. He just wasn't coming to terms with the new reality. I walked up to Mark, Leland giving me the mean mug the whole time.

"What are you going to do with these guys?" I asked Mark.

He looked at me for a moment and said, "I don't know."

"You going to take them to Tavares and put 'em in the jail?" I asked.

"You ain't taking us no-fucking-where!" Randal shouted and he started to move toward me, but a tug on his collar by Rick brought him back in line.

Mark said, "You know as well as I do there's no way to lock people up. Who's gonna watch them? We're stretched thin as it is."

"I hear you," I said.

Randal surged forward again and when Rick grabbed at him, he slapped his hand away, but he stopped short of charging me.

"What are you going to do? Really. I'm curious," I said to Randal.

Randal was just like the troglodytes that had spawned him; his mouth worked faster than his brain. "I'm gonna fucking kill you!"

From where she was sitting on the ground, Pat spoke up, "You think you're some big shit, Morgan. Just 'cause you got power and water. You won't share it with no one, and now we all know you have food too. All those girls of yours don't look hungry." She looked back at the crowd. "His kids aren't hungry, are yours?"

I shook my head and looked at the crowd. "So you people are ready to take what you think I have, is that it?"

"We're all hungry! We're having to get water out of the damn pond!" someone from the crowd shouted out.

"Have any one of you people ever come to me to ask for water?"

All I got was blank stares in return, so I continued. "Has anyone here asked me for anything? I know Pat thinks I'm sitting on some mountain of food, but I'm not, and even if I were, it's mine. I bought and paid for everything I have. You people could have bought food for your families. Your situation isn't my fault. So what's going to happen? Are you going to come to my house and threaten my family like you did here? Which one of you is going to shoot *my* wife?" I pointed at a man in the crowd. "You?"

The man looked away.

"We'll deal with you soon enough," Pat said from where she sat slumped on the ground.

"Damn straight," Leland added.

I looked at Mark and asked him again, "What are you going to do with these people?"

Again, he just looked back at me. "I don't know."

"So you're gonna kill me?" I asked Leland and Randal.

Leland glared at me. "Damn straight, asshole," he replied.

"Big talk," I said.

Leland lunged for me. I stepped back and kicked him in the nuts as hard as I could. He dropped to his knees with a groan. Randal bolted for me next. I drew the XD and brought it up level with his face and pulled the trigger. The round went into his left eye and blasted out the back of his head. As his body hit the ground, Pat began to shriek. Leland looked at the body of his son lying in the dirt, dark red blood oozing from the crater in his head. When he looked back toward me, the muzzle was already lowered at him. I pulled the trigger again and he collapsed. Mark rushed over and grabbed my arm. Rick was standing there with a look of shock on his face.

"What in the hell are you doing?" Mark screamed into my face.

"What you should have. I'm not spending the rest of my

life looking over my shoulder. They clearly stated they would kill me, and they threatened my family. Everyone heard it. Now it's over," I yelled back at him and jerked my arm from his grip.

Pat screeched and tried to tackle me. I jerked away and looked down at her, then looked at Mark. I was looking right into his eyes and there wasn't anything there, really: no malice, no approval, nothing. I raised the muzzle slightly and shot Pat in the top of the head.

Looking back up at Mark, I wasn't sure what to expect. He stared back at me. The lights were on, but no one was home. I looked over at Rick, and he was still standing there slack-jawed, so I turned back to the crowd gathered behind. The first person I saw was Reggie. He was grim-faced but nodded his head at me. My knees were starting to feel a little weak.

The crowd displayed a mix of expressions: shock, revulsion, and even a kind of approval. No one spoke, no one moved. I slowly holstered the XD, then looked back at them.

"I know some of you think what I just did was wrong, but these people just threatened me. They came here to Mark's house and threatened to shoot his wife. They came to try and take what they felt they were owed. They weren't owed anything, and Mark's the last person anyone should be trying to steal from. Mark went to the county today for *you* people. What did you do while he was trying to make sure you could feed your families? You came here with people who pointed guns at his *wife*."

The crowd shuffled in shame.

"I know most of you haven't been outside of here since things went down, but I have. I walked over two hundred miles to get here. One night my friends and I tried to help some people, a family with kids. Turns out they wanted what we had and were willing to kill for it. I ended up getting shot in the head as a result of it." I turned my head to show them the scar.

"We were hunted like animals, and all we were carrying was a pack and a little canned food. What you need to think about is what kind of person you want to be. Sure, lots of you are going to say you just showed up here today to see what was going on, but who spoke up when Leland and Randal threatened Mark's wife?" No one in the crowd said a word.

"That's right: nobody. And which one of you was going to go home empty-handed after you looted Mark's home? Today's the day you have to decide what kind of person you're going to be. And I'm telling you, if you make the wrong choice, chances are you'll end up like them." I nodded at the bodies on the ground. "I know damn well most of you are good people, moral people. But for those of you who aren't, this is the chance for you to understand why you want to respect people's property and their rights.

"It's a new world now. There was a time back in the past where people handled their own business. If you mouthed off to someone, you might end up getting your nose broke. Or, like happened here, you threaten someone's life, you might end up dead."

A woman from the crowd, another of those neighbors that I barely recognized from my trips to the bus stop, stepped forward. She stretched out a finger and jabbed it in my direction. "Those people were no threat to you, and you ain't the law! You said Mark and Rick are, but you aren't! You can't be the judge, jury and executioner. Mark, you need to arrest him for murder!"

I shook my head and said, "You weren't too concerned

about the law when your friends were threatening to shoot Mark's wife." I looked over at Mark. "What's it gonna be?" He was on the spot now; he had to make a decision.

Mark stood there for a minute looking at the crowd, then back at me. He shot a quick glance at Rick, who just shrugged his shoulders. Mark looked back at me, then to the crowd. He cleared his voice and started into it: "Today in my meeting with the sheriff, I was given the power to enforce law in my area of control as I see fit. That doesn't make me the supreme lord of the land; I still have to follow the law. But things are different now.

"There is no more going to jail for some minor bullshit"— he gave me a quick glance—"or major bullshit, for that matter. While I do not agree with what just happened here, it was bound to happen. Things *are* different now. If you commit a crime against someone, you better damn well expect to pay for it. And what you all don't know is, Morgan has already been deputized, so he is a deputy, as is Danny back there." Mark pointed to Danny, whose head popped up. I don't think either of us thought that was a real deal that day at the barricade.

The woman spoke up again. "It still ain't right. You gonna kill the rest of us soon too?"

Mark stood there for a moment, and I broke in, "If you try and come take what you want from someone else, then yes. You threaten another's life or their family, then yes."

She said, "Well, I don't like it. I don't want to live here." She looked at her husband standing beside her.

I said, "Then you're free to leave. Look people, we need to work together. What I saw out there—most of you don't know how good we have it. If we don't hold together as a community, I guarantee you someone from outside's going to show up and take everything we have. We have each other or we don't have anything. I know I don't know many of you, but I can be the best friend you ever had, or the worst enemy you ever come up against." I looked over at Mark and said, loud enough for the crowd to hear, "Don't we have some food to distribute now?"

Mark looked over at Rick and said, "Can you go help pass out the food?"

Danny climbed off the quad and met Rick at the back of the truck. The folks in the crowd slowly began to move over to form a line, where the two men started handing out MREs. Mark came over to me, and he did not look happy.

Through clenched teeth, he started in on me. "If you ever try any shit like that again, you can bet your ass I will shoot you down, you got me?"

"I do, but this little issue is now dead, pun intended. If they had walked away from here, *I*—you got that? *Me—I* would have had to deal with them. They would choose when and where, and what fucking good am I to my family if I'm dead? Or what if they came after you again, or picked someone else to go after?" I fired back at him.

"Well, you damn well picked a fucked up way to do it," Mark replied.

"Mark, you're a good guy, but you need to open your eyes. What were you gonna do to those assholes, the guys who pointed guns at your wife? Arrest them? It's like you said: there's no jail time anymore. Fear of being arrested isn't going to keep anyone safe nowadays. The only thing that's gonna keep the assholes in line is knowing that they might end up dead. You're damn lucky something worse didn't happen here, and I'll tell you what: what I did here just made *your* family safer.

"It was done in public; everyone saw it, heard it and can't argue with it. It's done," I said, then added, "I think we should go and check out their house, and everyone who wants to be there should come."

Mark looked at me, confused. "Why?"

"I have a feeling is all, just a feeling," I said.

"'Bout what?" Mark asked.

"Let's all just go and have a look," I said.

Chapter 7

Thad went home and told Anita what had happened. She cried angrily for a while and then Thad went outside to the barn and started pulling boards off. Once he had what he thought was enough in the bed of the truck, he told his wife he was going back over to Mr. Jackson's house. He hadn't yet told her that they would soon be moving there and decided to wait a little before doing so.

Little Tony came running up, seeing his father at the truck, and asked if he could go. Thad told him to stay home with his mother for now, that he would come and get him for a ride later. It wasn't until he was heading out the door that the bullet fragment in his arm reminded him of its presence. Thad slipped off his coat and his arm was covered in blood. The cuff on the sleeve had kept the blood from running out. Thad went back in and called to Anita. She came out and took a look at it, ordering him to the kitchen table.

Anita had Thad sit at the table while she cleaned the small wound and then probed around for the fragment. Unsuccessful in her search, she wrapped up his elbow and told him to keep it clean and dry. He kissed her and took down his other coat from the hook by the front door and headed out. When he got to Mr. Jackson's place, everything was just as he left it. The three bodies were still lying in the front yard, the front door was still open and the two trucks were still loaded with plunder from the house.

Thad drove his truck around to the rear of the house, pulled up to the barn and unloaded the planks into the little shop attached to the barn. He went and started up the old Ford tractor in the barn and drove it around to the front of the house. Lowering the bucket, he climbed off and started piling the bodies of the killers into it.

He spent the rest of the day building the coffin and burying the bodies, taking special care with Mr. Jackson. Loading the man and the woman wasn't too big a deal to him; the girl was something else entirely.

Thad picked up the small body and gently laid it in the bucket. Once she was in the bucket, Thad looked down into her eyes, which were still open, but lifeless and empty. Blood ran across her face and into her hair. Thad slowly reached down and closed her eyes. Standing back up, he looked at her again. The regret washed over him in a wave. He was suddenly ill and had to kneel down, resting an elbow on the bucket. He had killed this young girl who was probably only doing what her parents told her, what they thought they needed to do to survive.

Thad slowly stood up and climbed onto the tractor. Putting it in gear, he headed out through the pasture, having to stop and open two gates to do it. On the far side of the field, where the tree line started, Thad found what he was looking for: a hole that the old man had used as a trash pit. Pulling up, and without any more thought to it, Thad dumped the three bodies into the hole. After a few minutes of work with the bucket, the hole was full and the bodies were gone.

Thad went back to the barn and went straight to work

on the coffin; he didn't want to see the old man's body until he had to. Having built one before, this box went a little faster, and after about two and a half hours of work it was done. Thad went inside the house and looked at the old man lying on the floor. Mr. Jackson was considerably bigger than his mother. Thad had to lay a blanket out on the floor and roll the old man onto it. Using the blanket, he pulled Mr. Jackson out to his truck, where with a little effort he managed to get the body into the back.

Out at the barn, Thad laid the coffin on the ground at the rear of the truck. This made the job of lowering the body into the coffin much easier. Thad went back into the house and into the old man's bedroom. On the dresser was a picture of Mr. and Mrs. Jackson at their wedding. Thad took the picture and a Bible from the nightstand and went out to the coffin where he put them into the box. In the barn Thad found a logging chain and carried it back out to the truck. Thad took the chain and wrapped it around the coffin, then lowered the bucket on the tractor so he could hang the chain over the hooks on the top of the bucket.

Using the tractor, Thad carried Mr. Jackson out to the small plot behind the house, where one headstone already rested. After setting the box off to the side, Thad dug as much as he could with the bucket, then stepped off into the depression and began to shovel out the dirt. When the old man was finally in the ground, Thad took a rake from the barn and dressed up the grave. With all the bodies taken care of, Thad took a few minutes to feed the livestock. In the chicken coop he counted seven eggs and took them home with him.

When he got home, Anita already had dinner ready:

northern beans cooked with a smoked hock and some corn bread. Anita sat with her husband while he ate, but they didn't really talk.

Anita brought Thad another glass of water as he was finishing his last piece of corn bread. After washing it down, he looked up at her and said, "We're moving tomorrow."

Anita looked at him with surprise. "Where? Why?"

"We're going to go to Mr. Jackson's house. There's a lot of food there, as well as a fireplace and the log stove. It's a better place to try and make it than here. And the old man told me it's what he wanted before he passed," Thad said.

Anita nodded her head slowly in response.

Thad woke early and slipped out of bed without waking his wife. On the nightstand was a candle. Striking a match, he touched it to the wick to light the room. Thad liked the soft light of a candle, more so than the harsh, bright, artificial light he had lived his whole life with. After dressing, he went down the hall to Tony's room and sat on his bed. Putting a big hand on the little boy's shoulder, he gently shook him. "Wake up, little man."

The little boy rolled over and rubbed his eyes. "Daddy?"

"Yeah, it's me. I need your help. You wanna come help me today?" Thad asked with a smile.

Little Tony bolted upright. "Yeah, Daddy, I do!"

"Shhh, don't wake your momma. You get dressed while I get things ready."

As Thad walked out of the room, he could hear the boy ripping open dresser drawers and shuffling around the room. Thad went into the kitchen and took a pad from a drawer and a pen from a cup on the counter. He wrote Anita a note telling her he and Tony were down at Mr. Jackson's place and they would be back in a couple of hours. Thad took the note back to his bedroom and laid it on the bed, where he was sure she would see it. Thad met Little Tony in the hall. He was dressed and ready to go. Thad knew if he didn't get him moving soon he would vibrate through the floor.

"You ready?" Thad asked, already knowing the answer. Tony's head bobbed up and down quickly. He was wearing a black watch cap on his head pulled down over his ears like the one Thad always wore and a fleece-lined denim jacket, and who knew how many layers under it. Thad put his arm around the little boy and they headed for the door. Outside, Tony started around to the passenger side of the truck, but Thad called to him, "Hey, come on over here."

The boy walked around to the driver's side as Thad climbed in. Thad looked at him, then patted his lap and asked, "You wanna drive?" The response was immediate and overwhelming, and Thad thought Tony was going to stomp him to death climbing up into his lap. Thad backed the truck out of the drive and straightened it out on the road and then let go of the wheel. "You take it from here," he said. Thad worked the gas and brake and let the boy steer the truck in a wobbly path toward the old man's house.

The two of them fed all the animals and brought in the few eggs laid overnight and then, using a wagon from the shed, they brought all the items the thieves had carried out back into the house. Thad put all the food back in the pantry and placed the guns back in the gun rack. By now Tony was hungry, so Thad went into the kitchen, where he found three biscuits on a plate on the table, covered with cheesecloth. Laying a plate on the table, he took a spoon from the drawer and set a jar of honey out. Little Tony needed no more explanation.

While Tony ate, Thad went through the house. Mr.

Jackson had lived there a long, long time. He felt like he was trespassing, that being there was just wrong. Then he thought about what the old man had said to him and that eased his tension a bit. The house was well suited for life without electricity, as it had been built before there was power in the area. In the living room was a big fireplace made from large pieces of stone. In the kitchen was still an old wood stove. There was a gas stove as well, but Thad was certain there wouldn't be any gas for it. Out back of the house was a pitcher pump that still worked and a springhouse over a small spring that ran clear, cold water, so water wasn't going to be an issue.

The more Thad walked around and looked at the house, the better he felt about things. As he was coming down the hall toward the living room, Tony met him, honey on his face and hands. "I need to wash my hands, Daddy," the boy said, his face shiny with honey and a quick tongue working all the places he could reach. Thad smiled.

He took Tony into the bathroom and grabbed a wash-cloth, then spotted some cotton balls on a shelf over the toilet. With a big smile on his face he took one and walked back out to the hall and handed the cotton ball to the boy and said, "Here, wipe your hands with this." Thad had a big evil grin on his face. Tony took the cotton and tried to wipe at the honey. The cotton fibers stuck to the honey and the more he tried to wipe the more fibers separated. Soon his hands were matted in sticky cotton. Tony looked up at his dad in confusion. Thad broke out and started to laugh, but Tony still didn't understand. His hands looked like he was the abominable snowman or something.

Putting a big hand on his back, Thad said to him, "Come on, let's go get you cleaned up." As Thad walked him out to the old pump, Tony was still trying to get the cotton out from between his fingers. Once Tony was cleaned up, they hopped into Mr. Jackson's truck, it being in far better shape than the one Thad had been driving, and headed home. Pulling up in front of his house, Thad could see warm light glowing inside and smoke issuing from the chimney. He found Anita inside cooking eggs while sipping a cup of coffee. She set a plate on the table for Tony, and he dove into them without hesitation. Anita looked up from her son and gave Thad a kiss. "Good morning."

They spent the rest of the day moving the things they needed and wanted from their house to the new house. Anita asked Thad about exactly what happened and he told her everything. Everything except the part about one of the raiders being a young girl and him shooting her in the top of her head as she looked up at him. Thad knew it was a much harder world now and that Anita would ultimately be faced with it, but he loved her enough to spare her what he could while he could.

It was a mutual decision between Thad and Anita to move their bed into the bedroom; they just couldn't bring themselves to sleep in the old man's bed. The next few days they spent settling in. Both of them felt like they were trespassing in the house, but as the days wore on they became more comfortable. Little Tony was the only one that took to the new house like a fish to water. He was up every morning helping his dad feed all the animals, clean up after them and perform the general work of maintaining a farm. For the first week after settling in, they saw no one.

Chapter 8

Sarge and the boys had their orders. Against his wishes, Sarge had been pressed into military service again. He was finally convinced when a full-bird colonel made a trip out to the little cabin to press upon him the gravity of the current situation. The colonel reminded Sarge that he had once taken an oath to defend the Constitution against all enemies, foreign and domestic, and it was now time to put the latter part of that oath to action. The nation was in turmoil, and the federal government was using the opportunity to purge the land of those they saw as unfit. It was like the Soviet purges or the Civil War all over again: family was turning on family, friends on friends and neighbors on neighbors.

Sarge's new mission was guerrilla warfare, to be conducted on all FEMA and DHS targets of opportunity. In addition to these two target pools was another that actually disturbed the guys, the US postal service. When Mike pressed the colonel as to why they were to target letter carriers, the colonel explained that the postmaster general had been tasked with finding people and assigning them to work brigades. While on the surface this sounded benign, it was in fact an effort to press people into work camps where there was only one way in and one way out. The government touted these camps as "relocation and assistance" facilities, but they were internment camps, closer to Soviet gulags than refugee camps. While most of the population was unaware of the operations being conducted, they were starting to come around. In the early days, people had flocked to these camps, where they were processed according to a myriad of factors.

It was at one of these processing stations that the seeds of the current course of action had taken root. While some of the military went along with the plan, there were others that saw the situation for what it was and decided their loyalty was to the Constitution and the people of the United States of America. This was the problem that Sarge, Ted, Mike and Doc found themselves faced with, and they took it on without hesitation.

With all this in mind, Sarge held a meeting with the guys to discuss the situation. He told them about the truck at his house and that he wanted to go get it.

"You got to be out of your fucking mind, wanting to go back to the house after what we did there," Doc said.

"I don't expect to just waltz in there, ya fuckin' patata head. We'll go down the river and set an observation post and watch it for a couple of days. If it's clear, we'll slip in after dark and get the truck," Sarge said. "Mike, you're going with me; pack for three days. Ted, you'll drop us off and Doc will hold down the fort."

Mike suggested that they take a radio with them so if they made contact with unfriendlies the others could act as a reaction force. Sarge agreed, and they set up a frequency to use in case of emergency. Doc and Ted would monitor the radio twenty-four seven. They packed for three days, just in case of an escape and evasion scenario, and they took as much ammo as they could carry. Sarge carried the SPW and a carbine and Mike took the 203 and an AT4, along with a couple of claymores. Don had been sent out onto the deck while the guys had their little meeting and finally stuck his head back in the door at the sound of all the activity, asking, "When's lunch?"

Sarge gave him a look of disgust and threw an MRE at him. "Here."

Don looked at the bag, then looked back at Sarge. "What's wrong with makin' some taters and onions?"

"We ain't got time for that shit now; that's as good as it gets at the moment," Sarge said.

Don sat down at the table, muttering to himself about eating out of a damn bag, but settled down to his lunch. While Don ate, the rest continued on preparing for the mission. They had the boat loaded by four. Sarge wanted to head out about nine and ordered Mike to get some rack time. Ted and Doc kept watch and Don was kicked out of the cabin, Sarge giving him a fishing rod to keep him busy.

At nine o'clock they eased the boat out of the slough into the Suwannee. They ran the boat blacked out, all three of them wearing night vision goggles. The trip down the river was uneventful. Sarge paid attention to the houses where he saw lights, but they were few. Sarge motioned Ted to the side of the river at a bend. His place was just on the other side and down river about a half mile; the others would walk from there. Sarge reinforced the instructions to monitor the radio, and a rough plan of what to do in the event they made contact with the bad guys. With a quick shaking of hands, Mike and Sarge slipped into the night.

It took the two of them almost two hours to move the half mile or so to a spot they could see Sarge's house. Even in the dark, Sarge didn't like what he saw. In the greenish glow of the goggles, all he could see where his house had sat on the bank was a big black spot overlooking the river.

Mike eased up to Sarge's side. "Doesn't look good, boss," he whispered.

"About what I expected, but look, the garage is still there; they didn't burn it," Sarge said.

The two of them took a few minutes to set up their hide and settle down for a long look. Sarge set the SPW up to cover the river, and Mike tapped him on the shoulder and whispered in his ear that he was going to set up claymores about thirty yards either side of their position. Sarge gave him a nod and Mike picked up his pack and moved off into the darkness once again. Sarge unrolled a foam sleep mat and laid it on the ground, then took up a position behind the Minimi. Listening to the pitch dark all around him, Sarge could hear Mike moving around faintly to his right.

Mike came back, giving a low hissing whistle so Sarge wouldn't shoot him, then moved off to Sarge's left to set up the other mine. It didn't take him long before he was back in the hide. He was taking up position to watch their six when he tapped Sarge on the shoulder. Sarge looked back at him.

"Hey, what's this, you getting soft?" Mike said in a breathy whisper, jutting a thumb at the foam mat.

Sarge kicked him in his thigh, then whispered back, "Just wait, dipshit, you'll get old too. Now keep your damn eyes open."

Mike laughed inside, thinking back to the days when the old man would make them lie in the rocks, mud and thickets on the range, the whole time screaming about "not having that fucking sissy mat in the real world." He thought about reminding Sarge of that, but he didn't want to get kicked again.

The rest of that night went without incident, with one exception. About two thirty in the morning they heard a helo overhead to their south. Even though they scanned the skies with their goggles, they never did see the ship. The only thing worse than hearing a helo working over your head was not knowing where it was or what it was doing. At five in the morning, Sarge told Mike to catch a couple hours of sleep. Mike pulled his sleeping bag over him. He knew not to get into it, as it could easily become a body bag if he needed to move quickly. He was out in under five minutes.

Sarge reached into his pack and pulled out a small stainless thermos of coffee and poured himself a cup. He would stay up and see what the dawn brought. The boat wouldn't be back for them until tomorrow evening, so he had plenty of time.

Mark looked at me for a minute. He said, "All right, we'll go have a look, but me and Rick go in, you stay outside."

"Fine by me, boss," I answered.

I had to give Mark credit, what he did next surprised me. He walked over to the people gathered at the back of the truck and called for their attention.

"Listen up, everyone." He paused to give them all a minute.

"Considering the situation we are in, everything, even things we previously took for granted, has a new value. We need to utilize every asset we have, take every advantage that comes our way. With that said, and considering what just happened here, we are going to search Pat's house for anything that can be used. We will distribute these items on an as-needed basis, and to ensure that everyone knows what we find and this is on the up and up, anyone who wants can come with. Rick and I will conduct the search; no else is going inside, but you will all see what's there. Everyone understand?"

There were several glances in the crowd and some murmuring, but no one objected. I guessed the thought of getting something overrode their objections to pillaging the house of the dead. Pat's house was less than a block from Mark's, so the walk over was short. Our little procession down the road brought a few more people out of their houses. Pat and her husband had a ten-acre spread; there were three horses and a couple of cows as well as a chicken coop. Most of this, except for the horses, couldn't be seen from the road, but once everyone was past the hedge of cedars, you could see it all. We weren't even in the house yet and people were already talking about the chickens.

Mark and Rick walked up to the front door and brought their weapons up to the ready. Rick reached over and opened the door and Mark stepped in, sweeping the room with the muzzle of the AR. They were inside for quite a while, the crowd was alive with rumors about what was in there. They were already trying to divvy up the stuff outside the house they could see, like the grill and the tractor. I stayed well off to the side of everyone, just watching and listening. Mark emerged from the house and called me over.

"What's up?" I asked him as I walked up, the crowd starting to press in.

Mark looked past me and said, "Everyone stay back, no one is going inside, just wait."

Then he looked at me." I can't fucking believe this, there's a fucking pile of food in here."

"I kind of thought so. What did you find?" I asked.

"There's a pile of canned food and a shelf full of dry beans and rice. I mean, it isn't a mountain or anything, but it is enough to last them several weeks," Mark added, his eyes big, that bewildered look on his face again.

"Well, what are you going to do?" I asked him. People in the crowd were craning their necks trying to see into the house. "Whatever it is, you better do it quick," I added.

"I guess we'll bring it all out and divide it up."

"If I can make a suggestion, bring it all out and pile it up out here so they can all see it. If we can't divide it evenly, and I mean to the ounce, then maybe you should take custody of it and we work out a way to prepare one meal a day and everyone comes and gets fed. And think about it this way: if people have to come to you for a meal, that'll reinforce your authority. Having people feel like they owe you can't hurt," I offered.

Mark thought about that for a minute. "That may be best, but if they don't get something today, they may riot; if we're hauling it all out here, they could take it when we're inside, and they might accuse me of taking it. I don't need that kind of trouble."

Danny stepped up, having been off to the side listening. He said, "Then have some of them go in and bring it out. Have Rick stay in there to make sure they don't pocket anything, have someone out here to inventory it all and assign someone else to keep track of the inventory. Make them all part of the system so they can't point fingers."

Mark and I looked at one another, then back at Danny. "That's a damn good idea," Mark said.

Mark turned and went back into the house to give Rick the plan, then came back out with a notebook and pen in his hand, looking at the crowd as he called out some names. "Reggie, Luis, can you two come in and help carry some stuff out?"

The two men moved toward the house and Mark scanned the crowd again. "Marie, can you come over here and write down everything they take out, what it is and the amount? Get someone to help you if you need." Marie was the woman who had spoken out about me at Mark's house. She looked around at the people standing around her, waved to another woman and the two of them went up to Mark and took the notebook and pen.

Reggie and Luis started carrying out canned goods and bags of rice, pasta and beans. The two women noted every item that was carried out and the items were laid out on the front yard. When it was all said and done, there was a substantial pile of food. It wouldn't feed everyone for very long, but it could for several days. As the spread of food increased, the crowd pressed in. People were talking amongst themselves about what they wanted, how much they would get and, in a couple of cases, the best way to cook what they saw.

Once everything was brought out, the anticipation was building into a fervor in the crowd; it was obvious that some of these people hadn't had much to eat recently. Mark stepped between the crowd and the food and said, "All right, everyone, back up a little."

Someone from the crowd shouted, "Just pass it out already!" This was followed with a round of "Yeah!" and other approvals. Mark waved Rick, Danny and myself over; we joined him in a semicircle.

"All right, everyone can see what's here. Marie, you got it all down?" Mark asked.

Marie held up the notebook. "Every last ounce," she announced.

"Good. As you can all see, some of this we can't just break up and pass out, so here is what we're going to do. Marie is

83

in charge of the inventory of this food; she will keep track of how it's used and how much," Mark called out.

Marie had a look of horror on her face. Mark said, "What we are going to do is secure this food and we will prepare community meals." This was met with some jeers and protests; the crowd was turning decidedly hostile. Mark raised his hands, trying to quite the crowd, but to no avail. Rick fired a shot from his pistol and they quieted down immediately.

Mark looked over his shoulder at Rick and said, "Thanks, you scared the shit outta me." That got a few laughs from the crowd. Mark told them, "Look, if we all take a little of this, then we all might have something today, but if we pool it and prepare community meals, then it will go further. Everyone will get a meal. We're going to track the food and everyone will know how much is left and how many more meals we can make. It's the fairest way to do this."

"So who decides when we get to eat, and what we get to eat? You? Now the law is going to feed us?" Someone from the crowd called out.

"Yes. This isn't *your* food; this belongs to all of us, to the community, our neighborhood, and it must be done equitably and fairly," Mark said.

"Well, how are we to know someone isn't taking it when no one is around? Marie has the list; what's to keep her from taking food?" another voice called out.

I stepped forward and asked, "Mark, you going to store this in your shed?" Mark nodded. "Then we'll put two locks on it. Marie will have one key and Mark the other. That way they both have to be there for the door to be opened and no one will be in there alone."

There were no more objections from the crowd. The last

detail to work out was when the community meals would be served and where. Once that was sorted out, Mark asked me to bring my Suburban over, which I did, and then a couple of the guys loaded the food. I drove Mark, Marie and Reggie back to Mark's house, where all the food was stored. Mark had two new locks in his shop. They were hung on the hasp and Marie took one set of keys and Mark the other. There weren't any further objections, especially once Mark pointed out the fact that he had just passed out the county food to them all.

Not everyone was at the food distribution, but it didn't take long for word to spread that there was food being handed out and those who weren't there started to trickle into Mark's yard. I told Mark I was done for the day and was going home. He stopped me, saying, "You aren't done yet."

"Now what?" I asked.

"You have three bodies that need buried in a decent manner," he said.

All I could do was look at him. I just wanted to go home. I was spent, done and tired. "Are you serious?"

"Damn right I am. You aren't going to leave them in my yard overnight. You made the mess, you can clean it up."

My head dropped to my chest. The thought of having to dig three graves seemed beyond me right then. Reggie walked over from the shed where he had finished storing everything and said, "I'll help you, Morg."

"There you go, get it done, it's going to be dark soon," Mark said.

When Mark was gone, Reggie looked over at me. "Where we gonna plant 'em?"

"I guess on their property. Let's go over to their house and get some sheets to wrap 'em up in, then we'll load 'em in the Suburban and drive them over. Digging three holes was not on my list of things to do today," I said to Reggie with a sideways glance.

"Well, if I had fuel for my tractor we could use the bucket to scoop out most of it. That'd make it a hell of a lot easier," Reggie said.

"Tell you what: you go find the sheets, and I'll get some fuel," I said. Anything that would keep me from digging until midnight was fine by me.

"Sounds like a plan," Reggie said as he started off toward Pat's house.

I jumped into the truck and headed toward home. I drove around to the shed where the fuel was stored and parked the truck. In the shop I found the pump I'd picked up at Harbor Freight, one of the ones that screwed into the bung and had a handle to crank out the fuel. As I was heading back toward the shed, my neighbor Howard called out to me from the fence. I gave him a wave and said I'd be right there and set the pump on the drums and walked over.

"Hey, Morgan, have you been listening to the radio at all?" he asked as I came up.

"No, been dealing with other issues. Why, what's up?" I asked.

"Just get on the twenty-meter tonight and work the band. There is some bad stuff going on, real bad," he said.

"There's bad stuff here, my friend, real bad," I said. Howard just looked at me with a questioning look.

"You'll hear about it soon enough," I told him

"Yeah, Pat should be down any time to fill me in," Howard said.

"No, she won't either, ole buddy."

"Is she all right?" he asked.

"No, her husband and son too," I said.

"What the hell happened?" Howard asked.

"I'll check out the twenty-meter tonight. I gotta go right now, talk to you later," I said as I walked off toward the drums.

I had already filled one five-gallon GI can and was filling the second when I heard a small sniffling voice call out, "Daddy?"

Looking over my shoulder I saw Little Bit standing there, tears running down her face. Stopping the pumping, I knelt down. She walked over and fell against me, crying. "What's wrong, baby?" I asked.

Through the sobs and tears she told me how she was no longer allowed to play with her friends next door. Their parents told her she was no longer welcome there and that her father was a horrible man. I squeezed her tight and kissed her on the head.

"I'm really sorry, honey. Something bad happened today, really bad, and some people are angry at me for it. I did it 'cause they said they were going to hurt me, and I didn't want anything to happen to you, your sisters and Mommy," I told her, trying to comfort her and at the same time spare her the details.

She looked up at me with those tearstained cheeks. "But who am I going to play with now?"

"I'll talk to them and see if we can fix it, okay? Why don't you go inside and ask Mommy to put on a movie for you?"

"What are you doing? Can I come with you?" she asked, rubbing her nose.

"No, baby, I'm sorry. What I have to do, you can't be there, sorry. But tell you what: tonight we'll play a game together, all of us."

"They won't play, they never play with me," she said, referring to her sisters.

"They will tonight, I promise," I said.

"Okay, Daddy," she said and gave me a kiss on the cheek. I squeezed her tight again and she ran toward the house, yelling that she was going to go and pick out a game for us.

After finishing the second can, I loaded them into the back of the Suburban and headed for Mark's house. As I approached it I didn't see Reggie out front so I passed by and went to Pat's place. Reggie was standing in the front door with some sheets draped over his arm, looking at something in his hand. I pulled up and called out to him, "Jump in and we'll go over to your place and fuel up the tractor."

He looked up from whatever it was in his hand, then turned and started toward the truck. Reggie was a big man, a diesel mechanic by trade. He was bald-headed and sported muttonchops; he had "outlaw biker" written all over him. He walked up to the driver's side of the truck and stuck his hand out. He handed me a driver's license. I took it and looked at it; it was a pretty young girl with blonde hair. The sort of woman that would drive the young rednecks around here wild.

"Who is it?" I asked.

Stern-faced, he replied, "My niece."

I looked back down at the little card in my hand. "Where'd you find it?" I asked without looking up.

Reggie pointed back at the house without looking away. "In there. In Randal's room."

I looked back up at him. "Yeah, well, it wouldn't surprise me, but now we'll never know."

"If he were still alive, we would." Reggie fixed a cold gaze on me.

I handed the card back to him. "Well, if you think he had something to do with it, then he's already been dealt with. I hate to say it, and I'm sorry, but she's gone and nothing's going to change that."

He stood there another minute, then walked around and climbed into the passenger side. He didn't say another word. We fueled the tractor, he drove it back over to Pat's, then we went over to Mark's and wrapped the bodies in the sheets he took from Pat's house and loaded them into the back of the truck. Back over at Pat's house, Reggie went to work on the pit. He started scooping out the earth, working progressively deeper, like an inverted ramp. With the way he was going there wouldn't be any hand digging.

The sound of the tractor brought people out. A small group gathered and watched as he worked. I guess some were curious, others were just plain bored and this was better than the view from the porch. Others were looking decidedly unfriendly. The way Reggie had dug the hole, I was able to back the Suburban down into it. Together, we slid the bodies out one at a time and laid them on the ground, careful not to just toss them or drop them. We laid them out side by side, with Pat in the middle.

When I tried to drive the truck out of the hole, it got stuck. Being only two-wheel drive, it slipped in the soft sand. There were some snickers from the gawkers when I got out and went to the back for my tow strap. I didn't have to say anything to Reggie; he was already backing the tractor up to the front end. I put one loop over a tow hook on the front end and dropped the other over a hitch on the back of the tractor and we pulled it out without incident.

Reggie pulled around to the other side of the hole and started pushing the dirt in. He pushed slowly, allowing the earth to roll in and gradually cover the three bodies. As I stood there watching, I thought back to James on his tractor doing the same thing. I wondered how he and Miss Edith were doing. I missed them and the time I had spent with them. A wave of uncertainty washed over me. How many was it now? Six? Seven? I ran through it in my head: no, it was eight, or more. At least eight people I had killed. And why? What kind of person could kill that many people? I thought back to earlier in the day and looking down at Pat, that and the impact of the bullet. What had I done? I had to, didn't I? There was nothing to stop them from doing what they had threatened to. It wasn't like I could have called the sheriff and had a restraining order placed on them, not that that even worked before. And it wasn't that I had been making a point: I didn't doubt that Randal and Leland would have lain in wait for me. Maybe not today or this week, but eventually.

But could it have gone differently? I was still standing there when Reggie shut the tractor down. I looked at the smoothed-over fresh dirt and couldn't even remember the hole being filled. Reggie walked up to me and stood there, looking at the spot. He said, "I hope we don't have to do this too many more times."

I looked over at him. He was still looking at the bare dirt. I said, "Me too. Thanks for the help. I really appreciate it."

"No problem. The way I figure it, you need all the friends you can get around here right now," he said, finally looking over at me. I glanced up and nodded my head.

One of the onlookers called out, "Is anyone going to say anything for them?" No one spoke up; the few that were there just looked at the bare soil, then at me.

I walked over to the Suburban and drove home. It was

almost dark by the time I got into the house. Mel was in the kitchen, fixing dinner: chili with rice.

She asked, "You okay? What happened today?"

I looked at her and said, "I just don't feel like talking about it right now."

She stood there looking at me for a minute, then gave me a hug and stepped up onto her toes and kissed me. "You hungry? You never came for lunch."

I was starving, and I told her so, but first I needed a drink. Going out to the shop, I pulled some buckets out from under the shelves, then got on my hands and knees and pulled a case of Benchmark No. 8 out. It was cheap whiskey that I had bought on a whim and put away for "just in case," and today was just the sort of case that called for it.

Mel came into my shop before I got a chance to open the case. "You going to come in and eat?" she asked.

"Yeah, I guess so."

She was standing in the door looking at me. "What's wrong? What happened?"

I didn't want to have this talk with her, but there was no way around it; better she hear it from me.

"Okay, hang on a second, though," I said and went back and opened the case, pulled out a bottle and walked over and leaned against the workbench. Mel looked at me like my head was on sideways when I unscrewed the bottle and took a shot. I held the bottle out to her. "Want one?" She just shook her head at me with a look somewhere between curious and annoyed. "You might want one when I'm done," I said.

I went into what had happened, from the trip to town to the return, and what had happened at Mark's house and afterward. I told her what Randal and Leland had said, what

Pat had said, and then of course what happened next. She stood there looking at me, her eyes growing wider as I went along. When I got to the shootings, her hands went to her mouth. She stood there without saying a word.

When I finished, she was still standing there with her hand covering her mouth and her eyes wide. I picked up the bottle and took another shot. She finally came out of it. "I can't believe you did that. What's going to happen?"

"I don't know," I answered.

"Are you going to go to jail?" she asked.

That actually made me smile; it was just another example of how people were not coming to the realization of just what was going on. "No, honey, I'm not going to jail. But there are some people that are not happy about it, so we need to be careful," I told her.

We went inside, where a bowl of chili sat at the table waiting for me. I asked Mel where the girls were and she told me they were all in their rooms reading or something. I ate my dinner without much enthusiasm. When I was done, I went into the girls' rooms to check on them. The two big girls were both reading books. I talked to each of them for a minute, lying on their beds to spend a couple of minutes with each of them. Little Bit was in her bed with a Bass Pro Shop Monopoly game in her arms, sound asleep. I slipped the game out and covered her up, then went out to the living room.

Mel was sitting on the couch reading a book as well. I sat down for a minute, then told her I was going to go out to the shop and listen to the radio for a while; I just couldn't sit inside right then.

"Bring some wood back in when you come. There isn't any more on the deck," she said as I stood up to go.

"Okay."

Back out in the shop I turned on the radio and spun the top off the bottle. I poured a couple of fingers of whiskey into a canteen cup and started to scan the frequencies. The traffic on the radio was really picking up. I heard people from several states. Even though radios had been outlawed, it didn't appear to be stopping anyone from transmitting.

Most of the talk was what you would expect: conditions where the various people were, food situations, water situations and security. Rumors were being exchanged about where food was being distributed or where the government was using force. This was a little disturbing to hear, that they were actually going after people. I wanted to ask questions but wasn't about to transmit. Sarge had made it clear about how careful I had to be, and that thought made me think of him and the guys, where they were and what they were doing, how they were doing.

I was roused from my thoughts of the guys when I heard someone talking about a mailman. They reported seeing a mail truck go down their road with a uniformed mailman driving it. This brought about a lively conversation about whether or not the government was starting to function, some saying it was now just a matter of time before the power would come back on and things would start to get back to normal. The chatter on the radio deteriorated on the frequency I was listening to, so I started to scan through the band.

It wasn't long before I found another that caught my attention when I heard "mailman" again. Stopping on the frequency for a second, I heard the end of the exchange.

"Asked me a bunch of questions and was filling out a form."

"What'd he ask ya?"

"What I did for a livin', did we have any food, then he asked if'n I had any guns. That's when I told him it was none of his business. Then this other feller got out of the Jeep and came up. He was wearin' a uniform and carry'n a rifle, an' he told me to settle down an' answer the questions."

"What'd you do?"

"I called my boys outta the house, then tole them to git the hell off ma land."

"Did they leave?"

"Damn straight they did."

This conversation too went off in another direction so I just shut the radio down. Draining the canteen cup, I went inside.

Chapter 9

Thad and Anita had been in the house for almost a week when Pastor Fish showed up one afternoon. Thad was out back cleaning out the pigpen when Pastor Fish came out the back door and called to him. Thad looked, up leaning on the shovel he was using and waved a greeting. He met the pastor as he crossed the yard toward the pen.

"How ya doin', Thad?" Pastor Fish said, sticking out his hand.

"Good, Pastor Fish, how you doin?"

"Fair ta middlin'. How's things here?"

"Good as can be, considering what brought us here," Thad replied.

The pastor's face turned sour. "What happened?"

Thad told him everything except what Mr. Jackson had said about the girl and the way she had died. He pulled his arm out of his coat to show the wound where the piece of bullet still resided. Pastor Fish took Thad's arm in his hand and looked at it.

"Thad, that's startin' to look angry, you taking anything for it?"

"No, sir, ain't got any antibiotics."

"We'll see what we can do about that. Where'd you bury Mr. Jackson?"

Thad motioned for him to follow and led the pastor to the

oak tree where he had buried the old man. The two men stood there for a couple of minutes, not saying anything. The pastor took a look around the area, then said, "You couldn't have picked a better spot. It's a wicked world we livin' in nowadays."

"Getting worse ever day too," Thad said.

The two men walked back up to the house in silence. As they came up to the back porch, they could hear voices on the front side of the house. The two men shared a quick glance and Thad drew his Glock, which he always carried now. He walked around the side of the house. Pastor Fish stayed behind Thad as he peeked around the corner. Holstering the pistol, Thad and the pastor stepped out to see Anita talking with a uniformed man.

"Is that a mailman?" the pastor asked.

"Sure looks like it."

Anita saw them coming, and Thad could see some apprehension on her face as he approached. The man looked up as the two of them came up. "Good morning," he said with a smile.

After a brief exchange of niceties, the man got down to business. The postmaster had been tasked with conducting a census of sorts, to figure out where people were, what their skills were and, most importantly, what their needs were. The uniformed man went down a form asking questions and making notations on it. When Thad asked what they needed all this information for, the answer to the question caused the three of them to share a quick glance.

With a smile on his face the uniformed man replied, "To facilitate the relocation of people to the area where they will be able to provide the most benefit to the reconstruction of our nation." He said it as an actor would recite a well-rehearsed line, or like a used car salesman trying to close a deal.

Thad looked the man straight in his eyes. "We don't plan on going anywhere. We're taking care of ourselves and will continue to do so. Thank you for coming out." He put an arm around Anita and turned toward the house, motioning with his head for the pastor to follow.

As Pastor Fish stepped by the uniformed man, the man stepped in front of him and asked, "Where do you live?" again with that plastic smile on his face.

Thad motioned for Anita to go into the house and stepped between the two men. "I'm gonna ask you to leave now." The man took a step back, still smiling, and flipped through the papers on his clipboard.

Looking down at the sheaf of papers, the man asked, "Where's Mr. Jackson?"

Thad took a step toward the man, but Pastor Fish put a hand on his shoulder. Thad looked at the Brother, who nodded with his head toward the road. Standing by one of the old-style mail Jeeps was another man. This one wore a military-style uniform and carried an assault rifle. Thad turned and the Brother put a hand on his shoulder again and the two of them walked toward the house.

From behind them the mailman called out, "You will be receiving a letter in the coming days with instructions. Failure to follow them will be . . ." The man paused for a moment. ". . . unpleasant to say the least. There are jobs that most would rather not have, do you understand?"

Thad and the Brother continued into the house, Thad shutting and locking the door behind them.

Inside, Anita was in a near panic. "What are we going

to do? They can't just send us off to work someplace, can they?"

The Brother spoke up before Thad could. "If martial law has been declared, then they could."

"Well, they already did that," Thad said.

The old Brother looked over at Thad in surprise. "How do you know?"

"I have a radio and someone I trust told me."

"You have a two-way?" the Brother asked.

"Yeah, I got it on my way home. My friend gave it to me."

Anita said, "What are we going to do, Thad?"

The conversation went on for some time between the three of them, trying to figure out what they should do. Anita's biggest concern was that they might be split up and sent to different places. Thad tried to assure her that would never happen, and Anita reminded him he was useless to them dead. Thad sat there for a minute chewing on that.

"I'm gonna set up the radio. I need to talk to some folks if I can reach them," he said.

Ted showed up with the boat the next evening. They hadn't seen anything to make them think there was anyone around. Sarge figured the DHS goons weren't worried about it since they had torched the place. Using the boat to cross the river, Sarge slipped up to the little garage that sat between the river and the scorched spot where his house had once stood. Pulling the door open, he saw the old truck was still sitting there.

The truck was an old Dodge Power Wagon that Sarge had owned before he went into the army. It had spent many, many years in storage. Since his retirement, Sarge had spent some time getting it back into running order. A new Crate 360 sat under the hood now, and the rest of the running gear had been rebuilt and were now as good as the day they had come off the line in Detroit. What he had not spent any time on was the looks of the beast. It was mostly a flat black of sorts and the interior was in wretched condition, with the springs showing through the seats.

The rotor cap and the coil were in an old Glad garbage bag box on a shelf. Sarge pulled the box down and installed the two pieces in a matter of moments. Ted and Mike stood watch, Mike out front and Ted behind the building watching the river. After a quick check with the two guys to make sure the coast was clear, Sarge cranked the old truck. Dead, not even a click. Sarge ran out to Mike and told him to go pull one of the batteries from the boats and get it back up here pronto.

Mike did as instructed, giving Ted a quick rundown on his way. Mike had the battery back in a few minutes and Sarge hit the key. This time the truck cranked for a minute, then fired to life. Sarge feathered the gas for a moment, the old beast revving its response. Satisfied it was ready, Sarge stepped out to Mike and told him to get Ted and head for the swamp, he would meet them on the old road they had scouted prior to this little exercise.

"Be careful. If anything happens, call us and we'll be there," Mike said.

"Just keep the radio on. Let's go," Sarge replied.

Mike gave him a nod and jogged around the garage. Once they were in the boats and turned out into the river, Sarge grabbed his gear and tossed it into the truck. Opening his pack, he pulled an old flannel shirt out, then took off his vest and threw it on the front seat and put the flannel on.

Swapping his boonie hat for one of his 101st trucker-style hats, he would look like any other old cracker driving down the road, if there were any driving.

When he made it to the gate, he found it had been pulled down by something heavy; the six-by-six posts anchoring either end of it were pulled completely out of the ground, and the gate lay twisted and mangled. Then he spotted something in a tree and he climbed out to look at it. It was a WANTED poster. Actually it was several, like the ones he had seen for the FBI's most wanted, only this one had his picture and name on it. The others had photos of Mike, Ted and Doc on them. Their posters gave their names and ranks and labeled them as deserters, and armed and dangerous. The line under WANTED made his blood run cold: it said DEAD OR ALIVE. Sarge was standing in the road beside the truck looking at the poster and suddenly became aware of the rumble coming from the two Thrush glass packs on the old truck. Looking down the road, he saw a man he recognized as one of his neighbors standing in the road looking at him.

Looking back to the poster in his hands for a moment, he read the part about the reward. Instead of cash, the reward was offered in "food credits, redeemable at any FEMA facility." Lowering the poster, Sarge looked down the road again. The man was still there, but he put his hands in his pockets and walked off the road, trying too hard to look casual. Climbing up into the truck, Sarge put it in gear and deliberately drove toward the man's house. Coming abreast of the house, he saw the guy still in his yard. Sarge pushed the clutch in and gunned the engine, looking right at the guy, who quickly went inside.

Seeing the mistake of those glass packs clearly now, he took a bit of a roundabout way out the area, knowing anyone around could easily hear the old beast. He was on edge for the entire drive to the rendezvous with Mike and Ted. The more he thought about it, though, the less it seemed to him like there would be anyone out here looking for him. Sarge knew the DHS just didn't have the personnel to watch these sticks too closely; they would let their reward offer do the work for them.

Rounding the corner where he was to meet the guys, Sarge saw the trees move out from in front of his truck. He was impressed with Ted for this one. Instead of cutting brush to build a blind for the truck, Ted had dug up some of the small pines and planted them in five-gallon buckets, then dug holes in the ground for the buckets to fit in. After driving in, the guys dropped the buckets back in the holes and spread pine needles out at their bases. Sarge got out, popped the hood and grabbed a piece of wire from the seat. Mike came over to him and asked, "What are you doing?"

"Just a little surprise for anyone who tries to start the truck," Sarge answered.

He went around to the front of the truck and fished the wire through the firewall, telling Mike to find it and pull it through. Once the wire was pulled into the cab, he connected the other end to the coil after stripping it. Inside the cab, he stripped that end and wrapped it around one of the seat springs from the bottom. He rerouted the positive side to the ignition. If anyone tried to start it, not only would they get the shock of their life, but the horn would sound too.

The three of them quickly spread the camo net Sarge had over the truck and headed back to the shack. He told them about the posters. Doc seemed to take it worse than the other two, who brushed it off with typical morbid humor.

"So now everyone is looking for our scalps in exchange for a can of beans," Doc said.

"Get used to it, son, this is only the beginning. It's going to get a lot worse soon enough," Sarge said.

"Thanks for that, really cheered me up."

Sarge said, "Look at it this way: this makes it easier for us."

Doc looked at him like he was stupid and Sarge said, "Anyone we come across is either for us or against us. No gray area now."

Doc said, "You may be ready to kill everyone you meet, but I'm not. Everything I've ever done was aimed at protecting these people."

Sarge said, "Let me make this very fucking clear right now: I don't *want* to kill everyone I come across. You and I both took an oath once: all enemies, foreign *and* domestic. I've done my part for the foreign ones, now comes the time to deal with the domestic. Anyone who isn't part of the solution to the current problem is part of the fucking *problem* and will be dealt with accordingly." He paused for a moment to look at all three men. "No quarter will be given, none will be expected. You all heard what the colonel said. We have a defined enemy, we have a defined mission." He paused again and looked squarely at Doc, his expression softening some. "You want to overthink this. I get that, it's the way you're built. So think about it this way: how many times have you wondered why the average German didn't stand up to Hitler? Lots, I bet. I know I have. And I don't know the answer to that, but I do know I'm not gonna have people fifty or a hundred years from now asking the same thing about me."

Mike reached out and slapped Doc on the back. "Come on, man."

Doc said, "I'm with you."

Sarge put a hand on his shoulder. "Ain't no one asking you to like it. I sure as hell don't. Just keep thinkin' about who we're doing this for. Friends, family, anybody under the DHS boot."

"Yeah, which reminds me, I got a call from Thad earlier," Doc said.

Sarge asked, "How's he doing?"

"Not good. Said a mailman came by his place and was asking a lot of questions, basically told them they may be relocated to areas where their skills would be best utilized for the *common good*."

"Damn, they're moving faster than I thought they would," Sarge said, looking down at the trail as he walked.

"You expected it?" Doc asked.

"Well, sorta, yes. Under martial law the postmaster can be tasked with conducting a census and compiling lists for things like work details and relocations. I guess they are getting to work on it already. Shit. I really thought it would take them longer. How many of them were there?" Sarge said.

"He said there was one guy in a postal uniform and one in a DHS uniform who was covering him. The guy told them they would be getting a letter in the next few days with instructions, and then there were threats. He wanted to know what you thought he should do."

Sarge walked for a moment and then said, "We'll have to think on that one for a while."

Chapter 10

The next week went by without much happening. Food was the growing concern for almost everyone in the neighborhood. We had managed to conserve ours and were in pretty good shape, especially since I had shot a deer one night in the front yard.

I had been sitting on the porch when I heard something and clicked on my flashlight and saw three sets of lights shining out in the yard. At first I was shocked to see them there; after all, with so many hungry people out there I thought the deer would have been wiped out, but there they were. I stepped inside and got my .22. It was an old Mossberg bolt-action. The best part about it was the scope I had put on it. It had an illuminated reticle that used a 2032 coin-style battery.

Turning the sight to the lowest setting, I held the flashlight in one hand and propped the rifle on the porch rail. Centering the crosshairs between the set of glowing eyes, I fired a Stinger. The other two immediately bolted and were gone. I found the deer right where it had bedded down for the night. Since it was so cold out still, I gutted the deer, saving all the organs except for the digestive tract, and hung it high in a tree where I usually processed deer for the night. All the organs I took inside and put in a bowl in the fridge. My plan was to save them for the dogs, as dog food was getting scarce.

Hanging the deer had unintended consequences, as the neighbors to my east saw it the next day. This just added to the hard feelings in the neighborhood. I had killed a deer and everyone knew I had meat. They already suspected that I had other food, since I didn't take any of the food Mark got from the county. Maybe I should have, but it felt like the right thing to do. It was five more meals a day for those in the community when my family wasn't there in line. But it didn't gain me any points with anyone. Mark, Danny, Rick and Reggie were the only ones that would work the barricade with me, or even speak to me, for that matter.

When I was butchering the deer I took a ham over to my neighbor and offered it to him. He refused, acting like the meat was tainted. I just looked at him and said, "Then just let the kids eat it. They won't care." He finally relented and took the meat after looking back at his two children playing in the yard. They already looked skinnier than I had ever seen them.

Even that act of generosity didn't help, and it seemed to only make matters worse. Danny and I were on the barricade one morning early when some of the folks from down the road came up. They were going to go out hunting in the forest down the road a bit.

"Where you guys headed?" Danny asked.

One of the three men, one from down on Danny's end of the road replied, "We're going to go and see if we can kill something, anything, to eat." He paused for a moment and looked at me. "We can't all kill 'em in our front yard."

I thought I would offer some helpful advice, maybe try and break the tension. "Try looking for them at night with a flashlight. That's how I got mine."

"That'd be great if I had batteries for a flashlight," the

man replied and then the three of them walked through the barricade heading toward the forest.

I looked over at Danny. "How in the hell can they be pissed that I got a kill? It's not like I took it from one of them."

"They all think you have a mountain of food you're sitting on. What Pat said really stirred them up. Some of them feel like you killed them just to shut 'em up."

"That's not why I did it and you know it," I said.

"I do, you do, but that's about it. And you gotta admit, it was fucked up."

"If I hadn't have done it they would have done me just to get what they think I have. Hell, you have almost as much as we do. Why aren't they beating your door down?"

Danny gave an evil little grin. "I guess 'cause you killed Pat before she could talk about me."

We stood in silence for a few minutes, and then Danny said we should start a fire in the barrel. As he was putting together the makings of a fire I thought I heard something. "Hey, man, you hear that?"

Danny stopped what he was doing and walked over to where I was standing, cocking his head to listen. "Yeah, I do. What is it?"

The sound was a low rumble of sorts, but was definitely getting louder. "Almost sounds like a big truck," I said.

"Yeah, it does."

We stood there listening for a few minutes, the sound getting louder until there was no doubt that's what it was. It didn't take long before we could see the truck coming down the road, heading north on 19. "Check this shit out," I said.

As we stood there, a large tanker truck came rumbling past us. It was escorted, front and rear, by Humvees. As the Hummers came toward us, the gunners in the turrets trained their weapons on us. We both stepped back from the barricade with our hands held up in front of our chests. The M249s mounted to the turrets were way more hardware than I wanted to tangle with.

The rear gunner kept his weapon on us until they were out of sight down the road. Danny and I exchanged looks. "What was that?" Danny asked.

"Had to be a fuel truck; that's the only thing that would warrant that kind of security. You know folks would do about anything for several thousand gallons of gas right about now," I said.

"You're probably right, but where was it going, and why was it coming through here?" Danny asked.

"The only thing I can think of is the bombing range. Remember those guys I told you about, the ones that tried to shoot down the helicopter? They said there was something going on over there on the range. Maybe that's where it was headed."

"But why come through here, and where was it coming from? There's a fuel depot in south Orlando, but I would have thought that was used up long ago by now."

"Maybe coming from Tampa and just varying the route to prevent ambush," I said.

Danny went back to making the fire and we didn't talk about it anymore. I made a mental note to tell Mark about it, for no real reason other than the curiosity factor.

For most of the morning the sound of a chainsaw had come from old man Howard's house. He was busy cutting wood, and from the sound of it, a lot of it. The saw would run for a while then stop for a while in irregular intervals, but always in the same manner. You could tell when he had cut enough to stack or haul or whatever he was doing with it, so when the saw stopped abruptly, I turned to look back that way.

With the saw stopped it was quiet, the air was cool and it was a nice morning. Then the air was ripped by a bloodcurdling shriek, followed by shrill, short screams.

I took off at a run toward Howard's house. It was one up from mine toward 19. His gate was closed and locked, but I was over it in a flash. As I ran up his drive I saw his wife on her knees off to the side. She was holding Howard and she was covered in blood.

I skidded to a stop on my knees beside her. Howard was on the ground, his right leg severed just below the knee. He had his hands wrapped around his leg just above the knee, but with every beat of his heart, bright red blood spurted from the leg. The ground in front of him was covered in blood; the chainsaw was lying on his severed foot. Without saying anything, I tore the trauma pack off my vest and pulled out the tourniquet. Wrapping it around his leg, I found it was still attached by a thread of skin. I placed the tourniquet just above his knee, pulled it tight and began cranking it down. The spurts of blood slowed, then stopped.

I grabbed the Sharpie out of the kit, looked at my watch and wrote a big T on his leg, then 7:47. Howard's wife was still in hysterics, and Howard looked like he was going into shock. I pulled out a casualty blanket and covered him with it, then elevated his other leg. He was still conscious, but he didn't look good. Pulling the JetScream whistle out of a pocket on the vest, I blew three long blasts, paused and blew three more, then repeated it a third time. I told his wife to go in and get a blanket for him. She didn't move, so I grabbed her shoulder and shook her. This brought her around and I finally got her moving.

I could hear people coming over the gate and it wasn't long before Danny, Rick and Mark came running up. When Rick got close enough to see the scene, he stopped abruptly and said, "Oh shit!"

Mark and Danny were both looking down, mouths agape. Mark looked at Rick and said, "Go get the Mule and bring it up here. Shoot the lock off if you have to."

Howard's wife came back out with blankets and we covered Howard, who was still conscious. He was one tough old man. Out at the gate came the sound of three rapid shots, then the sound of the Mule racing up the drive. Laying a blanket down in the bed of the Mule, we picked Howard up and laid him in.

"Where are you taking him?" cried his wife.

"Up to the forest vet," Mark said. This was something we had discussed earlier, even paying a visit to Doc Peters to talk it over. He was the only kind of doctor around. The fire department in Altoona had an ambulance, but it didn't run and was seldom manned given the current situation.

"To a vet?"

"You got a better idea?" Mark said.

Mark jumped into the Mule, then looked at her. "You coming?"

She made her way around to the passenger side and climbed in. Rick managed to wedge himself into the bed with Don to help stabilize him during the ride. Mark kicked the buggy into gear and took off down the drive toward the road, leaving Danny and me standing there. Danny looked down at all the blood on the ground. "Think he'll make it?"

"He's a tough old man," I said.

After they were gone, Danny and I walked back up to the barricade. We still had about an hour before we would be relieved. We talked a little about Howard and what we thought his chances were. Neither of us gave him much of a chance, and both of us were glad it wasn't us. We had both been doing some cutting, though we both had quite a bit of wood already cut and stacked. With wood being the only real source of heat, and the abnormal cold, having a pile of wood on hand was a good thing.

Our conversation turned to power after Danny commented on what the guys going out this morning had said about batteries. Since things had gone bad, Danny had been bringing down his rechargeable batteries to the house for me to charge. That got me to thinking, and I said, "You know, I have two spare panels and a spare inverter."

Danny paused for a minute. "No, I mean, I guess I did, but I never thought about it."

"We could take them to your house and set them up, maybe use your deep-cycle batteries from the boat. It wouldn't be a lot, but it would be something for you," I said.

His eyes lit up. "Dude, that would be awesome. Having some power would be great."

"Even better than that, I have three sockets you screw into a regular lamp and it makes them take the twelve-volt bayonet-type bulbs, which I also have. We could wire it to one of the circuits in your house and you could have some light."

"That would be great. I'm also running low on lamp oil," he said.

"I have more of that too," I added.

"When do you want to do it?" Danny asked.

"We can do it today if you want, after we get relieved."

"Sounds good to me."

We were interrupted by a group of people coming down the road. They were quite a sight to see, probably ten or twelve of them. It looked like an extended family group. They were pushing and pulling every sort of cart and wagon you could imagine, with one boy of about eight or nine pulling a Radio Flyer. As soon as they saw us, the group moved almost as one to the opposite side of the road, with the men staying between us and the women and children.

As the group got closer, two of the men broke off and walked over to us. They were both carrying rifles and one had on a pistol belt with a revolver in it. One of the two said, "Mornin'."

"Mornin', what do you hear?" Danny asked. This had become a most universal question when two people met.

"Not much. We saw one of them utility vehicles haulin' ass down the road earlier, looked like someone was hurt." I took this guy to be the leader of the band.

"Yeah, he's one of our neighbors, bad chainsaw accident," Danny said.

"That's a shame, probably a death sentence," the other man added.

"Where you folks headed?" I asked.

The leader pointed down the road, "Into the forest, trying to get away from some of the damn people. Things are starting to get bad in town."

"Where are you guys coming from?" I asked him.

"We all lived in Eustis or Mount Dora," the other man said, then, pointing to the Igloo cooler sitting on a little stand by the burn barrel, added, "Is that water?"

I glanced over my shoulder at the cooler. "Yeah, it is. Y'all need some water?"

The leader spoke up, "If'n ya could spare it. We ran out of the bottled water a long time ago. Water went out in town a couple of weeks ago. We stored water in everything we could find, but we're almost completely out now."

"You're welcome to it. It's almost full. Just have one or two of your people bring the bottles over, no offense," I said.

"None taken. You just can't be too careful these days," the leader said.

He turned to his group and called out to a couple of the ladies with them. They started pulling out bottles and jugs, old soda bottles and milk jugs from the looks of it. The two women carried them over and Danny walked them through the barricade to the Igloo. They emptied it, filling what they had, and still had empty jugs.

After the women were headed back across the street, the leader came up to the barricade and stuck out his hand. "Fellers, I can't thank you enough. Everyone we've seen so far keeps their distance and gives ya the stink eye. It's nice to know there's still some good folks in the world."

"No problem. We're nice to those who are nice to us," Danny said and shook the man's hand.

We talked to him for a few more minutes. He was vague about exactly where they were headed, just as we were vague about how many people were on our street. I did tell him that everyone was armed and we had a security system, stretching the truth a bit about that part. Then he made me a little uncomfortable by asking about food. We told him that we were all barely getting by, then I turned it on him. He told us that was another reason they were heading into the forest: "There's more to eat out there," he said.

I didn't say anything, but inside I knew better, and it

made me think that soon the right to hunt on land that had been public might be another source of conflict.

They finally moved off down the road. Once they were gone, Danny said, "More to eat?"

"Yeah, I wasn't going to say anything, but if that's the reason they're going, unless they got Euell Gibbons with 'em, they're going to freakin' starve. There's some stuff in the spring and summer, but you know the winter is damn thin out there. I hope they like palmetto hearts and swamp cabbage."

Danny laughed. "That's what I thought, but you know more about it than I do. Hell, Little Bit shows me stuff."

"Yeah, she thinks it's the coolest thing in the world to pull something off a vine and eat it. The women at the bus stop like to have had a heart attack one day when she pulled the tip off a greenbrier and ate it. I was sitting in the truck and saw the woman try to stop her. Little Bit told her I said she could, so the woman comes over and asked if I let her do that. I told her I let her. Hell, I encourage her."

Danny laughed again. "I bet. She cracks me up. Maybe you can bring her down when you come."

"Shit, you'll probably see all three of them. They haven't been down to your house in a while."

"Just feed 'em first; this ain't like the old days," he said.

I asked how they were doing with food and told me they were still all right. I had given him a hindquarter off the deer, and he was making jerky out of some of it, and they had cooked up some already as well. The rest was hanging on the back porch since it was still so cool out.

Hearing an ATV coming up the road, we looked back to see our relief coming. It was Lance and another guy, a young kid. I didn't remember his name, but I knew he was Reggie's nephew who had come to stay with him. We told them about the procession that had been by and to keep an eye out for them, just in case. Lance then had a great idea. He said, "We need something like a bell or something up here to sound in case of an emergency."

"I have that old bell out on that post in the front yard. It's probably rusted and won't move right now, but I bet I can clean it up," Danny said.

I looked at Lance, then at Danny. "That's a damn good idea. Great idea, man, we'll bring it down here later and put it in."

Lance smiled and walked over to the barrel to warm his hands. I grabbed the empty Igloo and climbed onto the back of Danny's Polaris as he started it up. We headed down to my house and when we pulled in I told Danny to hold on for a minute so I could refill the jug, then he could take it back before heading to his house. We agreed that I would come down around noon, using the Suburban to move the panels and inverter/charge controller. Danny wheeled the ATV around and headed for the gate.

Chapter 11

After talking to Sarge, Thad had a lot of work to do. He and Anita loaded almost all the food into the old Scout and drove out into the woods behind the old home place. He had looked around until he found an old drum that was empty. Old man Jackson apparently didn't believe in recycling old motor oil and had a couple hundred gallons of the stuff in drums around the property. In a junk pile, he found a top for the barrel but never did find a locking ring. Picking out a spot, Thad laid a drop cloth on the ground and started to dig, laying the spoil on the cloth. It took him about an hour, but he got the hole dug. Little Tony wanted to help, but Thad was in a hurry.

Once the hole was big enough, he set the drum in a couple of times to ensure it fit. They filled the drum up almost two-thirds of the way with cans and jars, making sure to leave some cans for his personal pack. Thad filled the rest of the space with clothes, some water, a little ammunition and other assorted stuff. Once the drum was full, Thad caulked the lid with silicone and then backfilled the hole. When he was done, he still had a sizable pile of dirt on the drop cloth. It was an effort, but with Anita and even Little Tony pushing, he was able to tie the corners together and get the bundle into the back of the International.

Back at the house, he collected all their guns and went to

work on hiding them. The house's interior was done in paneling, so using some tools from the shop Thad pulled out the brads, being very careful not to damage the panels. He chose spots where less than a full sheet was used, near corners or doorways, and removed these smaller sections. In the little piece between the front door and the wall that was behind the door when it was open, Thad put the SKS and one pistol. Then he mounted a hook he had found in the shop to the panel with a nut and bolt, putting a washer on the inside behind the nut. Using some of the brads that weren't bent, he put just enough in around the edge to make the panel snug, having to add three to the top to keep it from bowing. Even with those he knew he could pull the panel out with one hand if he needed to.

He kept his old shotgun and his Glock out, Anita had her Glock as well, just in case. Then they went about preparing bug-out bags in case they couldn't get to the trucks. Anita had a pack she used for school, and Little Tony had a decent pack. The Transformers graphics and bright colors would have to go, though. Thad told himself to look for some spray paint for it, and he knew Tony would not be happy about that.

Thad made up the packs with the basics. Little Tony came up to Thad with a couple of his favorite Transformers in his hand. These, he told his father, were required. Thad took the toys from the boy and made room in his little pack for them. As he was doing so, he thought about the transition in his son. Here he was, making a pack for him in case they had to run for it, and the little boy carried over some toys to add to it, as if they were packing to go to Anita's sister's for the weekend.

They didn't have enough sleeping bags, but Mr. Jackson

had several nice wool blankets. Thad took these and rolled them up, then put them inside garbage bags and tied them to the bottom of the packs. Thad had a sleeping bag, but it was for Tony; he and Anita would use the blankets. Thad had his poncho, but they didn't have any other ground cloth, so he went out to the old man's shop to see what he could find. There was a nice old canvas tarp, probably ten by ten, but it was so heavy that he had to dismiss it. Digging through the shelves he finally found something that would work: half a roll of thick black plastic.

Thad took the plastic and cut four pieces to six-by-eight and folded and compressed them as best he could. He figured these would work well for ground cloths and, should they need it, overhead shelter. He also distributed the few MREs he had left from his trip home between Tony and Anita's pack. In his own he put as much canned food as he felt he could reasonably carry. In addition to the food, clothes and shelter items he packed, Thad also had his knife and Leatherman tool. He strapped a small camp axe to his pack and a bow saw to Anita's. He found his first aid kit and stuck that in his pack.

Thad set the packs by the door and stepped back to look at them. Then it hit him: fire. He had a lighter and the magnesium block he had gotten from Sarge, but that was it. Going back into the kitchen, he found a box of strike-anywhere matches and filled a pill bottle from the medicine cabinet with those. Looking through the kitchen drawers, he found two more Bic lighters and put one each into Tony and Anita's packs. Little Tony thought it was cool he got to carry a lighter, and Thad told him it wasn't a toy and he wasn't to use it except in an emergency. Little Tony nodded.

He had done all he could; now all they could do was wait.

Anita prepared dinner for them: a canned ham and some home-canned green beans and mashed potatoes. They sat down to dinner at the dining table, an oil lamp lighting the room. Thad cut up with Tony, and Anita admonished them both to knock it off at the table and eat their dinner; they didn't really listen, though. Before long, even she was laughing and joining in. Thad paused for a moment, taking the whole scene in. It was like a hundred years ago probably: no TV to interrupt dinner, no phone calls, just his family sitting and enjoying their time together.

Sarge had ordered that they all stop shaving, not that the guys really cared. It was worse on him than them; he had shaved every day for so long that he simply couldn't stand the feel of the stubble on his own face. He hoped DHS was looking for clean-shaven men with a military bearing; he wanted to change that as much as possible.

After a week of no shaving and little washing, Sarge deemed them all sufficiently grubby to start their recon. Sarge called a meeting and laid out his plan. He and Ted would take one of the boats and go up to Suwannee. They would dock the boat outside of town and walk in. Both of them would be wearing civilian clothes and carrying only pistols. Mike suggested they take rifles and stash them near the boat in case they had to break contact with any bad guys. Sarge thought this over; he didn't like the idea of taking the long guns in the boat in the event they got searched on the river. Mike reasoned they were going to engage the bad guys at one point or another anyway, so why worry about it.

Ted said he agreed with Mike, and Sarge relented and agreed to take the rifles. He modified the plan to include possible engagements on the river. If anyone attempted to search them, they would engage them on the water. A radio was put in the boat they were taking, and Doc and Mike would stand by with the other boat as a reaction force in the event they ran into any big trouble. With the plan set, they all set about getting ready to launch the mission.

Don had been sitting in the corner, eating the leftovers from breakfast. He spoke up as Sarge was changing into an old pair of jeans and an insulated flannel shirt. "Hey, Linus, see if you can get some beer in town. I'm dyin' over here."

"This ain't the fucking Hilton."

"I know that, but this is getting old; can't go anywur, can't do nuthin' and no damn beer. Just take me to town an' drop me off, then," Don said as he started to stand up.

Sarge pushed him back into his chair. "You ain't going anywhere. We drop you off in town and they'll grab your ass up in a heartbeat."

"I ain't worried 'bout them; I ain't done nuthin'."

"Maybe you ain't worried, but I'm worried what you would say to them."

"I wouldn't say anything 'bout y'all," Don snorted.

"You have no idea what they would do to you. You'd be making shit up, admitting to shooting Kennedy when they got done with your sorry ass. Not to mention that you'd sell your momma out for a case of beer," Sarge shot back.

"Now, you just wait a damn minute—"

Sarge told Mike, "You watch him. If he tries to do anything, shoot his ass."

"Hey!"

"This ain't no fucking game," Sarge said.

Don eased back into his chair, slumping down. He stared at the floor, then he looked up at Sarge. "So no beer, then?"

Mike started to laugh. "You gotta admire his spirit. Man knows what he wants."

About noon, Ted and Sarge headed out into the river and turned west toward Suwannee. They were surprised to see several boats on the river, though most of them were under oar power. Everyone they passed waved at them and they waved back. It seemed like any normal day on the river. Most of the boats were fishing. They saw several people throwing cast nets; this was about getting food, not sport.

Approaching Suwannee, Sarge beached the boat. He and Ted took a minute to look around. Then they took their rifles and moved off to the west a bit and hid them in the palmettos. Satisfied with the job, they moved off toward town. Sarge had an old canvas tool bag, the kind masons use, with some barter items in it. He thought this would help their cover. As they came into town they saw very few people, so they headed toward the docks. Approaching the post office, they saw a line of people coming out the door.

Sarge set the bag down and knelt down like he was looking in it. Ted stood in front him, between him and the post office. "What do you make of it?" Ted asked.

"Remember what Thad said about the mailman? Can't be a good thing," Sarge replied.

Sarge was looking past Ted at the post office when he noticed the bus. It was an old YellowBird school bus sitting out in the street. As people came out of the post office, some of them would get on the bus. There was a fairly heavy security presence there as well. Everyone in line had papers in their hands and a badge clipped to the outside of their coats. As they approached the building, one of the guards would look at the badge, then rifle through some papers on a clipboard, then wave them through the door.

Sarge closed the bag and stood up. "Let's go this way. We don't need to get any closer to that shit."

The two turned and headed down a lane that paralleled one of the many canals, heading south. After a block they turned to the west again, trying to find their way to the center of town, where all the big docks were. As they came out from between two buildings to the road on the next block, Sarge saw two men in black uniforms under an awning to a little shop. Sarge and Ted kept their heads down and kept on walking. They went across the street and into an alley on the other side. Sarge took out the handheld ham radio he had under his shirt and stuck an earbud in his ear.

"Swamp Rat, this is Swamp Rat Actual."

Mike came back over the radio. *"Swamp Rat Actual, have you five by five, go ahead."*

"It's getting a little hinky here. Move up to jump off and stand by for fire support," Sarge said.

"Roger that, we're ten mikes out," Mike replied.

Sarge and Ted came out of the alley and they were in the dock area. Here there were a number of people and also a number of boats that looked like small ferries. The two men stopped short near the corner of a building and looked the area over.

"What in the hell is going on here?" Ted asked.

"Looks like they're moving people," Sarge replied.

A man and a woman were walking down the board-walk toward the two of them. Sarge could see the badges clipped to their coats. As they came closer, Sarge tipped his hat to them. "Howdy, folks."

The couple looked at them and the man said, "Morning."

"What's all this about?" Sarge said, gesturing to the scene at the docks.

The man looked at them, looking at their chests and noticing neither of them were wearing badges. "It's the relocation act. People are being sent to the camps where they're needed."

Sarge was looking at the badge on the man's chest while he spoke. On it was the man's picture and his ID info, including his Social Security number and a thumbprint. He also took note of the red field the man's name was printed on.

Sarge looked back up just in time for the man to ask, "Where's your ID? You know you can't be out without it."

Ted jumped in quick. "Oh, we just came into town to get ours. We live way out and just heard about it. Where are they sending you to?"

The man looked at him with a suspicious glance. "We don't know yet; we haven't been told."

He looked at his wife, who was tugging on his arm. The man looked down the boardwalk and said, "We have to go." And they walked off.

Ted glanced over his shoulder and saw two men coming their way. He looked at Sarge and cut his eyes toward the alley. The two of them turned and started back down the alley. "We need to get the hell out of here; this place is crawling with goons," Ted said.

As they started across the street, a voice called out from behind them, "Gentlemen, can you hold up?"

Instead of stopping, they kept their heads down and kept walking. As they approached the next alley, the voice called out again, "Stop and identify yourself!"

Sarge keyed the mic on the radio. "Swamp Rat, we need to draw these guys off us now."

"*What's your location?*" Mike asked.

"We're on the east side of town, near the river," Sarge answered.

"*Roger that, be there in two mikes,*" Mike replied.

Sarge and Ted were heading for edge of town at a quick trot. The two men behind them came out of the alley. "Stop or we'll shoot!"

They dove to the ground at the sound of shots. Sarge looked up to see Mike laying down a stream of fire with an M249. The two goons that were behind them were taking cover, their faces in the dirt. Sarge and Ted jumped up and took off running for the boat. They grabbed their rifles from where they were stashed and quickly boarded the boat, Ted shoving it off as Sarge started the engine.

"Swamp Rat, we're clear. Head for the Alamo," Sarge called into the radio.

Doc called back, the sound of the M249 in the background. "*Roger that, Actual. Breaking contact and heading for the Alamo.*"

Sarge looked down the river and saw the other boat heading their direction. Mike was still firing at the shore. Doc's voice came over the radio as Sarge opened the throttle on the boat. "*Actual, we have two fast movers coming up behind us!*" The sound of the Squad Automatic Weapon, or SAW, was almost constant.

"Shit!" Sarge yelled.

"What's up?" Ted shouted from the front of the boat.

"They have two boats after them!" Sarge yelled as he swung the boat in the center of the channel, heading toward Mike.

"*Mike's hit, Mike's hit!*" Doc screamed into the radio.

"Fuck!" Sarge yelled as he pushed the boat wide open. "Mike's hit!"

A. American

Ted knelt down in the bow of the boat, his M4 ready. He reached into his coat pocket with his left hand, took a frag grenade and pulled the pin.

"Swamp Rat, we're going to pass you on your left, put the hammer down, son!" Sarge yelled into the radio.

"*Roger that, on the left!*" Doc shouted back.

The two boats were gaining on Doc and Mike and when they were about thirty yards out, the SAW opened up again. Sarge could see Mike leaning on the transom of the boat, resting the weapon on it for support. The lead boat suddenly yawed to the right, but the other boat kept closing. Sarge veered to the right, passing Doc's boat, and Ted opened up with his M4. As they came almost abreast of the second boat, he threw the frag. It missed and landed in the water, shooting a geyser into the air behind it. Sarge had his M4 up, firing with one hand and steering the boat with the other. One of the goons in the boat dropped. The boat wheeled in the channel and turned to the west again. Sarge turned his boat to trail Doc. Ted fired at the DHS boat as it headed west.

Back at the shack, Sarge had Ted jump out at the creek mouth, just in case. He waded ashore and took up an over-watch position. Running the boats up to the end of the creek, Sarge jumped into the boat with Mike. Blood was smeared on the deck. Sarge lifted him off the deck with Doc's help, and the two of them got him out of the boat and onto the boardwalk to the shack. Approaching the shack, Sarge kicked the door open, causing Don to jump with fright. He was tied to a chair and he fell over onto the floor with a thump.

Doc swept the little table with his free arm, knocking plates and coffee cups to the floor. They laid Mike out on the table and Doc began ripping his body armor and assault gear off him. There was an entry wound on the left side of Mike's chin and an exit wound under his ear. Doc threw his pack onto a chair and tore into it, pulling out sponges and stuffing them into the wound. Mike howled in protest, but Sarge grabbed his arms and pinned him to the table. Don was still on the floor trying to yell through the duct tape over his mouth.

Doc turned Mike's head and examined the exit wound. "He's going to be all right; it missed the artery, but I'm going to have to cut away some of this tissue. It's pretty tore up."

"Hold on, son. Doc knows what he doin'," Sarge said.

Chapter 12

After loading the spare panels and the inverter/charger into the Suburban, I went back into the house and asked the girls if they wanted to go down to Danny and Bobbie's, and I was met with a chorus of "Yeah!" Mel said she wanted to go too, so we locked up the house and chained the gate and headed down.

Danny had already pulled up the post with the bell on it and had it lying by the drive. All the girls headed into the house, except Little Bit; she wanted to hang out with Danny and me. We decided to put the bell up before working on the panels, so we loaded it into the Suburban with a set of post-hole diggers and a shovel. There was no way Little Bit was staying behind, so we loaded her up too and headed for the barricade.

We shot the shit with the guys at the barricade while we planted the post. Little Bit amused herself by climbing on the big logs used to construct it. I had to give her a piece of paracord from my vest because she "needed some rope." I asked if the guys had seen anyone on the road and they replied no, no one had passed.

"No news is good news," I said.

Danny had already oiled the old bell, and it worked great. We came up with a simple code: one ring simply meant they needed Mark or a deputy. Three rings in rapid succession meant there was a problem. If the bell was being rung continuously and fast, then the shit had hit the fan at the barricade.

With all that sorted out, we loaded up and headed back to Danny's, stopping by Mark's to tell him about the bell and the code for the rings. He thought it was a great idea and wondered why no one had thought of it sooner. After talking with him for a minute with him, we headed back to Danny's. We installed the panels on the roof of the rear porch. It faced south and would have the best exposure, plus it put them close to the electrical panel.

Once the panels were mounted, we installed the inverter/charger on the porch under the panel. Danny already had the two deep-cycle batteries sitting there and I wired them up, using the cables from the boat. Once it was all hooked up, I used an old Simpson analog meter to check the voltage: ten volts was all they had in them. The charge controller indicated the batteries were getting almost four amps of charge, not bad for only two panels. I told Danny to let them charge for the rest of the day before we tried to connect anything and see what they looked like tomorrow.

We spent the rest of the day hanging out there, just like old times. Mel and Bobbie cooked some venison steaks on a grill Danny had set in the fireplace and even managed a pot of rice and a couple cans of green beans. There wasn't a lot, but it was enough, and as we ate we talked of how we were more fortunate than some of our neighbors. As we sat around the fire after eating, Danny asked about water.

"Do you think that will run my well pump?"

"No, your pump is 240 volts; that only has 120 volts," I said.

He sat there for a minute thinking. "What if we took that

irrigation pump from your place and hooked up to my well. Are you using it?"

"I'm not using it and the inverter will run it, but it will be a pretty big draw on the batteries."

"All I want to be able to do is fill a drum every few days; it should be able to do that," Danny said.

"Yeah, as long as you aren't doing too often, it would do fine. We'll do it tomorrow if you want."

"It would be nice. I've been dipping water from the pond, and it's getting old."

"All right, tomorrow. I'll pull it off and bring it down," I said.

I had never thought of his water situation. Danny had a small pond on his property, but it was the color of strong tea, and I could only imagine what it was like having to deal with it. We finally said our good-byes and Mel and the girls headed for the Suburban. Danny went out and opened the gate for us and we drove out, everyone waving to him as we did. The drive to our house is short, just five minutes, and in the past was never something to give a second thought to. Tonight, in the dark and in light of recent events, I was look-ing at every shadow on the side of the road. Some of the houses had a little light, but most were dark. There was still the assortment of dogs that ran along with the old truck as we went along, stopping when they hit the fence at the prop-erty line.

When we pulled up to the gate, Mel started to get out and open it, but I told her I would do it and to keep her eyes open. As I got out and headed for the gate, Meathead came running up, tail a wagging and that silly almost-smile on his face. Seeing him made me feel a little better; if anyone was out there he would let me know. After pulling in and closing the gate, I pulled up to the house. It was pitch-dark, since leaving the porch light on was a no-no these days. I told the girls to all stay in the truck and I got out and walked up to the house with my rifle at the ready.

At the door I turned on the Surefire mounted to the rail and lit up the front door. I opened it and let Meathead go in. He ran in and sniffed around, then ran to the sliding glass door in the dining room and started to bark and jump at the door; something had his attention out there. I doubled back to the truck, made sure Mel had her pistol and told her to get in the driver's seat, and that if it got loud to go back to Danny's. I walked around the edge of the house toward the gate in the split fence. The gate was closed so I just sat and listened.

It was an eerie quiet, like in a horror movie right before someone goes, *Hey do you hear that?* and a chainsaw starts up and cuts that guy in half. That was a little less funny when I remembered what had happened to Howard. I went back to the house and got the dog and brought him out, opened the gate and tuned him out into the yard. He took off like a shot, barking his ass off. I could hear him running toward the back fence, and then he turned and headed back toward me. Raising my rifle, I flipped the light back on and saw the three sets of eyes reflecting back at as they ran toward the spit fence just to my right. Instinctively I centered the sights on one of the deer and fired two quick shots. The deer fell about ten feet from the fence and the other two went over.

Hearing the old Cummins rumble to life, I ran around the side of the house and waved at Mel before she drove off. I was surprised when I almost ran into her. "Who's driving the truck?" I asked in genuine surprise and relief that neither of us had shot the other.

"Taylor is! I told her to get ready to go if I gave her the signal," she replied.

"Why weren't you in the truck?" I was a little upset.

"And just leave you here? What happened back there?"

"It was a deer. Meathead chased three deer."

"And you shot one?" she asked.

"Yeah, I didn't really think about it, just did it."

"Oh, the neighbors are going to love you. Are trying to piss them all off? I mean, it's nice you got the meat, but you have a bow, and everyone in the neighborhood heard that shot."

And she was right. It wasn't long before an ATV could be heard coming down the road. It went past our house and to the barricade, so I didn't think anything of it. Mel went to get the girls in the house and I went over to the deer, which Meathead was licking like a popsicle. Looking down at it, all I could think was that I really didn't want to mess with it right then. But I had given away half of the last one, and this one would certainly help. I decided to give some to Danny, but the rest was going in the freezer.

I was brought out of my thoughts by the sound of the ATV coming back up the road. I listened as it slowed in front of my house, then the distinct sound of my gate opening and the machine started up the drive. I walked out to see who it was and could tell from the headlights it was Mark.

"What was the shooting about?" Mark asked as he shut the machine down.

"Meathead jumped a deer and I shot it, reflex more than anything else," I replied.

"You shot another one? Are you trying to piss everyone around here off?"

"Yeah, I heard that one already."

"What? Whatever. Everyone knows you got the other one and now you get another one, and when they find out about it they'll be pissed."

"First off, they're free to get their own deer; I'm not stopping them. And second, how are they going to find out when right now only you and I know about it?" I replied.

His entire demeanor changed. Mark crossed his arms and stared back at me. "What do you mean by that?"

"You said 'when they find out about it.' I'm not going to say anything, are you?"

"No, I'm not, but they will find out. Look, these people are hungry, their kids are hungry, they are getting desperate and we need to be working together. Everyone needs to pitch in so we can all get through this," Mark said.

"That's a good idea. Everyone should get together and do just that," I replied.

"So you're on board, then?"

"Me, no. I'll take care of my family and myself."

"What's wrong with you? Why won't you help?" Mark asked.

That pissed me off. "I *am* helping. I use my truck for the benefit of all, I pull security—one of few that do around here—and I don't ask for anything. You haven't seen my family or me in the line for the food you got from the county."

"No, and everyone has noticed it too."

"So what? They should be happy that the five of us stayed away; it was more for them. These people need to start worrying about taking care of themselves and stop worrying about what someone else has. I've shared food too, did you know that?"

Mark was silent for a moment. "I know you gave some to Danny."

"Yeah, and I gave some to him." I pointed to my neighbor's house. "He didn't want to take it, but I told him his kids wouldn't care where the meat came from."

"No, he didn't bother saying anything about it."

"But they were probably bitching with everyone else, right?"

Mark just looked at the ground. "Look, I need to know how much food you have."

"That's none of your, or anyone else's, business. I'm not asking anything from them or you, so everyone needs to leave me the hell alone." I practically spit the words out.

"You don't get it, do you? No one saw this coming. If we don't work together, no one is going to get out of this alive. Do you enjoy this shit?"

"No, I don't enjoy this shit, what the fuck is wrong with you? But implying that because I was more prepared than others and that as a result I'm responsible for them is pure bullshit."

"I have to do what is best for everyone. If you have food, it needs to be distributed," Mark said. Now he was starting to get pissed.

"And for what? You take what I have and give it out to people that are sitting on their asses waiting for someone, not them, but someone else, to come along and give them what they need and want. So what happens then? Then my family is starving and we're back where we started. And besides, that isn't going to fucking happen, and I think you know that," I replied.

"What are they supposed to do? You can't go to the store and buy food. There isn't any food."

"I got two deer; they can hunt. There's rabbits and squirrels, dove and quail, why the hell can't they go out and get their own food? I mean, what the fuck are they doing all day? Waiting in the bread line complaining? Tell 'em to go hunting, set snares, whatever. Hell, we have a library—tell 'em to do some reading, figure it out. Tell 'em to get ready for planting season. Tell 'em to get off their asses and take care of themselves."

"These guys *are* trying. You shot your deer at night, but no one else has flashlight batteries, and during the day there are so many people out in the woods that no one is seeing anything. So they're getting pissed that you go out at night with a bright-ass light and knock deer down with no effort," Mark said.

"What the fuck, man? You're turning into one of the mob that was at your house. Have you forgotten that? That bunch that stood there while Randal pointed a gun at your wife? Some of these people who are whispering in your ear were at your house ready to take what they thought you had, and now you come here and try to do the same to me."

"This isn't the same thing. There's no mob here, it's just me."

"No, but it *is* the same thing: you want what I have. You going to shoot me in front of my wife and kids? Are you ready for that fight?"

"Dammit, Morgan, no one is talking about shooting you! But something has to happen or it's going to get damn ugly around here. It's getting hard for me to keep these people under control," Mark snapped.

"Then organize them! There *are* things to eat: organize hunting parties so that not everyone is out in the woods at the same time. I mean, how many houses are out here, thirty or forty? What's that, a hundred people or better? Get them all working together. I don't see anyone doing anything but sitting around and waiting. Well, guess what: no one is coming. They need to step up and take responsibility for themselves."

"It's my responsibility to take care of them."

"No, it's not. You're law enforcement; if you want to take that on, then that's on you. But if that's the road you're gonna take, you have to think about something: people look up to you. They trust you. What you say *means* something, and more important, what *they* say in front of you means something. You got guys talking about taking what I have. If you don't say something, they're gonna figure you think it's okay. And where does that put us? I mean, look, this is a pretty heated conversation, but I don't think for a minute you're gonna come after me. But what about them? What happens when half a dozen guys drink the last of their liquor some night and head my way? How does that situation end? Them dead, me dead, my family dead? How does any of that benefit anybody?"

Mark was shaking his head, but he looked uncertain.

"I'm *for* this community, I am. I know we have to stand together, I do. But I have to stand for my family first, just like everybody else. And if you're not telling them I'm with them, that I've already done a lot for everybody, then what the fuck are they supposed to think? Look, I'll do everything I can to help, but get it in your head now: what I have is mine, period."

Mark stood there for a minute thinking. "Sorry, man; it's just getting really bad. You know Miss Janice at the end of the road?"

"Yeah, she has the forty acres, right?"

"That's her. She's in bad shape. She has no food at all. She actually ate the canned cat food she had. Plus, she told me she saw three men on the other side of her fence, toward the forest."

"Well, that's not good. We need to start doing roving patrols, that way anyone who tries to sneak around will at least think we have our shit together. As for her food situation, I'll take her some of this venison and some other stuff I can spare tomorrow. I'll also walk her fence and see what I can find there."

"Thanks, man. Things are just getting bad and I'm not sure I can keep things together much longer."

"I'll help you any way I can. If anyone is in desperate shape, I'll try and help, but don't think that makes me the food bank. You heard what I said, right? They're looking to you for leadership. And I'm sorry as all hell you don't want it, but you've been elected. No one wants to hear you're not sure, okay? You have to dig deep and give the people what they need, even if it's not what they want."

Mark was quiet for a minute and kicked at the dirt. "Yeah, I hear you. It's just—"

"I know, man, I know. Nobody asked for this. But nobody's asking if we asked for it either. We just have to do what we gotta do. They picked you. You can't just give up, and you can't let them call the shots. I mean, shit, what is civilization? It's having someone in charge who thinks about what's best for the group but who stands up for the rights of the individual."

"You're laying it on kinda thick, Morg."

I shook my head and said, "Don't pretend you don't know what I'm talking about. We can't afford that shit right now. They picked *you*, man. You gotta *lead*."

"Fuck me," Mark said.

"I hear you, man."

Mel came out of the house and called, "Hey, you coming in? Oh, hi, Mark, everything okay?"

"Yeah, everything's fine. I was just checking on the shots I heard." Then he looked back at me and said, "Well, I gotta go." We shook hands and he headed out for the gate. I still had a deer to dress, and as much as I didn't want to do it, I knew that being in Mark's shoes was worse.

Chapter 13

Thad had got up early the next morning to tend to the animals, and he saw the feed was almost gone. He knew that in the past people would turn their hogs out into the forest and let them free-range. He decided that later today he would walk the fence and see if it was good enough to keep them in and if it was, he would turn them out. After letting the chickens out to run for the day, he went back inside.

Thad found Tony sitting at the table eating a wedge of cornbread that Anita had poured some condensed milk over. Thad sat down and pulled the plate over in front of himself. Little Tony reached out and grabbed the plate. He had a big smile on his face with a mouthful of cornbread and milk running out of the corners of his mouth. Thad smiled and pushed the plate back over to the boy and Anita came over and set a plate down in front of him. Taking a bite, Thad understood why Tony didn't want to share.

Anita set a cup of coffee down in front of him and he washed the cornbread down with it. Anita carried the pot over and asked, "Want more?"

"Sure," Thad said and he held his cup out.

"Enjoy it while it lasts. There's one more can and it's gone."

"Damn, that'll be a bad day."

After his second cup of coffee, Thad went outside. He felt

anxious and didn't know why, but he had seen enough bad in the new world to pay attention to the feeling. Coming around the side of the house, he saw the old Scout sitting there and suddenly he knew what he was anxious about. He went over and sat down in the old truck and turned the key. The little truck turned over and rumbled to life. The gas gauge showed half a tank, so Thad drove the truck around to the barn and went inside. He found one full five-gallon can and one with about three gallons in it. He took them both out to the truck and put them in the back. It was the first time he thought that maybe having a hybrid might be worth it, and that made him smile. There wasn't a hybrid ever built that was big enough for him to fit into.

He told Anita that he was going to take a short ride and would be back soon. Thad drove the old truck back around the house and out the gate and made a left. The road was just a dirt track and went out into the woods past the house. He was watching the side of the road that the house was on for a place to pull off. After about a mile he found a spot that looked right and pulled off into the woods. The four-wheel drive worked good, and he was able to push the truck out into the bush a pretty good distance.

Satisfied it was far enough out, he got out the big bowie knife that Morgan had given him to cut some branches to cover the truck with. Once he had it covered enough, he looked back toward the house. The cache that he had made out in the woods behind the house was to the south of him, and he was going to try to find his way to it. Thad used the knife to cut a small trail to the cache site. That way if they had to get to it in a hurry they could. After about an hour of cutting his way through the bush he came to the fence. He had overshot the cache site and walked down the fence until he found the tracks from the truck.

Finally locating the cache, Thad started back out toward the Scout again, cutting a trail. After about twenty minutes, he cut his first trail and connected the two to make a good trail to the truck.

Thad was in the kitchen drinking a glass of water when Anita came in. He told her what he had done and why and what he was going to do with the pigs to save on the feed. As he was talking to her, her eyes suddenly got wide.

Anita pointed to the door, "Out! Get outside and take your clothes off!" She ordered.

Thad looked at her, "What?"

"You got ticks all over your coat! Get outside and get them clothes off, then you need a bath. You ain't coming back in here till you do."

Thad looked down at his coat and saw two ticks on it. He started to reach up and pick them off, but Anita slapped his hand.

"Out!" She shouted and pointed to the door.

After getting Mike's jaw cleaned and sewed up, Doc had him lay down on one of the cots. Don was still on the floor raising as much hell as he could in his trussed-up condition. Sarge pulled him upright in his chair and started to untie him, making clear he wasn't in the mood for any of his shit at the moment. Ted was still up at the head of the little creek, keeping an eye on the back door. Once Don was untied, Sarge went outside and sat down in one of the chairs on the little deck. Doc found him sitting there with his head in his hands.

"You all right, Sarge?"

Sarge looked up and said, "We shouldn't have gone in there. That was a dumbass stunt and it almost got Mike killed."

"Don't be so hard on yourself, man, it was just a sneak 'n' peek. It shouldn't have been a big deal."

Sarge looked up at Doc and said, "But it sure as shit turned into a big deal, didn't it? I should have known better. These assholes have been jerking off for years thinking about what they would do given the chance. We aren't dealing with a bunch of ragheads from some third-world shithole."

"Maybe not, but since the shoe is now on the other foot, why don't we take a move from their playbook? I mean, we've known since Vietnam you don't win this kind of fight going head-to-head."

Sarge sat there staring at the old worn boards under his feet, and after a moment he stood up and put a hand on Doc's shoulder. "That's a damn fine idea, son. No more head-on shit. We're going to be like hyenas biting the lion's ass every time he ain't looking. And I promise you one thing: I won't ever put anyone in position like that again if I can help it."

Doc laughed. "Shit, Sarge, we're all big boys. We know what can happen. All of us have been down range. Let's just make it hurt."

Sarge smiled and gave Doc a nod. "I feel like a beer, want one?"

"Sure, why the hell not."

Sarge went to the back of the old shack with Doc in tow. Kneeling down on the deck, he pulled a string out from between two boards and pulled up a milk crate full of Bass. Doc started to laugh, and over his shoulder, Sarge said, "If that fat fuck inside had found it, there wouldn't be any left."

He took three of them from the crate and lowered it back into the water. He handed one to Doc and went around to the front and opened the door. Don was sitting in a chair, staring at the floor. "Hey," Sarge barked, and when Don looked up, Sarge threw the bottle to him. This brought an immediate smile to Don's round face. Sarge shut the door and went back out to the deck and sat down.

"You think Ted can come back?" Doc asked.

Sarge was taking a pull on his bottle. "Yeah, go get him."

Doc climbed into one of the boats and headed down the creek to get Ted. Sarge sat back down in his chair to finish his beer. It wasn't long before Don came out the door with an empty bottle in his hand and an expectant look on his face. Sarge looked up at him and said, "What?"

Don looked around the deck. "Uh, you got any more?"

"That's it for today, my friend," Sarge said, then turned up his bottle and drained it.

"One beer? What the hell good is that?" Don whined.

"As good as it gets," Sarge replied as he stood up and headed for the door. He went inside to check on Mike. Mike was still on the cot asleep. *Doc must have given him something*, Sarge thought. He pulled a chair over to the side of the cot and sat down. He was sitting there with his hands folded and his elbows on his knees when Ted and Doc came in.

"You all right, boss?" Ted asked as he came through the door.

Sarge looked back over his shoulder and said, "Yeah, I'm okay."

"Don't blame yourself, boss. Shit happens; at least we're all still alive," Ted said.

"How's he doing?" Doc asked, coming over to kneel down beside the cot.

"Sleeping like a baby," Sarge said as he stood up.

"Yeah, an ugly fucking baby," Ted said.

Sarge looked down at Mike, then back to Ted, "You ain't shittin'. The best part of him got smeared on some Charmin."

Ted started to laugh, and without looking up Doc said, "Damn, you guys are hard. He can't even defend himself."

"Yeah, Doc, you should be warned: don't pass out around the old man or you'll wake up in some bad shit," Ted said.

After Doc had finished checking on his ward, he, Ted and Sarge sat at the table. They discussed their options, how to harass the DHS goons while limiting their exposure to them. They came up with a number of ideas, all of which had varying degrees of risk and complexity. IEDs were considered the safest way to engage their enemy, but triggering was the problem. They didn't want to accidentally harm civilians, so if they went that route they would have to use command-detonated devices.

The next-best consideration was sniping. Sarge had his M1A and could drive tacks with it out to nearly five hundred yards. This would eliminate the civilian casualty issues but ran the risk of being engaged by a flanking force or a sweeping action after the initial engagement. The last thing they talked about was basic ambushes. It was agreed that this could be a viable tactic on select targets. Single vehicles or small groups were deemed acceptable targets. Anything with armor was out, as was anything with a large security presence. Air cover was an absolute deal breaker; if air cover was ever present, then whatever action they were planning was to be abandoned. The colonel had told them they were working on a solution for the air issue. It was the key: they had to assume air superiority for their plan to work.

"Have you guys heard anything on the radio from Morgan?" Sarge asked as the conversation was winding down.

"No, not a word. Mike and I were just talking about him yesterday wondering where he was and what was going on with him," Ted said.

"Is the computer still hooked up on the other rig?" Sarge asked.

"Yep, it's listening. Nothing yet."

"Well, keep listening," Sarge said.

The group wasn't going to do anything until Mike was mobile again, so they had to find other ways to occupy their time. Sarge decided he was going to wash his clothes. When he said this to the two guys, they said they wanted to wash theirs as well. Sarge told them to follow him outside and he would show them the laundry facility. Sarge's laundry facility consisted of a big old galvanized washtub, one of those industrial-size potato mashers and a bag of the cheapest laundry powder he had been able to find.

Out on the deck, Sarge dumped his dirty clothes in the tub, scooped water from the creek with a bucket and poured it in. Adding a scoop of powder he started to pound the hell out of them. "And you don't need much powder either," Sarge said as he was working the masher. When he was done, he put them in a mesh laundry bag and hung them in the creek for the "rinse" cycle.

Ted and Doc just stood there and watched the whole presentation, and when Sarge was done Doc said, "You gotta be shitting me."

Sarge looked up. "Well, just run into town and hit the laundromat, then."

Both Doc and Ted did their clothes the same way, and

when they were done there were three bags of clothes hanging off the deck in the creek. Doc said he would stay outside on watch for a while, so Ted went in to find Sarge messing with the radios. He had a set of headphones on and was scanning the bands to see what he could hear. Ted knew that the old man was taking what happened to Mike hard and he wanted to get him outside for a little while. He suggested the two of them go fishing and after a little prodding, Sarge finally agreed.

Both of them were wearing civilian clothes when they got in the boat. Sarge had the SPW lying in the bottom of the boat covered with a tarp, and they both had carbines and sidearms. They weren't going to go far, just up to the mouth of the creek where Sarge said he always caught big channel cats. For bait they had a can of SPAM. That and couple of poles and they were in business. Sarge asked Don if he wanted to come, but to his surprise he didn't. *After all that bitching about being stuck in the cabin for so long and he turns down a chance to get out. Figures*, Sarge thought. Sarge told Doc to keep an eye on him, and he and Ted headed up the creek for a little fishing.

They anchored inside the creek, keeping close to the bank to try to provide as much cover as possible. The two of them sat and fished for a while, and the fishing was pretty good. In fewer than two hours, they had eight nice cats in the live well. Sarge decided they had enough, and they headed back for the cabin. As they pulled up to the shack, Sarge was pissed not to see Doc.

"Where the hell is he?" Sarge growled as Ted tied up the boat. He went to the door and threw it open. Doc was kneeling down on the floor, and Mike was beside him.

"What the fuck is going on in here?" Sarge barked.

When Doc looked back, Sarge could see they were leaning over Don, who was sprawled on the floor. The little shack had a strange smell, something antiseptic.

"He found that shine we took off them pirates; he drank two pints of it straight down," Doc said.

"Holy shit, I forgot all about that shit, where was it?" Sarge said.

Mike looked up, his bandaged jaw preventing him from speaking, and pointed to the shelf under the little kitchen sink.

Chapter 14

The next morning I got up and had breakfast with the girls. This was going to be their first encounter with fried mush, and I was extremely interested to see how they would take it. I was in the kitchen when they came in, and the smell of bacon filled the room. Mel was still asleep; this would be her introduction to the dish as well. Last night before going to bed I had taken a few minutes to boil up some corn meal, the first step in making fried mush, and put it in the fridge before going to bed.

There was a twelve-inch cast-iron skillet on the old Butterfly stove, and I had dropped two big spoonfuls of bacon grease into it. Cutting slices of the boiled cornmeal about a half inch thick, I laid them into the grease, and they landed with a satisfying sizzle. I lightly browned both sides and then took them from the grease and put them on a paper plate, glad I had stocked up on those. Lee Ann and Taylor came in. Taylor loves bacon, and I knew the smell of it drifting through the house would get her out of bed.

As she came into the kitchen she said, "Mmm, bacon."

"Not quite, but just as good," I replied.

Lee Ann walked over and looked at the plate, "What is that?" she asked in her best disgusted-teenager voice.

"It's fried mush," I said with a shitty grin on my face.

"There is no way I'm eating that," Lee Ann said.

I knew that was coming and probably shouldn't have told her what it was called. I took a piece from the paper plate and put it on another, then drizzled honey over it. "Here, just try it," I said, handing her the plate.

She took the plate and eyed it suspiciously, looked at Taylor and said, "You try it," and handed her the plate.

Taylor took the plate and smelled it. "Smells like bacon," she said, then picked up a fork and cut a corner off and stuffed it in her mouth. A huge grin spread across her face. "Tastes like soap," she said, which is a running joke in our house for something that is good.

Lee Ann had a look on her face that said she didn't buy it, but took the next plate I prepared. Then I made one for myself and started to eat. She finally took a bite, "Hey, that's pretty good. What is it?"

I told them what it was and we all had a second piece. By now we were making enough noise that Little Bit came out, rubbing her eyes and dragging Bobby Jack, her stuffed monkey, behind her. Bobby Jack was a constant fixture with her, it was one of those stuffed animals you go to the mall for. Go in the store, pick out a carcass and then they stuff a tube up its ass and pump it full of polyester foam. I guessed if kids ever really thought about that process, the bear shop would have gone out of business. I felt a sudden pang for the stupid stuffed animal shop. The world that had supported something so far removed from keeping your family safe and feeding them was gone. And for all its flaws, I missed it.

She came over to the island and climbed up onto a stool. "What's that?" she asked, looking at the plate.

Before I could say anything, her sisters shouted, "It's mush!" Anything they could do to try and torment her.

She gave them both a look then asked, "Is it good?"

The girls finished off what was left on the plate. Fortunately I had put two slabs aside for Mel and I went into our room to see if she was awake. "You up?"

From under the covers came a muffled reply. "It's cold, did you start a fire yet?"

"Yeah, the girls are sitting in front of it now. I made breakfast and the coffee is ready," I replied.

As she pulled the covers off her head she asked, "When are you going to get that stove set up in here?"

This was on her constant "nag" list. I had the wood stove but had never gotten around to putting it in our room. I guessed I was going to have to break down and do it.

"As soon as I get some time. I have to help Danny get some water going at his place and I have to take some stuff to an old lady at the end of the road who's having a hard time. Maybe tomorrow if nothing goes to hell today," I told her.

"What are you taking and who is it for?"

"The old lady that has the forty acres down past Danny and Bobbie. She's been eating cat food, so I'm taking her some of the venison from last night's deer and some other stuff."

"Miss Janice? She's been eating cat food?" Mel had a look of disgust on her face.

"Yeah, can't imagine it either," I said.

"Don't give away too much. We have three girls to take care of."

"Yeah, I had that talk with Mark last night."

A chorus of "Danny's here!" from the living room let me know that he was here to help pull the pump. I walked into the living room as he came in with a "Yo," his standard greeting. Little Bit jumped on him and he picked her up and played with the monkey for a minute, then set her down.

"You ready?" he asked.

"I was just heading out. Let's get this thing broke apart and see what we can do at your place," I said.

We went out the sliding glass door into the backyard. "What the fuck, man, you kill another one?" Danny said when he saw the skinned deer hanging from the tree in front of the shop.

"Yeah, Meathead jumped it last night and I dropped it. I wasn't looking to, but it was running right at me. Let's cut a quarter off for you guys when we're done."

Danny just shook his head. "People are going to hate you."

"Let 'em hate. We're taking a quarter to Miss Janice down the road from you too. We'll have to bone that one out and cut it up for her, though," I said.

"She out of food?"

"Been eating cat food," I said.

"Shit!" was all he said.

It took us about fifteen minutes to pull the pump—when I installed it I had used unions for both connects to make replacing it easier. I carried the pump out to the Suburban and when I came back around the house, Danny was already cutting the deer up.

"Thank God it's winter, I don't know what we're going to do in the summer. Damn sure won't be able to hang 'em like this," he said.

We worked together to cut a quarter off for him, then we cut a front shoulder off and carried it over to the cleaning table. Working together, we cut all the meat from the bones and put it in freezer bags, making sure to cut all the pieces small. When that was done, we wrapped Danny's hindquarter in some butcher paper and loaded it in the truck with the freezer bags.

Danny headed out on his Polaris and I drove the Suburban. On the way down to his house, Mark came out of his drive in the Mule. Danny stopped in the road. I stopped behind him and walked up to Mark. He and Danny were shaking hands when I walked up.

"Hey, Mark, you heard anything about the old man?" I asked.

"Morning, Morg. He's still at the doc's house. He's keeping him there. Doc said the wound is healing, but he's still worried about infection."

"How much of the leg did he lose?" Danny asked.

"Doc managed to save it just below the knee. He still has the joint, not that it will do him much good. I think the prosthetics industry is probably closed now. He did say that tourniquet you put on saved his life."

"Well, that's good. I couldn't just stand there and let him bleed to death," I replied, feeling a little awkward. "Think anyone will remember that?"

"Good luck," Danny said.

"I don't know," Mark added. "Can't hurt, I guess."

We stood there for a minute talking over some of the news, which consisted of food, water and the weather. As well as firewood, which was talked about almost as often as the others. "Where you guys headed?" Mark asked.

"Down to Miss Janice's place. We have some food for her, and I want to take a look around her fence," I said.

"Let me know what you find. I'm curious if she really saw something or if she's having hallucinations," Mark said.

Anita carried clean clothes out to Thad while he washed in a bucket set under the old pitcher pump outside. The water was cold as hell, but his wife had made it plainly clear he wasn't coming back into her house till he took a bath. He actually needed a bath, so it wasn't a bad thing. He thought of what she had said: my house. He smiled to himself and shook his head thinking about how fast a woman takes possession of something, be it a house or man.

After dressing, he went back inside where it was warm. Anita had lunch ready, beans and rice today. He couldn't complain: every day his family got fed was a good day. He didn't know what she did to make it taste so good, but he enjoyed it. Little Tony, however, was not a fan. But he had been raised not to question what was put on his plate, and he ate it. When they were done, the little boy cleared the table and Anita started on the dishes. She had to carry water in from the pump in a bucket and pour it in the sink. All the washing was done with cold water. That was the one thing that Anita complained about.

Thad went out and drove the truck around to the barn. He was going to take the radio out to make it more portable in the event they had to bug out and didn't get the truck. This way he could put it in the Scout if he needed to. Thad was sitting on the ground cutting wires under the dash when the little man came outside.

"Daddy, Momma wants you."

"What she need, little man?" Thad asked

"Somebody's here."

Thad jumped to his feet and headed for the back door. He

came into the kitchen and didn't see Anita and headed for the living room. Anita was at the front door, standing behind it with it only partially open. She heard him coming and looked back. Thad stepped past her and pulled the door open. Standing there was the mailman again, with that same shitty-ass grin on his face.

"Thadius Jones?" the mailman said as the door flew open.

"What do you want?" Thad demanded.

"Well, I told you that I'd be back with instructions for you, and here I am."

Thad started to tell the guy to go to hell, but thought better of it. Instead he reached out and took the envelope that the man was holding out. Opening the envelope, Thad pulled out a folded-over form typical of all government forms, full of all kinds of information except what you want to see. After scanning it for a minute, he finally saw what he was looking for. In a box labeled UNIT ASSIGNMENT, he saw the name "Avon 4."

From his travels across Florida, he assumed this meant Avon Park. Looking the document over further, he saw another box labeled ASSIGNED DISCIPLINE. Inside this box were three words: "Driver/Manual Laborer." He knew exactly what that meant: he might be driving a truck, but more likely he'd be digging ditches somewhere. Folding the paper back up, he unfolded the second piece, the one with Anita's name on it. Thad took a quick look and saw that her unit assignment was Avon 2.

"Why does she have a different unit assignment than me?" Thad asked.

"I cannot answer any questions. I am just here to drop off the information. As you can see, you have a departure date here." The mailman reached over the top of the paper and tapped a section of the form. It was two days away.

"And what are we supposed to do?"

Raising his clipboard again and, going through the sheaf of papers, the mailman said, "It says here you are to depart from Lutz."

Thad looked at the man. "And how in the hell are we supposed to get to Lutz? You know how far that is?"

"You have two days. It's just down 41. Should be an easy walk."

"Anything else?" Thad asked.

"Yes. Don't miss your bus. You will be bussed to your final destination, and you do not want them to come looking for you." As the mailman spoke, he pointed to the security man he had with him. He was the same as the last time, black uniform with a big DHS patch on the sleeve.

"Oh, you won't have to come get us, I promise," Thad replied and shut the door.

Thad stood and looked through the little fan-shaped window at the top of the door as the mailman walked back to his Jeep. Leaning on the hood, he looked back at the house while he spoke to the security man. He reached into his shirt pocket and took out a pack of smokes, pulled one out with his teeth then produced a lighter and lit it. He tossed the pack and lighter on the hood and the security man picked them up and lit himself one.

They stood there leaning on the white Jeep smoking their cigarettes. Thad watched them through the little window, wondering if this was something they did to get a rise out of people who had been through forced withdrawal from nicotine.

I don't smoke, assholes, Thad thought as they stood there. It didn't take them long to finish their smokes. They flipped the butts into the yard: not the edge of the yard, but out into it. Eventually they climbed into the Jeep and drove off.

Thad stood there for a while looking at the road. The Jeep was gone and he didn't see anything that worried him. After a moment he heard Anita behind him and turned to her. "We gotta go."

"Where?" She asked, and again that look of fear was on her face. It hurt worse than anything he had ever felt in his life. Just knowing she was afraid made Thad mad. He was supposed to take care of her, protect her; that was a man's job, after all. "I don't know, but we have to leave from here."

Anita sat down on the old sofa in the living room. "When?"

Thad stood there for a minute and thought about it, then looked at her. She looked so small to him and her went over and sat beside her. "Tomorrow night. We'll wait till it gets dark, then we'll leave." Thad reached out and wrapped his arms around her. She leaned into him and almost disappeared into his huge shoulders.

Little Tony came in the room and looked at his mother, he could tell she was scared, and that scared him. He walked over and sat on one of her knees and looked up at his dad. Thad looked down at the boy and smiled. It was a forced smile, but he wanted to make him feel a little better.

"What's wrong, Momma?" Tony asked.

Anita reached out and put a hand on his head. "Nuthin', baby, I'm okay."

"You look sad."

Anita stood up and looked at Thad. "Well, I guess we got work to do if we're leaving tomorrow."

"Where we goin'?" Little Tony asked.

She looked back to the boy with a smile on her face, one that didn't look as forced as Thad's. "On a trip. You wanna go for a ride in the truck?"

"Yeah!"

Thad had already prepositioned most of what they thought they would need, but they made another pass through the house, looking for things they could use. Thad piled the few items they came up with on the back porch along with some assorted tools that he grabbed out of the shop. Now he just had to get everything loaded into the Scout.

The Scout was in the woods about a mile away, the cache was buried in the woods out behind the house and they had things there they needed to take with them as well. Thad sat on the swing on the back porch thinking about it. The most logical thing to do was to go get the Scout and drive it around and load everything up. But he was nervous to do it, afraid that someone would be watching and the moment he tried to move anything they would swoop in.

More important than when and how to go and get his supplies was where he was going to go. Thad sat there rocking in the swing going over the options in his head. He wished he could get back to Sarge, but he hadn't talked to him in some time. Then he thought about Morgan, but the thought of just dropping in on someone unannounced was a bad idea. He needed to get on the radio and see if he could reach anyone, maybe get some ideas from the guys.

Thad went back in the house and told Anita he needed to go for a walk to use the radio and try and get ahold of someone to see what they should do.

The radio was still lying in the front seat of the old truck where he had left it when he was interrupted while removing it. Picking it and the antenna up, Thad started out through the back of the property toward where the cache was buried. He didn't want to walk down the road and he had put the trail in from there to the Scout, so he figured it would be the safest route to get to it. Crossing the fence, he picked the trail and headed for the old truck.

After stringing the antenna in the tallest tree he could find, he opened the hood and connected the power cable directly to the battery using his Leatherman tool. Taking out his notebook from Sarge, he started going through the frequencies, listening for any transmissions. He heard a lot of talk, just not from the people he wanted to talk to. Some of the chatter caught his attention and he stopped on a frequently to listen.

A man from Jacksonville was on the radio, an old man from the sound of his voice. He was going on and on about what he called the Hessians. He told of how groups of armed men were going around the city killing, robbing, raping, basically doing whatever they wanted. He claimed they had working vehicles, motorcycles and ATVs, and were running rampant. When he paused, another voice came over the station talking of the same thing. He was in Atlanta and said that groups like that were also there. They ran through parts of town where there was no federal presence, which had been growing by the day.

The two men talked and Thad listened as they exchanged stories of how these groups would show up when the people of the area refused to cooperate with the FEMA plan and how they thought it was the government doing it. When the groups showed up, they stayed to a fairly defined area, raising general hell. After several days of this, the FEMA/DHS troops would move in and the thugs would move out. The man in Atlanta claimed that he witnessed what he called a mock firefight, the two groups confronting each other in the open streets. He said there was lots of gunfire but no casualties on either side.

As the federal troops moved in, the thugs would gradually pull back and out of the area and were not pursued. The two of them were in agreement that these were government-sanctioned thugs sent in to intimidate the local populace into submitting to the federal authority. Thad listened to this for a while, then moved on to other frequencies. As he scanned the bands, that name stuck in his head: *Hessians*. He thought about that, trying to remember where he had heard it. Then it came to him: German mercenaries used by the British during the Revolutionary War.

He was rolling that thought around in his head when he heard a pop, or thought he did. Looking up from the radio, he surveyed the area around him. Nothing was moving, no sound. Then he heard it again, one pop. This time he knew what it was and took off at a run toward the house.

Chapter 15

He's going into arrest, I'm going to start CPR," Doc said.
Sarge stepped over and put a hand on Doc's shoulder.
"No, you're not. Don't waste your energy on him."

Doc looked up at Sarge, and the look on his face told
the old man he was pissed. "Look, son, he's gone, and even
if you bring him back, then what?"

Doc looked back down at the rotund man on the floor
and dropped his hands onto his BDU-clad thighs. He sat
there shaking his head. "I guess you're right, it's probably
what he was trying to do."

Sarge made Mike go lie back down while he, Ted and
Doc dragged Don's body out of the shack. Out on the deck,
Doc asked Sarge what he was going to do with the body.
Sarge told him that tonight they would take him downriver
in the boat and drop him in. When Doc tried to protest,
saying that was where people, including them, were getting
their drinking water, Sarge reminded him of how many gator and fish carcasses had probably been thrown into that
river in the last several weeks.

The three of them got the body into one of the boats
and covered with a tarp. Sarge wanted to wait until it was
pretty late to go out on the river, so there was time to
kill. Going back inside, he sat down at the radios again and
played around with the bands. With his headset on, he

looked over to one of the other radios that was tuned to a preset band and connected to a laptop. A program was running on it and there was a map of the southeast. He looked at the screen for a minute, then turned back to the big box in front of him.

Ted stayed outside to keep watch while Doc tended to Mike. His wound looked good. Doc changed the dressing every day, but that was putting a dent in his supply of bandages. While applying a Telfa pad to Mike's jaw, he thought they would need to find a source for more. The typical places ran through his head: pharmacies, hospitals and the like. Pharmacies would surely be looted out and hospitals would be too damn dangerous to even think about, but it didn't change the fact that they were going to need more.

Mike was conscious and getting a little restless. Doc told him he needed to take it easy, but Mike told him he needed to get up for a bit or he was going to lose his mind. Doc finally relented and Mike got up and went to the kitchen. He was hungry and wanted something to eat. The bullet had passed along his jaw, but the wound was only in the soft tissue. He knew it would be painful to eat, but he was damn hungry. He started some soup and sat at the table with Sarge.

Sarge was going through the bands and stopped on one. He unplugged the headset and the speaker squawked to life. Mike and Doc both looked up at the same time as the sound of a man's voice filled the room. Even Ted opened the door and stuck his head in at the sudden sound. They all stood there listening as a voice filled with panic came out of the speaker. The man was screaming into the radio about gangs rampaging through town, how the feds were just outside of town and weren't doing anything about it. He had tried to leave, to get away from the chaos, but was turned back by armed men in black uniforms with DHS patches on their shoulders.

He said he had begged them to let him and his family out, told them what was going on in town, but they wouldn't let them leave. There were many people there trying to get out, but none of them were let through. Women were begging DHS to at least let the children through, but all were turned away. Now he was back in his house trying to hide from the terror in the streets. They could hear gunfire. It was not very loud or frequent at first, but the tempo and volume increased along with the panic in the man's voice.

It wasn't long before they heard screams intermixed with the gunfire. Ted had opened the door and all four of them were standing there listening as the scene unfolded in their minds. By then the man was shrieking into the radio. A crash came out of the speaker, then screams, closer screams and other voices. These voices were angry, hate-filled and loud. A woman screeched in the background, then another female did, too, and that one sounded much, much younger.

The man was still yelling when the station cleared and silence filled the shack. The four of them stood there not wanting to look at one another. Mike stood up and walked over to the little stove and turned off the burner, then went back to the table and sat down, suddenly no longer hungry.

Later, Ted was on the radios listening for anything that might be out there. The military radios were all silent, but the ham had plenty of traffic on it. As Ted listened he heard people from all over the country talking, and then he caught a transmission that grabbed him. A ham in England was talking with another in Maine. According to the English ham operator, while there had been some damage in the UK associated to the solar flare—power lines down, substations burned out and many structures burned as a result of the power lines overloading and setting them on fire—there was no damage to cars, and most electronics still worked in the areas that had power. Power was out in most of the country, but there were small pockets that had it and the other areas were being restored.

The citizens of England had been told that restoring power to the entire country would be a slow process, as the large transformers used at power plants and substations would take time to manufacture. There were even cases of transformers sitting in storage yards catching fire and burning. It had been determined that the stored units had not been properly grounded and had absorbed the load from the flare, causing the damage.

Ted listened for a few more minutes then went out to let Sarge know what he had heard. He sat on an old wire reel and relayed the information to the old man. Sarge sat there listening, taking it all in, not saying anything. Ted finished with, "What'cha think?"

Sarge sat there for a minute and then said, "I guess that proves my theory."

"What theory is that?"

"Remember when I said that an EMP could have been set off, either as an act of terrorism or deliberately by our own government?"

Ted thought about it for a minute. "Vaguely. You think that could be it?"

"What the hell else would do all this? Sure some of it may have been from the flare, but the rest of this had to be something else."

"Who do you think did it?"

Sarge rocked his chair back on its rear legs. "Doesn't really matter, does it?" "I guess not."

"Go tell Doc that we're going to go drop Don off."

When they had found a likely place on the river and lifted Don to drop him over the side, Ted said, "Kinda messed up just dropping him in the river."

"Best we can do for him," Sarge said. He went back to the console and turned the boat back down the river.

"Let's go drop off the food before we start on the pump. If she really is out of food, then I want to get it to her quick," I said as Danny climbed onto the Polaris.

"Cool. Let's go by the house and drop mine off. I'll ride with you."

I nodded my head as he started the machine. I followed him down to his place and waited at the gate while he drove it up to the shop and parked it. Danny walked back out to the gate and climbed in and we headed down toward Miss Janice's house. She had forty acres at the end of the street, which turned into her driveway. Her gate was closed and Danny got out and opened it. I drove through and he closed it behind me.

Pulling up in front of her house, I honked the horn as we got out. Danny went toward the house and I went around to the back of the truck to get the food out. I could see the old woman talking to him at the front door as I walked up with what we brought. She looked frail and sickly, but she was very warm and welcoming.

"Come in, come in," she said as I came up, holding the door for the two of us.

We went in and the old woman was upset she didn't have anything to offer us except hot water with a little lemon juice.

"Don't worry about us; we're here to bring *you* some stuff," I said.

I set the bag of venison on her little kitchen table, then a cloth shopping bag with a couple pounds of lentils, five pounds of rice, a couple dozen tea bags, a Ziploc bag of sugar, some assorted cans of veggies and two cans of SPAM. When I looked up at her, she had tears in her eyes. Her thin hands were pressed together in front of her mouth and were shaking.

"You okay?" I asked.

She stepped over and reached out and wrapped her arms around me. Patting her on the back, I tried to comfort her. "It's okay. Mark said you might need some help, so we came down. I just wish we had known earlier."

Through her tears she thanked us, hugging Danny as well, and told us how desperate she had been. How she couldn't bear the thought of asking anyone for anything when no one had anything to give. She didn't know what she was going to do and had prayed to God, then there we were, and she knew it was an answer to her prayers. I told her I didn't know about an answer to her prayers, but it would help for a while. I told her that it was very important that she not tell anyone.

She didn't understand why I wouldn't want anyone to know; she had heard bad things about me from some of the people in the neighborhood, but what she had been told couldn't be right. "You can't be as bad as they say; here you are bringing me all this."

I told her I appreciated the vote of confidence and let her

know she was in the minority for thinking that way. Looking around her place, I saw a big fireplace in the living room. It was an older-style one that had a big black iron hook on one side for suspending a pot over the fire. That answered my question about where she was going to cook.

We finally got around to asking her about the men she had seen on her property. She told us she had seen two men on the other side of the pasture. They were standing on the outside of the fence looking at her house. When I asked if they had guns, she just laughed, "Sweetheart, these old eyes can't see that far." She couldn't tell how they were dressed either. When I asked if she was sure she saw people, she replied, "Unless Bigfoot is wandering around out there, they walked down the fence yonder," and pointed across the field.

Danny told her to take care of herself and that if she needed anything to drop by his house. He then asked if she had a gun. "Hang on," she said, and walked out of the room. She returned with a 1903 Springfield. It looked kind of comical. Before us stood this little old woman, not more than five foot two, her frail hands wrapped around the stock of a big old rifle held up at her waist. It was something out of an episode of *The Beverly Hillbillies*: Granny goin' out possum huntin'.

Danny was shaking his head. "You know how to use that thing?"

The old woman smiled, opened the bolt and closed it with a slap. "You betcha."

I couldn't help but laugh. "You be careful with that artillery. We're going to go and take a look at the fence."

We finally got out of her house, after several rounds of thank-yous and good-byes. We went to the Suburban first to get our rifles, then headed out across the field. We were both laughing about the '03, how big it looked in her hands and what we thought would happen if she pulled the trigger. Once we got to the fence, Danny went right and I went left. We were going to walk the length of it to see if we saw anything. I was almost to the north end of the fence line when Danny called out, "Over here!"

Walking back down the fence, I saw what he was looking at: on the other side of the fence were several sets of footprints. The prints went off into the bush on the other side of the fence. "I'm gonna hop over and see where they go," Danny said.

"I'll come with you," I said. "We need to be careful, though."

The tracks went down a little trail that intersected with a larger one where there were tracks from an ATV. It looked like there were two people that came in on it. Worse was that it looked like they had been there more than once. The trail went off into the Ocala National Forest; they could have come from anywhere. We talked about the possibilities for a minute, then about how long since they had been there. The tracks were not fresh; it looked as though it had been several days at least.

Danny had the idea to sweep the trail. If anyone came again the tracks would be clear, and if they came in and saw the trail swept, then they would know someone knew they had been there. We cut some scrub oaks and took a few minutes to wipe out the tracks for about twenty feet of the trail. We'd done everything we could for the moment and headed back to the truck to go and get the pump installed at Danny's.

The pump installation didn't take long, but if it weren't for the huge pile of PVC parts Danny had it wouldn't have been possible. Danny liked yard sales and always looked for those boxes or buckets full of miscellaneous parts that seem to be at every yard sale. He had piles of assorted stuff; PVC parts were just part of that inventory. Initially we were just going to connect a hose bib to the discharge side so he could fill a drum every few days, but I had another idea.

Using the wires that were already there, I spliced them into the cord of the pump. I went to his panel and moved those wires to a single pole breaker in his panel on the same phase as the inverter. Wired like this, the pressure switch for the pump would control this pump as well. When the pressure dropped, the pump would kick on and pressurize the tank, then cut off. It would function just like the in-well pump. Bobbie was positively thrilled when she realized she could use the toilets again.

Chapter 16

As Thad ran back down the trail toward the fence, he heard automatic weapons fire, then nothing, save himself crashing through the brush. His mind was racing, his heart was pounding and he was scared shitless. He gripped the old side-by-side in his right hand, and all he could think was, *Let me just get there, let me just get there.*

He let out a cry as black smoke started to rise into the sky. As he got closer to the fence, he caught glimpses of the flames through the trees. He didn't know it, but he had started to cry. Reaching the fence, he could now see the nightmarish scene in full. Flames leapt from the roof of the house, and thick black smoke was pouring out the kitchen door. Thad put a palm on a fence post and vaulted the fence. Without thinking about his own safety, he ran toward the house. Smoke poured from the open front door.

He stopped there for a second looking at his worst nightmare unfolding before him. He took a quick look up the road just as a white mail Jeep turned off the road. Thad put his forearm over his mouth and ran through the front door, but it was futile. The smoke was so thick it burned his eyes. They teared up immediately to the point he couldn't see. He dropped to the floor and tried to crawl in, but the thick smoke was now less than a foot from the floor. He crawled out the front door coughing and gagging. Once outside, he fell on the ground still gagging.

Finally getting a breath, he stood up, screaming for Anita and Tony, but there was no reply. Kneeling down, he stuck his arm in the front door and groped around beside it. He felt a pack and pulled it out: his. Sticking his arm back in, he felt for the others, and his heart sank when he found them and pulled them out. He sat there holding little Tony's pack, crushing it against his chest and wailing. He was crying so hard he was convulsing. Reaching out, he pulled Anita's pack over and cradled it in his arms. Looking into the hellfire behind the door, he again screamed for Anita, and again, there was no reply.

Thad got to his feet and remembered the SKS in the wall. Reaching around the corner, he grabbed the hook and yanked the panel off, then knelt down and felt for the rifle. Finding it and the other stuff he'd put in there, he took it all out. He chambered a round in the SKS. The fire was growing in intensity and he had to back away from the house. He carried the three packs over to the truck and dropped them in the bed. Lowering the tailgate, he sat down. All he could do was wait for the flames to die down.

Thad sat there as the fire consumed the house, its progress marked by small pops, windows falling out, the roof falling in and then the walls collapsing. Thad sat and watched, feeling completely and utterly impotent. He pushed away the thought that his wife and little boy were in the house to a deep part of his brain. He sat in the bed of the truck and cried throughout the night.

The fire burned itself out in the early morning. The thoughts of Anita and Tony were clawing to get out, but he succeeded in pushing them back in the hole in his chest.

He tried to look around in the ruins of the house, but it was still hot and too dark. It would be several more hours before the sun came up, several more hours to keep those thoughts shut up.

When Thad opened his eyes, the sky was just starting to lighten. It was overcast and the layer of clouds looked like slate. He knew he needed to go into the house, but he didn't want to. He stood there for a moment, surveying the scene before him. Rubbing his chin, he stepped up to where the door once was and looked again.

Inside the angular blackness was what one would expect to find after a house burned: the springs from the living room furniture and the beds. There was a pile of pots and pans, the cabinets having turned to vapor around them. In the center of the black was the bowl from the toilet, the tank lying in shards around it.

His eyes settled on a form in front of the springs of the sofa. A rather large charred lump with soft curves was covered with ash and charcoal. He wasn't consciously observing it, but his eyes were fixed on it. It was the lines of pink and white that brought him around; in all the black there were cracks of pink and white under the char. Thad slowly walked through the ash and debris, stopping just short of the form. As he stepped around it and turning his head, the form slowly took on a recognizable shape.

In an almost detached manner he made out a head, then an arm. Under the arm was another head, though smaller. Though he was looking at the charred remains of his family, that wasn't what he saw. He saw Anita lying on the floor holding Tony. That was how he would always remember them, not this: this wasn't them. Turning away from them, he went out to the barn, which hadn't burned, and found a shovel. Going out to where he had buried the old man, Thad started to dig.

The digging lasted into the midday. Thad dug without stopping. When the first grave was complete, he stepped out and shoved the spade into the ground to start the second. With the spade buried in the ground and his foot still on it, he paused, looking into the hole. Pulling the blade out of the ground, he stepped back into the hole and started to cut the side out, enlarging it. Widening the hole didn't take long. With the digging complete, he stepped back out of the now-larger hole, walked over to the old pump and took a long drink.

Walking back out to the front of the house Thad reached into the bed and took out the two smaller packs. Setting them on the tailgate, he opened them and pulled out some items out of each. From Tony's pack he took a Transformer. He held it and looked at it. After a moment, he opened his pack and stuck the toy inside. In Anita's pack he found her hairbrush. It was an old heirloom she'd had for as long as Thad had known her. The silver was tarnished and the bristles worn, but she treasured it, and now he would. Holding it to his face, he breathed deeply, taking in her scent with his eyes closed. Letting out the breath, he stuffed the brush into his pack as well.

He took the two ponchos from their packs and went back into the scorched remains of the house. Unrolling the ponchos on a fairly flat spot, he steeled his nerves for what came next. He was standing there flexing his fingers, tense, anxious and nervous. Looking down at his hands, it suddenly struck him that he could not do this bare-handed. The thought of having their . . . of having them on his hands was too much. Thad went back out to the truck and pulled the old work gloves from his pack and returned to them. With the gloves on, he knelt to the task at hand. It was gruesome, grisly work. For the first time since the sun had risen, the tears returned to his eyes. Getting them both out and wrapped, Thad went back to the barn and returned with a wheelbarrow. They were so small he was able to move them both at the same time.

He gently placed them in the grave still wrapped up. Looking at the two bundles, it didn't feel right. As gently as he could, Thad unwrapped them, leaving one poncho underneath them both. He placed Tony's little form back into his mother's arms, then covered them both with the second poncho. He stood and looked down at them, the tears running down his nose, small round spots shining on the poncho where the tears landed. Thad reached up and pulled the watch cap from his head and ran his hand over his stubble. He looked at the cap, then back at the poncho. Leaning down, he lifted the poncho and placed the cap between the two of them. That little act made a difference to him. He suddenly felt better. He had them to keep with him and now they had him, for eternity.

Thad filled the grave slowly. He worked steadily, and the grave was full too soon. He decided against a marker. If he marked the grave, then others would be able to find it, and he would prefer that no one ever know where they lay.

Realizing there was nothing more he could do, Thad looked down at the fresh dirt. The mound barely rose above the surrounding grade.

He said, "I love you, and I always will. I will see you again, and until that time I will carry you in my heart."

With that he went back out to the front of the house and began putting his gear together. He was going to go get the Scout and all the stuff he had in the cache. He knew what he needed to do and where to start. How wasn't important; getting it done was. He'd move the Scout closer to where he would need it. With what he had in mind, the old pickup would be useless shortly.

Thad knew the post office was on 45 in Land O' Lakes, and that was where he was going to start looking for that son of a bitch. The problem was going to be getting there. He couldn't just drive the truck into town; that was guaranteed to get him snagged. He had to find another way to get there. At his old house he had a mountain bike. He, Anita and Tony used to go for rides together, but that was not something he could think about right now.

Parking the Scout at the burned house, he took the truck and went over to get the bike. Pulling up in front of his house, the house where he had lived for so long with his wife and son, he almost couldn't get out of the truck. There was no way he could go inside, so he walked around the house to the barn out back. The bikes were leaned against one wall, covered in a tarp. Thad pulled the tarp off and dropped it to the ground. He stood there for a minute, looking at the three bikes leaning against the old boards of the barn. He remembered the day he had put the basket on the front of Anita's bike, and the day he had taken the training wheels off Tony's. He was starting to well up thinking about them, but he pushed it back down, grabbed his bike and returned to the truck.

He tossed the bike into the bed of the truck and headed back to where the Scout was parked. Having seen the way the mail truck turned when it left the house, Thad knew which way it had to be going to get to the post office, if that's where it had gone. The opposite end of Swift Mud Road dead-ended into Pump Station Road. It was a county road and was usually blocked by gates at either end, but it was the most direct route into town. They must have opened it up for their use, Thad figured. If they were using that road, that was where he was going to get him.

Thad drove past the road to the burned house and headed toward Pump Station Road and just as he had thought, the gate on that end was open. About halfway down the road was the pump station, and just before he came to it Thad turned off the paved road onto a dirt road off to the right. He drove the truck down the little dirt road until he was a pretty good distance into the swamp, then pulled off the road and concealed the truck in the swamp. He cut limbs and palm fronds to hide the truck. Once that was done, he got on the bike and headed back to where the Scout was parked.

Riding the bike was another trigger for the memories to surface; they had ridden on this very road many times before. It had been a safe place for Tony to ride, as there wasn't any traffic on it. Again, he pushed those memories back into that deep, dark place, the pit that was getting bigger every hour. He was back at the Scout in just a little more than a half hour. Once there, he loaded the bike on the roof of the old truck and headed back to where he had hidden the pickup. He hid the Scout farther down the dirt road and on the other side. Since it was four-wheel drive, he was able to drive it farther out into the swamp before concealing it.

Thad got on the bike and headed for town. He wanted to see if the mail truck was at the post office. He took his pack and pistol with him. In the pack he had some MREs and two canteens of water.

Sarge and Ted made it back to the cabin without seeing another person. Ted was securing a line to a cleat on the little dock when Sarge jumped off and started down the little boardwalk. Ted met him on his way back. He was carrying his M1A and a pack. "Where you going?" Ted asked.

"Hunting," Sarge replied as he jumped into the boat. "Keep an eye on things here, I'll be back later."

"You going to keep an eye on Don and see who shows up?"

"Yep."

Sarge backed the boat down the creek and motored down toward its mouth. He nosed the boat into the back behind a couple of cypress trees and tied it off. He found a suitable hide under a couple of downed trees not far away. Climbing under them, he started to make the hide comfortable for his stay. He cut some limbs out of his way and put down the foam mat. Once he had his hide ready he took the suppressor from the pack and screwed it on the M1A. Laying the pack in front of him, he laid the rifle across it and put some camo cream on his face. Once he had his face painted up, he got comfortable and waited.

He had his thermos of coffee with him and he passed the time sipping on it. Using his NVGs, he scanned the river from time to time but didn't see anything. As dawn approached and the sky began to lighten, he began to hear boats on the river and saw them soon after: mostly canoes and rowboats.

It was one of the canoes that spotted the body floating in the river. There were three people in the canoe and they carried on a conversation amongst themselves. Eventually the person in the middle held onto Don's shirt and the other two paddled the canoe to the other side of the river and pushed the body against some snags to keep it in place. The spot where they hung the body was at Sarge's two o'clock and about three hundred yards away.

Now that he had a target distance, Sarge made a couple of adjustments to his scope and settled down again. The canoe started down the river and soon disappeared from Sarge's line of sight. Now it was a waiting game. Sarge was screwing the cup back on the thermos when he first heard the sound of someone in the swamp behind him. Now he wished he had brought his carbine with him.

Drawing his .45, he rolled over so he could look behind him and waited. After a moment a low whistle came out of the swamp. Sarge shook his head and whistled back. In a moment, Mike's face appeared under the logs. He had a big goofy smile on his face, all the more goofy because of the wound to his jaw.

Sarge was shaking his head. "What the fuck are you doing here?"

"I had to get out of there. I'm going stir-crazy."

"Well, get your ass in here before someone sees you."

Mike wiggled his way into the hide, elbowing Sarge in the ribs in the process. Sarge rolled onto his side, put a boot against Mike's hip and shoved him over, both of them cussing. Adding Mike to the small hide was bad enough, but he had also brought the SAW with him and they had to make room for that as well. Mike took a few minutes to cut away some limbs to give him an unobstructed field of fire. Eventually they were both settled into the little hide and they got as comfortable as they could.

They laid there talking in low whispers, Sarge asked how his jaw was and Mike told him it was getting better. Doc was pretty anal about the dressings being changed and made sure he took the antibiotics. After an hour, Mike elbowed Sarge and nodded his head downriver. Sarge looked up to see a boat coming slowly upriver from the direction of Suwannee.

Lowering his head to the scope, he looked at the boat. There were two men in black uniforms, and while he couldn't read the patches on their shoulders, he could see enough to know they were DHS patches. There were also two other people on the boat in civilian clothes, and one of them for sure was from the canoe. Without lifting his head, he told Mike to keep an eye on the river for any other boats. The boat eased up to the body at the direction of the civilians. While one of the DHS goons controlled the boat, the other three men leaned over the side of the boat to where the body was snagged on the logs.

As the three men were trying to pull the body back into the boat, Sarge settled the cross hairs on the side of the boat driver's head. As the body was clearing the gunwale, Sarge let out a slow breath and squeezed the trigger. The driver fell into the boat and the other looked back. Sarge already had the cross hairs lined up on the second uniformed figure, and when he turned to look back, Sarge squeezed the trigger again. The black-clad figure fell over the side, taking Don's body with it; the two civilians ducked down.

Sarge watched them as they crawled around. A bloody hand reached up and pulled the boat into reverse, then took hold of the steering wheel and started backing it out into the river. Once the boat was out in the channel, one of the civilians stood up and opened the throttle and headed downriver. As soon as the boat was out of sight, Mike and Sarge immediately started to clean out the hide. They took everything with them, leaving as little trace as they could.

Chapter 17

I left Danny and Bobbie to once again marvel at the miracle that is indoor plumbing. Mark was out in the yard at his shed when I went by, so I pulled up to his gate and let myself in. He was going through the boxes we had gotten from the county labeled HUMANITARIAN AID. He had several of them laid out in front of the little shed.

"What'cha doing?" I asked.

"Looking at these. Check this out."

I looked at the boxes scattered around the door to the shed. Inside was an odd assortment of items. There were boxes of water, flour, salt and sugar. There was also a box of multivitamins. The most interesting thing was that all the packages had labels in several languages. It looked like the kind of stuff the US usually gave to starving people around the globe, not here. Some of the boxes also had things like baby formula, lentils and something like Cream of Wheat, but it wasn't Cream of Wheat.

"What are you going to do with this stuff?"

Mark was on his knees on the ground, one of the open boxes in front of him. His hands were on either side of the box and his head dropped down to his chest. "We're out of the food we got from the county; I need to do something for these people."

"From the looks of it, they aren't going to be very grateful. I think you should put that stuff away for a while. When they're really desperate, they'll appreciate it more."

Mark looked up at me, and the expression on his face disturbed me. "You're one to talk. It's easy to talk shit about food when you're not hungry."

That caught me off guard; it was definitely no longer a friendly conversation. "Just a thought," I said. I thought we had settled at least some of this the other night, but now it was sounding like Mark was even more in the "let's take Morgan's stuff" camp. I filed that away.

I told him about the tracks we had found at Miss Janice's house and what we did to the trail. He told me to keep an eye on it and let him know if there were any further tracks. I told him I would and said good-bye. We didn't shake hands. Mark went back to digging around in his boxes and I headed for the gate. His comments about the food really bothered me, and that was something to worry about.

Back at the house, the big girls were busy hanging laundry out on the line and Little Bit was climbing a tree with a piece of 550 cord. Mel was in the kitchen washing some dishes. I came up behind her, wrapped my arms around her and kissed her neck.

"Nope," she said without pausing from her washing.

"What?"

She looked over her shoulder. "Maybe later."

I smiled and kissed her again. "How's it going?"

"Just trying to get some stuff done around here. How did your trip go?"

"Good. We dropped off the food and she was really happy to get it. I don't know what she's going to do when it's gone."

"You did what you could. We can't feed the entire neighborhood."

"That's another thing. Tonight we need to move some of our food and bury it in drums. Even Mark is starting to get a little weird."

She stopped her washing and turned to look at me. "You really think he would come here after it?"

I thought about that for a minute and said, "He might, and that's too close for me."

"Where are you going to put it?"

I had been thinking about this on the way home. "I think I'm going to take it down to Danny's. We can bury it out in the woods behind his place."

"Well, if you think it's coming to that, then let's do it. I'm not going to let the girls suffer because other people didn't prepare for themselves."

"I agree, but people don't think that way. They're getting hungry and desperate."

"Should we just share it all, let everyone know what we have, and distribute it?"

I looked at her for a minute before speaking. I had thought about this very thing. It might bring us closer to our neighbors, create a little more community in our little world. But I said, "No, if we did that they would just come back when whatever we gave them ran out. We would never be able to convince them all that we didn't have more. Right now they just *think* we have it; if they *knew* we did we wouldn't be able to fight 'em off."

She turned back to the sink and said, "Do what you have to. You know we're depending on you. No else is going to look out for us."

I thought about what Mel said as I went out the sliding

glass door. I was going to go out to the shop and start trying to figure what and how to cache. The girls were still hanging up clothes on the line and I stopped to look at them. Lee Ann saw me and waved, a big smile on her face. My girls were not living the reality of most on our block. They were fairly removed from the suffering all around us. There was one reason for that, and it was that I had taken the time when things were good to prepare. I had no way of knowing that this was in our future. Even in my worst imaginings, this had never even made the list.

Sure, I had thought of an EMP, but the totality of it didn't even come close to what I imagined. Not having transportation or water were things I thought of, but you really can't get a feel for it until you're there. We had always had power and running water, and even during the worst hurricanes we could go to town for some ice or other supplies we needed. Maybe the folks that lived through Katrina had a better idea of what it took, but I damn sure hadn't.

I was surprised at how much was still on the supply shelves: everything from canned food and toothpaste to lamp oil and feminine hygiene stuff. There was shampoo and soap, first aid stuff, rice and bags of beans and lots more. I wondered where to start and what to take. For many years I had been buying ten-pound bags of rice and beans and storing them in mylar bags with oxygen absorbers, then placing the bags in five-gallon buckets. There are a dozen buckets I can see, plus the ones under the bottom shelf. While not the most appetizing combination in the world, it will keep you alive. Thankfully I thought to store a lot of salt as well.

My pack was lying on the bench and I went over to it and opened it up. I hadn't really messed with it since I had gotten home. There wasn't much left in it: just MREs, my mess kit and my sleeping bag. I pulled the sleeping bag out to hang up and let it air out for a while and I saw the envelope in the bottom of the pocket. I opened it and found a note and a thumb drive.

I remembered Sarge had said something about putting it in there. He had asked if I had a computer. I had my old laptop in the shop, but the battery would need to be charged before I could use it. I was walking across the shop to get it when I heard the bell at the barricade: three rings, then three more. It caught me off guard.

I was standing there looking out the door of the shop when the bell started to ring continuously. Running outside, I yelled at the girls to get in the house. I was still yelling at them and waving them toward the house when the first shot rang out. It started as a couple of pops, but it turned into a fusillade of continuous cracks. The girls ran for the back door and I ran in behind them. Picking up my carbine, I headed for the door. Mel yelled at me, "Where are you going?"

"To the barricade! You hear that? Get the M1 and stay inside!" I shouted as I ran out the front door.

The bell had stopped and the crackle of gunfire had slowed. I was running down the driveway when a figure ran in front of my gate, a man in dirty clothes. He had a short beard and wore a Ford hat on his head. He stopped and looked right at me. He was breathing hard and his eyes were huge. He held a rifle at his waist and turned toward me as he brought it to his shoulder.

I dove to the ground and shouldered my AR while prone, and he fired before the rifle got to his shoulder. I brought the sights up and started to fire at him. My first couple of rounds missed, but the third hit him in the left thigh and he spun in the road. He was sideways to me when I finally got a good sight picture and put two quick rounds in his ribs. He fell like a sack of meat. The sound of gunfire started to rise again. It sounded like it was coming from down the road, farther into the neighborhood.

I slowly got to my feet and in a crouch moved toward the gate. The sound of guns going off and the crack of the rounds as they passed grew louder. As I got closer to the gate, I was able to see up the road a little. There were several people in the road, standing upright and firing at something. One of them was the guy who had talked to Danny and me at the gate when we gave the group heading into the forest water. He had a rifle to his shoulder and looked back and yelled at someone. I knelt on one knee and lined him up in the sights. Two quick rounds and he went down.

In my peripheral vision, I caught some movement to my right and swung the carbine around. Mark was in a crouch, firing his carbine and moving toward the barricade. I moved to the gate and called to him. He didn't look up, so I checked the road and saw two men running for the barricade. One of them fell and the second turned to shoot back and was met with a hail of fire from Mark, me and Rick, who was behind Mark. He went down just inside the barricade. The three of us spread out and started up the road, looking for anyone else. Once we made it to the barricade, Mark and Rick checked the road to see if there were any others out there. The road was empty of the living, but there was one body lying in it.

With the area secure, we started to look for the two guys that should have been on the barricade. My gut tightened when I saw two bodies laying on the right side of the road. One of them was face down, his rifle lying under him. The other was laying back, his legs folded under him as if he had been on his knees when shot and he fell back. From where I was I could see the wound was to his face, and I didn't want to get closer to see who it was.

Thad had about a six-mile ride to the post office. He could have gone through the nearby neighborhood but decided instead to go down to 41 and straight into town. There were a couple of reasons for his decision. First, if he went through the neighborhoods he ran a much higher risk of encountering people. A big black man on a bike riding through a predominately white neighborhood under the current circumstances would surely not be warmly received. Second, he wanted to see what things looked like on the highway; if there was anything organized going on, it would be out there.

Thad rode down Pump Station Road past the water treatment plant, and the smell coming from it was awful. Past the plant he turned onto Ten Cent Road and continued on it as it turned into Ehren Cutoff Road. At the split in the road where Caliente Way went off to the right, Thad stayed on Ehren. That way wouldn't take him through neighborhoods. Up ahead he would pass the entry to a couple of the preplanned communities Florida was notorious for.

Approaching the first of these, he could see some men standing around the ornamental wall entry. When one of them noticed him coming, he slapped another man on the shoulder and pointed. They both went back just inside the entry to take cover behind a car that had been pushed up to block it. Thad moved to the opposite side of the road away from them and tried to look as casual as he could. He kept his eyes fixed on the road in front of him, using his peripheral vision to see what they were doing.

He wasn't sure, but it looked like they were pointing rifles at him. Thad just kept on pedaling and passed them without incident. He passed three more little miracles of modern housing with names like Magnolia Point and Caliente Casita Village. These others were likewise manned, but no one made any trouble. After the last neighborhood, the post office was only a mile or so down the road.

Thad stopped the bike on the far side of the ball field across from the post office, where there was good tree cover. He took a canteen out of his pack and took a drink, then replaced it in the pack and took out a small pair of binos. After hanging the pack by a strap from the handlebars, he used the binos to glass the building across the street.

There were several vehicles there, mail trucks and others. One thing that caught his eye was the flagpole. The US flag that typically flew there was missing; in its place was a FEMA flag. Thad just shook his head as he went back to looking at the building. The driveway was blocked and manned. There was a Humvee sitting at the barricade and four armed men in black uniforms loitering about.

The one thing Thad had was time. He sat down under the big oak with his canteen and waited. From time to time he would raise the binos and take a look at the building, but most of the time he just sat there. Late in the afternoon a group of men came out the front door. Three were in postal uniforms and two in the black tactical-looking ones. Thad raised the binos and watched as they all fished packs of cigarettes out of various pockets and lit up. He chuckled to himself at the thought that even under the current circumstances, they still couldn't smoke in the building.

His big head rocked back and forth with a big smile on his face at that thought, and then the smile faded and he became rigid as a board. He would never forget the man's face, and there he was. Thad moved the binos away for a moment, then looked through them again. It was him, no doubt about it. He watched as the man walked over to one of the mail trucks parked in front of the building. He leaned in for a moment, then returned to his friends. Now Thad knew which truck was his as well.

The men finished their smokes and went back inside. Thad lowered the glasses and sat there thinking. All he knew was where the guy was today. If he left, he wouldn't have any idea where he went tomorrow. It was late in the day, and Thad decided he would stay there for the night to see where the mailman headed in the morning. He had no sleeping bag, but he had enough hate running through him to keep him warm no matter how cold it got.

Thad pulled the pack down, pulled out an MRE and ate it cold. The sun started to drop and he hadn't seen anyone come back out, so he knew the man was still in there. Thad watched as the security on the barricade changed, a new crew coming out to relieve the ones on duty. Those being relieved went into the building. *They must be staying in there*, Thad thought. *That's good.*

Thad pulled the pack over, made a sort of pillow out of it and leaned back to try and get some rest. He had just closed his eyes when a bright light caused him to open them again. There was one of those diesel-powered light towers in the parking lot lighting up the area. He hadn't noticed it before, and couldn't imagine how he hadn't seen it. It lit the surrounding area up with a bright white light. He was sitting under and behind the oak trees, and his spot didn't light up too much. He spent the rest of the night listening to the hum of the diesel engine. He slept little.

At six in the morning, he was pissing on the back side of the big oak when the light tower shut down. He looked up and saw a few people out in the parking lot. He picked up the binos and again started to watch the mail truck. He alternated between it and the front door, just waiting for the son of a bitch to come out. He didn't have to wait long. Around seven thirty he saw the face he was looking for. The man came out and lit another smoke, and as he did Thad wondered if the lighter he used was the one that had started the fire.

When it looked like they were getting ready to leave, Thad put his pack on and readied his bike. He waited as the mailman and his security escort got in the truck and pulled toward the barricade. The security personnel manning the barricade opened it so the truck could pull out. It was the first of several. The truck turned north on the highway, the next two turned south and the last one turned north as well. After they were all out, Thad hung the binos around his neck and started to ride along the left field fence, parallel to the road. At the end of the park, he pulled out onto the sidewalk and kept his eyes on the lead truck, pedaling as hard as he could.

At the intersection of Ehren Cutoff, the lead truck made a right and the second one kept going north. Thad pushed himself to go faster. He angled the bike across the road toward the intersection, and making the turn he saw the truck up ahead just as it rounded a curve in the road. As Thad reached the curve, the truck was nowhere in sight, but he kept up the pursuit. As he approached the entrance of the neighborhood on the right, Thad called out to the men manning the barricade, "Did a mail truck come through here?"

From behind the car a man stood up and pointed down the road. From there the options were pretty limited. They had to be going back out to Pump Station Road. He knew he couldn't catch the truck, but now he hoped he knew where it would be sometime later today. With that thought in mind, he began to ride at a more manageable pace.

Turning onto Pump Station Road, Thad looked at the little dusting of sand where the road curved away from the plant. He skidded to a stop when he noticed his bike tire tracks in the sand had been cut by the larger tires of what Thad knew was a mail truck. Back at his truck, he took a minute to drain a canteen, then several to eat everything left in his pack.

After eating everything he could find, including the sugar packets from the MREs, Thad pulled the truck up to the end of the dirt road and inside the tree line enough that it wouldn't be seen. To pass the time, he went through the glove box, messed around with every knob on the dash and when he was out of things to turn twist or flip, he pulled the pack over.

He found a pack of apple jelly, tore the top off and sucked its contents out. Reaching back in the pack, his hand landed on the Transformer. He had it sitting in his lap when he finally opened his eyes to look at it. He remembered Tony lying on the living room floor playing with it. He held it up, making it walk along the top of the steering wheel. A slight smile came to his face as he made laser sounds just like Little Tony had.

The smile faded and Thad shoved the toy back in the pack. He had spent the day sitting in the truck, getting out occasionally to take a piss and stretch, and he was standing in front of the truck looking down the road when the mail truck rounded the corner onto Pump Station Road.

Thad climbed behind the wheel, started the truck and put it in gear. He watched up the road, waiting for the truck to come into view. It didn't take long. The mailman was on the left, on Thad's side of the truck. Through the windshield he could see the security man sitting beside the driver. As the truck came closer, he held the brake down and stomped the gas pedal to the floor. When the Jeep was almost in front of him, Thad let off the brake and the truck leapt forward.

He could see the driver as he raced toward it. He was looking over at the security man, who was looking out the windshield, and just before the truck slammed into the Jeep the driver looked over. His eyes went wide and his mouth opened in a scream that never made it past his lips. The truck hit the Jeep square in the driver's door. The two men were thrown to the far side of the Jeep. Thad kept the accelerator to the floor and pushed the Jeep to the opposite side of the road.

The road was raised about a foot and a half and as the Jeep's wheels dropped off its edge, it fell over onto its side. Thad didn't let off the gas and pushed the Jeep around so that the rear of it faced the road with the bottom of the Jeep pressed against the passenger side of the truck. He jumped out of the truck and ran to the front of the Jeep. The windshield was shattered but still in place, and through it he could see some movement. Raising one of his size-thirteen boots, Thad kicked the glass in with one thrust. The glass fell in on the mailman, who was trying to get up. Thad reached in and grabbed the man by the collar of his coat and snatched him out through the hole.

The postal worker looked up, sudden recognition on his face, and said, "No!"

Thad released the collar and wrapped his left hand around the back of the man's head, like an NBA star palming a basketball. His right hand was in a tight fist and Thad smashed the man's face with a slapping, crunching sound. The body went limp. Thad turned his attention to the security man, who was trying to crawl out of the Jeep. Seeing Thad's feet, he looked up, blood streaming from his nose and mouth. Thad's right leg came forward, his boot crashed into the man's chin, snapping his head back, and he too went limp and fell half out of the Jeep.

Chapter 18

Sarge and Mike double-timed it back to the shack. Rushing inside, Sarge yelled for Ted to get the claymores. Ted looked up from the radios he was monitoring and asked, "Why? You been followed?"

Sarge set the M1A down, leaning it by the door where the weapons were kept. "No, we're going to ambush them again." He picked up the Minimi.

Mike said, "They'll be expecting us next time."

Sarge put the sling of the machine gun over his head. "Correct, but they think we're on this side of the river, and we're going to be on the other side, above them on the bank. Now hurry the fuck up." Sarge looked at Ted and said, "Get the SAW. Mike, grab one of the AT4s. Doc, you're going to take us to the other side of the river then come back into the canal here and wait. Take the 203 with you; if we get in trouble, start dropping some heat on 'em."

Sarge saw the younger men thought it was a bad idea, but they did as they were told. Soon Doc was in the boat and all the men climbed in. Sarge directed Doc to a point upriver from their last ambush.

When they hit the bank, the three men jumped out. Sarge said, "Listen to the radio. I'll call you when we're ready to be picked up. Stay far enough back in there that no one sees you."

Doc nodded and backed the boat back into the river, looking downriver for any sign of their targets. Sarge directed the guys to the high bank overlooking the now two bodies in the river. He pointed out the locations for the three claymores they brought and indicated the positions he wanted the guys in. Each of them would have a clacker for setting off a claymore. They would be spread out on the ridge about thirty yards apart. Sarge and Ted would be at either end of the ambush, each of them with a SAW, and Mike would be in the center with his carbine and the AT4. Sarge instructed them that he would set off the ambush. If there was a security boat that stayed out in the river, Mike was to hit it with the rocket if the ambush was triggered.

It was getting late in the day and Sarge had begun to wonder if anyone would be back that day when he heard the helo. Looking over his shoulder down the ridge, he could see Mike had his index finger above his head, twirling it around. Sarge nodded and put his hand out, moving it up and down slowly, telling Mike to chill out. Sarge looked downstream and the helo shot right over his head, coming from behind him and going out across the river.

"Shit," Sarge muttered under his breath.

He watched as the bird banked hard and turned on a bright spotlight. It was searching the side of the river where they had set the previous ambush. The pilot was making fast passes up and down the bank, dangerously close to Doc in the little canal. If they spotted Doc in the boat, they'd be fucked. The helo made another fast pass, the door gunner leaning out of the ship, a SAW held to his shoulder, looking down into the swamp.

On the next pass, the gunner pointed down into the swamp and talked into his headset. Mike pointed out at the helo and held his hands up in a WTF? Sarge shook his head, holding his fist up and shaking it at him, telling him to hold fast.

Again the helo returned to the mouth of the little creek. Sarge watched as the gunner stepped out onto the skid. He had to be looking at the boat Doc was in. The gunner looked toward the pilot and started to talk into his mic. Suddenly three boats came roaring down the river, two fiberglass boats and one rigid-hull inflatable, or RIB. The RIB was orange and had USCG painted on the side and the crest of the Coast Guard on the aluminum wheelhouse of the boat. Mounted to a hard point on the bow of the boat was a .50 Browning Machine Gun. Sarge knew the ambush had been a mistake, but they still had the advantages of position and surprise. That didn't make up for the other side's air cover, but it helped.

Between the three boats there were more than twenty men. The boats went to the other side of the river, moving toward the creek mouth. Sarge dropped his head. "Motherfucker!" he said into the grass under him. He cradled the machine gun in his arms and crawled toward Mike and then waved at Ted to come over.

"What the fuck are we going to do now? I told you this was a bad idea!" Mike said.

"I know, but we're over here an' they don't know it." Sarge said.

Ted made it to them and said, "What the fuck, man?"

Sarge cut him off. "Don't tell me it was a bad idea, I got that already. The question is what are we going to do about it? We can't leave Doc over there alone."

"You're damn right we aren't leaving Doc over there. We got to draw those bastards off him and then we got to try and get the fuck out of here," Ted said.

"Ideas?" Sarge asked.

Ted looked at Mike. "Can you hit that bird with the rocket?"

"Oh, sure, just as soon as it goes into a hover and gives me the 'go' signal. Fuck no, I can't hit that damn thing!"

"Then what the fuck are we going to do?" Ted asked.

"Knock it off, dammit. Ted, you go back to your position, I'll go to mine. We're going to open up on the bird. Mike, you hit that RIB. We put enough rounds on that ship, they'll bug out. Maybe we can even knock it down. As soon as it's gone, Ted you and I open up on the other two boats," Sarge paused and looked at Mike. "You have to get that boat. If they get that fifty into action we're fucked to the max, got it?"

The two men nodded. Sarge said, "Let's get Doc's ass out of there." With that he crawled back to his position and Ted did likewise. After settling back into his hide, Sarge looked down to Mike, who gave the old man a thumbs-up and shouldered the rocket. Sarge set out another drum for the shortened SAW and sighted down the barrel at the helo, which was now making slow orbits over the mouth of the creek.

As the bird came out into the river, closer to them and with the gunner on their side, he took a deep breath and settled his sight on the gunner hanging out the door. He squeezed the trigger and the little machine gun started to spew lead and tracers at the ship. Ted's gun joined Sarge's and the gunner was hit numerous times. Sarge immediately changed his point of aim to just in front of the engine cowling, and at the same moment the ship banked hard and started to climb. A loud bang and a whoosh erupted from Sarge's left and through his peripheral vision he saw the rocket streak out across the river.

The orange RIB erupted in a violent explosion. The

other two boats immediately opened their throttles. One of them was too close to the bank and launched itself up onto the knees of the cypress trees on the side of the river. Ted and Sarge were both still firing at the ship as it raced to get out of range. Sarge could clearly see tracers from both his and Ted's weapon sink into the fuselage of the retreating helo.

The last boat had moved upriver and was now putting rounds into the bank Sarge's tracers were coming from. The stranded boat exploded and the few men that hadn't been on it turned and started firing into the swamp.

Ted opened up on them and another explosion went off in the tree line. The man he was shooting at went down. Sarge ran out of ammo and had to change belts. The men on the last boat were getting a better range on him, and their fire intensified. The boat started to move slowly back toward them. Mike and Ted both were looking for any signs of life on the other side of the river when a geyser of water erupted beside the boat. Mike looked upriver and began to fire at it with his carbine.

Sarge was just closing the feed tray cover when another geyser of water erupted. The boat turned and started upriver, throttle wide open. Mike continued to fire at it until it rounded a bend out of sight. The RIB was gone and the other boat that had got hung up on the cypress knees was burning, thick black smoke billowing up from it. The sound of an outboard revving up brought Sarge back around and he looked across the river just as his boat came flying out of the creek mouth. Doc came across the river hard and fast, running up onto the soft mud just down from their location.

"Come on, come on!" Doc shouted.

Ted and Mike came at a run. Sarge asked, "Did you get the claymores?"

"We got ours; head to the boat and I'll get yours!" Ted shouted.

Sarge picked up the clacker and pulled the wire out. He picked up his SAW and pack and ran for the boat. Mike was already down on the bank, and Doc had his weapon up and was looking upriver. Sarge jumped into the boat and Ted was soon behind him. Mike was the last on board, and Doc backed the boat into the river and opened the throttle as he raced across the river toward the creek.

"This one's still alive!" Rick called out from the road. He was standing over the body lying on the road in a spreading pool of blood.

I looked at the two bodies lying inside our barricade. I could see them both lying there but I couldn't see their faces, and I really didn't want to look at them. I looked up and saw Mark kneeling down beside the man on the road. I walked over toward the bodies. The one on his back with his knees bent was Lance. His arms were wide out to his side as if he were making sand angels on the side of the road. Seeing him there with a bullet hole just above his right eye really hit me. I hadn't seen anyone I knew and cared for killed, and it landed on me like a ton of bricks.

I walked over to the second form just behind the log barricade. He was on his side facing away from me, but without seeing his face I could tell he was a smallish young man and then I knew who it was. Reggie's nephew had moved in with him a week or so before and, not wanting to feel like a mooch, he had been taking his turn on the barricade. As a reward for his efforts, he got a bullet in his chest.

I went over to him and turned him over. His mouth hung

open in a silent scream. His left eye was open and his right closed. I reached down and closed his eye. I sat there and wept over his body. I couldn't control it, it just came out. My hand was still on his face when I finally managed to get my shit together. I looked up to see Danny, Reggie and a couple of others heading our way. Danny was on his ATV and Reggie was at a full run.

I looked over at Mark, who was still kneeling over the man on the road. Rick was covering him, his head constantly scanning the area. Danny skidded to a stop and hopped off the Polaris. "What happened?"

"We got hit. Don't know what they wanted exactly, but you see what happened."

Reggie was almost to us and I went out to meet him, to stop him. At my approach, Reggie slowed, huffing to get a breath. "What the fuck happened?"

I shook my head. I didn't know how to break it to him. Reggie looked me square in the eye and simply said, "Robbie?"

"Yeah, man, I'm really sorry."

Reggie walked over to the boy's body. Danny was standing there looking at him as Reggie came up. The big man stood there looking down in silence. Rick walked over to us and looked at the bodies, then looked at the three of us. "It's the same group that came by a few days back, the ones heading into the forest. They were hungry and desperate and they thought they'd come back here and scare us into giving them some food."

Without looking up, Reggie asked, "Did any of them get away?"

"Yeah, he doesn't know how many, though."

Reggie looked out at the road. "He still alive?"

Rick looked up at Reggie, oblivious to what was coming, "Yeah, Mark's trying to find out where their camp is."

Reggie started out toward the road. Mark was still there by the man, who was now only barely alive. Reggie stopped by Mark's side and looked down at the stricken man on the pavement. "You get what you needed from him?"

Mark looked up. "Yeah, I got a pretty good idea of where they are."

"Looks like he needs a bandage," Reggie said. He knelt and pulled his Buck 110 from its sheath and rammed it into the man's chest. The wounded man couldn't even muster a scream. His mouth opened, he raised his head from the road, the veins on his neck bulging with the little blood still in him. Reggie twisted the knife and the man twitched with every rotation of the blade. The dying man looked at Reggie as he let out his last breath, and as his head fell to the road, Reggie said, "That's for the boy," before pulling the blade out, wiping the blood on the tattered shirt before standing to sheath the blade.

Mark sat on the road looking up at Reggie. He rose, his eyes locked on Reggie. The big man just stood there looking at the deputy as he stood. Mark raised his carbine and pointed it at Reggie. "What the fuck is wrong with you damn people?" he screamed.

Reggie didn't reply, he just looked back at him. Mark flipped the safety off his carbine and demanded, "Why? Why did you do that?"

"He was responsible for Robbie; he earned it."

"We can't just kill everyone we come across." Mark shouted, the carbine still pointed at Reggie.

I took a step toward Mark. "Lower the rifle, man."

"No! We can't keep doing this. You fucking people can't keep killing people whenever you want!"

"He killed two of ours! What were you going to do with him, put him in jail?" I asked.

Mark kept the rifle trained on Reggie. "He was already dying. I was just going to let him die on his own. Now put your fucking hands up, Reggie!"

"Take it easy, Mark, chill out," I said.

"Shut the fuck up, Morgan. Get on the ground, Reggie!" Mark shouted.

I raised my carbine, pointing it at Mark. "Mark, you need to chill the fuck out."

Mark cut his eyes toward me, but before he could speak I said, "Mark, lower the weapon. You're out of line. They killed his nephew, his niece is already dead, what the fuck do you expect him to do? They killed two of ours; what the fuck do you care how he died anyway?"

Danny ran out into the road. "What the hell is wrong with you guys? Mark, you're pointing a rifle at Reggie; Morgan, you're pointing a damn rifle at Mark; you guys all going to start shooting one another now? We need to work together! This is bullshit! Put the damn guns down!"

Mark and I both glanced at Danny, and I lowered my rifle. "He's right, Mark, put the rifle down."

Reggie looked at Mark and said, "Shoot me if you're going to. Otherwise get that shit out of my face." He stepped past Mark and walked toward the barricade, passing Danny in the road. Reggie gave him a little nod and asked, "Can you take him to the house for me?"

"Sure, let's load him up."

I gave them a wave and headed down the road toward my

house. From behind me I heard Mark call out, "Who's going to man the barricade?"

I turned in the road. "You are. I'm going to Lance's house to tell his wife he isn't coming home for dinner. Get one of these guys to tell your wife you're okay." Turning around, I headed for the house. As I passed the man in the road that I shot while in the driveway, I paused and knelt down. He was dead, way dead. The two rounds I put in him did the job. He had bled out on the road. I patted his chest and then his pants. In his right pants pocket I found five 30-30 rounds, and in his back pocket was a wallet.

The wallet contained what it probably had on the day things had fallen apart. There were three one-dollar bills, a Blockbuster card and a driver's license with the name Clint Arnold. There was also a picture of him, his wife and kids. The woman looked vaguely like one of the women who had come up to get water from the keg the day they came by. I could only imagine the desperation he must have felt to attempt this. I could see his wife and kids huddled under a thatch of palmettos with a small smoky fire in front of them. And now he would never come back to them. I could just see my girls sitting there, Mel dirty, hungry and cold, and I vowed it would never happen, not as long as I was alive.

Tossing the wallet on his chest, I stood up and started to the house to get the Suburban to go back and pick up Lance's body to take home to his wife. Mel met me in the driveway as I came up. "You okay?" she asked.

"Yeah, but Lance and Reggie's nephew were killed."

"What happened?"

"They were a group that came through a few days ago. They had some women and kids with them, so we gave them water and talked to them a little. They seemed okay, but they were heading into the forest. I had a feeling they wouldn't make it, and they didn't. They ran out of food and they thought they would come back here. Mark found one of them still alive and he said they thought they would scare us, get some food from us."

"Did you shoot any of them?"

I nodded. "One for sure, and I may have hit another, but everyone was shooting at him. The one I shot is lying out there on the road in front of the house. I looked in his wallet and he has pictures of his family in it; you know, mom, dad and the kids all together. He was just trying to feed his family."

"We can't feed everyone. The girls come first." Mel crossed her arms. "If people want to come and try and take what we have, make our kids go hungry, then they need to pay the price."

"You're right, and they did. But think about it this way: if we didn't have what little we do then I might be faced with trying the same thing they did."

"But you planned ahead. We sacrificed for a long time to prepare for this and I'm not about to give it away to anyone."

I looked at her with a little half smile. "Yeah, we sacrificed all right, and you bitched the whole time as I recall."

She pressed her lips together, lowered her chin and looked up at me. It was her "you're an asshole" look, and I knew it well. "What are you doing now?"

"I'm going to take the truck and get Lance's body, take him home to his wife. Thank God they don't have any kids."

"Be careful," she said as she turned and headed for the house.

I went back to the shop and opened one of the cans of loose rounds I had bought from Palmetto Armory. I topped off the mag and saw I had fired twelve rounds. I started thinking about the whole thing for a minute. I remembered firing at the first guy, but I didn't remember how many and I hardly remembered the rest of it. They had invented that camera technique called "bullet time" for the Matrix films, the one that made everything super slow-motion. But my bullet time was the opposite; everything was too fast and the details were all jumbled together.

I knew I had to take Lance home, but I took a few minutes to clean and field strip my rifle. It was kind of cathartic, sitting on a stool scraping the carbon out of the chamber of the Bushmaster.

"What'cha doin, Daddy?"

I looked over my shoulder to see Little Bit standing in the door. "Cleaning my rifle, what're you doin?"

"I'm bored. Lee Ann and Taylor won't play with me."

"I'm sorry, baby, I'll talk to them," I responded as I ran a chamber brush into the rifle without looking up.

She came into the shop and looked into the open ammo can. She knelt down and reached into the can and grabbed a fistful of rounds. "These are big bullets, Daddy. The ones for my Crickett are a lot smaller."

I slid the bolt carrier back into the upper I looked over at her. "Yeah, they're a little bigger," I said with a smile, then closed the upper onto the lower and snapped the pin back in. With the carbine back together, I slid the mag back in and pulled the charging handle back to chamber a round. Putting the rifle on safe, I told Little Bit, "Let's put these away, okay?"

She stood up and I closed the can, securing the lid with the latch. She said she wanted to put it away, so I moved back so she could try and pick it up. With a grunt she grabbed the handle and pulled, but it didn't budge. She stepped over it with one foot on either side and grabbed it with both hands, and again with a groan she strained against the can. This time it actually came off the floor a little. She dropped it back to the floor and hung her tongue out of her mouth. With wide eyes she looked at me and said, "That's heavy!"

I smiled at her and she cracked up. "It sure is." I pushed the can back into its place under the shelves.

I went over to the other side of the shop and grabbed a roll of clear plastic off one of the shelves. As I turned to head for the door, Little Bit asked if she could go with me. I wanted to take her—I liked hanging out with my girls—but this wasn't something for her to see. "Sorry, baby, you can't come with me for this."

She said, "Why not?"

I decided to tell her the truth. "Because I'm going to get a man that was killed earlier. He's dead and I'm going to take him home to his wife."

She stood there for a minute. She asked, "It isn't Danny, is it?"

"Oh no, baby, Danny's fine, it's not him."

She stood there for another minute. "I want to come. I want to help."

She sure looked determined, and I thought maybe I should let her see it. She'd never seen a dead body before, and maybe she needed to. "Okay, Little Bit, if you want to come you can, but remember what I said I'm going to do; it isn't going to be fun."

"I know, but I'm going. Let me get my stuff."

"Hurry up, I'll meet you at the truck."

She took off at a run and disappeared into the house. God only knew what she was going to get.

Chapter 19

Chuck started to come around. His head was pounding and his face hurt like hell and his DHS uniform had blood on it. His vision was blurry, but he was able to make out Marty tied to a chair beside him. It looked as if he was in a barn of some sort, but he couldn't see much other than the metal siding and all the crap scattered around. He tried to pull his arms up, but they were tied tight and there was no way he could get them out. His legs were likewise tied and he couldn't even move his feet. Outside the barn he could hear some animal noises. He *hoped* they were animals.

Thad had never really thought the whole thing through. His plan only went so far as to try and get the men responsible for the death of Anita and Little Tony. But now he had them and he wasn't sure what to do. Like he did every evening, Thad had put a couple scoops of the dwindling feed into a bucket. He went out behind the barn and thumped the side of the bucket with his hand while shaking the feed. It wasn't long before the eight hogs he had turned out to forage came running toward him. He fed them every night; no sense in wasting the hog feed.

As the hogs came trotting up, Thad looked back at the pen behind him and the big old oak in the center of the pen. He swung the gate open and walked into the pen. The hogs dutifully trotted in behind him. Thad dumped the feed into the trough and went out the gate, closing it behind him. He turned and looked at the old tree again, then back at the hogs, who were noisily consuming the feed he had dumped. He had an idea.

Chuck looked up when he heard the door open and a big black man came in, leaving the door open. He was still having a hard time seeing. His broken nose and all the blood on his face added to the hangover effects he felt from whatever happened earlier.

The black man walked past him, not even indicating he saw him. "Hey, what the fuck do you think you're doing? You know who we are?" Chuck asked.

Thad didn't even acknowledge him. He picked up a hank of rope hanging from a large nail driven into a pole on the far side of the barn. As Thad headed back out, Chuck said, "Hey, fucker, untie me! You'll untie me if you know what's good for you!"

The black man never showed anything to indicate he had heard and continued outside. Marty started to come around after the black man went outside. "Marty! Hey, Marty," Chuck whispered.

Marty raised his head and said, "Chuck, that you?"

"Yeah, it's me."

"Where are we? What happened, last thing I remember was a truck coming at us."

"Can you move? I'm tied tight and can't move a damn muscle."

Marty tried to move his arms, hands and legs but he was trussed up tight as well. "No, man, I can't move shit. Where the fuck are we?"

The black guy stepped through the door again. Marty said, "What the fuck, man! What the fuck are you doing?"

Chuck looked over at Marty. He didn't know what was going on, but Marty's reaction scared him. He said, "Dude, what the fuck is wrong with you?"

Before Marty could say anything, the guy stepped up behind Chuck and wrapped his forearm around his neck. Chuck tried to drive his chin down, but Thad was too strong.

"What do you want, you big black—"

The man applied more pressure to his neck and he was out. Marty went apeshit.

"What the fuck, man, what are you doing, what do you want?" he screamed.

The black guy picked Chuck up still tied to the chair and carried him out of the barn. Marty's imagination ran wild as to what was happening outside and what was surely about to happen to him. He began to cry and called out, begging for his life, asking what he wanted and shouting threats. It felt like an eternity to Marty as he sat tied in the chair, but soon the black man came back through the door. Marty started to bounce up and down in his chair, and spittle flew out of his mouth as he cried and pleaded. The man never said a word and simply carried him, chair and all, outside.

He set Marty down beside the fence facing a pigpen. Marty could see Chuck still in his chair sitting in the middle of it. There were several large hogs and sows milling around the pen. A couple of them were checking Chuck out, pushing their big wet noses against him. Chuck came around as one large hog shoved his snout into his crotch.

"What the hell?" Chuck cried out as he came to. He tried to rock in the chair, but there was nothing he could do.

Both men were startled by the rumbling sound of a tractor starting up off to the side of the pigpen. The two men looked over to see the big black man sitting on the tractor and looking back over his shoulder at them. Before they could say anything, the tractor lurched and started to inch forward. Chuck's arms were tied behind his back and they started to rise, pulled up by the rope running through a block on a large limb of the tree. The other end was connected to the three-point hitch of the tractor.

When the tractor stopped, Chuck was completely off the ground, the chair still tied to him and his arms pulled up over his head, dislocating both of his shoulders. The black guy climbed off the tractor and went into the pen. Chuck was screaming in pain and this caused the pigs to squeal, adding to the racket. The black man drew a big knife and cut the chair off of Chuck, then bent down and untied his boots and took them off, tossing them to the side.

Chuck was in so much pain he could hardly speak. With the boots off, the man stood and looked at Chuck. "You the one who killed my family?"

In a low breathy voice, Chuck replied, "Fuuck yew."

The answer came from Marty. "He did, he shot them, I swear to God, I didn't do it!"

The man looked back at Marty. "Why?"

"We came back to the house, we knew you weren't going to go and we were going to try and scare you. She shot at us and he shot her."

Chuck was slowly spinning around from his rope. In a pain-filled voice, he said, "You sorry fucker, *you* set 'em on fire."

Marty said, "They were dead, he shot 'em both, they were already dead!"

The man turned back to Chuck. He tilted his head to the side to look into his eyes. "You kill my boy?"

Chuck tried to spit in his face. The man stepped back, a little of the sputum landing on his coat. He quickly stepped forward and landed a quick right-left combination to Chuck's ribs. The wind left him and he could hardly get a breath. The man turned and walked back into the barn and came out with a small jar and a paintbrush, one of those cheap blond-bristled throwaway-type brushes. Chuck couldn't see him as he came up. He opened the jar and dipped the brush in and then, taking it out, he held it down to the pigs. One of them started to lick the bristles, and then another pushed in.

The man pushed past the pigs to Chuck, dipping the brush again. He began to brush the stuff Chuck's bare feet. Chuck could smell molasses. He tried to protest, but he was in too much pain. Marty was still in hysterics, and shouted, "What the fuck are you doing!"

The pigs could smell the sweet goo on the feet dangling just over their heads. The man went over to the tractor and took up the strain on the rope Chuck was hanging from. He pulled on the tag end of the line, and the half hitches came loose. He lowered Chuck down toward the pigs. Chuck tried to pick up his legs to keep his naked feet away from the snouts of the swine below him. The man hitched the rope off when Chuck's feet were just in reach of the pigs.

Thad stood there looking at the man. He said, "What's your name?"

Chuck looked up and said, "Chuck. Chuck Henry."

Thad said, "You killed my boy an' my wife, Chuck Henry. Now you're going to pay for both of them." He turned to the mailman. "And you're next."

Chuck yelled, "They weren't dead!"

"What?"

"They weren't dead when Marty set the fire," Chuck groaned through clenched teeth.

Thad turned and looked at the mailman—Marty—who began to babble incoherently. Thad did manage to make out, "He killed 'em, it was his idea!"

"Don't worry, you're next," Thad said to Marty.

Thad turned back when he heard Chuck let out a little yelp. The pigs were nipping at his toes and, when Chuck didn't push them away, they began to bite harder. Thad took the jar and, pushing the swine out of the way with his knees, made his way over to the hanging man. He brushed the dark, sweet goo all over Chuck's feet and calves. The man began to cry, "Just kill me, you sick fuck, for cryin' out loud, just fucking kill me!"

Thad looked the man in the eyes. "Oh, I'm going to, but you said they was alive in the house when y'all set the fire. That means they suffered, bad. So you gonna suffer too."

Chuck began to whimper and cry. He tried to keep his feet from the pigs, but he simply couldn't hold them up that long. Every time he dropped them a little, one of those damn animals would hop up off its front feet to get at his, biting his toes. As time went on, his toes turned into a bloody mess and Chuck began to howl in pain as the little appendages were ripped off and consumed by the swirling mass of pork below him. Thad stood and watched as the pigs slowly chewed and tore at the bloody feet.

The screams became louder. Chuck had found a renewed vigor from someplace and his cries grew louder and louder. He begged Thad to kill him and cursed him, asking what kind of sick son of a bitch does something like this. Thad stepped over to the man, making his way through the writhing swine, and said, "You want to die?"

In a low, whimpering voice, Chuck replied, "Yes! For the love of fucking God, yes!"

"All right, then," Thad replied. Taking a step back, he flipped open the straight razor he had found on the bench in the shop. He had put it there to sharpen and forgotten about it till today. In one quick motion, Thad swung the blade at Chuck's stomach. The blade went through the skin, tissue and muscle of Chuck's abdomen. Chuck let out a scream as the blade went through him, but that was nothing compared to what followed.

Thad stepped back and punched Chuck just below his diaphragm. The force of the blow caused his lower GI, large and small intestines to fall out in a large mass, trailing down his legs. Chuck looked on in horror as he felt the tugs. The hogs were tearing at his insides. He hung there watching in stark terror as a pig grabbed a mouthful of small intestines and ran to the other side of the pen, a streamer of the small wet vessel trailing it. He let out a scream, a wail the likes of which no one present had ever heard.

Thad stood there watching as the pigs consumed the organs in a frenzy. Marty, still tied to his chair, began to scream, "Kill him, for fuck's sake, just kill him!"

It didn't last too long. One of the hogs pulled on a piece of Chuck's innards and a blood vessel ruptured. Dark red blood began to pour down Chuck's legs, his face started to go pale, and after a couple of slight tremors ran through what was left of his body, Chuck died. The only way Thad could tell was that he had stopped crying out. The pigs were still at work and his body still swung and twisted on the rope. Accepting that he was dead, Thad turned to look at Marty. Marty was sitting there with that wide-eyed slack-jawed expression he'd had since he came around. Looking at Thad he went into a fit, violently shaking and rocking the chair. He was screaming total nonsense with spittle flying from his mouth and tears in his eyes. Thad started toward him, and Marty managed to fall over onto his side.

Entering the mouth of the creek, the boat came under fire from the west shore. Ted yelled out, "Contact left!" and opened up with the SAW he still held. Sarge joined in with his SAW and Mike set down his M4 and picked up the 203 that Doc had and started lobbing high explosive rounds at the muzzle flashes. The sudden overwhelming response quickly silenced the two men firing at the boat.

Doc turned the boat toward the shack. When they arrived, Sarge launched himself out as it came up to the little dock and began shouting orders out to the guys as they secured the boat. He wanted all the radios packed up in the cases, the solar panels down and the ammo secured. They needed to move everything they could get to the truck as fast as possible; the boot was surely about to come down. To get to the truck they had to hump a little more that three hundred yards through the swamp.

They got everything packed, hauled to the truck and loaded up. Things went so well that they had time to go back to the nice-to-have pile and pack that stuff up as well. The last thing they did was to booby-trap the shack. One corner of a piece of plywood was pried from the floor and a pressure switch, sacrificed from one of the weapon lights, was placed under it. Ted adjusted the plywood until the circuit was open, wired it into a nine-volt battery and connected it to a claymore. He ran another wire under the floor to the kitchen area and a claymore was hidden behind the propane tank for the stove. That wire was then connected to the blasting cap of the claymore, creating a daisy-chain charge.

Another claymore was rigged to one of the boats outside. A piece of the inner braid of a section of 550 cord was pulled out and tied around the speedometer pickup tube on the stern on Sarge's boat. The string was run over to the dock and connected to a small piece of wood that was holding a clothespin open. The clothespin had the stripped wire from the positive side of the circuit from another nine-volt battery wrapped around it, so that when the boat was moved, the string would pull the piece of wood out, closing the circuit. This claymore was suspended under the dock with an additional one-pound block of C4 pressed to its face.

With the welcoming goodies set, Sarge and Ted headed for the truck for the last time. Doc and Mike were already there on watch. As they came out of the swamp, Sarge asked that one of them get on the military radio—the green gear— and try to make contact with their army contacts. He wanted them to know what had gone down and also find out if there was a safe place to run to.

Mike turned the radio on as soon as he got in the truck. He put the headphones on and started to tune the radio, and as soon as he was on the proper station he heard, *"—calling Swamp Rat."* He sat and listened for a minute and heard the full transmission when it was repeated: *"Clementine calling Swamp Rat."*

"This is Swamp Rat, go ahead Clementine, break," Mike said.

"Swamp Rat, what's your situation, break?"

"Swamp Rat is E&Eing out of our AO, break."

"Roger, are you in contact, break?"

"Negative, Clementine, we broke contact and are looking for a new home, break."

"Swamp Rat, are you feet wet or dry, break?"

"Swamp Rat is feet dry and mobile, break."

"Swamp Rat, you need to move toward Dallas. OPFOR reaction force is en route to your location via Serpent, you need to exfil immediately, how copy, break."

"Roger, Clementine, I copy. Heading for Dallas, OPFOR reaction force en route via Serpent, does OPFOR have air assets committed, break."

Mike handed Doc their map case and said, "Find Dallas."

"Unknown, Swamp Rat, assume assets are in play, notify Clementine when you reach Dallas, Clementine out."

"Roger, Swamp Rat out."

Mike thumped the cab of the truck. Sarge looked back and Mike leaned around so he could hear him. "Clementine says there's a reaction force coming down the river. They want us to head for Dallas."

"Where the fuck's Dallas?" Sarge asked.

"I don't know, Doc is looking for it on the map."

"Give me the fucking map."

Mike turned back to Doc. "Find it?"

"Not yet."

"The old man wants the map." Doc handed it over and Mike passed it Sarge, who immediately started scanning the map and the various rally points that were marked on it.

Chapter 20

I was sitting in the Suburban when Little Bit came trotting out of the house. She was carrying a little white plastic case with a red cross on the front of it. When she climbed up into the truck, I asked her, "What's that for?"

"It's my first aid kit. We might need it."

I just shook my head at her. I sure wished a first aid kit would help Lance. I drove out the drive and made a left at the gate. As I passed the raider I had shot, she stood up in her seat to look and said, "Is that him?"

"No, that's not him. That's one of the bad guys."

She turned and sat back down in her seat without saying anything more and we drove to the barricade. I backed up to where Lance was lying. Mark and Rick were still there, as well as a couple of other people from the neighborhood. Mark came around to my side as I got out. "Seen any others?" I asked.

"There were a couple of people way down the road, but they didn't come up here."

"Can you help me load him up?"

Mark looked back at the body. "Yeah, sure. You going to put him in the back?"

"Yeah, I brought some Visqueen to wrap him in, then we'll load him up and I'll take him home."

I grabbed the plastic out of the back seat and walked back

to where he was lying. Little Bit got out of the truck and walked back. She stood there watching as we laid out the plastic. Mark and I picked him up and set on the sheet of plastic film, and Little Bit came over and looked down at him.

"Looks like he's sleeping," she said.

"He is, forever," I replied. Mark gave me a look asking why she was there.

I told him, "She'll see it sooner or later."

Little Bit was looking at the blood. There was a lot on the ground where we moved him from, and his shirt and coat were soaked. "Is that where the bullets hit him?"

"Yeah, remember those bullets you had in your hand earlier? This is what they do."

She looked thoughtful for a moment. "How do they do it? Do they explode?"

That took me by surprise, and I tried to think of how to explain it to her. "No, they don't explode, but the bullet is going very fast and it's really hard; it just sort of cuts a hole."

"I have some Band-Aids." She opened her little first aid kit.

"No, sweetheart, a Band-Aid won't fix it."

She looked up at me and said, "Daddy, I'm gonna go wait in the truck." She turned and walked around to the passenger side of the truck.

Mark asked, "Why in the hell did you bring her with you?"

"Look, man, she's probably going to see more of it, the way things are going. She asked if she could come. I told her what I was doing and she still wanted to, so I brought her."

"I don't want my kids to see anything like this." He was looking at her through the rear window.

"I don't really want mine to either, but this is the world we live in now. Let's load him up."

I dropped the rear gate and we loaded Lance into the back. Mark asked, "Can you come help bury these guys later?"

I looked at the body in the road, then back down our road at the others. "I'm not going to bury 'em. I'll drag 'em off into the woods if you want, but I'm not spending hours digging holes for 'em."

Mark turned with a disgusted look on his face. "We have to bury them; we can't just leave them here."

"No, we can't just leave them here, but I ain't burying them. I say we just drag 'em into the field across the road and leave em there; the buzzards will make short work of 'em."

"You are one sick bastard, you know that?"

"What the fuck do want from me? They just tried to shoot their way in here, and they killed Lance and Robbie. Fuck 'em, I don't give a shit about 'em. I already have a grave to dig today."

I turned and climbed into the truck, started it up and was about to pull off when Mark came up to the window. I put it down and looked at him. He said, "I almost forgot, the doc says Howard is ready to come home. Can you go pick him up later?"

"Yeah, after I do this, I'll go get him." I put the truck in gear and then put it back in park. I said, "Look, Mark, you have to decide who I am. Am I some sick bastard, or am I the guy who's going to pick up Howard? The guy who brought food to Miss Janice, the guy who came running when the shooting started? The guy who volunteered to tell Lance's wife that he's dead? Here's a thought: why don't you get some of those people who want my food, the same people who weren't here to defend the barricade, and put them on grave detail? Then maybe they'd appreciate what the rest of us are doing for them."

Mark looked at the ground and then back at me. He said, "Yeah, maybe."

I put the truck in gear again and pulled out. I looked over at Little Bit. She was looking out the window and being quiet—very unnatural for her. "You okay, kiddo?"

She turned and gave me a weak smile, then looked at my carbine lying on the seat between us. "Yeah, Daddy. Is that going to happen to you? Is a bullet going to cut a hole in you?"

I reached out and took her little hand in mine. "Well, Monkey, I sure hope not, but there's bad people out there and we have to try and protect ourselves. If bad people come, then we have to try and stop them."

Her little face contorted and she started to cry. "I don't want you to get shot with a bullet. Can't we just run away? Why do bad people have to come? Can't you just stay home with me and Mommy?" She was crying hard and I felt horrible.

I stopped the truck and she climbed over into my lap. I hugged her hard and she wrapped her arms around my neck and squeezed with all her might. "I'm going to be okay. You don't think I walked all the way home just so someone could shoot me when I got here, do you?"

She sat up and looked at me. "No, but I'm worried. I'm scared that someone will try and shoot you."

"Don't you worry about that. I'll be okay. No one is going to shoot me." She didn't know I had already been shot once, and I was damn glad of it. I asked if she wanted to drive. Just as quickly as the tears had started, they stopped. She sat in my lap and steered the truck. As we approached the gate to our house, she asked why we were going home and not to the man's house. I told her I wanted her to stay home and not go there with me. She started to protest, but I told her that it would be sad and she had already seen enough sad things for the day, and she didn't say anything after that.

Little Bit hopped out of the truck. I told her to tell Mommy I would be back soon and waited for her to go in the house. She stopped in the door of the house and gave me a little wave.

I drove to Lance's house, which was off a little spur road from the main road into our little heighborhood. As I pulled into the driveway I suddenly realized I didn't know his wife's name.

I honked the horn and saw a young woman look out the window. I stepped out of the truck and waved to her. The door opened and she looked around the side of it. "Can I help you?"

"Ah, yes, ma'am. I'm sorry, I don't know your name, but does Lance live here?"

"Yes, but he isn't here right now."

"I know. I'm Morgan. I live on the main road."

"I know who you are." She stayed behind the door.

"I'm sorry, I don't know your name." I was trying to figure out how to do this, but there was no easy way to do it.

"I'm Tina, what do you want?"

"Tina, can you come outside so I can talk to you?"

"We can talk right here; don't come toward me."

I had no doubt that she had a gun behind the door. I said, "I don't know exactly how to say this, but Lance was killed earlier."

She didn't say anything. She just stood there staring at me.

"He was shot by a group of people who were trying to get

in to steal food." She still hadn't moved. "Tina, did you hear me?"

"You're lying," she said flatly.

"I wish to God I was. I'm so sorry to have to tell you. I have his body in the back of the truck. I thought he should be brought here to you."

She told me I was wrong and called me a liar again. I tried to get her to come out so I could show her, but she refused and eventually she told me to go away and she shut the door. I didn't know what to do. I had envisioned crying and wailing maybe, but not a flat refusal to accept it. Finally I did the only thing I could. I carried Lance up to the front of the house and laid him out, then pulled the plastic off so she could see him. I could see her in the window, but when I bent over to set him down and straightened back up, she was gone.

I sat in the truck for a few minutes waiting to see if she would come out, but I never saw so much as the curtain move. After about half an hour I started up the old Chevy, backed out of the drive and headed down the road. I turned left toward Danny's house and drove down. Danny met me on the porch with a "Yo."

"You get the boy to Reggie's?" I asked.

"Yeah, he's pretty tore up. I gotta go tell his sister that her son is dead now too."

"Damn, first the girl and now him. I can't even imagine it."

I asked him if he would come and help me bury Lance. I told him how Tina had reacted and he just shook his head. He suggested we go get Mark and have him go with us, being as he was the one that everyone looked to. I agreed it was a good idea, and Danny went over to the shed and grabbed a couple of shovels. Mark was still at the barricade talking to a couple of the guys from the block and we motioned for him to come over.

He agreed to help and went back to the barricade. He asked one of the guys there to stay at the barricade and back up Rick, handing the man his carbine. Mark returned and climbed in, and we went back to Lance's house. His body was still lying in the yard and looked just as I had left it. Danny and I stayed in the truck and Mark went to the house.

He knocked on the door a couple of times and there was no response. He called out several times, still nothing. He tried the door, but it was locked. He waved for us to come up and we met him at the door, not sure what to do.

"What do you think?" Danny asked.

"I don't like it. She has to be in there, and now I'm concerned for her safety. We need to talk to her," Mark said.

"I'll go around back and see if I can see anything. You want to stay here in case she comes to the door?" I said.

"Yeah, I'll wait here. Danny you go around the right side, check the windows and doors, see if anything is unlocked."

We both gave a nod and headed around either side of the house. I was checking the last window on my said when I heard Danny call me. I walked around to the back of the house. He was standing on the back porch and the sliding glass door was open.

Pointing to the open door, I asked, "You open it?" He shook his head. He had his carbine at low ready, directed at the door. "Let's go see," I said. He nodded and stepped through the door. The kitchen was empty. It was small and very neat and clean. We stepped into the living room and it was empty too. I called out, "Tina, you okay?"

From outside Mark called to us. "You guys inside?"

"Yeah, we're in the living room, we're going to check the rest of the house," Danny called back.

There was a hallway to our right. Danny took the lead and lit the hallway with the light on his carbine. The first door opened onto the bathroom and it was empty. Across the hall from that door was another. Danny stepped in front of it. I reached out and grabbed the knob. Looking at him, I gave a nod. He nodded back and I threw the door open, Danny stepped in quickly and checked the room. It was empty. Again I called out, "Tina, you in here?"

We checked two more rooms but she wasn't in them. I threw the last door open and Danny stepped in with me following him. Tina was lying on the bed in a fetal position on her left side facing the door. She was clutching a picture frame in her left arm, and a Ruger .357 revolver was on the floor beside the bed, her right hand hanging off the edge. We stepped up to the side of the bed and looked down. The Surefire on Danny's rifle revealed an entry in her temple. The skin was burned and puckered; she must have had the pistol pressed against her head when she pulled the trigger. I told Danny I was going to go get Mark and left the room. Opening the front door, Mark could tell from the look on my face what we had found. "Where is she?" he said.

Stepping into the room, Mark was visibly shaken. "Dammit!"

We looked around the house for a note and didn't find one. I didn't know Lance real well and I didn't know Tina at all, but I could only imagine that her grief over Lance was what brought her to do this. We wrapped Tina in the bed linens and carried her out the sliding glass door and out to the back yard. Setting her down, we went around to the front and carried Lance around. The three of us stood there around the bodies, not saying anything, just looking down at the two wrapped bundles. Finally Mark spoke up. "Can you guys handle this?"

Danny and I just nodded, and Mark said, "I'm going to search the house for anything the community can use. Whatever I find I'll put in the back of your truck. Can you drop it off at my place when you're done?"

"Yeah, man, you need a ride back?" I asked.

"No, I'll walk."

Mark headed back to the house while Danny went back to the Suburban and returned with the shovels. We picked a spot out near what had been a small flower garden. We walked off a plot big enough for each grave and then I took off my vest and leaned my carbine against a fence post. Danny did likewise and we began to dig. It took about three hours to dig the two graves. When we had them about five feet deep, we put the bodies in. Once they were in, we stood there looking down at them. I'm not a religious man and neither is Danny. I couldn't begin to know what to say, and after a brief silence we began to fill the graves. Once the dirt was mounded up, Danny and I collected our gear and went back to the truck.

We threw the shovels in beside two boxes Mark must have put there. The whole time we were digging the graves and lowering the bodies, Danny and I never talked, and even in the truck we were silent as we drove back to Danny's house. Pulling up at the gate, I stopped and Danny hopped out. After shutting the door, he looked in. "I'll see you later, man."

"Yeah, later, man."

Thad picked Marty up and set his chair upright. The man was still crying and whining, asking what Thad was going to do to him. Thad walked out of the barn, returned with another chair and set it down in front of Marty. Marty looked around, not sure what was about to happen. Thad spun the chair around so the back was facing Marty, swung a leg over and sat down, resting his arms on the top of the chair's back.

Thad sat for a full minute without saying a word. Marty's eyes shifted from side to side nervously and he licked his lips in apprehension. Thad sat there with his forehead resting on his forearms, looking down between the slats of the chair back. Finally Thad looked at Marty with an expressionless face, this just served to unnerve Marty even further and his chest started to heave as he sucked air and blew it out through clenched teeth.

Finally Marty couldn't take it anymore. "What do you want?" he asked, crying as he did.

Thad sat there for a moment. "You got a family?"

Marty answered immediately, "Yes, yes, I have a wife and son, he's twelve."

Thad cocked his head to the side. "You love 'em?"

"Of course, more than anything."

Thad pursed his lips and nodded his head before dropping it again to look at the slats. "Me too, I loved my wife and boy too," he said as he looked back up.

Marty's newfound hope quickly faded, his face yielding to the contortions once again. "Look, man, I'm really sorry. It wasn't my idea. Chuck did it."

"You lit the fire, didn't you?"

Marty's eyes grew wide once again, his lips trembled, mouthing words that never sounded. Finally a weak "Yes" issued from his lips.

"Why? You say Anita shot at you, so you two shot her and set the house on fire while they're still alive? Why not just let 'em be and leave?"

"You don't understand these people. They tell you to do something, you do it, that's it. There is no discussion. Burning the house is standard procedure for them. People don't do what they're told, they teach 'em a lesson."

"So then you're only doing this cause they make you, huh?"

"Yeah, yeah, this kinda thing isn't me. I only do this because I want to take care of my family."

"Ya know, I walked a long, long way to get home to my family. I did a lot of crazy shit to get home, the only thing that kept me going was the thought of them, and you set them on fire."

"Look, I'm really, really sorry. I . . . I didn't want any of this," Marty managed through the renewed tears.

Thad sat looking at the man. "You want a cigarette?"

Marty wasn't sure how to respond. He wasn't sure if it was a genuine offer or would open this whole thing to a new level of hell. "Uh, yeah, sure."

Thad pointed to his breast pocket. "In there, right?"

Marty looked down at the blue postal service coat he was wearing and nodded. Thad leaned over, fished the smokes and lighter out of his pocket and tapped one out, holding it up so Marty could grab it with his teeth. Thad struck the old trench-style lighter and held the flame up so Marty could get to it. Marty took a long, hard drag on the cigarette, then thanked Thad. Thad nodded his head and held the lighter up between himself and Marty, looking at it.

Marty was sucking the cigarette down hard and fast, looking at the lighter Thad was turning between his fingers. Reaching the filter, Marty spit the butt out, making sure to turn his head so it didn't look like he was spitting it at the big man. Thad looked up and shook another one out, holding it up in a manner that asked if he wanted another. Marty nodded and Thad leaned over so he could get to it and lit it for him. Again Marty inhaled deeply, letting out a cloud of smoke.

Thad held the lighter up once again. "This the lighter you used to light the fire?" Thad was looking past the lighter at Marty.

Marty moved the cigarette from side to side in his mouth nervously. He took another long pull on the smoke, squinting his left eye as he did. Without saying anything he slowly nodded his head. Thad was still holding the lighter with two fingers between the two of them. In one quick motion he snapped his fist around the lighter. The quick movement startled Marty causing him to spit the butt out. It landed in his lap, causing him to gyrate in the chair, "Hey, hey!"

Thad stood up. Marty was still looking into his lap at the glowing butt resting on his crotch. Thad paid no attention to him and walked over to a corner of the barn. Marty finally got the butt out of his lap and noticed the big man was gone. He craned his neck around looking for him. "Hey, where'd you go? Hey, man, where are you?"

Thad walked out where Marty could see him. He had a pack over his shoulder.

"What are you doing," Marty asked.

"I'm gonna leave you now."

"What?"

"I'm going."

"You're just going to leave me here?"

"Yeah, you're on your own."

"Thank you," Marty said.

"Don't thank me. I said you're on your own," Thad replied. He then struck the lighter and tossed it into a corner of the barn onto a pile of hay that he had soaked in kerosene. The hay caught immediately, the flame growing with rapid intensity.

Marty said, "You're leaving me here." Then he said it again, as a terrified screamed question, "You're leaving me here?!" He began to thrash his upper body back and forth like a child restrained in a high chair might. It was the only part of his body he could freely move and he was doing everything he could to move it. Thad stood there for a moment looking at Marty as he started to scream and shriek. Marty the postman called for help, he begged Thad to release him, and then he cursed him using every vile epithet he could imagine to impugn Thad's race, manhood and heritage. When none of that drew a response from the big man, Marty screamed out, "That bitch screamed her lungs out! She begged for her life and we burned her ass!"

Thad stood there motionless. "You've already begged for your life, guess that just leaves the screamin' and burnin'."

Marty's face was expressionless. His mouth hung open with drool running from the corner onto the postal service patch on his coat, but only for a moment. He went into another fit of fighting against the ropes, thrashing back and forth violently, succeeding once again in tipping the chair onto its side. Thad walked out of the barn and over to the Scout. He set the pack on the hood, leaned against the fender and watched as the flames grew up the side of the barn where he'd set the fire. Through the open door he could see the man lying on the ground, squirming to try and free himself. He could hear the man screaming and cussing.

By the time the roof of the barn caught and began to

burn, the heat was enough to make Thad back the Scout up. He then got out and leaned against the fender once again. Inside, the heat must be unbearable. Thad had never heard anyone scream that loud. The pigs in the pen were also screaming, more from fright than the heat as they were far enough way to be safe. In one loud crack, the beams supporting the roof finally gave and fell in, silencing the man. The only sound in the air now was that of the fire and terrified swine. Thad sat there for a moment looking at the tall flames, the sparks climbing up into the pitch-black, cloudless sky above. He stood there with his face raised to the heavens and said, "I'm sorry."

Walking over to the pigpen, he opened the gate and went in. Thad drew the big blade and slashed the rope holding the body. It fell into the swirling mass of hogs at his feet. The light from the fire played off the rumps of those closest to it and lit the faces of those opposite. Thad looked down at the ghoulish, bloodstained grin of one of them, and it almost looked as though it were saying thank you. Thad left the pen, leaving the gate open, and went back to the Scout. He climbed in and sat behind the wheel, looking at what laid before him. It was a familiar scene, with the only difference being there was no innocence under these flames.

Chapter 21

Sarge turned the map around a couple of times till he had it oriented. He stuck his index finger out and ran it over the map, and, finding what he was looking he for, he tapped the map with the finger. He told Ted to turn left when he hit the dirt road. Ted nodded and hung a hard left onto the white sand road, fishtailing the truck as he did.

Dallas was an old shack eight and a half miles due north of the Sarge's shack. It was in a huge undeveloped area crisscrossed with roads, paths and trails. Mike and Doc sat in the back of the truck, trying to hang on as the truck careened around the corners.

"What the hell is he trying to do, turn the damn thing over?" Doc said to Mike. He was leaning against the tailgate with his right arm hooked over the top of it.

Mike was sitting on top of the stack of camo nets close to the cab, his right leg stuck out against the far side of the bed to brace himself. He shook his head. He had a big smile on his face, as much as he could smile with the wound. He looked like a kid who was enjoying the ride.

The trip to the little shack didn't take long. When they got close Sarge called a stop and Ted pulled over to the side of the road. They got out and huddled around the map. "I was worried they saw you," Mike said. "I was scared shitless."

Doc was stretching his back. "They would have, but I climbed out and hid in the woods. They saw the boat and that had their interest. I didn't know what to do, and then you guys opened up and all hell broke loose."

Mike asked, "Were there Coasties in that RIB?"

"All I saw were DHS guys. There may have been one operating it, but none on the deck."

Mike shook his head. "Man, I hope not. My old man was in the Coast Guard."

"You fire that rocket?"

"Yeah."

"Hell of a shot," Doc said.

Sarge stepped between them. "Story time's over. Mike, you and Doc head through the bush here, take a due east heading. You're looking for a little shack over there. Make sure there aren't any surprises waiting for us. If you make contact, turn due south and we'll pick you up on the first dirt road you come to."

"Anything to get out of that damn rattletrap," Doc said, and then the two of them headed into the bush.

Sarge went to the passenger side. "Saddle up, Tonto, we gotta be ready if they need us," he said over the bed.

"What do you mean 'we,' white man?" Ted said.

Sarge chuckled and they climbed in and waited.

Mike and Doc were both wearing NVGs and communicated with hand signals as they worked their way through the bush. They were approaching the shack from the east side, and when it came into sight they took a knee and waited, watching the shack for any movement, anything that indicated someone was there. They waited for twenty minutes without moving or saying anything. Finally Mike looked over at Doc, raised his index finger and twirled it, then pointed to the south. Doc nodded and the two men stood up and moved out.

The shack sat in a small clearing, maybe half an acre. The two moved silently around the eastern edge of it, and coming to the southern edge, they stopped and took a knee to look and listen. They continued this process around the western and northern borders. Satisfied it was clear, the two men went across the road that passed just to the north and checked it as well.

The two men moved back to the clearing, skirting the western edge and approached the small shack from that side. At the edge of the shack they paused again, listening. Mike was paying particular attention to the ground around the shack. Doc motioned and Mike followed him to the northern edge of the shed. They carefully checked that side then moved to the eastern side where the door was located. There were no windows in the shack, no way to look inside. Mike stepped around Doc at the door and checked very carefully around its four sides. Finding nothing, the two of them prepared to open it. Mike positioned himself in front of the door with his carbine shouldered and at low ready. When he triggered the green laser on his weapon, Doc jerked the door open.

Mike stepped inside quickly, turning to the left, and Doc immediately followed him in and turned to the right. The shack was big, thirty by forty feet, a big set of double doors on the south side. It looked like it had been used to store equipment, but not recently. Mike found some old oil filters, big ones, piled in a corner, but otherwise the place was empty, save for black widows and a population of antlions that must have numbered in the thousands. Mike told Doc to hang out while he went back and got the old man.

Mike went back through the woods to the truck. As he approached, he gave a little whistle. It was answered with another and he came out of the bush and walked up to Sarge's side of the truck.

"Well?" Sarge asked as he came up.

"It's clear, boss, big place too. We can park the truck in it."

"Well, let's go see this palace."

Mike jumped into the back of the truck again and Ted drove off toward the shack. As they pulled in, Doc came out to meet them. The four men went into the tin-clad shack to look it over. Just as Mike had said, the structure was big enough to drive the truck into and they agreed that for the night they would drive in. The next day they would again make a hide for it in the woods. Sarge didn't like the idea of having the truck in there with them in case they were discovered. In the meantime they decided to set up camp for the night.

As they went back out to the truck, a low whump drifted across the forest. "Looks like they found the party favors," Mike said.

Ted just shrugged his shoulders and went to the truck to get his pack. Mike hopped into the truck and drove it around to the south side where Doc was opening the doors. Mike backed the truck until it was against the far side of the building before shutting it down. This way it gave them some room to get some speed if they needed to get the hell out of Dodge.

The rest of the evening was spent setting up camp for the night and prepping the comm gear. While they wouldn't transmit tonight, Sarge wanted it ready for the morning. Mike volunteered to stand the first watch and went outside and moved off into the tree line. Inside, the rest of the guys sorted out their gear and broke out some MREs. Sarge dug around in the bed of the truck looking for his stove; he was out of coffee and getting damn irritable. Ted came over and liberated it from under the camo nets and handed it over. "Here, before you go completely insane."

Sarge grabbed the stove and set it on the tailgate. "Believe me, you don't want to see me without coffee."

Ted leaned on the top of the bed. "You know that day's coming, right?"

Sarge was busy priming the stove and didn't look up. "What day?"

"The day when there's no more coffee."

Sarge stopped in midstroke, his thumb still over the end of the plunger in the tank of the stove. He looked over at Ted with his teeth gritted. "You watch your mouth! Don't start no shit; there won't be no shit!"

Ted laughed and turned away. "I'm jus' sayin'."

I had to go Mark's house after leaving Danny's. It was on the way anyway, so I stopped and dropped off the boxes. When I set them out at the little shed in his front yard, I opened them to take a look. There were two cans of beans and half a bag of flour and some hygiene products. In the second box there was a can of salt and a box of pepper. Seeing how little the guy had struck me. If these two boxes were any indication of how the others around there were doing, then people were about to get damn desperate. I admired Lance for never having said a word about how thin things were at home, but I knew most people weren't as stoic.

Mark was still at the barricade when I pulled up on my

way to get Howard. I told him I had left the boxes in front of his shed. He gave me a look then said, "Thanks, I'll have to get Marie over to open her lock." He shook his head and said, "Putting two locks on there was a good idea at the time, but she is a real pain in the ass."

"What do you have left in there?"

"Not much. We're down to the mush that was in those humanitarian aid boxes. I guess it'll keep you alive, but it tastes like shit."

"What is it?" I asked and suppressed a smile.

He thought for a minute. "Kinda like plain oatmeal and Cream of Wheat. It's hard to explain; the package has all the nutritional info on it, and it's got everything in it, except for taste."

I couldn't hide my grin anymore. Mark noticed it and said, "What?"

"I was just thinking of all those commercials we used to see on TV that had those kids with bloated bellies eating slop from a bowl with flies buzzing around it."

"And you find that funny?" He kinda glared at me, like I was crazy for saying that.

"No, no, it's just that it reminded me of the *South Park* episode where they made fun of Sally Struthers. Remember how she used to always be on those commercials?"

Slowly, a big smile spread across his face. "What was that character's name, the little Ethiopian kid that they brought over?"

I started to laugh and so did he. "I don't remember his name, I just remember him chasing shit down trying to get some food and her fat ass eating everything that wasn't nailed down."

Rick looked over. "What's so damn funny?"

Mark looked at him with tears in his eyes. "*South Park.*"

"*South Park?*" Rick asked.

"Never mind," Mark said with a wave, still laughing.

We both recovered and talked for a minute about some things in the neighborhood, Miss Janice for one, and how we needed to check on her. He asked again about the raiders that were still lying in the road, if I was serious about not helping to bury them. I assured him I was, but that I would still help haul them off into the woods or the field across the road and dump them. The look on his face made it pretty clear that he wasn't happy with my position. He said, "I'll let you know when you get back."

I drove out the barricade and headed down to the doc's place. Parking in front of the office, I walked around back to the house. It was connected but the doc was usually in the house and not the office. I knocked on the door and a woman opened it. I introduced myself and told her I was there to pick up Howard. She introduced herself as Nancy Peters, the doc's wife, and invited me in. She told me Howard was doing well and was more than ready to go home. I gave a little laugh and said I was sure he was. She led me out to the Florida room, where Howard was sitting in a wicker chair with his good leg up on a stool.

"Hey, old man, you ready to go?" I asked as I came in.

He looked up and said, "More than ready. What took so dang long?"

"If you were in a hurry, you coulda called a cab."

Howard laughed as the doc walked in. "Is this your ride?"

"Yeah, his chariot is outside," I replied.

"Nancy, can you gather up Howard's stuff while I go over some things with—" The doc paused and looked at me. "Sorry, I don't know your name."

"Oh, I'm Morgan," I said and stuck out my hand. He took it and we shook.

"Follow me, Morgan, I need to go over Howard's after-care."

We went out to his office, where he pulled a few items from a cabinet and put them in a box. There were rolls of gauze, gauze pads, a bottle of antibiotics and some pain-killers. He gave me a concerned look. "Howard doesn't like the painkillers, but take them with you; he may need them. Make sure he takes his antibiotics three times a day."

"How about the wound? Does it still need cleaned, or is it closed up?"

"The staples are still in, and yes, it needs cleaned and the dressing changed once a day. I'm putting a bottle of Betadine in the box too."

"You have any saline? I like to mix the two for wound irrigation."

He looked up at me, a little surprised. "Yeah," he said and he took a quart bottle from a shelf and dropped it in the box along with a big irrigation syringe.

"You have training?"

"Just OJT."

"Well, if you need anything, just let me know. If he develops a fever or anything, bring him in."

We went back to the Florida room where Howard was still sitting. There wasn't a wheelchair for him, so he had to use a pair of crutches to get out to the truck. I helped Howard in and put his crutches in the back along with the box Doc packed for us. Doc and Nancy were standing in the driveway waving as we pulled out. The ride back to our road was short, less than a mile, and Howard sat quietly as we drove. When we passed a family walking down the side of the road pushing a shopping cart, he finally spoke up. "We're fucked, aren't we?"

I looked at the family in the rearview mirror. They had moved to the side of the road when we passed them. "Things sure are different now."

He stared out the window in silence for a moment. "Just think of all the lost knowledge, things that everyone used to know how to do that now no one knows anymore."

"It's all still out there, in books. We'll just have to learn it all again." I looked over at him and smiled.

He was still looking out the window. "What good is an old one-legged man going to be? I can't even collect firewood to heat my home or shoot limb rats for food."

"You can still shoot limb rats. Phyllis will just have to go get them for you. As for firewood, I'll keep you stocked, and there is one thing you can do that is very important."

Howard looked over at me, trying not to look too interested in what I had to say.

"You have your ham rig, right? You need to spend your time listening and making notes. We need to know what is out there and what is coming our way. You can do that, can't you?"

"I guess even with only one leg I can do that."

"I know it doesn't look too good today, but think about the future. You can still stand guard at the barricade, can't you? If you're doing that, it means some of the younger guys will be freed up to plant when spring comes, stuff like that. Hell, at some point we're gonna need a school, and a teacher. Maybe you'll do that. Point is, we don't know everything we're gonna need, but we know that we're gonna need everyone. You hear me?"

He looked over and nodded. "I hear you."

I smiled, and he smiled back at me and asked me to stop at the barricade. Mark came up to the truck when I stopped. He said, "How ya feelin', Howard?"

"Pretty good for someone who lost half a leg. I wanted to say thank you to you and Morgan. You guys saved my life."

"Shoot, all I did was drive you down to the old saw-bones." Mark pointed at me and said, "He's the one who really saved your hide."

"It was just some first aid. I couldn't let you lie there and bleed out."

"Well, it saved my ass," Howard said.

Rick called out, "There's a motorcycle coming."

I stepped out of the Suburban, put the sling of my carbine over my head and walked out to the road. The scooter was coming out of Altoona and was loud as hell. I've always heard bikers say that loud pipes save lives, but damn. The bike slowed as it got closer and coasted to a stop in the road in front of the barricade. The man sitting on it was wearing a pair of clean jeans and a leather jacket. His boots looked like Hi-Tecs or something like them. There was a rough-looking scabbard strapped to the right side of the bike with a rifle butt jutting out of it.

He sat on the bike for a moment then put the kickstand down and stepped off. He was wearing a helmet, one of the little skullcap kind, and took it off. "You guys have any clean water?" he called out.

I was standing in front of the barricade with my carbine at low ready. He wasn't holding a firearm and was standing there with his hands on his hips. After a moment I told him we did and waved him over to the barricade and the keg kept behind it. He opened one of the hard boxes on the side of the bike and pulled out a couple of one-liter water bottles. When he was about halfway to the barricade, I asked him if he had any other weapons on him. He said that he did and opened his jacket to show a Glock in a high-ride holster on his belt.

"Is that the only one?" I asked him.

He smiled and replied, "No, there's another one on the bike too."

"Just keep it in the holster and we'll be fine," I replied.

He held his hands up in mock surrender. "No problem, man, all I want is some water. Besides, from the looks of you guys, I don't have enough guns."

He went over to the keg and filled his bottles. Mark came up to me as he was filling them and said he didn't like the looks of him. I told him his cop was sticking out and laughed when he looked down at his zipper. That got me a hearty "Fuck you." As biker dude was screwing the cap on the second bottle, I walked over to him and asked where he was coming from. He told me he had been down in Miami, but he was from Phoenix. He had come down to pick up the bike he was riding, bought online from an old Cuban dude and had come down with his truck and a trailer to pick it up when things "went to shit," as he put it.

"How's Miami?" I asked.

He just laughed. "Worse than ever, if you can imagine. Liberty City was on fire when I pulled out, Alpha 66 was trying to put together a navy so they could invade Cuba, and the Cubans and Haitians were in the business of wholesale murder of one another." He said to hang on, then went to his bike and came back with a black case. When he opened it I suddenly thought I was dealing with someone a few sandwiches short of a picnic. He pulled an iPad out of the case. I kind of raised my eyebrows at him and he just smiled and hit the POWER button. To my complete astonishment, the damn thing came on. He winked and said, "Check this out."

He played a video taken with the iPad. It was the skyline of Miami and it was burning. The view panned down and there were bodies on the road. The vantage point appeared to be from across a large canal and from at least the second floor of a building. I watched the video in total amazement as the thick black smoke billowed into the sky, and the crackle of gunfire could be heard in the background. He explained that what we were seeing was Overtown in Miami. He had been on the roof of a building watching the chaos. Miami was a cesspool; mounds of uncollected garbage were piled everywhere. Many of the residents of the city and suburbs of Miami came from third-world countries, and when the power failed and the country started to slide backward, they naturally went back to what they knew. Sewage was simply dumped into the street along with the carcasses of animals killed for food. The latter included everything from cats and dogs to chickens and iguanas.

He told me how he had watched three Haitians try to kill a donkey with a machete. The donkey had brayed and screamed when they struck it with the big blade. They had the poor creature tied to a palm tree and it fought against the rope but couldn't escape. He said he would never forget the look on that animal's face, how big its eyes were, wide in abject terror. At that point it was the worst thing he had ever seen in his life. He couldn't take it and used his Mosin—he nodded his chin at the rifle on his bike—to put the animal down. He said when he shot the damn donkey, the Haitian with the machete stopped with the blade poised over his head for another strike. The man was covered in blood from his face to feet. Hearing the shot and seeing the animal drop, they simply began to cut it up.

He finished up by saying, "Hell, I'm a hunter, but that was just awful."

I pointed as the iPad and asked, "How?"

He smiled real big and waved me over to the bike. Opening one of the boxes, he pulled away the felt from the top to reveal a copper wire mesh. I guess the look on my face was enough of a question so he went on to explain how he had some of his stuff in a Faraday cage he built. When he had had to downsize to fit everything on the bike, he took it apart and lined the box on the bike with it. I shook my head. He was pretty sharp. "Hey, what's your name?"

He stuck his hand out and replied, "Jeff. Jeff Collins."

I introduced myself to him and asked about his trip up. He walked over to the bike and I followed him as he spoke. I was curious why he was no farther from Miami than he was, since I had walked from Tallahassee in far less time. He told me he didn't have any family and wasn't in a rush to get anywhere. He was just cruising around, finding fuel where he could and getting a feel for things. He opened the box on the bike, put the iPad in and pulled out a big bag of Bazooka bubble gum, reached in and grabbed a handful and then offered it to me.

"I don't want any, but can I take some for my kids?"

"Sure, man, help yourself," he replied as he unwrapped a piece and stuck in his mouth, then unfolded the little comic.

I reached in, grabbed a few pieces and stuck them in my pocket. He read the comic and laughed to himself then proceeded to open four more pieces and stuff them in his mouth as well. I laughed when he looked up with a mouthful of the hard squares, trying to get them all mashed up.

"Like bubble gum?" I asked.

He swatted at a gnat that was harassing his ear and replied, "You gotta enjoy the little things in life, especially nowadays."

"Yeah, I guess so."

He swatted at the gnat again. "What the hell's with these damn flies?" he said as he was trying to draw a bead on one in front of his face.

"Gotta love dog-peter gnats."

He stopped with his fist clenched tight in front of his face, an unsuccessful attempt at capturing the pest and looked at me with one eye half-squinted. "What'd you call em?"

With that huge wad of gum lodged in his jaw, he looked like the cartoon baseball player on the bag of Big League Chew bubble gum.

"Dog-peter gnats. Where do you usually see the damn things?"

He folded at the waist and began to laugh. He said, "That's funny as hell. I've never heard that before."

"There's only one surefire way to get rid of 'em."

He chewed the wad for a moment, then asked, "How?" with more than a hint of suspicion.

"Cut a hole in the seat of your pants. Buzzing around your face is only their second choice."

The gnats were buzzing around his head when it rolled back and he began to laugh. I watched as one of the little bastards flew right up his left nostril, like a Goldfish crumb caught in the suction of a Kirby vacuum.

What happened next startled me. He stopped in midlaugh

and went to take a breath to try to snot-rocket the pest out, but the sound that came from his throat was like a half-full bathtub draining, when the little vortex of water forms and that deep-throated slurp comes up from the drain. That sound was followed immediately by the sound the little rubber stopper would make when, caught in that vortex, it found its way over the hole and plugged the flow of water.

Jeff reached up and grabbed his neck. His eyes were wide, and his mouth hung agape. I looked at him for a second before I realized he couldn't breathe; his face was growing progressively redder, and the veins in his neck and forehead bulged. I ran around him and tried to perform the Heimlich maneuver on him to no effect. I had my arms around his midsection, jerking upward against his sternum, trying to dislodge the wad of gum in his throat. After a couple of attempts, his knees buckled and with all his weight on me, he slumped to the ground. He was still trying to get a breath, but it just wasn't happening.

I knelt down and pounded on his back: nothing. After another brief moment, he fell to the side. Tears were dripping from his nose as he lay there on the road. Opening his mouth and holding his tongue down with my thumb, I stuck my right index finger into the back of his throat to try and get the pink mass out. All I managed was to pull a long sticky string out of his mouth. He was motionless by then. I tried a sternum rub to see if he would respond, but he was gone. I heard a scuffing sound and looked up to see Howard hobbling over. He stopped at my side looking down at the body. "Why'd you kill 'im?"

I looked up at the old man. "Look here, kickstand, you start any shit and you're going straight to the glue factory." He just shrugged his shoulders and stood there.

Mark walked over, looking confused as hell. "What in the hell just happened?"

He stepped up and knelt beside Jeff and put his index and middle finger to his throat. Looking up, he said, "There's still a pulse." He stood up and straddled Jeff's motionless body, raising his right foot. Mark stomped on his chest, planting his boot right on Jeff's sternum. Jeff let out a coughing kind of sound, and that big pink wad shot straight up into the air. Reflexively, Howard stuck his hand out and the mass landed in his hand.

Jeff took in a deep breath and let out a long moan. "Oh, my fucking ribs," he said as he wrapped his arms around his chest and rolled onto his side. "I think my ribs are broke," he moaned.

Mark, Howard and I stood there looking down at him for a minute. Jeff looked up and asked who hit him. Howard pointed to Mark and replied, "He did, 'cept he put the boot leather to ya."

Jeff rolled onto his back and looked up at Mark. "You a cop? That's police brutality, man."

Mark smiled. "You're welcome."

I reached down and pulled Jeff to his feet. He was still holding his ribs and leaning forward slightly. Howard held out the wad of gum. "Want this back?"

Jeff looked over, "Hell no, I don't want that shit. My throat is killing me."

Howard tossed the wad off into the palmettos at the side of the road.

"You gonna be all right?" I asked.

"I need a place to sit down for a while."

I told him to come with me. He was worried about his bike, but I assured him it would be safe there. We had to push it behind the barricade before he would agree. I loaded Jeff and Howard up and headed for Howard's house. I managed to get Howard delivered to his place, but helping him into the house was bit of a pain. He needed a ramp, and I added that to my mental list of things to do. I asked about their firewood situation and his wife said they were fine for now. I told them both if they needed anything to come and get me. They were both a little hardheaded, saying they didn't need any help, and I said, "Well, if you do, you know where to find me."

With Howard finally home, I took Jeff to my place. He wasn't saying much, and I couldn't blame him for it. At the house I took him in and deposited him on the sofa. He protested at first, not wanting to burden me, but I told him not to worry about it, to take it easy for little while and that he could stay the night and leave in the morning. I went to see Mel in the kitchen and told her about our guest. By the time I got back to the living room, Jeff was sound asleep. I left him there and went back to the kitchen.

"He's asleep," I said as I came in.

"Is he armed?"

"Uh, yeah, he has a pistol that I know of."

"And you bring him here, with our girls?" she said, leaning against the island with her arms crossed.

"Well, yeah. I don't think he is going to be a problem. He seems like a pretty good guy." I told her what had happened and she said she wouldn't be comfortable until I had Jeff's pistol. I nudged him and when he didn't wake, I slipped it out of the holster and showed it to Mel.

"Good, now I don't feel like I'll be killed in my sleep. Now that that's settled, why in the hell did you take her with you today to load up a dead body?"

"She wanted to go. I told her what I was doing and she wanted to go. You think we can hide this sort of thing from them forever?"

"She's seven; of course she wanted to go with you. The only dead people she has ever seen were on TV. She doesn't understand it."

"She has a better understanding of it now. Look, I knew she wasn't ready for what she was going to see, but I would rather that first encounter be under a somewhat controlled situation than when we are running for our lives and she freezes when she sees a dead body. We're all going to be seeing more of them."

She stood there for a moment, looking right through me. "Why are you so damn morbid? Why do think we're going to go all *Mad Max*?"

I was stunned. "Have you looked around? Do you have any idea what is going on, how bad things are?"

"The power's out, so what? It's like the hurricanes a couple of years ago. It's not that big a deal."

That made me pause. All this time I had been worried that Mark and other folks weren't really getting it and it had never occurred to me Mel wasn't either. I said, "It's not that big a deal? Are you out of your damn mind? We're doing better than most because of what we put away, but for most folks out there the shit has hit the fan in a big way, and let me clue you in to something, we're going to be in the same boat as everyone else is soon enough. The food we have stored is going to run out, the fuel is going to run out, and we'll be like everyone else: hungry and desperate."

She said, "I don't think it's that bad. Is it?"

"After we buried Lance and his wife today, Mark went through their house. They had two—*two*—cans of food and a little flour, that was it. Everyone around here is probably in the same boat."

Mel cocked her head. "Why did you have to bury his wife?"

"She wouldn't come out. She called me a liar when I told her he was dead, so I left his body in the yard and went to get Mark. When we got back, we found her dead in the house. She shot herself."

Mel stood there silent for a moment and then said, "Oh."

Chapter 22

Thad loaded everything from the cache into the Scout. When he was done, he examined the rifle he had taken off the security man. It was an M4 with an ACOG optic sight and a light on the foregrip.

He had no experience with the weapon and started trying to figure out how it worked. He pressed the mag release, and the magazine fell out and landed on the ground. He turned the weapon over and looked at the mag well. He re-inserted the mag and tapped the bottom, then shook the weapon to make sure it was in tight. He pressed the release again, this time with his hand under it, catching it. After setting the mag on the hood he grabbed the charging handle and pulled it to the rear and the chambered round ejected. Thad picked up the round and put it back in the magazine. Once he had it back in, he put the mag back into the weapon and pulled the charging handle back and let it go. It closed with a solid slap.

Thad put the rifle to his shoulder and looked through the sight. He aimed at a live oak about twenty yards from him and squeezed the trigger. It was stiff and wouldn't move. Thad lowered the rifle and looked it over. Finding the safety, he flipped it up and once again put it against his shoulder. Pressing the switch for the light, he squeezed the trigger, and this time the weapon barked and kicked slightly against his shoulder. He settled the rifle and fired a couple more rounds at the tree. It didn't look like he had hit it, but walking up he could see the small holes in the bark. Thad flipped the safety back to the safe position. Feeling a little more comfortable with the rifle, Thad put it back in the truck and climbed in.

Leaving the farm for the last time, he drove by the burning barn and headed toward his house. Thad pulled up in front of his house and sat there looking at it. After a moment, he got out of the truck, went to the back and took out a blue plastic jug. He let himself in and left the key in the lock.

He poured the kerosene out on the floor of his bedroom and lit it. He went to Tony's room, where he did the same thing. He poured the rest of the kerosene on the sofa and lit it as well. With the flames building, he walked out on the front porch and stood there for a minute, stuffing his hands into the pockets on his coat. He rolled his shoulders against the chill in the air and took in the scene from his front porch for the last time. His hand found Little Tony's toy in his coat pocket and he clutched it, thinking about the Transformers movie he had watched with Tony, the part where the bad guys had burned the Transformer's home world and the good guys had to go on the run.

Thad climbed back into the truck, started it and sat there for minute. He backed the truck out onto the road and paused again. After a moment he turned the truck north on Swift Mud Road and started to drive. As he drove, Thad thought about where he was going, where he could go. He knew Sarge had left his place. Then he had a thought and stopped the truck in the road. Reaching into the back seat, he pulled his pack to the front. He dug around in the pack and finally came out with a piece of paper. He sat there looking at it, rubbing it between his fingers. Finally he laid it on the seat beside him and took out his atlas, something he was thankful he had managed to salvage from the old truck.

Once he knew where he was going there was nothing left to do but get started. It was a long way and he was not looking forward to the drive, but he wanted to get away, and he never wanted to see Land O' Lakes again. It was late and Thad didn't expect to see anyone out, but he didn't really care either way.

He made his way to I-75. He drove until he reached the exit for Lake Panasoffkee and got off. The exit ramp dead-ended into another road and Thad needed to take a right. As he approached the T in the road ahead of him, Thad saw a makeshift roadblock. The area around it was dark, and as the headlights swung around to light up the area, it appeared to be empty. Nonetheless, he reached over and picked up the old coach gun and laid it in his lap.

Thad went off the left side of the road and was passing the barricade when he saw the tent. As he looked at it, a head popped out of it. Much to his relief, the man didn't come any farther.

After making his turn, he reached the intersection of CR 470. This road would take him through a couple of small towns. One large intersection up ahead was his only real concern; it crossed 301 and was the one place where he would certainly encounter people. Once past that, he would go through Yalaha then Howey-in-the-Hills. There he would turn onto 19 and face his next major obstacle: the bridge over Lake Harris. This one worried him the most, as any detour around it would add many miles to the trip through heavily populated areas.

Thad kept his eyes on the road, occasionally scanning the

sides of the road for anything that looked out of place. He was at ease as he drove. The road he was on would end ahead and he would have to make a left to continue through Sumterville. Up ahead he could make out what could only be the overpass on the turnpike; this could be an issue, but he hoped not. Once again he laid the old shotgun in his lap and moved the Scout to the center of the road. There was no trouble, and when he reached Howey-in-the-Hills, he knew the bridge over Harris was coming up.

Just outside of the town proper he turned onto Highway 19. That side of the lake was mostly orange groves, the trees stripped of any leftover fruit. As he approached the bridge, Thad slowed the Scout to a stop and strained to look out across it. It was impossible to see across, but from his side everything looked peaceful enough. Putting the truck in gear, he started onto the bridge. He was going slowly as the thought of the Scout careening off the bridge into the alligator-infested lake below sent chills up his spine. As he drove, he looked out into the lake, and save the occasional reflection of the moon off the lake it looked like a bottomless abyss.

Halfway across the bridge he was looking out into the water when he was blinded by light. Snapping his head around, he saw two sets of lights high off the ground, each of them with four blindingly bright beams. Thad slammed on the brakes and put the Scout into reverse, and an amplified voice came at him from the opposite bank, but with the windows up he couldn't make out what it said. Thad stretched his right arm out across the passenger seat and looked back to back off the bridge, but his heart sank when two sets of lights began to accelerate from the opposite end toward him. He stopped the truck and looked forward again.

Silhouetted in the light coming from the other end, he could see men walking toward him, armed men. He looked in the rearview again and saw that men were climbing out of some sort of ATVs, and they too were armed.

Thad's head dropped onto the steering wheel. He bounced it a couple of times, finally letting it rest on the wheel, and shook it from side to side.

Sarge made coffee and told the guys to get some rack time. The guys went about digging out their sleep gear. Since they probably weren't going to be here long they took out only what they needed: sleeping bags and mats and some MREs for chow. They didn't talk much. They were on the wrong end of the game now; they were in E&E mode and none of them liked it. Sarge went over to the radios and checked the settings on the green gear, the military crypto radios, then picked up his carbine with his free hand and took his coffee outside.

He went outside and flipped his NVGs down. He took a sip of his coffee and scanned the area around the little shack. He walked around the building, returning to the door and set his cup down beside it before walking off toward the nearby tree line. He made a circuit around the edge of the clearing and finally picked a spot off the southwest corner and sat down under a big live oak. If any trouble was coming, it would probably come from the west or the south, so it was a good spot to keep an eye out.

Inside, Mike unrolled his bag on his mat. He thought he heard something and stopped to listen. Hearing it again, he walked over to the tailgate of the truck where the radios were set up, picked up the headset and put the speaker to his ear. After a brief pause, the transmission crackled through: *"Clementine to Swamp Rat."*

"Go for Swamp Rat," Mike replied. Ted looked up and Mike gave him a nod with his chin.

"Swamp Rat, you need to rendezvous with Stump Knocker two-point-five clicks north of your current location at 0500, how copy?"

"Roger that, rendezvous with Stump Knocker at 0500 two–point–five clicks north of current, wilco."

"Clementine out."

Mike set the headset down and looked over at Ted. "Who's Stump Knocker?" Ted asked.

"Don't know. I'm gonna go get the old man."

Mike slung his carbine, picked up his NVGs and turned them on and headed for the door. He put them on as he stepped through the door and dropped them down. He stood there for a moment as the green gloom began to form into a recognizable picture. Once they were warmed up, he walked out from the building looking for Sarge. He saw him when Sarge stood up, the motion caught Mike's eye and started toward him. They met at the back of the building. "What's up?" Sarge asked.

"Clementine called and wants us to meet up with an element called Stump Knocker at 0500 tomorrow."

Sarge looked down at the ground, scuffing the brown grass with the toe of his boot. "What'cha think?"

"I think we need to be there early and see who comes a-callin'," Mike replied as he rubbed his jaw.

Sarge looked at him for a minute. "How's the head?"

"Still sore, but getting better."

"All right, you wanna go? You up to it?"

"Yeah, I'm good. You going?" Mike asked.

"What the fuck do you think?"

Mike laughed softly. "When you wanna leave?"

Sarge looked at his watch. "It's 2330 now; let's pack our shit and head out now. We can catch a little sleep once we get there."

The two of them headed back inside where Ted was sitting beside the radios on the tailgate. As they came in, he looked up and smiled. "What's the plan?"

Sarge told him that he and Mike were going to head out now and be in position when Stump Knocker showed up. He wanted him and Doc to stay behind and keep an eye on things. They would take the Green Gear with them and the handheld radio. If they needed to, they could communicate over that. Ted nodded and Sarge and Mike went about getting their packs ready. With all the noise, Doc sat up and said, "What the fuck, man? I'm trying to sleep."

"You'll have plenty of time when you're dead," Sarge replied over his shoulder as he dug around in the bed of the truck.

Sarge was on point. They moved slowly and deliberately, stopping often to look around and listen. They were in position a little before 0300 and found a spot between two big palm trees where Sarge set up the Minimi. Mike moved off about twenty yards to Sarge's right behind the trunk of a huge sand pine. They could see each other from their positions and went over a few hand signals. Once in position, they each reapplied camo paint to their faces and added camo in the form of vegetation to their immediate fronts as well their sixes.

The two men tried to get comfortable and fought the urge to sleep. It was quiet and still in the predawn and all they could hear was the ringing in their ears. As the dawn came closer, Sarge stared out into the trees, not really focusing on anything in particular, just watching for movement. It didn't take long for him to pick up what looked like three men moving through the trees across the small clearing. After a few more seconds of looking, he was sure he could see three, though there surely would be more.

Sarge looked at Mike and held up three fingers. Mike nodded and went back to scanning his section. As the three men approached the small clearing, they veered off to the north and kept walking, disappearing from view. After a couple minutes of their passing, two more men came into view; these would be the rear security element. These two men moved through the little clearing extremely slowly. With them out in the open, Sarge was able to get a good look at them and their gear. These two were wearing the same multicam that they were. They were carrying M4s and wearing sidearms in drop-leg holsters.

They paused in the clearing and spoke in a very low whisper. After a brief pause they split up. One of them continued in the same direction the previous group had gone and the other continued out the other side of the clearing and disappeared into the darkness. Sarge checked his watch: 0434. It had to be them. He would stay in position for a while, then he would contact them on the radio. After the men moved through, the woods fell silent once again. The sky was changing colors, going from the deep black of night to the cobalt of early morning.

A few minutes before 0500, Sarge reached over and turned the radio on. In a low whisper he called his contact element.

"Swamp Rat to Stump Knocker." He waited and repeated the call.

"*Go for Stump Knocker,*" came the hushed reply.

"What's your ETA?"

"*Stump Knocker is on station.*"

"How many in your lead element?" Sarge whispered in the mic.

There was a pause, then, "*Three.*"

"How many in your security element?"

Another pause. "*Two.*"

"Roger that, retrace your route in. We'll identify ourselves when you reach us. Leave your security element out."

"*Roger that, Swamp Rat. Stump Knocker's inbound.*"

Chapter 23

I came through the door with an armload of wood, leaving the big garden cart out front. The fire was down to a bed of coals, and I added some of the smaller limbs I'd collected to them. Jeff was sitting on a stool in the kitchen, and Mel was leaning against the counter.

"What's for dinner?" I asked.

"Biscuits and gravy," she replied.

"Sounds good to me. How you feeling?" I asked, looking at Jeff.

Rubbing his throat, he said, "Better, thanks."

We sat and talked while the biscuits in the little oven browned. Jeff was from Phoenix and had been the supervisor of an IT department. He worked for a company that did contract work for the federal government. It was a good job and paid well, but it kept him inside more than he wanted. He enjoyed shooting the Mosin he had left on his scooter. He had modified it and told me, "It's no peasant's Mosin."

I asked if he wouldn't mind helping me on a little project I was working on.

"Not a problem, man," he said.

Taylor and Lee Ann came trooping in through the sliding glass door. They stopped when they saw Jeff and stared at him. He smiled at them and said, "Hi." They just stood there, Taylor slowly closing the door behind them. After I let them know it was okay, they said hello in return and lightened up a bit. They wanted to know what was for dinner and bopped around the kitchen pestering Mel.

Mel told them to go get Ashley and bring her out for dinner and to make sure they all washed their hands. They ran off and I asked Jeff if he would like to get cleaned up and showed him to the bathroom in our bedroom. As he was stepping into the bathroom, he looked at me and asked, "I assume my Glock is in safe hands?"

I let out a little laugh. "Yeah, sorry about that, but Mel insisted I get it. With three girls in the house, she's pretty protective. You can't be too careful these days."

"If I hadn't been so tired, I wouldn't have come in here. Like you said, you can't trust anyone these days. But after my little near-death experience, I was kinda wore out."

"Did you see a white light?" I asked with a smile.

"Nope, but I did see the face of my ex-wife. Her head was bouncing up and down and her mouth was going a mile a minute, just like the last time I saw her. Now I'm scared of where I was headed," he said.

I had to laugh. "Come out when you're ready. The water works here, so do what you need to," I said.

The girls were all at the table and there was some jockeying going on as to who would sit beside me. Mel was setting out plates with a couple of biscuits each and big ladle of sausage gravy. The stocks in the freezer were starting to run low, but we had decided to use them up so that if anything were to happen, that food wouldn't go to waste. Jeff came out and took the empty seat. He was between Little Bit and Taylor. Little Ash had never met a stranger and immediately asked, "What's your name?".

He told her, then she asked, "Were you the man asleep on the couch?"

He laughed and nodded his head. We talked a little while we ate, nothing serious, but the girls peppered him with questions and he politely answered them, never showing any irritation with their constant probing. Then I made a huge mistake. I was telling Mel about the video he had on his iPad, and as soon as I said that little four-letter word, all three of the girls looked up at him, just staring. Jeff's eyes darted around the table from girl to girl. Finally he asked, "What?"

Taylor, with a forkful of sausage gravy dripping onto her plate, said, "You have an iPad that works?"

"Yeah, but there's no Internet or anything, so you can't do much with it."

Little Bit looked up with wide eyes. "Does it have Angry Birds?" she shouted.

"Yeah, it does."

"Oh, can I play it, please, please, please?"

"It's not here right now. It's on my motorcycle." Looking up at me, he said, "Which I would like to go get."

I told him we could after dinner and he promised to let Little Bit play Angry Birds, at which she giggled with delight. The other girls wanted to know if had any music on it that they could listen to. He said he would be happy to let them look at what he had. They told him they had MP3 players, but not much in the way of new music.

As we were finishing dinner, Mel surprised everyone by bringing a peach cobbler to the table to a chorus of cheers. She told us not to cheer until we tried it. Everyone got a big scoop, pretty much finishing off the pan, and we were all more than impressed with it. Jeff was particularly happy. He said, "This is great. It's been a long time since I had a meal this good."

Mel said, "I think your hunger is clouding your judgment."

The girls and I all piped up about the same time, voicing our approval. Once dinner was done, the two older girls took care of the dishes and Jeff and I headed for the door. Little Bit was clamoring to come with us, but it was dark out and I had a pretty strict rule about them not going out after dark. She persisted, but finally got the point. I put my vest on and slipped the sling to my carbine over my head. Jeff looked at me. "My Glock?"

"Oh yeah, hang on," I said and headed for the bedroom. When I handed it over, I said, "Sorry about that."

"No worries, I've got it back." He looked over at Mel who had took up a spot on the end of the sofa closest to the fire. "Thanks for dinner. It was great."

"You're welcome. We were glad to have you."

We walked out the drive heading to the road and chatted as we went. I asked what his plans were and again he said he didn't really have any. I asked if he would be interested in hanging out here for a while and he said he'd think about it.

"Why do you want me to stay?" Jeff asked.

"Well, to be honest, I'm not the most popular guy around here. I have one solid friend that I can count on and a couple of others that are all right, but that's it."

He looked at me with a sideways glance and asked why that was. I went on to explain my trip home to him, the whole thing, and what had happened after I got there. I told him about Pat and her kin. He looked at me with raised eyebrows and said, "Little harsh, don't ya think?"

"I have a wife and three daughters. They're my first

priority, and there's no way I can keep my eyes open twenty-four seven. Would you turn your back on someone who you knew was coming after you?"

We reached the gate and I glanced over at him. He had his head down and his hands in his pockets. I said, "I can tell from the look on your face you've already had to make that decision."

He nodded his head without saying anything. We turned up the road and headed for the barricade. It was cold out and there was a low layer of clouds; it looked like rain was coming, and I hate rain when it's cold out. Reggie was at the barricade with my neighbor. They had a fire in the burn barrel and were standing over it when we walked up.

"Hey, Morg, who's your friend?" Reggie asked.

I made the introductions and we all stood around the fire, warming our hands. Reggie asked about the scooter. "That's a nice ride. What year is it?"

Jeff looked over at the old scooter with pride. "It's a 1960 Panhead Duo-Glide. She's all original too, even the paint."

"Damn, that must have cost a pretty penny." Reggie was shaking his head as he stared into the fire.

"Yeah, but what the hell, the thirty I spent on it wouldn't be worth shit now anyway."

We all nodded in agreement, and I asked what had happened to the bodies of the raiders. Reggie said that Mark and Rick had loaded them up and hauled them off, but he didn't know what they did with them. We stayed there with them for a little while just shooting the shit, nothing too deep, then Jeff said he wanted to get his bike somewhere safe. I told Reggie I would see him later. He asked where he could put it and I told him to take it to my house. I said he could crash on the couch tonight and if he was interested in staying we could find him a permanent place later.

"The thought of sleeping in front of that fire sure sounds nice," Jeff said as he swung a leg over the old Harley.

"One thing, though, you gotta keep it going all night."

Jeff smiled. "No such thing as a free ride anymore, huh?"

I kicked his front tire. "Just this one."

He laughed and started the old scooter. The pipes on the damn thing were incredibly loud. Jeff rode off toward the house. At first he went slow so I could walk alongside him, but that beast was so loud I told him to just get it to the house and park it.

It was completely dark by then, and with the cloud cover there wasn't any moonlight coming through. The only light out now came from Jeff's bike. The headlights cast a cone of light that illuminated the trees above and on both sides of the road. Jeff turned off into the drive and headed toward the house. I was still a little ways away when I heard a woman scream.

The scream came from past my house, and I strained to look out into the dark. Then there was another scream and what sounded like several people yelling. I started to jog toward the commotion, and a light appeared, dull and yellow, two houses down from mine. As I got closer, I could hear two men yelling and saw someone run out of the yard and down the road, heading into the neighborhood, but the yelling continued.

As I walked through the open gate I could see two figures holding another on the ground. The one on the ground struggled a bit and was met with a hard blow from the bigger of the two on top of him. From where I was, it sounded like someone slapping a steak against the fridge. The figure on the ground let a howl of pain and went limp. Then I heard a man say, "That's what ya get, thief!"

Walking up to them, I hit the button on my flashlight and lit the group up. There was a woman standing to the side. She had on fuzzy slippers and some sort of flannel PJs, all wrapped up in a thick robe. She had one arm wrapped around her chest and the other hand over her mouth. On the ground was a young guy, somewhere between sixteen and eighteen. His right eye was already starting to swell and blood ran thick and slow from his nose, a string of it hanging from his face where it reached for the grass.

On top of him was a heavyset man in gray sweatpants and a black sweatshirt. He outweighed the kid he was on by better than a hundred pounds. He was one of those guys who had no neck—not muscled, but fat. He had those rolls of meat on the back of his head where it met his shoulders, and even in the cold he was sweating. With him was what looked like his son, who looked just as corn-fed as his old man. When the light hit him, the kid on the ground started to beg for help. "They're trying to kill me!" he shouted.

Boss Hogg looked over his shoulder, having to turn his upper body to get his head far enough around to see me. "He's a fucking thief! He was stealing our chickens. We done lost three, now I know wur they went."

"No, I wasn't! I didn't steal anything! They just jumped me!"

"You did too! I saw you with two of 'em in your hands. You callin' me a liar?" the woman shouted.

I could hear Mark's Mule coming down the road and looked up to see him turn into the drive.

Mark pulled up looking frazzled. He looked like he wasn't getting enough sleep and it was starting to wear on him. The robe-clad woman ran to him as he climbed out of the Mule. "He was stealing our chickens!"

"No, I wasn't! They jumped me and started beating me! Get him off!" the kid on the ground cried.

The cop in Mark was already in gear. "Then why you in their yard?" he asked with a sigh.

The fat man glanced over at Mark. "'Cause he was stealing our chickens."

The kid on the ground didn't have anything to say; what *could* he say? He was caught in their yard at night with a chicken in each hand. Mark asked them what they wanted him to do about it. They looked at him kind of confused. "You're the law; it's your job. You need to do something about it. We can't have people going around here stealing from us," the man said, loosening his grip on the kid.

"Well, what do you expect me to do? I can't put him in jail," Mark said, more than a little annoyance in his voice.

The man straightened himself up and looked at Mark. The boy rolled hard to the side and out from under the man. In a flash he was trying to get his feet under him to run. The man lunged for him, missed and landed on the ground. His son leapt for the kid and in a twist any football player could appreciate, the kid rolled out of the tackle and was at a full run. The man looked at Mark and shouted, "Shoot him!"

Mark just shook his head. "I'm not going to shoot someone for stealing a fucking chicken."

The big man stood up. "Then what damn good are ya if you aren't going to protect us?"

Mark just shook his head and walked over to the Mule. I looked at him as he passed me, but he didn't even acknowledge I was standing there.

The man and his wife watched Mark as he got back in the Mule. He said, "Next time I'll shoot him myself!"

Mark started the Mule. I walked over to him and rested a hand on top of the roll cage. "You look like shit."

He said, "Yeah, thanks." He sat there for a minute staring off into the darkness and then said, "What do these fucking idiots want from me?"

"They want what they always wanted: someone else to make decisions for them."

He hung his head and shook it slightly. "They wanted me to shoot that kid for stealing a fucking chicken."

"We need to come up with a way of dealing with little shit like this. If they had shot him I wouldn't have blamed 'em, but if people call for help or there's some other petty crap, we need something a little less permanent than a firing squad," I said.

"What are we going to do, put a set of stocks in the village square?" Mark asked.

I raised my eyebrows and looked at him. "That's not a bad idea. Then the next time something like this happens we have a way to deal with it. I think you should do just that. I mean, think about—I don't know, three hundred years ago. No small town had someone who could stand watch on a jail all day. But people who stole stuff, they were still part of the community. They were tied to the land, just like we are now. You couldn't just pack up and get a job in the next town over. So they used peer pressure. Some dumb kid takes a chicken, he gets shamed in front of everyone he knows. Chances are he learns not to do it again."

Mark didn't even look up as he put the Mule in gear. "Fine. I delegate it to you, then." And he drove away.

Thad sat rocking his head on the wheel while the men out-side shouted orders at him. He could hear them, but he just couldn't face the fact that he had only made it this far. Turn-ing his head to the side, he looked at the M4 lying on the seat. For a moment he thought of getting out with it and the shotty and just ending it right here, but he knew he couldn't do that. Slowly and with great effort he reached over and opened the door. The voices ordered him out of the truck.

"Put your hands up, turn away from me, get down on your knees, cross your feet, do not fucking move!"

Thad followed the orders. He was thrown to the ground, a knee on his neck, and people were grabbing at him, yank-ing his arms, shouting orders that seemed to contradict one another: "Give me your hands! Don't fucking move!" *Well, which is it?* Thad wondered.

He was quickly searched. "Gun!" one of them called out. "Knife!" shouted another. "Look at the size of this fucking thing!"

Thad was jerked up off the pavement and led toward the far end of the bridge. He heard the old Scout start up, then the lights went out, all of them. He was led in the dark, and no one talked to him, not that there was really much to say now. His hands were bound behind with those flexible cuffs. He heard the zziiiiippp as they tightened them on his wrists. He saw that one of them was wearing a vest with the word SHERIFF in big white letters.

"You guys cops?" he asked.

"Shut up and keep walking," came the terse reply.

At the other end of the bridge there were a number of

people, almost all of them in uniform. Thad was led to a tent and forced into a chair sitting in front of a folding table. Other than him and the man standing by the door to the tent, it was empty save the Coleman lantern hanging from a hook on the pole that supported the top of the tent.

He sat there for some time. He wasn't too worried: after all, it was the sheriff that had him and not some band of thugs. After a while, a man came in and sat in the chair on the other side of table. With a thud, he dropped some of the gear from the Scout down in front of him. The man sat there looking at Thad, not saying a word. Thad stared back at him indifferently.

The man rocked back in his chair, putting his hands behind his head and began to speak. "I'm Captain Taylor with the Lake County Sheriff's Department." He said this as though Thad should know who he was. Getting no response, the man added, "And you are?"

Thad sat there for a minute. "You can call me Thad."

Sitting back up and resting his elbows on the table, the man cupped his hands together beside his head, taking an exaggerated look at the items on the table. He looked up at Thad and spread his hands apart. "So, you wanna tell me where you got this stuff?"

Lying on the table was the M4 and the tac vest he'd taken from the security man, the DHS patch still on the front of it. Thad looked at it for a minute then asked, "What do you want to know?"

"Well, help me out here: where did you get a DHS rifle and tactical gear from? Are you a member of the DHS?"

"No, I'm not."

Captain Taylor sat there expecting more, but Thad didn't

say anything else. The captain spread his arms, raised his eyebrows and said, "And?"

"And I took it off the man who killed my wife and son."

Captain Taylor sat up at that. "The man who killed your wife and son? The DHS killed your wife and son?"

"Yes."

"And you know this for certain? You were there when they did this and they didn't kill you?"

"No, I wasn't there when they did it, but they told me they did."

"They? There were two of them, two DHS men?"

"No, the other was a mailman."

Captain Taylor sat back, his eyes wide. He interlocked his fingers and put his hands on his head. "A mailman?"

Thad nodded.

"A mailman and a DHS agent killed your family?"

Thad nodded again.

Captain Taylor raised his hands over his head. "You gotta know this sounds a little crazy, Thad." The Captain let out a little laugh. "That a mailman and DHS agent killed your family." He dropped his hands into his lap and rocked the front legs of this chair off the ground. "Where're this mailman and DHS agent now?"

Thad turned his head to the side a little, looking up, making a show of thinking it over. "I would think they's pig shit."

The Captain turned his head and leaned toward Thad a little. "Come again?"

"By now they're pig shit."

The Captain looked at him. "Pig shit. They're pig shit now?" He paused for a moment, looking down his nose at Thad. "You, you fed 'em to the pigs. You fed a mailman and a DHS agent to the pigs," he said, not a question but a statement.

"Well, the DHS soldier definitely is," Thad replied slowly. "The mailman . . . well, I don't know whether the pigs or the fire got to him first."

"Thad, would you humor me for a minute? Would you just tell me exactly what happened?"

Thad sat there, his hands still bound, and told the story exactly as it happened. He didn't leave anything out. When he got to the part of dealing with the two men, the captain had a look of horror on his face.

Chapter 24

Mike and Sarge stayed in their positions and watched as the three men slowly approached the clearing. There was enough light now that they could see the men without the aid of the NVGs. As they approached, the men stopped and took a knee. After a moment, the point man rose and stepped out. When he was about four feet out and twenty from Sarge, Sarge called out in a low voice, "Stump Knocker." The man froze and the ones behind him fell prone to the ground. The point man was scanning the area, looking for the source of the voice. After a moment, he answered, "Swamp Rat?"

Sarge rose up from under the palms. The point man immediately saw him and raised a hand, and Sarge responded likewise. The other two men in the element came into the clearing and joined them. Mike stayed in his position waiting for Sarge to signal him to come out. Two of the men moved to the edge of the clearing, and Mike watched as the man who had passed through the clearing earlier returned to the edge of it. With a security perimeter set up, the man with Sarge motioned for him to take a knee and did likewise.

"First Sergeant Mitchell?" the man asked.

"Correct."

"We called you guys out because they were about to bring the world down on you. The brass wants to bring you guys in. We're preparing to make some moves and will need all the help we can get."

"We left some welcoming gifts for them, heard one of them go off. What the hell is going on?" Sarge asked.

"From what the DOD has been able to determine, the solar flare was used as cover for an EMP strike. We're not sure who did it, but the intel geeks are working on it and developing a theory."

"What are your plans?"

"We're not going into that right now. We just came to bring you guys out."

Sarge sat for a minute weighing his options, though this was really his only one.

"What's our exfil route?"

"Our intended landing zone is a regional airport in Steinhatchee."

"Steinhatchee, that's over twenty miles away," Sarge snorted.

"I know, but we didn't want to bring any assets in too close to the shitstorm you guys started."

Sarge smiled at him, the camo paint on his face cracking when he did. "Just following orders."

Mike rose from his position, causing the men on the perimeter to snap toward him with their weapons raised. Sarge said, "He's with me." The men looked over and lowered their weapons, though they kept them shouldered.

Mike ran up to Sarge's side. "We got trouble."

"What's up?"

"Ted's got movement to the west, about two hundred yards away. We need to get back to them."

The other man asked, "How many?"

"He's not sure. Fifteen to twenty."

"We'll never get to them in time. They could try and get out, take the truck and run," Sarge said, looking at Mike, who was listening to Ted on the ham handheld. Mike shook his head.

"Stand by," the other man said and began talking into a radio headset he was wearing.

"Clementine, Stump Knocker, how copy?"

"Stump Knocker, Clementine, loud and clear."

"Clementine, we have foot-mobile hostiles closing in on Dallas, requesting air support."

"Stump Knocker, wait one."

The three men sat in silence waiting for a reply.

The voice in the headset crackled, *"Stump Knocker, Draco Three-One is inbound, coordinate on Tac 7, out."*

The man reached back and pulled the radio from its pouch on his back and changed the frequency. Keying the mic, he called, "Stump Knocker, Draco Three-One."

"Draco Three-One, Stump Knocker."

"We have estimated fifteen to twenty foot-mobile hostiles closing in on Dallas, can you verify?"

"Stump Knocker, Draco Three-One will be feet dry in two mics and on station at Dallas in five, how copy?"

"Roger that, Draco Three-One."

The man looked at Sarge. "We'll have an A-10 over them in five minutes. He was loitering just offshore and is inbound now. Tell your guys to sit tight."

Mike relayed the info to Ted and after another brief pause the headset the other man was wearing crackled to life. *"Stump Knocker, Stump Knocker, Draco Three-One."*

"Go for Stump Knocker."

"*Stump Knocker, I count two-two, repeat twenty-two, armed hostiles closing on Dallas from the southwest. There are vehicles on a dirt road about two clicks out.*"

"Roger that, Draco, wait one."

"Tell your guys to get flat. How close are they now?"

Mike called Ted on the radio and asked, then looked at the man and said, "One hundred fifty and closing."

The man shook his head. "They're too close for heavy ordnance; he'll have to use his guns."

Into the mic, he said, "Draco, you're cleared, guns hot, danger close; I repeat, you're cleared, guns hot, danger close, make your run north to south."

"*Roger that, Stump Knocker, inbound guns hot, danger close from the north.*"

After a couple of minutes the men in the little clearing could hear the whine as the A-10 lined up for its run; it was passing right over their heads as it started.

Ted and Doc were under the truck in the barn. They were sweating bullets and they just knew they were about to either be killed or captured. They had been told to get down, that close air support was inbound, but they could hardly believe it and were waiting for what came next. After what seemed like an eternity, the building shook and dust fell from the joists. They could hear fragments hitting the tin building, peppering the side, zipping through the thin metal.

Then came the sound: it was like someone was tearing a hole in the fabric of time. Then came the noise from the plane as it pulled out of its dive and climbed.

In the clearing, the men sat motionless as the growl reached them, lower, but just as intense.

"*Stump Knocker, Draco Three-One. The hostiles that are left are fleeing west.*"

"Roger that, Draco, stand by," the soldier replied. He told Mike to call the guys and tell them to get moving, to take the truck and head out to the east. Mike called them and Doc was in the driver's seat and starting the truck before Ted even got out from under it. Outside, they could hear moans, voices pleading for help. Ted ran over and threw the door open and Doc gunned the old truck through it. Ted jumped into the passenger side as it came out and Doc swung the truck around and headed to the north.

Mike reported their guys were clear of the area and the other man called Draco Three-One and told him that the friendlies were out of the area and that he was clear to engage any target of opportunity. While Mike was talking to Ted on the radio, they could hear the sound of the A-10 working the target over. Sarge shook his head. "I feel for those poor bastards," he said as he looked up at the operator.

"Where are they?" Sarge asked Mike.

Mike said, "They're on their way, on that road over there." He pointed to the east. The sound of the Warthog was still in the air, the big thirty-millimeter gun firing in short bursts, the high-pitched whine of the engines as the pilot dove and pulled out.

Sarge looked at the other man. "Let's—" And he paused for a minute. "What the hell is your name?"

"Captain Lewis."

"Well, Captain Lewis, when they get here let's use the truck to get to Steinhatchee."

"I'm going to get us a closer LZ now; hang on a sec." The captain tuned his radio. "Stump Knocker, Raven Two-Two; Stump Knocker, Raven Two-Two."

Before Raven could reply, another voice came over the

radio. *"Stump Knocker, Draco Three-One. I've got eyes on two inbound helos. I'm bingo fuel and buggin' out."*

Mike looked at Sarge, then at Captain Lewis. "What the fuck are we going to do now?"

Captain Lewis pressed his headset against an ear and held up a finger, listening. *"Raven Two-Two, Stump Knocker."*

"Raven we've got inbound hostile helos, requesting immediate extraction at LZ Tiger."

"Roger that, Stump Knocker. Raven's inbound to Tiger, Bronco Three is providing cover. Do you need them to assist with the helos?"

"Roger that, if they're available."

"Stump Knocker, Bronco Three." Yet another came over the radio.

"Go for Stump Knocker, Bronco Three."

"We're inbound, ten mics out."

Mike called Ted and told him there were two birds inbound and to hurry the hell up. Ted asked where they were; he needed an exact location. Mike told him they would move out to the road and to just keep coming.

"Tell him to step on it, Mikey. They need to get here before those damn helos do," Sarge said.

"Guys, we've got a pair of Apaches coming in to take care of 'em. If they don't bug out, he'll blow 'em out of the sky," Captain Lewis said.

Sarge looked over at him. "What *don't* you guys have? Do we have the entire army on our side?" Sarge, Mike, Captain Lewis and the other three men with him started to move to the east toward the road, Mike looked over at the Captain and asked, "Hey, where's your other man?"

Captain Lewis looked back at Mike and grinned. "Don't worry, he's around." To Sarge he said, "No, not yet, but we're working on it. We have our assets at Camp Riley that we are using. There is an assault happening right now on the DHS side of the base, and we're trying to consolidate the entire facility."

Captain Lewis went on to explain that most of the air assets at their disposal had been airborne when the assault started. Fixed wing aircraft were loitering in a couple of areas, rotary wing assets were either assisting with the assault or helping with the recovery of Sarge and his crew. Raven Two-Two was the Black Hawk coming in to pick them up, Bronco Three was the lead in a two-ship sortie and Bronco Four was his wingman.

As they reached the road they heard the truck. Mike got on the radio and told Ted to keep coming, that he could hear him. It wasn't long before they could see the truck bouncing down the road. Once it was close, Mike stepped out in the road and waved at Ted. The truck skidded to a stop in the road. Doc was white knuckling the wheel, and his head was twisted out the window looking up for the two helos.

With seven men needing to get in the back of the truck, some of the gear had to go. Captain Lewis grabbed a Pelican case and went to throw it to the side of the road, but Sarge grabbed him by the wrist. "Let me sort out what we dump," and took the case from him and put it back into the bed of the truck. Sarge went through the bed, dumping the nonessential stuff.

As they were all climbing in, the first of the two helos roared overhead. Mike started to beat on the roof of the truck. "Go, go, go!"

Doc slammed the truck in gear and floored it, shouting, "Shit!"

The ship arced up and to the right. They all could see the door gunner sitting with one foot out on the skid, looking back at them. Captain Lewis got his radio. "Bronco Three, Bronco Three, we've got a hostile helo overhead, we need you here ASAP!"

"Roger that, Stump Knocker, be there in three mics."

Doc had the pedal to the floor and it was all the guys in the back could do to hang on when they hit one of the many, many bumps that threatened to launch them out of the bed. Sarge was screaming at Doc, but either he couldn't hear him, or more likely, he just didn't give a shit.

As the ship passed, the emblem of the Department of Homeland Security was clearly visible. The pilot kicked the tail around and lined up on the truck. They were stuck on the dirt road, which was straight as an arrow and lined with trees on either side: they were a sitting duck. Captain Lewis was looking over the cab of the truck as the nose of the bird dipped and started toward them. All of the guys were looking at the ship wide-eyed, each of them waiting for the gunner to open up. Captain Lewis's headset crackled, *"Stump Knocker, Bronco Three."*

"Bronco Three, you need to hurry the fuck up!"

"Stump Knocker, are we weapons free?"

The gunner in the DHS ship opened up, the rounds hitting the road in front of the truck. Captain Lewis keyed his mic and screamed into it, "Yes, yes, weapons free, you're weapons free, bring the fucking heat!"

I looked back at the people standing in the yard. The man looked up and said, "Why didn't you do anything?"

I just turned and walked away. Back at the house, Jeff was still outside at his bike. He looked up as I walked over and said, "Where you been?"

I told him about the little incident and he said he had heard the yelling but didn't know where it was and since he wasn't from around here he wasn't about to go walking around. He thanked me for letting him stay the night. When he did, I told him to hold off on that as I had a condition.

He looked up. "Yeah, what's that?"

I said, "Let me keep your weapons."

He stood there for a minute thinking about it, propped his elbow up on his chest and rubbed his chin. "You know, ordinarily there is no way in hell I would consider that, but I know you're thinking of your wife and kids." He paused for a moment. "And to show you that I'm not a threat, I'll agree, but I'm keeping the key to my bike." He smiled.

"I appreciate you understanding, and I wouldn't dream of taking the key from you. Hey, tomorrow can you help me with something?"

As he pulled his pack off the back of the bike he said, "Sure, what is it?"

I told him about the little package Sarge had sent home with me and tried to explain what it was for. He knew exactly what I was talking about and said he could certainly help out. Jeff reached into one of the saddlebags and pulled out the iPad. I shook my head when he did. "You know what you're starting with that, don't you?"

He looked up with a grin. "Let 'em have some fun. They're teenage girls and probably could use the distraction. Hell, you think I haven't been playing Angry Birds? It gets lonely on the road."

I agreed he was more right than he knew and we headed into the house. Mel was sitting on the end of the sofa closest to the fireplace. She said, "We need wood."

I stopped in the door and looked at Jeff. He just shrugged,

but I wasn't about to let him off that easy. I said, "Uh, it's your job to keep the fire going tonight, remember?"

He looked like I had let the air out of his balloon. "Aww, come on," he pleaded in mock protest. I waved him into the house and called the girls. Little Bit came right out. In the manner of typical teenagers, Lee Ann and Taylor finally came out and flopped onto the sofa, Taylor landing on her mom's feet, and looked up. I looked at Jeff with a little nod and he unzipped the iPad case. Their faces immediately lit up.

One of them was certain to get upset with who was going to use it first, and I wasn't sure how to go about establishing the pecking order. Before I could say anything, Jeff said, "Okay, girls, there's three of you and only one iPad, so you're going to have to take turns, and I'm sure you all want to know who gets to go first." They all nodded in agreement, smiles on their faces so wide they pushed their ears back.

Jeff reached into his pack and took out a Crown Royal bag, holding it by the gold cord and bouncing it in his hand, a faint clicking coming from it each time he did. "What you're going to do is stick your hand in the bag and take one marble. Keep your hand closed and don't look at it. When each of you has one you'll put your hands out and open them to see which color you have. Whoever has the white one gets to use it first, and the other two will do it again to see who goes next, got it?"

I looked at Jeff with raised eyebrows. "I got nephews," he said.

Jeff held out the bag and one at a time they drew their marbles. Taylor got it first, Little Bit second and Lee Ann last. Jeff handed it over to Taylor, but before they ran off I stopped them and said, "Look guys, this belongs to Mr. Jeff and it is literally irreplaceable, so treat it that way. If he comes and asks for it, give it back immediately. If there is any fighting over it, you'll never see it again, got it?"

They nodded and ran off to Taylor's room, shrieking as they went. I looked at Jeff and he smiled, then to Mel. Her eyebrows were raised. "What?" I asked.

"You two are starting some trouble there, you know that, don't you?"

"Yeah, probably, but they'll have fun and it'll take their minds off things," I replied.

"It will do that. Now go get some wood. And when do you think you'll get that stove put in our room?"

I shook my head, looking at Jeff, but he just shrugged and raised his hands. "Hey, man, don't get me involved."

We went outside and he followed me to the woodshed. On the way I asked how his carpentry skills were. His reply made me laugh. "Well, as far as IT guys are concerned, I'm an awesome carpenter."

"I'll keep that in mind."

We filled the big green cart with wood and hauled it back to the house. As we were stacking the wood on the porch I told him that we were thinking of building a set of stocks to deal with folks who couldn't keep out of trouble. He shook his head and commented on what a weird world we were living in now. We moved some of the wood into the rack beside the fireplace. Mel came out of the bedroom with a pillow and a couple of blankets for Jeff and laid them on the sofa. He thanked her and looked at me and said he'd be right back.

Jeff went outside and came back in with his Mosin. After handing me the rifle he gave me a Glock, then reached into his coat and drew the one in the holster and handed it to me as well. The look on my face must have revealed my surprise. "I told you I've got two of them," he said.

I was looking at the first one he'd handed me. The barrel protruded out the end of the slide and the threads were hard to miss. "This what I think it's for?" He nodded. "You have it with you?"

He nodded again and reached into a pocket of his coat and took out a Surefire suppressor and held it up for me to see. "It's a nice little accessory," he said with a smile before putting it back in his pocket.

Mel went back and told the girls it was time for bed. They protested, what with the new distraction they had. I came into Taylor's room and closed the door, and Mel looked at me curiously. I told the girls that Jeff was a guest in our house, but we didn't know him and while they were to treat him with respect, they were to also treat him like a stranger. If anything weird happened in regards to him, they were to call for help. I stressed the importance of this to them, making sure they got it. The girls all asked if they could sleep with Taylor and play with the iPad for a while. We agreed; all of them together would be better than in their separate rooms.

Mel and I went back out and I told Jeff I would get with him in the morning about our little project. He said he would keep the fire going, thanked Mel for the blankets and we headed to bed. I put Jeff's weapons in the safe and locked it up. Mel asked if it was a good idea to let him stay. I told her I didn't get any kind of a bad vibe from him, and I was usually pretty good at sizing someone up as soon as I met them, something she had always hated about me. Mel is very outgoing and likes to talk to people. I could be on a deserted island all alone and be fine. We could meet someone and talk to them for a while, Mel would say something like, "They were nice" and I'd reply with "He's a douche bag and full of shit" and more often than not, I would be right.

I woke up once and looked out in the living room. The sofa was empty, so I slipped on my moose-hide wool-lined slippers and walked out. There was fresh wood on the fire. Jeff wasn't in the bathroom, but as I passed through the kitchen I saw him on the back deck. I stepped out and Jeff said, "You can't sleep either?" He was looking up at the sky.

"I haven't slept through the night in so long I don't remember what it's like."

"Yeah, me too." He paused for a minute. "You ever seen stars like this?"

I looked up. "It's amazing, isn't it? When I was walking home, I mainly traveled at night. It's beautiful."

He said, "Yeah," and just stared up into the night. He seemed lost in thought, maybe remembering something, something that might be a little painful.

"Hey, man, you alright?" I asked.

"Yeah, man, just thinking about home, about all the shit that used to be and may never be again. I lived in a world of ones and zeros, computers. That was my life, and now there'll probably never be another one."

"I know, but at least we're still alive. I'll see you in the morning." I left him on the deck staring at the stars and went back to snuggle up next to a warm Mel.

The next morning Jeff was buried under blankets on the sofa when I came out. The fire had burned down to a bed of coals. I quietly laid a small piece of lighter wood on the coals, piled a couple of logs on and went into the kitchen. Turning the knobs on the Butterfly, I let the wicks prime while I took eggs from the fridge, filled the coffeepot from the Berkey and pulled a canned ham from the cabinet. Since I had introduced everyone to the fried mush it had become a frequent part of our breakfast, and there was some in the fridge.

I had just taken the coffee off the burner when Jeff came in rubbing his head. I said, "Mornin', Sunshine."

"Damn that smells good," he looked into the pan that a couple slabs of ham and mush in it and pointed at the slices of mush. "What is that?"

"It's called fried mush, made from cornmeal. How do you like your eggs?"

"Sunny-side up," he replied absentmindedly as he took down a coffee cup and poured a cup. After taking a sip he let out a groan. "Damn that's good."

By the time Mel got up I had her plate ready and a pan full of scrambled eggs for the girls. Mel, Jeff and I sat and ate breakfast together, and amongst the three of us we killed the pot of coffee. Jeff asked if I could make another and I obliged him. We still had nearly two dozen cans, though the day was coming when it would be gone. Little Bit came out of Taylor's room. She was wearing the jammies with the feet in 'em and was cute as hell. She had the iPad, and I could hear the theme music from Angry Birds. She came to the table and climbed up in a chair.

Mel got up and fixed her a plate of eggs and mush and set it in front of her. She didn't even look up from the game. "We got any honey, Mom?"

"You have honey?" Jeff asked.

"Yeah, I keep bees, a couple of hives out back. It's not a lot, but it keeps us in honey," I replied, Jeff raised his eyebrows and nodded his head, then took another sip of his coffee.

Mel came back with the honey and set it on the table and took the iPad from Little Bit's hands in one fluid mom motion. "Hey!"

"Eat your breakfast."

"I was in the middle of a game!"

"It'll be there."

She reluctantly picked up her fork and started to push the eggs around on her plate. I asked Jeff if he was ready to start on our little project and he hopped out of his chair. "Yeah, man, let's go!"

I laughed at him, "Been without coffee for a while?"

"Yeah, man I don't ever remember it making me feel like this!"

We went out to the shop and I showed him the little package that Sarge had sent home with me. Opening the laptop up, I showed him the text file and after giving him a minute to read it asked if it made any sense to him. He said it was pretty simple and he could have it ready in an hour or so. I told him the shop was his, he could use whatever he needed to get it done and that I had a couple of things to do and I'd be back later.

Going back in the house, little Ash was done with her breakfast and was sitting in front of the fireplace with the iPad glued to her fingers. I told her I was going down to Danny's house and asked if she wanted to go. She never looked up and replied with a "nah." Taylor came out of her room and said she wanted to go.

While she was getting dressed I put on my vest and grabbed my carbine and pistol, then thought about Jeff's. Going to the safe, I took out his two Glocks and the Mosin and set them beside the safe. Mel was in the bathroom, and when she came out I told her where I put them and that if he asked about them to give 'em to him. She didn't protest, just nodded and wrapped her arms around me. "This would be better if you weren't wearing all this. Where you going?"

"I'm going down to Danny's. We have a little project to work on. Taylor's going with me." I gave her a kiss and told her I'd be back later. As I walked away she swatted me on the ass. "Looking forward to it."

Taylor was bummed when she found out we were walking, but fuel was at a premium. We went out the gate and turned right, heading into the neighborhood. She walked along, not saying anything, just looking down. "You okay?" I asked. She just shrugged her shoulders. This was her usual response when something was bothering her, and it was all the confirmation I needed. I put my arm around her and pulled her close. "What's up?"

She shrugged her shoulders again but with a little more prodding she finally opened up. She was lonely, missed her friends from school and, more importantly, she was afraid. She was worried what was going to happen, what her life was going to be like and if she going to be able to go to college. I tried to reassure her but was honest about the fact that we didn't know. I told her not to worry right now. We were all still together and I wasn't going to let anything happen to her. She asked if she could go to her friend Rene's house. She was Taylor's age and lived on one of the side roads we were approaching.

I turned onto the little dirt road and we walked down it toward Rene's house. I knew Rene's dad, though not well. His name was Tom and I had no idea what he did for a living. There was smoke coming from the little tin stack. Like many houses out here, Rene's family's had a wood stove in the living room that was more for decoration and setting the cozy scene on a cold night than to actually heat the house.

"Looks like they're home," I said and jostled her shoulder.

"Hey, Tom!" I called out as we approached the house. I didn't want to get shot at dropping by to see a neighbor.

The front door opened, and the long barrel of a shotgun slid out the crack. Behind it I could see a figure but couldn't make out the face. "Hey, Tom," I said with a wave and waited for him to realize it was me. After a moment the door opened and Tom stepped out on the small porch, closing the door behind him. He set the butt of the shotgun on the deck, holding it by the barrel. "Hi, Morgan." He was sporting a full beard and looked thin; his clothes were hanging from him.

We walked up to him, stopping at the foot of the steps to the small deck. "Hey, Tom, Taylor wanted to visit with Rene. Is she around?"

He shuffled his feet a couple of times and said, "Yeah, she's here, it'd probably do her good to see Taylor. Go on in, she's in her room." Tom opened the door and Taylor bounded up the stairs. After she was in, he shut the door again.

"Is she all right?" I asked.

His lips began to quiver a bit a tear ran down his cheek. "Uh, no, she's not well. You know, she was always so thin, and I think she's starving to death. She's so weak and can't hardly stand up without getting light-headed." His voice cracked as he talked.

"You guys out of food?"

He huffed. "We've been out of food for weeks. We've been eating the horse feed."

"Didn't you go to the community meals that Mark put on, the food from the county?"

The shame he felt was obvious; he couldn't look at me. "No, I was embarrassed for everyone to know I couldn't take care of my family. And now Rene is so sick."

"Can I see her?"

Tom looked up and wiped his eyes then sniffled. "Yeah, come on in." He opened the door and we went in.

Taylor was sitting beside Rene on her bed. She looked horribly thin. Taylor looked like she was about to cry. I grabbed Tom by the arm and walked out of the room. Once we were in the living room I told him I was going home to get some things for him, for her. He protested, saying he couldn't take anything from me, and I snapped. "This isn't a fucking offer! Do you see her, I mean do you really *see* her? I have two twelve-packs of Ensure at home. I'm going to get those and you're going to start pouring that into her. I'll get you some other food for her too, for you and your wife too, and you will eat it, you got it?"

He was crying openly now, nodding his head. Rene's mom was sitting on the couch. She was crying too, and just like Tom and Rene she was sickly thin. I left the house and jogged back home.

Chapter 25

When Thad finished, he slid his ass forward in the chair and leaned back. At this point he just didn't give a shit what happened. Captain Taylor had listened to Thad's story with great interest, occasionally making notes on a little pad. When Thad relaxed, Taylor rocked back in his chair, lifting the front legs off the ground and cupping his hands behind his head. He sucked his teeth for a minute, looking intently at Thad.

"Thad, if I cut those cuffs off you, are you going to give me any trouble?"

Without moving, Thad replied, "Not a bit."

Taylor stood up and walked around the table, motioning for Thad to stand. Thad stood up and heard the click of the flex cuffs being cut. He rubbed his wrists and rolled his shoulders against the stiffness they had caused. His elbow was particularly uncomfortable, and he pulled his shirtsleeve up and looked at it. Taylor looked over and said, "That doesn't look so good. What happened?"

Thad told him about the shootout at the house. He didn't tell him about executing the girl; he didn't want to remember it and damn sure didn't want to tell anyone else about it.

"Tell you what, walk with me over to the tent with the medics and let them look at it and I'll get you something to eat. You hungry?"

Thad hadn't thought about food in a long time, and until Taylor mentioned it he didn't realize how hungry he was. Now he was starving. He nodded and followed Taylor out of the tent. They walked through a series of tents. The path between them was lit with those little solar landscape lights. Thad made a mental note of that; it could come in handy later. Taylor stepped into another tent and Thad followed him. Inside there was an examination table in the center with tables and shelves around the sides. Medical supplies were stacked up everywhere, and two paramedics sat in a couple of folding camp chairs in the light of a Coleman lantern.

"Guys, Thad here has a bullet wound I'd like you to look at," Taylor said, pointing to Thad's arm.

The two men stood up and asked Thad to sit on the edge of the table. He did and they started the process of exposing his arm. When one of them reached for his shears, Thad told him to wait and stripped out of his shirt; he didn't have many. They asked the usual questions, and he answered them as best he could. When they asked what caliber it was, he said he didn't know if it was a bullet fragment or a piece of a Ford.

The wound was infected. The two medics cleaned it, a painful process that Thad endured without complaint, and then dressed the wound. After asking if he was allergic to any medications and, being told no, they gave him a bottle of penicillin and told him to take it three times a day. Thad said he would and turned to leave. Taylor was gone, so Thad stepped out after thanking the medics. Back outside he looked around and heard a voice call him from behind. He saw Taylor waving at him from the flap of another tent and walked that way.

Taylor held the flap open and Thad walked in. There was

a long table on one side full of big silver trays typical of a buffet. Under each one sat a can of Sterno, the blue flame licking at the bottom. This tent was lit with some lights, the kind from a construction site: little yellow cages strung out on a cord. Taylor pushed Thad toward the tables, other people, mostly in uniforms, were sitting at other tables in rows inside the tent, eating. Most didn't even take notice of him. Thad picked a paper plate and went through the line. There were scrambled eggs, institutional-grade bacon (but still bacon!), potatoes and a big vat of grits. Thad filled his plate and took a cup of orange juice and looked for a place to sit.

Taylor was right behind him and guided him to a table with two men sitting at it. They took the two free seats and sat down. Thad set to work on his plate immediately. The other three men chatted amongst themselves while Thad ate and he paid them no mind. Thad's big elbows were on the edge of the table and his head hung over his plate. After his second trip through the serving line, Thad dropped his fork onto the plate and finally sat back.

"Damn, I guess you was hungry!" Taylor said.

Thad patted his belly. "Guess so."

"When was the last time you ate anything?" one of the other men asked.

Thad glanced away and said, "It'd been a while."

"Thad, I'd like you meet Sheriff Billy Holland," Taylor said, nodding his head toward one of the other two men at the table.

Thad looked at him. He didn't look like a sheriff; he looked like everyone else around here. He wore the same BDU-style pants, black T-shirt and sheriff's jacket that they all wore. Thad looked at him and said, "Nice to meet you, Sheriff."

The sheriff nodded and sat there looking at Thad for a minute before glancing at the man beside him. The other man just raised his eyebrows and went back to swirling the coffee in his cup.

"Thad, Captain Taylor tells me you had a run-in with the DHS, that true?"

"I wouldn't say *I* had a run-in, but my wife and boy did."

"That's what I heard, and I also heard what you did about it. Was all that true?"

"Ever last word."

The sheriff nodded his head. "Well, I'm sorry for your loss; I only wish you had made it here sooner. Lake County will not be taking any shit off any federal acronym."

"That's nice to know, Sheriff. If I can do anything to help, just let me know. Far as I'm concerned we ain't even yet," Thad said.

"Where were you heading?" the sheriff asked.

"I was heading to a friend's house. We walked together for a long ways when we was trying to get home. He's the only person around here that I know now."

"You walked home? From where?" Captain Taylor asked.

Thad spent the next few minutes telling the story of his trip home and all the things he and Morgan had been through. When he finished, the three men looked at one another, then back at Thad.

"Where's your friend live, and who is he?" Taylor asked.

"The address is on a piece of paper in the front seat of the truck. It's somewhere in Altoona. His name is Morgan and he's a good man."

The sheriff looked at Taylor and motioned with his head. Taylor got up and left the tent. The sheriff went to the serving line and returned with two cups of coffee, handing one to Thad.

"Thanks."

"No problem. Your friend, his last name Carter?" the sheriff asked.

Thad nodded.

"Thad, this quiet guy over here is Captain Hall. He's head of the jail."

Thad nodded to Hall as he took a sip of the coffee and Hall did likewise. It wasn't long before Taylor reappeared with the slip of paper and handed it to the sheriff, who looked at it and handed it back.

"Thad, under our current situation I am having to confiscate all running vehicles. One as useful as yours would be a big help to us right now. But where you're going there are a couple of our men there. If I was to let you leave with the truck, would you turn it over to them when you got where you're going?"

Thad sat thinking for a minute, staring down into his cup. He wasn't sure what the hell was going on here. Were they actually going to let him drive out of here? If they did, he would turn the truck over, no big deal to him; he just wanted to get to Morgan's house. After draining the cup he set it down and said, "Sheriff, I've been an honest man my whole life. I've never taken anything from anyone and I always provided for my family. I don't have a family now. All I have now are a couple of friends, and at this point all I want to do is get to them. If you let me drive over there I'll be happy to turn the truck over to your folks."

The sheriff said, "Well, all right, then."

Thad pulled out onto Highway 19 and couldn't stop

smiling. He had a letter, on Lake County Sheriff's Office letterhead no less, that made sure he would get to where he was going. That they had taken the M4 and the tactical vest was an even trade in his mind. He reached over and picked up the hand-drawn map that Taylor had given him, and again he smiled and shook his head.

Thad kept an eye out for Lake Shore Drive. They had said it was the fastest way to Morgan's house. Lake Shore was closer than he expected, and he made the left on it without having to wait for the light. This was just getting better and better. Thad enjoyed the ride along Lake Eustis; it was a huge lake and the road wound its way along the shore under a canopy of oak trees. On the right there were some large houses that faced the lake to his left. Thad looked at those big houses and wondered about the people that lived in them, what they did to make all that money and what they were doing now.

As Thad crested the bridge over the canal for the boat ramp, he slammed on the brakes. Sitting in front of him in the middle of the road were two Humvees. On the road on either side were sandbag emplacements. In each of these there was a machine gun mounted and both of them were pointing at him. *Shit*, Thad thought as he slapped the steering wheel. Several men were approaching the old Scout with their weapons raised. They ordered him to put his hands up and, with no other choice, he did as instructed.

As the uniformed men approached, they ordered him out of the truck and he again complied. Two men on the other side opened the passenger door and looked in. "Clear!" one of them called out. A man that Thad assumed was in charge of the operation came up holding his M4 across his chest as the two men who had ordered him out were searching him.

"He's clean, LT," one of them said.

"Where you headed?" the lieutenant asked.

"Just trying to get to my buddy's house."

One of the men from the passenger side came around the truck and handed the lieutenant a piece of paper. He read it then looked at Thad and handed it back to the soldier that brought it.

"The sheriff give you that?"

Thad nodded his head. The lieutenant stared at Thad for a moment as if he were searching him for some sign of deceit. After a long moment he called over his shoulder, "Find anything in there?" One of the men searching the truck replied, "He's got some guns and shit, nothing major, though."

The LT pointed at the truck. "You can get back in."

Thad climbed in and shut the door. The lieutenant walked up and said, "Let me see your pass there," and held out his hand. Thad handed it over and watched as the lieutenant took out his pen and made a note on it then handed it back.

"There's another checkpoint you'll have to go through on the other side of town. Just show them this. I'll let 'em know you're coming, and they won't give you any trouble. If the sheriff says you're good to go, that's enough for me."

Thad gave the man a nod, and the lieutenant stepped back and waved at his men. "Let him through!"

It was early morning, the sun was up and it was still a little chilly out. Downtown Eustis had a mix of business and residential areas, all intermingled. As he drove down the quiet street, Thad didn't see any people; it was eerily quiet. He drove by the post office, then past a little strip mall. As he was negotiating a curve in the road, he again had to stop abruptly. In the road ahead was another roadblock. This time the men manning it didn't instantly raise their weapons. One of them simply walked out to the Scout. Thad waited for the soldier to approach and held up the pass.

"Mornin'," the soldier said as he came up to the window.

"Mornin'," Thad replied.

The soldier looked at the pass with a quick glance. "LT said you were comin'. Where you headin'?"

"To my buddy's place in Altoona."

The soldier stood there for a minute looking at the truck. "How'd you manage to hang on to this old relic?"

"Just lucky, I guess."

"Well, good luck."

As the soldier started to leave, Thad asked, "Is there any trouble up ahead?"

The soldier turned back. "Nah, not really. It's pretty quiet around here as far as we know. The farther you get from here the less we know, though, so be careful."

According to the map Taylor had given him, it was straight shot up 19 to Morgan's place. Thad made it to Umatilla in only a few minutes. There were a few people out, but not many. At the McDonald's, he passed two men on horseback, and they stared at him as hard he did them. Before, it had been an oddity to see people on horseback in the middle of the road; now it was odd to see a moving car. It was as if some rift in time and space had opened up and two peculiarities were brought face-to-face for just an instant.

Thad made it through town and continued down the road. After winding his way through the small hills on the north side of town, he saw the sign for Altoona. Picking up his map, he saw his next reference point was Highway 42. Just a moment after putting the paper down, he saw the three little stores that marked the intersection of the two roads. The parking lot of the big Kangaroo store looked like a flea market. Makeshift tables had been set up and people were setting up their wares for the day's trading.

The one thing that caught his attention was the two men in full camo holding rifles. He watched as one reached out and grabbed the other, pointing at Thad and his Scout. Thad kept his eyes on the two men as he passed them, and they also kept their eyes on him, talking between themselves and motioning toward the truck. In short order he passed the store, and as he passed the fire station Thad checked the mirror for the two men, but they weren't there. Thad noticed the field on the left, just where Taylor said it would be, and he slowed the Scout, looking to the right side for the road sign. There was a barricade with armed men behind it, and they were looking at him.

Mike was firing his M4 at the helo that was coming straight at them, but with the bouncing he probably wasn't coming close to it. Captain Lewis was still leaning on the cab, looking wide-eyed as the gunner raised the weapon to his shoulder. Doc, with his foot to the floor, was leaning over the wheel to look up at the approaching bird. Sarge was lying on his back, firing over the cab. His rounds too were probably ineffective. When the gunner opened up and the first rounds passed over the truck, Mike began to scream, a guttural, primal growl; flipping his weapon to full auto, he held the trigger back.

The first 30mm round passed through the rear compartment of the helo, coming in on the gunner's side and going out the other. The men in the truck watched as he jerked his head to the right and fumbled for the MIC button for his intercom. He wasn't fast enough, though, as the gunner in the

Apache let loose a six-round burst that slammed into the engine compartment and tail boom of the ship. The guys in the truck watched as the helo folded, found its way into the blades and exploded into a blur of flying metal. As the helo spiraled to the ground, the gunner was flung out of the spinning ship. Mike and Sarge looked on as the man was spun around the falling ship from the end of his safety lanyard.

The Apache roared overhead and behind the tumbling aircraft, then made a hard turn and raced to catch up to the other one that was chasing the second DHS bird. Shouts and cheers erupted from the bed of the truck as the flaming wreckage of the helo landed in the trees to the right of the road.

"Raven Two-Two, Stump Knocker."

Lewis grabbed his mic, and over the rush of wind and banging of the truck he replied, "Go for Stump Knocker!"

"Stump Knocker, we have you in sight. Looks like there is a clearing about half a click ahead of you that we can get into if you want us to."

"Roger that, Raven Two-Two. See if you can fit and we'll rendezvous there!"

"Roger, Raven's inbound."

Lewis slapped the roof of the truck and leaned around to the driver's door and told Doc to look for the clearing. As he was talking, the Black Hawk roared overhead.

A clearing opened up on the left side of the road and Doc pulled off. As the Black Hawk flared for a landing, the other orbited the LZ to provide cover.

Everyone bailed out of the truck before it came to complete stop and were getting their gear together. Sarge was handing Pelican cases out to be loaded up. Captain Lewis looked at Sarge and said, "We don't need any of that; let's get aboard!" He shouted above the roar of the Black Hawk.

"*We* may not need it, but *I* do. It's going!" Sarge made sure all of his radios as well as all of their weapons were loaded up and asked for an incendiary grenade. No one had one.

Lewis asked, "What do you want it for?"

Sarge pointed at the truck. "Burn it."

They all hopped into the Black Hawk and it lifted off. The crew chief was scanning the tree line for threats, swinging the GE minigun back and forth as he did. Sarge tapped the gunner on the shoulder.

Pointing down at the truck, Sarge keyed the mic for the intercom and said again, "Burn it." The gunner looked at Captain Lewis, who nodded, and the gunner lined up on the old Dodge and fired a short burst, missing the truck but quickly adjusted his aim and rounds began pouring into the truck. The other gunner, seeing the stream of red tracers spewing out of the other ship, began to fire on it as well. It wasn't long before the truck was burning, the sheer number of rounds hitting it setting it on fire.

Sarge sat there looking out the open door at the fireworks. It was a bittersweet moment for him. On the one side the damn DHS wasn't going to get his beloved old Dodge, but on the other side he was losing it.

Ted kicked Sarge's boot, and when he looked over Ted nodded out the door. Off the starboard side of the Black Hawk they could see the two Apaches come up in formation with them. Sarge looked back at Ted and smiled, and Ted gave him a thumbs-up.

Chapter 26

Running with a weapon slung around your neck is a pain in the ass. I am not an Airborne Ranger, and I don't want to be one. I had just rounded the corner onto my road when I saw an ATV start heading my way from the barricade. It was quickly gaining speed and I could see it was Reggie. He came past me in a blur, not even waving. I had to stop and stare at him; there was a person lying across the seat in front him, and while I couldn't see the head as it was hanging off the other side, what I did see was that the feet were bound.

I stood there looking at him as he sped down the road, slowing just enough to negotiate the corner onto his road. *What the fuck is that all about?* I wondered. At the moment, though, I had other shit to do and headed for the house. As I came in the gate, Meathead met me and followed me back to the shop. I was pretty out of breath when I jerked the door open. Jeff jumped and let out a howl, shaking his thumb then sticking it in his mouth and dropping the soldering iron he had in his other hand.

He looked at me with his thumb still in his mouth. "I booned ma tum."

"Sorry about that," I replied, still breathing hard.

He watched me as I crossed the shop and started to pull cartons from the shelves. I grabbed the two packages of En-sure then started looking for other stuff to take them. I was thinking high-calorie and high-protein. Grabbing an empty box, I threw in a jar of peanut butter, a few cans of sardines in tomato sauce (the big ones), a few cans of beans, a couple cans of spinach, canned corn, green beans, a couple packs of spaghetti noodles and two cans of sauce. All of this stuff I had a lot of—thank God for Aldi and Save-A-Lot.

"What the hell are you doing?" I heard Jeff say, his thumb now out of his mouth.

"One of our neighbors has a daughter who is starving to death and he's too damn proud to ask for help."

He raised his eyebrows. "Oh, need any help?"

"Naw, how's that going?"

Jeff looked back at the bench. "It's almost done. It should work fine; it was easy."

"I'm going back over and drop this off, then I have other shit to do. I'll be back later."

"Cool, I'll be in here probably; that laptop needs some work. Do you even know what a disk cleanup is, or how to defrag a hard drive?"

I looked at him kind of wide-eyed. "You mean you can do that?"

Jeff pressed his lips together and gave the finger. I took my box out and put it on the cart. Meathead was sniffing the box, and I pushed him with my knee. "Get out of there, nosy." That made me think and I looked at the box. While you couldn't see into it unless you were standing over it, someone might be out walking around, and it wouldn't take a rocket scientist to start wondering what was so heavy in the box that I needed a cart. I pulled it over to the woodshed and piled on wood to cover the box. It didn't take much, and I'd leave that with Tom too. At the gate I had to push Meathead back in and close it behind me to keep him from following.

At Tom's house I pulled the cart up close to the porch and carried the box inside. I took out the Ensure and handed it to Tom's wife. "Take these and mix 'em with water, half and half, for a couple of days. Don't give her too much at a time; take it slow at first." She nodded and carried the case into the kitchen. I followed her with the box and set it on a small table. Tom came in and looked into the box. He started setting the items out on the table. Tom's wife came over and watched as he unloaded the box, and both of them started to tear up.

Tom looked up at me. "I don't know what to say. There is no way I can repay you for this."

"It isn't much, but it's all I can do. I can't give you any more, understand?"

He nodded and looked at the table again. Tom's wife left the kitchen with a cup of the Ensure for Rene. Tom and I followed her back to the room and stood in the hall watching as Rene slowly sipped the mixture. I caught Taylor's eye and motioned for her to come out. She came out into the hall and we walked out into the living room. "I've got some stuff I need to do. You want to hang out here while I do it or do you want to come down to Danny's with me?"

Without hesitation she replied, "I want to stay here."

"Okay, stay here until I come get you. Don't walk home alone and don't talk about how things are at home, got it?" She nodded and I continued, "If anyone asks anything, we are just as hungry as they are and things are just as bleak, got it?" Again, she nodded.

I gave her a kiss on the top of her head. "All right, I'll be back later." She turned and headed back into Rene's room.

I didn't see anyone else on the way to Danny's. The quiet gave me time to think about Reggie and what the hell he was up to this morning, who was on the ATV and why.

I opened Danny's door as I knocked on it. They were sitting at the bar in the kitchen, eating oatmeal for breakfast. "What up?" I called out as I came through the door.

"Hey, man, what's up?" Danny asked.

"Wanted to see if we could press your carpenter skills into service."

He stuck a spoonful of goo in his mouth. "Sure, what do we need to build?"

"A set of stocks."

Bobbie looked over. "A set of what?"

"Stocks, you know, like from the Middle Ages." I mimicked the position, holding my hands up near my ears.

"What in the hell do we need that for?"

"Last night a kid was caught stealing chickens. The people called Mark over and wanted him to shoot the kid. Naturally Mark wouldn't do it, but what else can we do? Then Mark mentioned it as a joke and I said it was a good idea, so here I am."

"Makes sense; we need something other than execution. Let me finish this and we'll see what we can do."

We found enough four-by-fours and two-by-sixes at Danny's to put something together, but neither of us knew the first thing about building stocks. We leaned against the bench under the covered parking area and sketched some ideas out on a scrap piece of paper. After several variations and still no real idea of how to go about it, Danny said, "I wish the damn Internet were still up, then we'd know what the damn things are supposed to look like."

"If the Internet were still up, we wouldn't need 'em," I replied.

Danny let out a little laugh and shook his head. The sound of a four-wheeler coming up the road caught our attention.

Hearing them wasn't really anything remarkable these days, there were enough of them on our street alone, but it was coming up fast. We looked out toward the road and saw Reggie hauling ass on the other side of Danny's fence. He stopped at the gate and hopped off. We walked out toward him as he came jogging up.

When he got to us, he stopped and leaned over, resting his palms on his knees and heaving.

"You gonna make it?" I asked.

Reggie turned his head enough to see me and gave me the finger, and Danny laughed.

"There's someone at the barricade asking for you," he said.

"Who is it?"

Reggie finally straightened up. "Some big-ass black dude."

Thad sat in the truck weighing his options. After all, this was his destination, whether the men at the barricade knew it or not. The two men—one was really a boy, not more than fifteen—looked at him nervously. Both had rifles and while they weren't pointed at him, they certainly weren't welcoming. Thad opened the door and slowly stepped out, making sure he kept his hands where they could see them. The two of them immediately stepped back behind the log structure and clutched their rifles a little tighter. Once Thad was out of the truck, one of them called out, "What can we do for you?"

With his hands still where they could see them, Thad replied, "Is this where Morgan Carter lives?" The two men shared an uncertain glance and whispered between themselves. As they were talking, Thad heard a four-wheeler. The two men looked over their shoulders as another man, much larger than these two, pulled up on a quad. The big fella sat there for a minute looking at Thad. He climbed off the machine and walked over to his companions and they spoke in low whispers for a minute. As they did, the big guy would look over at Thad, neither with aggression or invitation. Thad started to wonder if he had the wrong street.

After a few moments of hushed conversation, the big guy walked out toward the road. "You looking for Morgan?"

"Yeah," Thad replied.

"You a friend of his?"

"Yes, I am. Is he still here?"

The big fella looked Thad over for a second. "You mind waiting here for a minute or two?"

"Not a bit. I'll be right here," Thad said and sat on the hood, resting his feet on the front bumper of the Scout.

The big guy whispered a few words to the other two then climbed up on his quad and raced away. Thad sat there as the other two watched him. Thad listened as the ATV went a short distance and stopped. After a brief pause, it started up again, and he listened as it faded away. *Morgan, your ass better be here*, Thad thought.

Reggie took me to the barricade and there was Thad sitting on the hood of an old SUV of some kind, made long before the term *SUV* was ever thought of.

He saw us coming and stepped down off the hood. A surge of happiness ran through me. I hadn't seen him in a while and it was damn good to see him. Reggie stopped at the barricade and I climbed off before he could. Reggie said, "You know this guy?" motioning at Thad. The other two guys at the barricade looked at me expectantly, and then Danny pulled up and shut his Polaris down.

I looked at Thad. "Naw, never seen him before."

Thad smiled. "Nice to see you too."

We met just in front of the barricade and shook hands. He had that ever-present smile on his face, but there was something lurking under it too, something dark.

"Damn, I'm glad to see you," I said, then looked past him at the old truck. "Are Anita and your son in there?" Not seeing anyone, I looked back at him; his face said it all. "Come on, let's go up to the house. Leave the truck there for now."

I asked one of the guys to pull the truck in behind the barricade, then introduced Thad to everyone. Reggie was still giving him a bit of the stink eye, so I said, "You guys heard about when I got shot in the head, right? Thad's the one who carried me out." That cleared the air, and Reggie stepped over to shake Thad's hand.

Danny rode beside us as we walked to the house. I didn't pry into what had happened and Thad wasn't offering. He mainly told me about how it had been when he was trying to get home, about a block being dropped on him from an overpass and about killing a man in front of the man's son. Thad told us about how the boy had walked over and kicked his old man in the ribs, then spit on him as he lay there dying. Apparently the guy hadn't been a good father or husband. He told us about some raccoons that had gotten in the back of the truck and had scared the shit out of him. By then we were at the gate and I opened it so Danny could go through.

As Danny pulled through the gate, Meathead came running up, his tail wagging, and then he saw Thad. I'd never seen a dog do a double take then backpedal, but he did just that, all the while barking his ass off. Thad smiled and said,

"I think your dog's a racist. He got a hood and shit like that?"

"He used to, but I got tired of washing the sheets. Never mind him, I think he's retarded."

"Him or his owner," Thad said. Danny laughed and I had to smile.

I said, "Hey, I resent that remark."

Mel was in the kitchen when we got to the house. "Hey, babe, this is Thad; he's the guy I told you about."

Mel leaned against the counter looking at him. "Well, you're not the little blonde who shot him in the head."

Thad smiled. "No, ma'am, I'm the big black one that drug his ass out."

She smiled and walked over to him. She said, "Well, thank you for getting him home," and reached up and wrapped her arms around his neck. He had to lean over so she could hug him.

She said, "Thad, would you like some coffee?"

"Oh yes, ma'am, if it isn't any trouble."

Mel poured coffee as Thad, Danny and I sat down at the table. She carried his cup over and set it in front of him, and he thanked her. Danny and I looked at her expectantly.

Pointing at Danny, she said, "You don't drink coffee"—then at me—"and you know where the tea pitcher is." Thad let out a laugh.

In my best Rodney Dangerfield voice, which was horrible, I replied, "No respect."

Mel walked back to the island and crossed her arms. "Oh, you want respect, I'll give you some respect." Thad and Danny smiled.

I said, "Honey, can't you wait? We have guests."

She snatched a scrub sponge off the island and threw it at

me as her face turned several shades of red, then left the room. Danny, Thad and I sat and talked for a bit about Thad's adventures. He told us about his trip home and encounters he had had: the block, the tricycle and some thugs chasing him down in an old Ford. Neither of us pressed him for details.

He ended it with a description of greeting his family in the driveway of his house; after that he was done talking.

To me, Danny said, "Damn, man, sounds like *you* had an easy trip home." Thad looked up and I nodded.

"Hate to say it, buddy, but I didn't have nearly the trouble you did. One little encounter with some good ole boys who tried to shoot down a couple of helicopters, but didn't work out real well for them. Then I ran into some hippies in the woods, but they didn't bother me none. I knew your trip to Tampa would be worse than mine, but I had no idea it'd be that bad."

Thad let out a grunt. "The trip home wasn't shit compared to what happened after I got there." He took a sip of his coffee and looked out the sliding glass door. "Morgan, you know there's a dude in your shop?"

"Oh crap, I forgot all about him. Let's go outside and I'll introduce you to Jeff."

As we were standing up, a ruckus erupted in the back of the house. In a blur of flailing arms and shouts, they boiled out of Taylor's room.

"It's my turn!"

"No, you just had it!"

"I haven't used . . ."

The argument came to an abrupt stop when they noticed Thad. They stood there for a moment staring at him, then looked at me, not sure what to think.

"Hi," Thad said and waved at them. Danny whispered in his ear, and a big smile spread across his face.

Thad looked at the girls and said, "I think it's my turn," and held out his hand for the iPad.

Suddenly none of them wanted it. The two big girls let go of it instantly, leaving Little Bit holding it. She looked down at it, then at Thad, then tried to hand it to one of her sisters, only to find they had both vacated the kitchen. Looking back and seeing they were gone, she quickly set it on the island and headed for the bedroom, shouting a muffled, "You left me!" as the door slammed shut. I doubled over laughing, Danny immediately followed my lead and Thad started that deep bass belly laugh of his.

We were still laughing when we went out the slider onto the deck. The door to the shop was open and Jeff looked up. I introduced Jeff and Thad and told him a little about the walk home.

"Nice to meet ya," Jeff said, shaking Thad's hand. Then he looked at me and said, "It's done and it works."

"Cool, you know how to use it?" I asked.

"Oh yeah, nothing to it."

Jeff walked over to the laptop and showed me how to type a message in the text box. "It's just like texting: just type what you want, hit ENTER and it will transmit." He hit ENTER on the keyboard and pointed to a little gray box sitting beside the computer. It had two LEDs that started blinking. "See? It's transmitting now."

"Looks easy enough. Later I'll figure out what frequency I need to be on and what to send and we'll see if my guy is out there or not," I said.

"Sarge?" Thad asked with raised eyebrows. I nodded.

"Well, Thad, what's your plan?" I asked as I leaned back on the bench.

He looked down at the ground. "Don't really have one. I just needed to get gone."

He didn't elaborate any further, but he didn't need to.

"Let's go see if we can find you guys a place to stay."

"Is there a deputy here named Mark?" Thad asked.

That caught me by surprise. "Uh, yeah, how did you know?"

"The sheriff asked me to turn over the truck to him."

Danny's head cocked to the side. "You met the sheriff?" Thad nodded and Danny said, "And they let you drive away?" Thad nodded again, and Danny raised his eyebrows.

"Well, that makes it kinda easy. Let's go see him and we'll talk to him about a house," I said.

We walked as a group to the barricade. The Scout had been pulled in behind it and Reggie was keeping an eye on it. As we walked up to the truck, Thad motioned to the log barricade. "Y'all need to do some work on this; nowhere to hide."

"Yeah, we've already paid the price for that," Danny said.

"I've got an idea," Jeff said.

"We're all ears, man," I said and he told us he would show us later.

I looked over at Reggie and said, "Hey, man, what was with the body on your four-wheeler earlier?"

"I'll tell you 'bout it later. Can you drop by 'round suppertime?" he said.

"Yeah, sure, everything all right?" I asked, and he nodded.

We got into the Scout and Danny directed Thad down to Mark's house. I was looking over the back seat at the guns. I said, "You collected quite the arsenal on your way home." He looked up into the mirror at me but said nothing.

Mark came outside before we were stopped in the driveway, holding his AR. When he saw Danny in the strange truck, he relaxed. If it was possible, Mark actually looked worse than when I had seen him the other night. After we all piled out and made the introductions, Thad told Mark that the sheriff wanted him to turn the truck over to him. Mark stood there for a moment thinking then said, "And you actually brought it here?"

Thad nodded.

"You two walked home together?" Mark asked, and Thad and I both nodded. Then Mark asked, "These guys staying with you, Morgan?"

"That's the other reason we're here. I was hoping we could let them stay in Pat's house. There's too many at my place to add Thad and Jeff."

For a moment he looked shocked. Even Danny looked at me like I was nuts. I said, "It's not like they're coming back."

Mark shook his head and let out a little grunt. "Yeah, I guess not. Whatever, I don't give a shit. And not for nothing, Morgan, but half the problems you got around here are because of the way you say shit like that. Something to think about."

I bristled at first, but I knew he was right. I wasn't sorry about what happened to Pat and her family, but yeah, some diplomacy might be in order.

We agreed to take the truck over to Pat's old place and unload all the gear, then we'd bring it back. As Mark turned to go inside he said, "Just leave the keys in it." Then he went inside, the door closed with a loud thunk, and the four of us were left in the yard looking at one another.

Jeff looked over at me and said, "I gotta ask, why aren't they coming home?"

I looked at him for a moment, then looked at Danny, then back at Jeff and Thad. "They're dead."

Thad said, "How'd they get dead?"

Danny replied before I could think of anything. "Morgan shot 'em, right over there," and pointed at the spot in Mark's yard.

Jeff said, "Oh, those people." He hadn't liked the story when I told it, and it looked like he was liking the idea of living in Pat's house even less.

We drove the truck over to the house and unloaded all of Thad's stuff. Jeff said he would ride the scooter down later with all his stuff. Inside, the house was untouched, much to my surprise. The outside, on the other hand, had been stripped of anything and everything that could be used. The woodshed had been nearly full and now was empty. All the feed was gone, as were all the chickens. It was obvious that the place had been cleaned out as soon as we left that day.

In the living room was a large stone fireplace, quite nice actually, and there was more than enough room for the two of them. I told them I would bring some wood down later and for them to come to the house later for dinner. We'd have to figure out what to do about food for them, water too. Danny and I left them to settle in and walked back to his house to continue on our project.

Back at Danny's house we finally settled on a design for the stocks. We used a couple of eight-by-eights for the upper and lower sections and mounted them on two four-by-four posts for the upright supports. A large strap hinge on one end enabled it to be opened. We cut the holes so they were snug on my wrists and neck, since Danny pointed out I had kind of a big head. A hasp for a padlock finished the piece off. It was getting late in the day, so we decided to finish it the next morning and I headed back home.

On my way back I saw the Scout was back at Mark's house. Thad hadn't wasted any time in returning it, and I knew that would go a ways with Mark.

I thought about Thad's family, and that got me to thinking about losing my own. I pushed those thoughts away and focused on the practical things we had to deal with. Our food would go a lot faster with Jeff and Thad around, and I knew it was past time to start looking at the long term, something I should have done as soon as I got home. Thad and Jeff were coming over for dinner, and it would be a good opportunity to see what we could come up with.

As I got to the paved part of the road, the sound of an axe brought me out of my thoughts. Looking off to the right, I saw the old man that lived there—I didn't know his name— trying to split wood. I wondered where his dogs were; they were usually out barking at whoever was in front of his place, but not today. The air was crisp as dusk started to fall, and the smell of woodsmoke filled the air. It really made it feel like winter.

Mel was in the kitchen again, poor woman; it seemed like she lived in there now. I said, "Hey, good lookin', what'cha got cookin'?"

"Salmon patties, macaroni and cheese and green bean casserole."

"Damn, sounds good. We should have company over more often."

"No, we shouldn't. I'm starting to get worried about food. Are we going to have to feed those two now?"

"I was thinking about food on the way home. We'll have to for a little while, but I'm going to start looking at some alternatives."

She got a sour look on her face. "What kind of alternatives?"

I just shrugged my shoulders. "Whatever I can come up with."

That statement didn't improve her mood any. "That's what I was afraid of."

"Where're the girls?"

With her spatula in one hand she pointed toward the door to Lee Ann's room. I found the girls gathered around the iPad still. It looked like they were drawing or something on it. They didn't even look up, though Little Bit and Lee Ann did say, "Hi, Dad."

"Hey, Taylor, when did you come home?"

Without looking up from the iPad, she replied, "Earlier."

"I know that. *How* did you get home? I told you to wait for me, remember?"

She looked up at me, her mouth hanging open, then said, "Rene fell asleep, so I left."

"And you just walked home alone?"

"No, her dad walked me home."

"Did he come up to the house?" This worried me; I didn't want anyone getting near the house right now.

"No. When we got to the gate, he turned around and went home. He told me to tell you thank you for the food." She swiveled around so she was sitting. "They were all crying and stuff."

"Did they give Rene the Ensure?"

"Yeah, they were giving it to her. She liked it a lot. Can I go back over there tomorrow?"

Before I could answer, Little Bit piped up, "I wanna go!"

Taylor looked at her with a scowl on her face. "You can't go; she's *my* friend!"

They began to argue, Little Bit complaining that she didn't have any friends to play with and was tired of being at home all the time; Taylor, being a typical big sister, didn't want her little sister tagging along. I'd heard enough, though, and said, "Knock it off! I don't want to hear it. You guys do what you're told. If you're told to wait for me, then you wait; if you're told not to leave, then don't leave."

As I turned to walk out, Lee Ann asked, "When's dinner gonna be ready?"

"Soon," I said as I closed the door.

Passing through the kitchen, the smell was wonderful. Mel asked, "Are we stuck here in this house forever?"

"Oh come on, not you too. You know we can't just go running around."

"I know, but I was thinking about my mom today." I looked over just in time to see the tears start. I had wondered how long it would be until she started to worry about her mom. She probably had been for some time and I was only just hearing about it. I walked around the island to where she was and wrapped my arms around her. She wiped the tears from her face.

"Babe, I'm sorry, but there's no way we can go to Orlando. We'd lose the truck on the way to either cops or bandits, and who knows what else could happen. There's just no way."

"I know, but I can't stop thinking about her."

I just stood there holding her. She knew there wasn't

313

anything I could do, she just needed to talk about it. I really felt like shit knowing there was nothing I could about it. Her mom lived in downtown Orlando, and I mean right downtown. It'd take a damn tank to get down there, and once we did we'd probably find she was gone. At least this way she could think of her as she was and not how we might find her. That sounded cold even to me, but the thought of finding her mom dead in her house was worse in my mind than wondering how she was doing. That's the logic I used about my mom and dad, and so far it had worked.

They lived on the St. Johns in Debary. I guess I could have gotten there on the river, but it was a long trip and who knows what would happen. I just hope the small community they lived in had come together. They were actually in a pretty good spot, or so I hoped.

I was stoking the fire when I heard Meathead start barking. I looked out and saw Thad and Jeff coming down the drive. Meathead was on the porch with raised hackles. I stepped out on the porch and waited for them.

Thad was looking at the dog as he walked up. "He gonna eat me?"

"Not in one sittin'," I replied, and they laughed.

"I think it'd take a herd of 'em to eat him in one sittin'," Jeff said.

"Come on in," I said.

As Thad stepped through the door he said, "Man, it smells good in here."

"After dinner we'll take a load of wood down to the house for you guys," I said.

Jeff asked, "Hey, Morgan, you got anything we could use for light? It gets freakin' dark in that house."

I hadn't thought of that. "I have some oil lamps, a bunch actually. We'll take a couple of them down too."

"That'd be nice. He's right, it gets damn dark in there," Thad said as he passed through the living room. "Evenin', ma'am," he said when he saw Mel behind the stove.

"Hi, Thad, you guys get settled in?"

"We're getting there."

Jeff walked in behind Thad, trying to look around the big man. "Man, what smells so good?"

Mel looked up with a smile. I was surprised at how at ease she was. Before, she had hated to have people just drop by. But then again, she hadn't been around too many people and maybe it was nice to talk to someone, anyone, besides me. "I hope you guys are hungry," she said as she took the last salmon patty from the skillet.

"Oh yes, ma'am," Thad said, followed quickly by an "Oh yeah!" from Jeff.

Mel called the girls out. Since Jeff and Thad were over they had to sit in the living room in front of the fireplace. The three of us guys sat at the table. Mel made plates for the girls and they took them into the living room and then she fixed plates for the rest of us. Once everyone had a plate, Mel took a seat and we talked while we ate. The talk centered around my concerns about food. Now that we had even more mouths to feed, we needed to come up with more. I asked the two guys if they had any ideas. Jeff said he was clueless; he was from the desert and didn't know shit about what you could eat in Florida, 'cept maybe alligators.

Thad was a little more help, though he didn't think of anything I hadn't already and didn't mention a bunch of things I was pondering. The result was that things were about to get serious. The menu was going to start to suck and everyone was going to have to work to find enough food for all of us. There wasn't much more to say about it right then and the conversation tapered off.

Jeff brought things back around. "Mel, this mac 'n' cheese is awesome. Is it from a box?"

"It started out that way, but I do my thing to it, gotta spice it up," she replied.

"Whatever you're doin', it's workin'. I really like the bread crumbs on top."

Thad held up a forkful of pasta as a salute and grunted.

I said, "It's great, Mel." I had to hand it to her; she did a good job on it. Mel had taken time to learn from some books like *Making the Best of Basics*, and had always written down recipes from a website called *Hillbilly Housewife*.

The girls all came in about the same time wanting more mac 'n' cheese as well. Mel was eating, so I got up and spooned them each some more out, then carried the pot over to the table, where Thad and Jeff immediately set upon it. I watched Thad and Jeff as they ate, thinking about the pretty basic dinner we were having. I remembered the day we had found those cans of French-fried onions on sale. Mel bought a bunch of them. It was a simple thing, one you wouldn't give a second thought to. But tonight, here, for the small group of people gathered around my table, it made a big difference. It made me think about what other things that we had acquired on a whim that would make a difference, be they food or something else.

When everyone was done I helped Mel clear the table. The guys offered to help but I told them we'd get it. As I was setting the last of the plates in the sink, Mel carried a stack of the paper plates over to the table. I hadn't heard anything about a dessert. She went to the fridge and came out with a cake, of all things. It wasn't very big, maybe eleven inches square, but it was two layers and frosted.

I said, "How in the hell did you come up with that?"

She smiled as she set it on the table, to the obvious delight of Jeff and Thad. "It's a Coca-Cola cake."

"A what?"

"A Coca-Cola cake. It's basically a box of that Jiffy mix, and I used Coke for the liquid. The frosting is some of the Jiffy powder as well."

Thad had a curious look on his face. "Never heard of that, but it sounds good."

With talk of cake in the kitchen, it wasn't long before the girls arrived. Mel cut the cake and handed out pieces to everyone. Little Bit naturally wanted a bigger piece, or to lick the knife used to cut it, or to scrape the crumbs off the plate, or anything she could think of to get some more. I finally shooed her out of the kitchen so we could eat ours. I had never heard Mel even mention Coca-Cola cake before, but it was excellent.

Once the table was cleared again, I sat back in my chair. Everyone was feeling fat and happy.

"Only one thing could make this any better," I said, pausing for a moment before continuing. "A drink."

Jeff looked up. "I would kill for a drink."

"Well, I have some medicinal whiskey in the shop, and right now I think it would be good for my health to have a nip," I said.

I went out to the shop and returned with a bottle of Jim Beam and set some glasses out on the table. I dropped some ice into each of them and poured a couple fingers of whiskey. Mel said she didn't want any and went to our room. The girls were gone to one of their rooms, so Thad, Jeff and I sat there and enjoyed our Beam. The first one went down so well we thought another was in order, so I passed the bottle for another round.

Before things got out of hand, I suggested we go out and load some wood in the Suburban to take back to their place. We donned our coats and collected our weapons and went out to the woodshed. I grabbed the old green cart on the way and we loaded it full of nice seasoned oak. While Jeff and Thad took it to the back of the truck, I went to the shop and grabbed a couple of oil lamps and two half-gallon jugs of oil. After putting them in the back seat, I grabbed a double handful of lighter wood from the old ammo can on the front porch.

Fortunately for me, our property is covered in old lighter stumps. When my stash gets low I just go out and cut about one foot off the current one I'm working on and split it up. I had been surprised to find a log almost eight feet long that was completely cured into lighter wood. On a cold morning, or better yet a wet one, it made it really easy to start a fire. After cutting the piece I split it out into pieces about a half-inch in diameter and piled them into the can by the front door. A pile of pine needles and piece of fatwood, and you had a fire in a matter of minutes.

As I was putting the fatwood into the back of the truck, the old bell at the roadblock sounded out into the night. Jeff and Thad both looked over at me. "What the hell is that? Little late for church," Thad said.

"That's not for church; it's the warning from our barricade. It means trouble. We need to go out there and see what's up," I said as I ran around the truck to the driver's side. Jeff jumped into the passenger seat and Thad got in behind him as I started the old Cummins up. We were in motion before Thad's door slammed shut. I flipped on the high beams as the old truck swung out on the road. In the light we could just barely make out the two guys standing behind the logs, the fire in the barrel off to the right cast a yellow light on the bush, but I couldn't see anyone on the other side.

Rick was at the barricade along with one of the young guys from the neighborhood. On the other side was a group of four or five people. I couldn't tell if they were men or women from where I was. Stepping out of the truck, I was able to clearly hear the shouting. Seeing the arrival of the three of us caused those on the outside of the barricade to pause and exchange glances.

Rick was crouched behind the logs with his carbine at his shoulder. He stole a quick glance our way then quickly looked back at the group on the other side of the logs. The three of us approached the logs, spreading out across the back side. Thad had his old coach gun laid over his shoulder. Jeff didn't have anything in his hands, but I knew there were at least one and maybe two Glocks on him. I had my trusty old Bushy slung around my neck. I'm sure the added firepower got the visitors' attention.

"What's up, Rick?" I asked.

"I want ma boy!" a short, fat pie-faced woman on the other side of the barricade demanded. Her hair was matted and she was red-faced. In the light cast from the old truck, she really looked rough. Beside her was a skinny man with long hair. He didn't look particularly dangerous or even interested in being there at the moment. With them were two other men. Those two had rifles with them, lever actions of some sort.

I looked over at Rick and said, "What?"

"She thinks her son is here or some shit and wants us to bring him out," Rick replied.

"He *is* 'ere, dammit, don'chu fuckin' listen?" the old woman cawed.

"Look, lady, I done told you, I don't know who in the hell you're talking about. I ain't seen anyone come in here. No one just walks in, as you can tell," Rick said.

"Ma boy come here to see Randal; whur's he at?" the skinny man asked.

Rick looked over at me. I just shrugged. Rick looked back to the gaggle on the other side of the logs and said, "He ain't here anymore."

The old woman squinted an eye and her upper lip curled up over her two top teeth. "Whur'd they go?"

Rick shrugged. "Don't know, they're just gone."

"If'n my boy ain't home tomarra, we'll be back," she said as she turned and headed over to an old Suzuki Samurai that I hadn't noticed. I was surprised that the thing would actually run. The skinny man got behind the wheel while the other two climbed into the back and that woman got in the passenger seat. It started with a loud rattle and headed off down 19 into the forest.

"Where're they from?" I asked Rick.

"I don't know. From the looks of them, I would guess a rock out in the damn woods somewhere. You seen anyone around here? Their kid maybe?"

I thought about the body I had seen draped over Reggie's four-wheeler. "Nope, haven't seen a soul." Rick looked as though he didn't believe me.

Jeff said, "Gabions."

I said, "What?"

"Gabions were fortifications used during the Civil War. They're baskets filled with rocks or dirt and stacked up to form defensive positions. That's what y'all need here."

I was thinking about that when Rick said, "I've seen those, that's good idea. It'd provide a lot better cover than these logs. I don't know what we'd make 'em out of, though."

I said, "We could use that stand of river cane back near Reggie's house."

"River cane would work real good. Use whole stalks for the verticals and split halves to weave around them, that'd work great," Jeff said, nodding his head.

"How big do they need to be?" Rick asked.

Jeff rubbed his chin for a moment. "Prolly three feet in diameter would be enough."

"Damn, that'll take a lot of cane and a lot of dirt to fill," Rick said.

"And a hell of a lot of manpower to complete. Just moving the dirt to fill them would be a hell of a job," I added.

"Well, these fuckers ain't doing anything else," Rick said, nodding over his shoulder toward the neighborhood. "If they're not gonna stand guard, they sure as shit can help make sure we don't get shot doing it for them."

We went on to discuss the logistics of such an undertaking and whether it was even worth doing. We could only block the road here; the rest of the neighborhood could be entered from the rear of any of the houses. Then we talked about whether or not the folks in the neighborhood would even help do it. I doubted that they would do anything to help out. Some would, but the majority of them wouldn't. They didn't even help man the barricade. Rick said he would talk to Mark about it and asked me to go and check out the stand of cane in the morning. Jeff said he'd go with me, and Thad, Jeff and I headed back to the truck.

I helped the guys unload the wood on their back porch, the closest approach to the fireplace. The lamps made a huge difference. Having my solar set up enabled me to use the lights in the house and I hadn't gotten used to how dark the nights were without them. Over at Thad and Jeff's place I was able to see just how dark it was. With the aid of the lantern it was no big issue to get a fire going. There was already quite a bit of kindling in the house and a large box of strike-anywhere matches. I told the guys to come down in the morning for breakfast and left them for the night.

As I was heading home, I slowed at the side road that Reggie lives off of. I thought about going down there to look at the cane, but really I wanted to go talk to him about his passenger and our visitors. Instead I went home to spend some time with Mel and the girls. The girls were already in bed by the time I made it back, so after banking the fire with a couple of logs I headed off to bed, where I found Mel buried in a pile of blankets.

After a breakfast of tasty casserole, Thad, Jeff and I headed down toward Reggie's house. As I was getting in the truck, Little Bit came out wanting to come with us. I told her to wait a bit and she could go with me later. I didn't pull into Reggie's drive, instead stopping the truck at the end of the road where the stand of cane started. The three of us got out to look it over, trying to figure out if there was enough there to make what we wanted.

While we were talking, Reggie came down the drive, "What's up, guys?"

"Hey, Reg, we're thinking of using the cane for something," I said.

"What?"

Between Jeff and I we explained what we were thinking of doing. Jeff offered a pretty fair idea of the design of the gabions, how we would need to split some of cane to weave in around the whole stalks. In the sand I drew a rough sketch of how we could set them up to improve the log barricade. When I finished my chicken scratch in the dirt, I stood up and waited to see what Reggie thought. He was standing thinking, reaching up and rubbing the stubble on his chin. I looked at his hand as he scuffed the beard on his face.

"Instead of using this cane, why don't we use some field wire? It'd be a lot easier to make 'em out of, find something to line 'em with to keep the dirt in," he finally said.

"That's a great idea, but where are we going to get the fence, start taking it down?" Thad said.

"I've got ten rolls of it." Reggie replied.

"What? Where'd you get all that?" I asked.

"I got it at an auction months ago. I was going to replace a bunch of the fence here and split fence the pigpen back there." Reggie jutted a thumb over his shoulder in the direction of the pasture.

"Reg, you have pigs?" I asked.

"Yeah, I moved 'em into the barn to keep 'em out of sight. They's seven sows and one boar in there. I'm waitin' for them sows to drop their litters, I know a couple of 'em are almost ready."

"Holy shit, that's a lot of bacon," Jeff said.

"That could sure help out some folks, if you're willing," I said.

Reggie looked at me with a slight squint. "Morgan, I ain't going to just give the meat away. There's a shit pile of people here who ain't lifted a finger to do a damn thing around here. Hell, most of 'em are just sittin' in their houses starving to death instead of doing anything about it." He paused for a moment. "But those folks who are working to keep things going are more than welcome to it."

"I think you know where I stand on that particular issue, Reggie," I said.

"How many people are back in here?" Thad asked.

"No one's ever done a count, but we guessed there are probably over a hundred, or there *were*, anyway," I answered.

"With that many bodies you guys should be able to get all kinds of stuff done around here if everyone was working together," Thad offered.

Reggie looked over at the big man. "That's just it: no one has really tried to organize a real effort to do anything."

"Who's in charge around here?" Jeff asked.

Reggie and I looked at one another. "I guess Mark kinda is," I said.

I had been thinking about the baskets and what to line them with while we were talking, and had an idea. "What if we used some tar paper to line the baskets with?"

Reggie said, "I have a few rolls of that too; that would work real good."

Jeff said, "That's perfect."

I said, "I have a few rolls too. I did half the roof earlier this year and had bought enough paper to do the whole thing, so I have a bunch."

"Well, then it sounds like we got a plan. Let's get to work. Morgan, back your truck up to the shop there and we'll load as many rolls into the back as we can. It'd be better to make these at your place since it's closer to the end of the road."

In the morning we met back at Reggie's and I backed in as Thad and Jeff followed Reggie up the drive. Reggie opened the big doors on the front of the shop and I was able to back the ass end up into it. They were already rolling the wire out when I got out. I went to the back of the truck, stood a roll up, leaned it over the back and hefted it up into the cargo area. Reggie came up and helped me muscle it in.

"Hey, Reg, what happened to your knuckles, man?" I asked, nodding at his hands on the roll of wire.

He just looked at me, then at his hands. He stood there in thought for a moment and said, "Follow me."

I followed him out a back door of the shop as Thad and Jeff moved another roll of wire past us. Reggie went to the barn and opened a padlock on a small door. He hung the lock on the hasp and turned to me. "Before you say anything, hear me out." He opened the door and stepped into what at one time was a tack room of sorts.

The early morning sunlight cut through the open door lighting up a rectangle on the floor. It took my eyes a second to adjust to the dimness of the small space. What I saw caught me off guard; in the center of the room was a man tied to a chair, a rag of some sort over his eyes. An old wool blanket was draped loosely over his shoulders. He had a flannel shirt on over a bloodstained T-shirt. He was unconscious and what I could see of his face told me why.

"Uh, Reg, who the fuck is that?"

"Remember we found that ID in Randal's room?"

"Yeah, but—" He cut me off.

"This here is the one who helped Randal. They killed them girls. They raped, tortured and brutalized 'em."

I looked at the figure in the chair, then back at Reggie. "You sure about that?"

Reggie nodded. "I've even got the names of the other girls. He knew where they were dumped too. Remember the tire tracks that Mark drew a picture of?" I nodded and he said, "I didn't need a damn picture of 'em. They were Super Swampers." He waved for me to follow him.

I followed him as he headed for the back of his property line, following a very obvious set of tire tracks. At the edge of his property under an old green canvas tarp was a red Nissan pickup sitting on a set of Super Swampers. Reggie pulled the tarp back over the bed and stood there looking into it.

"This is the last place she was. She was probably alive in here before they did what they did to her."

"Reggie, you positive about this?" He nodded. I said, "How'd you get the truck back here? No one saw it."

He told me that he and Luis had been at the barricade when the kid came by looking for Randal. Reggie didn't like the look of him the moment he pulled up and started to talk to the kid. From the conversation they had, he knew the kid was involved with what happened. I asked how he got him to his house, and he said he had caught the kid off guard with an uppercut to the chin. He loaded the kid up and took him home on his four-wheeler, then went back for the truck, driving it around through the woods to the spot at the back of his property.

"What about Luis?" I said.

"He knew my niece some. He won't say nothin'."

Reggie pulled the tarp back over the truck and we headed for the shop. When we got to the barn, Thad and Jeff were standing there looking in the open door.

"What's this, Morgan?" Thad asked.

I looked at Reggie. "You tell him."

Reggie gave the CliffsNotes version of what led up to the kid being tied to the chair. While he relayed the story, Thad kept his eyes on the kid in the chair.

"I guess this is who they were looking for, huh?" Thad said once Reggie finished.

Reggie looked over at me with a question on his face and I told him about the encounter at the barricade the night before. Thad looked at Reggie and me and said, "If he did it, then he needs to be dealt with. You can't let anyone find him here."

"Is he still alive?" Jeff asked and Reggie nodded.

"I guess we can bury him," Reggie said.

Thad looked past Reggie and said, "Them hogs in the barn here?"

Reggie looked a little confused. "Yeah, in there." He jutted his chin toward the end of the barn.

Thad said, "Morgan, we got five rolls into the back of the truck. Why don't you and Jeff head to your place and start on the baskets."

"Gabions," Jeff said.

"Gabions," Thad corrected himself.

"What are you guys going to do?" I asked.

Thad said, "Morgan, from what you have told me about things around here, you don't need any more shit on your head. I'll help Reggie do what needs done an' we'll come down in a little while."

The way Thad spoke surprised me, he had changed, and I didn't have to guess why. I looked at Jeff and jerked my head toward the shop. He followed me to the truck.

Chapter 27

Sarge looked out the open door of the Black Hawk at the Apache off the starboard side. He leaned back into the web seat with a smile on his face and closed his eyes. When he had retired from the army he thought he would never sit in one of these vibrating monsters again, but here he was. This was what he had missed, what he had tried to find out there on the airwaves of the world, the camaraderie of brothers in arms. He opened his eyes and looked around at the faces of the men with him, men who had chosen to fight the good fight.

Captain Lewis met his eyes and a smile cracked his face. His eyes shifted and Sarge followed them out the open door; they were crossing the fence line of Camp Riley. Smoke rose from several places around the base. Farther off in the distance they could see the air base, and there was smoke there as well. Sarge looked back to the captain and pressed the PTT button on his intercom. "Looks like they put up a fight."

Captain Lewis replied while still looking out the door. "Still are. We're mopping up right now, look out there."

Sarge followed his outstretched arm to a small runway. On the apron in front of a hangar were dozens of men sitting on the asphalt. They were on their knees with their hands on their heads and their ankles crossed. Standing around them were several other men. A loose ring of camo uniforms contained a fidgeting mass of black ones. Sarge could see a couple of camo uniforms walking amongst the captives, probably looking for the ones they wanted to interrogate.

"What are you going to do with all of 'em?"

Captain Lewis said, "I don't know what the plan is, but I think there's plenty to keep 'em busy." He finished with a smile.

"Look at all them jackbooted thugs," Mike said looking out the door.

The Black Hawk was descending toward the runway and the Apache banked away and flew across the base. As the helo approached the deck, a ground handler came out holding two small orange wands and began to give hand signals to the pilots. He was wearing the regulation earmuffs and goggles. Ted saw this and thought, *Even under the current circumstances the army is still the army.* The wheels touched the deck and took the load of the big bird. The pilots started to shut down the power plant as the ground man gave them the signal to kill power. Captain Lewis and his men bounded out of the ship with Mike, Ted and Doc in tow. Sarge levered himself out of the web seat and went to the door, looking out at the activity.

Here he was, over fifty and about to get back in the army. A grin cut his old face and he shook his head. Reaching out to brace himself on the door, he took a deep breath, and First Sergeant Linus Mitchell stepped out onto the asphalt of Camp Riley.

"What are they going to do to him?" Jeff asked as I turned the Suburban off Reggie's road.

"Not sure, but I could guess," I replied. "Look, you know I'm gonna need you to keep this a secret, right?"

Jeff said, "Hey, man, what you've done for me, I got no problem keeping my mouth shut."

"I get that, but I don't mean it's an obligation 'cause I helped you out. I need you to trust me. This neighborhood's seen some bad shit, and truth is, the guy who's supposed to be in charge is refusing to deal with it."

"You mean Mark."

"Yeah. He's not a bad guy, but he's not making the adjustment, you know? That guy's a murderer and a rapist. We're not gonna let him run around loose while Mark figures out how to have a trial or something."

"I get it, man. You got three girls."

"Yeah. That's it exactly. I'm not some vigilante, Jeff. It's just—"

"I get it, Morg. I get it. You can count on me."

"Thanks, man."

I was heading toward Danny's house; we were going to need his help with this. At Danny's, Jeff hopped out and opened the gate and closed it after I pulled through. Danny was in his shop working on a tiller when we pulled up.

"Yo," he called out as he walked up.

"Hey, man, what's up?" I said.

"Not much, just tuning up the tiller. I'm going to try and till the garden and build a greenhouse over part of it. Hey, Jeff, how's it going?"

"SOS, man, SOS," Jeff said.

I told him what we had in mind and asked if he could come help, and he agreed it was a good idea. I asked if he had any tar paper, and he said he had three or four rolls lying around. We went into the little tin building where he kept the tractor and lawn tools. In one corner was a pallet with a few bundles of shingles and three full rolls and one partial roll of paper. We loaded the paper up into the Suburban while he went in to tell Bobbie he was coming down to help. I pulled the truck up to the walkway and waited for him. He emerged from the house with Bobbie in tow and they climbed into the back seat.

"You coming to help too?" I asked Bobbie as she climbed in.

"I'm coming down to help Mel supervise," she replied with a smile.

"Oh, that'll certainly help," I said with a laugh.

"No shit," Danny added, and Jeff laughed as we headed for the gate.

I drove the truck around the back of the house to be closer to the shop, and as soon as I stopped Mel was coming out the back door with the girls in tow. When the girls saw Danny and Bobbie they ran up to them. Mel came up to me while the girls were giving their hugs and said, "You need to go over to Howard's house. His wife came over earlier looking for you."

"Is everything all right?"

"I don't know. She wouldn't really say, just that you needed to come over. What's her name? I can't remember it."

I thought for a moment but couldn't remember her name. "I can't remember either. Guess I'll go over and see what's up."

Jeff asked if I needed him to come and I told him no. He said he was going to dig my rolls of tar paper out and load them in the back with the others. He said the same thing I was already thinking: that it would be better to build the gabions out at the barricade so we didn't have to try to move them. Jeff and Danny went out to the woodshed where I told him the rolls were and I hopped the fence that separated Howard's and my yards. His wife saw me coming and had the door open as I came up.

"Hello, Morgan," she said.

"Hi, is everything all right?"

"Oh yes, come in, come in," she held the door, ushering me inside.

I found Howard in a bedroom he used for an office. His radio was set up in there and he was sitting in front of it with his leg propped up. I walked in and sat in a chair beside him. He smiled and said, "Hey, Morgan."

"What's up, Howard?"

"I thought you'd like to hear what's going on."

"What've you heard?"

"It isn't so much what I have heard as what I haven't." He paused, looking over the top of his glasses at me. "I haven't heard anything from the feds at all, but there is a lot of talk out there about what they're doing."

"Well, what's Uncle Sugar up to?"

"From what I've heard, they're moving people, lots of people—no one seems to know where or why, but that's what they're doing. The most interesting thing was a guy in up near Fort Bragg talking about a big firefight going on at the base."

Skeptical, I asked, "What, they fighting each other?"

"Don't know. All I know is what I heard."

Taking my hat off, I rubbed my hand through my hair. "You said they were moving people, know anything else on that?"

"I heard some nut job saying something about an executive order that gave the postmaster general the right to go out and round people up or some shit. I think he was batshit crazy, but he sure ran off at the mouth about it. Could you imagine the mailman showing up and telling you you had to leave? What would he do, whack you with a magazine if you didn't?" He laughed.

"I don't know, right now about anything is possible, I guess. How's the leg?"

Howard's face soured and he lifted the stump off the little stool it was resting on. "Okay, I guess."

The gauze was soaked with blood and fluid. I said, "Let me see it, Howard."

"You don't need to fool with it, I'm all right."

"When was the last time you changed the dressing?" I asked as I knelt down to inspect the leg.

"Been a day or two, I reckon."

As I got close to the leg, a faint putrid smell found its way to my nose. I said, "Dammit, Howard, you have to change it every day. The doc did a pretty good job, but if you fuck around and let it get infected, there isn't shit we can do about it. Where's the dressings and stuff the doc gave you?"

Howard fidgeted in his seat, but I gave a look that told him I wasn't going to let the issue die.

"Phyllis, can you bring them bandages in here?" he called out through the open door.

In a moment, she came in the room carrying the box the doc had given us. "Here it is."

"You guys need to change this every day; it's really important," I said.

"Oh, I know, Morgan, it's just there isn't much in here. If we change it every day, we'll run out pretty quick. We thought we could go a few days in between."

"Don't worry about running out. You can take the old

gauze and boil it and reuse it. As for the bandages, I have some, and there are other things we can use too. Cut up an old sheet and boil it and use that. Hell, we can use maxi pads too."

"Maxi pads!" Howard shouted.

I looked at him and said, "Think about what they do."

He just screwed up his face. I pulled on a pair of gloves from the box and started to unwrap the gauze, then removed the bandages. It didn't look good. In the box there were a couple of Betadine scrubs, and I asked Miss Phyllis to bring in a big bowl of water. Once I had the water, I used a scrub to clean the stub of the leg. While I'm sure it hurt, Howard never complained, though he did tense up a couple of times.

I made them promise to change the dressing every day, and once they promised, I headed for the door. I asked Miss Phyllis about their wood situation. She said they had plenty and not to worry about them. I told her I would check back in a couple of days and headed back to the house. I felt like I was getting too caught up in putting out fires. It's not that I didn't want to help folks out, but the big stuff, the long-term stuff, kept getting put off. There was hardly time to even make plans about what we should be doing and preparing for.

I found Jeff and Danny inside eating lunch and sat down to have a bite myself along with some tea. Mel and Bobbie were sitting in the living room with the girls. Danny asked how Howard was and I told him about his leg. He said we needed to keep an eye on him. Then I told them what Howard had heard on the radio and we all agreed we needed to keep an eye out. If it was true that they are forcibly relocating people, that could be an issue. Danny asked if I had checked on Miss Janice. I told him I hadn't and that we needed to. He volunteered to do it later that day. After lunch we headed for the barricade. Danny found the tools we needed and Jeff had loaded the paper up, so there was nothing left to do but get to work.

We had assembled four of the gabions when Reggie and Thad showed up. Danny was inside one of the baskets, tying the paper to the inside. We had laid the baskets over on their sides to make it easier to get in and out of. Jeff and I were unrolling wire when Thad walked up.

"Looks pretty good. Gonna take a lot of dirt to fill 'em, though," Thad said.

Looking up from the roll, I said, "Yeah, that's gonna suck. Weren't we talking yesterday about how some of the other folks around here could pitch in?"

"Yeah, we were," Reggie said, "but you know and I know that's gonna take an act of God to organize. I'd rather do it my damn self. Shit, if we had thought of it before, my nephew might still be alive."

We nodded at that. Reggie said, "I got an idea that'll speed it up. I'll bring my tractor down and we can scoop the dirt up in the bucket and bring it down here and dump it in."

Jeff said, "I like the way this guy thinks."

The five of us got busy and had assembled enough of them to cover the road in a couple of hours. The two guys that were guarding the barricade were all excited about our little project. After Lance and Reggie's nephew had been killed, everyone was nervous about being out on security. The logs provided little protection; they were designed to keep cars and trucks out, and there were precious few of those around now. I was lying in one of the baskets pushing pieces of tie wire through the paper so Reggie could twist them off when he stuck his head in the end. I said, "What's up?"

He stood there for a minute looking at me. I dropped my arms and propped myself up on my elbows. "You all right?"

Reggie hesitated for a tick and said, "Yeah, your friend there, Thad"—he motioned with his head in Thad's direction—"he tell you what happened to his family?"

"No, he didn't seem to want to talk about it, so I left it alone, why?"

"Jus' curious. I couldn't do it. I wanted to, but I couldn't"—again he hesitated, looking back down the road in the direction of his house—"but he did. I could never have imagined something like that."

Now he had my attention. "Like what, you mean kill that kid?"

"It wasn't the killing, it's what he did after."

"And what was that, after?"

Reggie dropped his head slowly shaking it back and forth. "Let's just say I ain't gonna have to feed them pigs for a while."

I looked at him; for an instant I was confused, then it struck me. "He fed him to the pigs?"

Reggie nodded. "I've been around them pigs since the day they was born, but they didn't hesitate. He cut him open an' when they smelled the blood an' guts they went right to it. Gawd, it was awful." Reggie stood up, hands on his hips, and looked over at Thad. "That man right there scares the shit outta me."

I climbed out of the basket and stood beside him. "Well, at least he's on our side."

"Huh, no shit."

With all the baskets assembled, we gathered around the back of the truck and were shooting the shit. I told everyone what Don said about people being forcibly relocated. Jeff laughed it off and Danny said they could have his asshole but nothing else. That got Jeff and I laughing until Thad cut us off.

He said, "Don't laugh." I looked at him. "Don't laugh about it. Best thing to do, if you see a damn mailman, you shoot his ass on sight."

Suddenly all the funny was gone.

"Why's that?" Danny asked.

"It was a mailman who came to my house, him and a DHS security man." Thad looked off to the southwest. "They killed Anita and Tony."

We all looked around at one another, everyone except Thad; his gaze was fixed out there somewhere.

When it was clear he wasn't going to say any more, Danny spoke up. "Hey, why don't we have a fish fry at my house tonight?"

That brought Thad back around. "Fish fry? You got fish?"

Danny smiled. "Yeah, but we got to catch 'em first."

"And that isn't hard either," I offered.

We all agreed a fish fry would be a nice diversion. Danny had a small pond at his place and it was full of bluegill. The girls had spent many an evening out there with bread balls and cane poles catching fish. But before we could run off to play we had to finish the task at hand.

We set the baskets up just behind the log barricades in a staggered line. The first one was set at the edge of the road and the next one was set just in front and beside it. The third

337

was set just behind and beside the second. This overlapping provided complete coverage, ensuring that a bullet couldn't find its way between two of the baskets. Doing it this way required more gabions than just setting them side by side, but it created a much more robust defense.

We had to assemble three more to complete the position and by then it was starting to get late in the afternoon. Everyone started to drift off toward their houses, agreeing to meet back at Danny's in an hour. Danny rode back to the house with me. Coming through the front door, we were met with an incredible smell.

"Damn, what the hell are y'all cooking?" Danny called out as he headed for the kitchen.

I followed him in and saw a big pot sitting on the stove just as Mel answered, "Beans."

We told them what we had in mind, the fish fry, and they were immediately excited. It was something we used to do a lot during speck season. Mel and Bobbie went about whipping up some corn bread real quick. The stove was already on, so it wasn't a big deal to throw the oven over the burner and get it heating while they mixed it up. I went and rounded up the girls, telling them we were going down to Danny and Bobbie's for a fish fry and that they had to catch the fish. That got them excited and there was a sudden flurry of bodies running around the house getting ready to leave.

Since there was no bread for bread balls, Danny broke out a can of corn. We'd set some aside for bait and use the rest for dinner. Danny kept several little cane poles on the rack that held his canoe beside the pond and it didn't take long before the girls were all catching fish. The fish bit as soon as a hook hit the water. It was all Thad, Danny, Jeff and I could do to keep the hooks baited and take the fish off; none of the girls were into that, though I was sure that would change.

There were nine people to feed, but we culled some of the smaller fish, which were many, and that told us that the pond could keep producing for some time. When the fish finally stopped biting, we had twenty-one nice bluegills. Mel and Bobbie were inside getting things ready. We were going to cook the fish on Danny's turkey fryer using a Dutch oven filled with oil. As was the tradition, the menfolk would cook the fish. Normally we would fillet the fish, but things being what they were I wasn't about to waste any meat, so we simply scaled and gutted them and cut off the heads. Thad said he preferred them this way; he liked the tails turning all crispy.

Taylor and Lee Ann went inside with their mom and Bobbie while Little Bit came out to help, touching the eyes and poking the guts as they were pulled out. With the four of us working it didn't take long before all the fish were ready for the oil. Danny already had it set up with the burner going and the oil heating when I carried the bowl of fish over. He had set it beside the picnic table and had all the stuff to season the fish set out on the table.

Thad said that he loved to fry fish and told us we wouldn't be disappointed if we let him take over. Not being one to hold a working man back, we stepped back. Thad went in the house and came back out with a couple of bottles of spices and a paper bag. He poured cornmeal and some flour in the bag and seasoned it, then added the fish one at a time and shook them in the mix before taking them out and lowering them by their tails into the hot oil.

The look on his face was hilarious; his lips were pressed

together as if he was whistling, though no sound came out. "Ohhh, this is gonna be good!" he proclaimed after lowering the fifth fish into the oil. The rest of us started to laugh. Danny had set out camp chairs and we were sitting around shooting the shit. It was another one of those instances of normality, if you didn't add in the all the rifles leaning around the picnic table and the fact that we all wore pistols. I got out of my chair and went to the truck, returning with the bottle of whiskey we had started on the other night. Danny went in the shop and came back with some Dixie cups, the little one you see in people's bathrooms, and I poured shots for each of us.

I thought to myself, *I could get used to this*. We joked and talked, drank and cooked and generally enjoyed ourselves. As the fish were ready to come out, Thad would pull them out of the oil with a set of tongs and put them on a baking sheet Bobbie brought out to us. It was one used for broiling and had a rack that held the fish above the pan, allowing them to drain. Paper towels were a thing of the past, but this worked just as well. We carried the pan into the house to a chorus of cheers from the women. It didn't last long, though; as soon as they saw the fish they started to bitch. They expected fillets, not this.

While they were still complaining, I picked a fish up by the tail and took a butter knife and ran it down one side. All the meat on that side fell off onto the plate, and I repeated the process on the other and held up the bones still in one piece. Seeing how easy it was, everyone immediately set about filleting their own. There was corn bread, skillet corn, and a pot of beans. Everyone came past the island and loaded their plates.

I was sitting in a chair on the far side of the living room

looking at the kitchen. The scene reminded me of a party and everyone was enjoying themselves. The house was lit by the flame from the fireplace and several oil lamps scattered around. Danny had some electric lights but used the lamps more often than not. Thad was sitting beside Little Bit, leaning down as she was saying something to him. He had a big smile on his face and was nodding his head and a moment later he leaned back and began to laugh, Little Bit looking up and cackling with laughter.

Taylor, Lee Ann, Mel and Bobbie were sitting at the table laughing about something. Jeff stood at the island picking at the plates, eating whatever was left. That brought a smile to my face: here was the smallest guy amongst us and he had the biggest appetite. He looked up and saw me looking at him and smiled as he stuck a crumb of cornbread in his mouth, licking his thumb as he did. A feast like this and such good company made me understand holidays like Thanksgiving better. A couple hundred years ago, there were probably only a few times a year when you could eat until you couldn't eat any more. I knew we wouldn't always have this much in the years to come, but I was glad we could appreciate it now, when we did.

If this was how life was going to be from now on, focused on family and friends, I could live with it. I thought about how much time I had used to spend on the road for work, missing my family. Things were a lot harder now, but I never went to bed alone far away from home and wondering what they were up to anymore.

Turning my attention from Jeff, I stared into the fireplace. The smile on my face faded as I watched the flames dance. I knew in my heart that this surely was not how life was going to be from now on. This was merely a moment of peace and happiness in an uncertain world. But why couldn't this be the new normal? Why did we have to suffer and worry? If we put our minds to it, as well as our backs, this could be the way we lived. The thoughts were still bouncing around in my head when I heard the first shot.

Chapter 28

Sarge followed the other guys into a large hangar. Passing through the huge open doors, he saw several rows of tables set up with uniformed men and woman sitting around them. Captain Lewis was off to the side talking to another man, and Sarge noticed when the captain gestured in his direction. He walked over to where Mike and Ted were setting their gear down.

At his approach Mike looked up. "What now, boss?"

"I have no idea, and from the looks of things, I ain't your boss anymore," Sarge said.

Mike looked at the officers then back to Sarge. "Aw hell, you ain't going to let those guys take over, are you?"

Sarge looked at the guys for a moment before speaking. "Look here, fellas, you're back in the army now. I suggest you get back in that mind-set. I don't know what they're going to do with me, but you boys are still property of the good ol' US government."

Ted dipped his chin in the direction of the officers. "Looks like we're about to find out."

Sarge looked over to see Captain Lewis and what turned out to be a bird colonel heading his way. Sarge snapped to attention, "Attenshun!" he shouted as the men approached. Mike, Ted and Doc all immediately followed suit. The colonel smiled and stuck out his hand as he approached. "At ease, gentlemen. First Sergeant Mitchell, I'm Colonel Fawcet. We spoke on the radio."

Sarge reached out and took his hand. "Good to meet you, Colonel."

Colonel Fawcet looked at the guys standing behind Sarge. "This your crew?"

Sarge glanced back over his shoulder and said, "Well, I wouldn't say they were mine. I'm sure they probably belong to you, but when I found 'em, I knew they shouldn't be without constant adult supervision."

The colonel smiled. "First Sergeant, I know you're retired now, but I need your help. Are you willing to come back aboard and help us out?"

"Colonel, when I took my oath it wasn't until I retired, it was forever. If you can use an old man like me I'd consider it an honor to help any way I can."

"You forming a geezer brigade, Colonel?" Ted asked.

Without turning his head, Sarge said, "No one's talking to you, dipshit."

"I think we'll get along just fine, Sergeant Mitchell."

"Can you tell me exactly what in the hell is going on, Colonel?"

"Let's get into that over lunch, Sergeant."

Sarge looked over his shoulder at the guys standing behind him. "These boys need some grub and probably some sleep, sir. Can you arrange that before we have lunch?"

"Putting your men first, absolutely." Colonel Fawcet turned to the people gathered at the table and said, "Lieutenant Cox, can you find these men some quarters and some grub?"

"Yes, sir," came the reply.

The colonel said, "If you guys will get with Cox there, he will get you sorted out."

"Roger that," Ted said.

The colonel beckoned to Sarge and said, "Sergeant Mitchell."

After the first shot we all looked at one another. I walked over to the front door and in the background I could hear some of the others moving. From behind me I heard one of the girls ask if that was a gunshot. I picked up my carbine before stepping out the door. I was listening for any sound; the absence of man-made noises allowed the natural sounds of night to really stand out. Aside from the crickets, I couldn't hear anything else.

Danny came out on the porch beside me. "Hear anything?"

"Naw, nothing."

"That damn sure sounded like a gunshot, though, didn't it? Maybe someone got a deer like you did the other night."

Before I could answer him, another shot ripped through the night, followed immediately by another. The shots were followed by shouts and screams. The sounds were coming from the back of the neighborhood, back toward the forest, and they were getting louder. Danny ducked inside and returned with his carbine and Thad and Jeff followed him out. The four of us were standing there in the dark listening to the chaos, not sure what it was, where it was or what to do.

"Look over there." In the light coming through the window, we could see Jeff pointing to the east. There was an orange glow in the sky that was rapidly growing in intensity.

"It's a fire," Thad said.

Danny dipped back into the house. I could hear him talking, feet shuffling across the floor and all the lights went out. He came back out on the porch. "We need to go check this out."

"Yeah, but someone needs to stay here," I said.

Before anything else could be said, the sound of ATVs coming up the road filled the air. There were several of them from the sounds of it, then shooting, lots of shooting. Through the trees we caught glimpses of small flames moving fast. Danny and I took off running toward the gate. I saw movement in the yard of Danny's neighbor: an ATV with two men on it. One of them was holding a torch of some sort. As they pulled up to the house, the man on the back lit something with the torch and threw it on the roof of the house.

Whatever it was rolled off the roof, spilling flames out onto the shingles as it did. When it hit the ground, the man stepped off the four-wheeler and bent over to pick it up; when he straightened and went to throw it again, there was a thunderous explosion to my right. I instinctively ducked but realized quickly it was Danny shooting. By the time I had my wits together enough to look back, the guy was down, the little flame lying in the grass beside him. The four-wheeler was turning to head for the gate. Danny was firing at it and I joined him. After three or four shots, the rider fell off and the ATV continued until it hit the fence.

"Look!" Danny shouted, pointing down the road where more men could be seen in the yard of another house. There was a large wash of flames running down the side of the house. Another man took a running start at the house and heaved a Molotov cocktail through the front window of the living room and the flames lit up the inside of the house. Danny and I both started to fire at them, though they were probably three hundred yards away and it was dark. Our fire drew their attention. I saw one of them point then shout at some of the others.

Suddenly there were three ATVs racing toward us. The passengers on each were firing wildly. We fired a couple of shots at them and turned to find some cover in the pine trees in front of Danny's house. As I slid in behind a tree, the first ATV raced through the gate. I thought we had closed it, but it was open. Danny started to fire at it, I joined him and the two men both hit the dirt. The second and third ATVs had already come through the gate.

I tried to angle myself to get a shot at one that was moving toward the front of the house. The passenger was standing up, one hand on the rider's shoulder, a Molotov in the other. They were going to try to run up to the house and throw it. I flipped over on my back and started firing and then there was an explosion. The Molotov turned into a fireball, consuming the men and their machine. They fell off and writhed on the ground, rolling around trying to put the flames out. I turned my attention to the third machine.

It was suddenly quiet. There was still some shooting, but it was a little farther away. We could see the one house burning and the glow from what had to be two more. The sound of the third ATV caught my attention; it was behind the house.

"It's around back!" I yelled to Danny.

As we ran past the porch, I wondered where Jeff and Thad were. As we rounded the house, we saw the four-wheeler sitting in front of the screen door to the back porch. Danny hit the Surefire on his carbine to light it up. One of the men was lying on the ground behind it and the second was lying on the stairs to the porch. Thad and Jeff were standing there. Thad had a bucket in his hands and water dripped onto a black scorch that still smoked where the stairs met the porch. Jeff was holding one of his Glocks, a tendril of smoke rising from the end of the stubby suppressor.

"We got 'em," Jeff said

We could still hear some ATVs running around along with some sporadic gunfire. Whoever this was, they were well equipped. "I need to go check on my house," I said.

"I'll go with you," Thad said.

We ran out to the Suburban and jumped in without saying a word. Thad had his old coach gun at the ready as I went through the gate and started down the road. The house next to Mark's was burning and I saw Mark out in his yard as we went by. I kept my eyes open for four-wheelers but didn't see any. My gate it was open, and I knew we had closed it. I turned into the drive, fishtailing the old truck and slinging rocks and dirt.

I floored it and took the drive to the backyard, planning to come at the house from the rear. As we passed through the gate in the split fence, I looked over at the shop. I had modified the door on it with a half-inch-thick piece of flat bar that I secured with two padlocks. It was a typical metal shed-style building and the door was nothing more than Styrofoam sandwiched between two thin veneers of metal. This with the bars on the inside of the windows was the best I could do to secure the building.

Two men were at work on the lower half of the door with an axe. There was already a sizable hole in the lower half and it wouldn't be long before they could get in. I swung the truck to face the shop and the headlights swept across it to light up one of the raiders, axe raised over his head for another strike. At the same time, Thad opened his door, the momentum of the turn flinging it open, and he stepped out while the truck was still moving. He raised his shotgun as the second man at the shop raised his rifle, an AK variant of some type, and fired as he backpedaled around the shop. His partner quickly followed him. Thad's shotgun went off as I jumped out of the truck. We ran to the shop, going wide to get as much of a view around the building as we could. The two men were running for the back fence. It was so dark we couldn't see them, but could we clearly hear their feet slam into the ground as they ran. Thad let loose another shot from the old coach gun.

We weren't about to chase them in the dark and went back to look at the shop door. They had done a hell of a job on it. Chunks of foam were scattered all around the front of the building along with torn pieces of the sheet metal cover. I was relieved to see that they hadn't made it in the shop.

"Don't look like they got in," Thad said.

"No, I don't think they did, but how did they know to hit my shop, of all the buildings out here? That's what worries me."

"You think they been watching us?"

I thought about it for a minute. "They had to be. I don't know if the attack on the back of the neighborhood was just a diversion or what, but it seems too well coordinated, don't you think?"

Thad said, "You're prolly right. I'll stay here. You go back down to Danny's and check on your girls."

"Thanks, I'll be back in a bit. If anything happens, just start shooting and we'll come a-runnin'."

"Don't worry 'bout me, go on."

Driving back down to Danny's, there were people all over the road. I saw Mark and his Mule racing around the houses, with Rick and his four-wheeler checking on others. As I was passing the side road to Reggie's house, I saw headlights coming down the road and stopped, unclipped the quick-release buckle on the sling of my rifle and switched it to my left hand in case I needed to fire out the passenger window. Reggie came sliding to a stop beside the truck.

"I got one of 'em tied up at the house. What do we want to do with 'em?" Reggie said.

"Where'd you get him?"

"He was running past my place heading for the woods. I was out in the barn trying to keep an eye on my place when I heard him coming. I hit him across the chest with a shovel as he rounded the corner. He's tied up in the barn."

Remembering what had happened to the last guy I saw tied up in Reggie's barn, I said, "Well, let's get him out of there. I'll follow you down to your place and we'll load him up in here and take him to Mark and see what he wants to do with him."

"Take him to Mark? You still beatin' that horse?"

"Shit, man, I don't know. Maybe this'll wake him up."

Reggie said, "Yeah, okay," and took off down the road with me behind him. We pulled up in front of the barn and found the guy tied up, in the same chair the kid had been tied to. What surprised me the most about the guy was how clean and well fed he looked. His clothes looked new, he was shaved and didn't look like he had been missing too many meals. And he didn't look scared either, which kind of freaked me out.

"Here's what he had on him," Reggie said, nudging a pile of gear on the floor by the door.

There was an AK variant, a pistol in some kind of tactical-looking holster, a chest rig with mags and a pack, the three-day assault style. The pack was black and didn't scream tactical until you really looked at it. He was wearing jeans and a camo jacket of some kind, definitely not military, but not Joe Civilian either.

Reggie had the guy's hands secured with tie wraps behind his back, and several wraps of rope secured him to the chair. I said, "We're going to take you out of the chair. I have no problem shooting you, so just walk out to the truck and we won't have any trouble. You fuck around and I'll drop you."

He never acknowledged I was speaking, but we got him out of the chair and into the truck without incident. Reggie threw his gear into the back and sat beside him in the rear seat with his well-worn Para Ordnance .45 stuck in the man's ribs.

We found Mark in the road in front of his house and showed him what we had. Reggie relayed the story of how he had caught him. Mark looked into the back seat at the man. "What the hell do we do with him now?" he asked.

"You tell us; you're the law," I said.

"I don't know what to do with him. Where can we put him?"

"How 'bout the stocks we built?" I said.

"You actually built that thing?"

"Yeah, Danny and me did."

"Go put him in there, I guess, but someone needs to stay there and keep an eye on him. I have to finish going through the neighborhood. We have seven dead so far."

"Seven?" Reggie said.

Mark looked over at him and nodded. "A couple of those are just assumed at the moment. Some of the fires are still burning, and we can't get in to look yet."

"Jesus, how many houses did they burn?" I asked.

"Four are totaled, three others were hit with fire bombs, but they either didn't catch or got put out."

"We took one out next door to Danny. They threw it on the roof but it didn't break, just rolled off, spilling fire the whole way, then Danny shot that dude. You know, this sure seemed awful coordinated. Where did they get all these damn ATVs?"

Mark shook his head and said, "I don't know," then looked into the back of the truck. "But we're going to find out."

Reggie and I took our prisoner over to the stocks and deposited him in them. Reggie had an idea and disappeared down the road in a cloud of dust on his four-wheeler, returning shortly after with a five-gallon bucket strapped to the back. He brought out a logging chain and a couple of padlocks. We wrapped the chain around the guy's waist and secured him to the four-by-four posts. Even if he got his head and neck out, he wasn't going anywhere. The strangest part of the entire thing was the fact that our new captive never said a word, never offered any resistance. It was like he was resigned to his fate and just went along with the plan.

Jeff was at the gate to Danny's when I pulled up. He was carrying the old SKS he had bought for a song from a guy he worked with. He opened the gate and I pulled through, stopping beside him. "You really need to start carrying that peasant rifle of yours," I said.

"I got your peasant right here," he said with a grin. "From now on I'll have it with me. How were things at your place?"

"Two guys were trying to axe their way into the shop, but they ran off when we showed up. Thad stayed behind to keep an eye on things."

"Sounds like we've been under surveillance."

"I was thinking the same thing. We need to get together with everyone and work out some better security. They knew not to come in the front door, and the back door was wide-ass open."

Jeff said he would keep an eye out on the front of the house.

Danny was behind the house, where the two had been killed by the steps. By the time I got there he already had dragged them out to his shop to get them away from the house, where the girls couldn't see them. He had a hose in his hand and was washing the blood off the steps when he saw me.

"We need to get the two from out front," he said as he ran the hose back and forth on the steps.

"How bad are they burned?"

He looked sideways at me. "Bad enough."

The two men were in pretty rough shape. Whatever they had used for fuel in those bottles had burned hot and long. The front yard smelled of burned cotton, plastic and rubber. Added to this was the sickly sweet smell of burned flesh and the rank odor of charred hair. One of them had been wearing some sort of a synthetic jacket, and it had melted to his skin and hardened into hunks of plastic in surreal forms. Their skin was mottled black and gray, with pink and white showing where blisters had formed and ruptured or where the heat simply split them open like overcooked hot dogs.

We used Danny's four-wheeler to drag them to the back. The ATV they had been on had suffered bad damage to all the plastic body sections. The seat was gone, two of the tires had burned pretty badly and most of the wiring was scorched. It would be useless except as parts. Danny was inspecting it, then looked up to where the one that we shot the two riders off of had stopped when it ran into the fence.

"Hey, man, these are all the same model. The colors are different on these two, but they're the same."

I looked over to the one tangled in the fence, then at the other one. Even with the fire damage on the one in front of us, it was obvious they were the same. I said, "That's weird. Maybe they hit a dealer or something and stole all of them."

"Maybe, but there isn't a dealer anywhere around here. They would have had to come from Leesburg or Ocala, or farther," Danny said.

"I guess you're right, but now I have a four-wheeler. I'm going to go get that one," I said, and pointed over to the fence.

As I started to walk away, Danny called out, "How much gas do you have at your place?"

I said, "I have a drum with some, don't know for sure, but with this many new machines around we're going to need more. Maybe tomorrow we should go up to the Kangaroo and see if we can trade for some gas."

Danny said, "Sounds good to me. You take that machine, we'll give this one to Jeff and Thad and I'll keep the burned one for spare parts. It's got the same motor that mine has."

The four-wheeler was still in gear and running sitting against the fence. I saw some blood on the seat. Swinging the light back across the pasture toward the house, I didn't see a body. I sure thought we had shot the guy off the thing as he was trying to run. I drove it toward the house. There was a body there. Back at Danny's, we talked about the bodies and agreed to deal with them in the morning. We went inside to check on everyone.

The girls were all a little frightened, and Little Bit was crying. The fire had scared Mel and Bobbie. They asked what was going on and we told them that the best we could figure some raiders had hit the neighborhood.

"What about our house?" Mel asked.

"Two guys were trying to break into the shop," I said.

"Did they get in?" Mel asked, worried.

"No, Thad and I got there before they could. He's down there now."

Danny said he wanted to take a quick ride around the neighborhood. The girls were all against that idea. Taylor and Lee Ann were scared and didn't want us to leave. I assured them Jeff was out front and no one would get in without some trouble from him. This did little to reassure them, but Danny and I went out and got our ATVs, heading for the gate. We told Jeff what we were going to do. He didn't have a problem staying to keep watch. Danny told him about the other ATV, that he and Thad could take it. "Thanks. It'll be nice to have something to get around here on," Jeff said.

There were still a bunch of people out, running here and there, shouting, crying. The houses that had been hit were still burning, casting orange light on nearby houses and creating dancing demons in the trees. We found Mark sitting in his Mule in the road down from Danny's with a group of people around him. He was being bombarded with questions, requests and accusations. He sat there staring into the flames of the house, taking no notice of the verbal assault.

We pulled alongside him, the crowd parting as we did. "What do you think?" I asked Mark as we eased to a stop.

His gaze never shifted. "Looks like we were hit by raiders."

"What are you going to do about it?" someone from the crowd shouted.

Still looking into the flames, Mark said, "Just what do you think I *can* do about it?"

"You're the police; you're supposed to protect us!" came the shouted reply.

Mark turned to the crowd, and his face was expressionless. "You fucking people *deserve* to die."

Everyone, including Danny and me, was speechless. Mark started his Mule and pulled away into the dark. I looked at Danny and he just shrugged. The crowd started to talk amongst themselves. When they started to look toward us, I started up my ATV and drove off to where we had left Reggie. He was still there at the stocks, sitting on the five-gallon bucket he had brought the chain in. As we pulled up and shut off the machines, I heard him say, "Then piss your fucking pants, asshole."

I looked at him with a little curiosity. "He's bitchin' he's gotta piss," he said with a jerk of his head.

I looked over at the guy. He didn't look particularly comfortable but wasn't showing any signs of stress yet. I asked Reggie if he wanted to be relieved. He said Rick told him he would do it later and he was good for now. We told him we'd get with him tomorrow; there would be some bodies to bury. Reggie said he would bring his tractor to make it easier.

Jeff was still at Danny's gate. He hadn't seen anyone or anything, but it was getting a little chilly and he asked for something hot to drink. Danny told him to come on back to the house. With all of us there again, there wasn't any reason for him to hang out. We went back to the house and I told Mel I didn't want to leave our place empty. If she wanted to stay with the girls, she could, but I had to go back.

Danny, Jeff and I talked about it and came up with a plan. Jeff would stay there with them and I would go home and ask Thad to stay over at the house. Like Jeff said, there really wasn't anything at their house that they were too worried about. After a round of kisses for the girls and a good-night grope with Mel, I headed out for the house. Most of the people that had been in the road had gone home. I saw Mark's Mule at his place as I went by and some lights on inside, and I worried about what had happened earlier.

Passing Reggie, I waved and was turning into my gate a moment later. As I pulled in, Thad's bulk stepped out of the azaleas with his shotgun half-raised, lowering it when he realized it was me. I pulled the Polaris around behind the house and parked it. Thad came up as I was inspecting the hole in the door.

"We'll figure a way to patch that up tomorrow," he said.

I nodded as I threw a piece of Styrofoam on the ground. "Yeah, we'll look at it tomorrow after we get all the bodies buried."

"How many?"

"Too fucking many," I said. "Probably seven people from the neighborhood, and maybe that many of the raiders."

I told him of our plan for the night and asked if he would stay. He agreed and we headed inside. The fire was almost burned out, but a handful of pine needles and a hunk of fat-wood started it right back up. I was laying in a log when Thad asked where the dogs were.

"Probably ran off when the shooting started. They're both scared of guns or fireworks, anything loud."

"I hope they come back. It's good to have 'em around."

The next morning the dogs were on the porch. Thad and I climbed on the ATV and headed down to the stocks without eating breakfast. Pulling out onto the road in the early morning cool, I was shocked to see the stocks were empty.

"What is it?" Thad asked over my shoulder.

"No one's here. Where's the prisoner?"

I turned and headed for Reggie's. After a couple of knocks, he came to the door, .45 in hand, wearing long johns. "Where's the prisoner?" I asked as a greeting.

Reggie rubbed his head, then scratched at his beard. "Hell, I don't know. Mark relieved me last night."

"Well, get your shit together and come down to Danny's house. We have two to bury there."

He acknowledged me by waving a hand as he shut the door. When we pulled in at Mark's house, I knew something was up. The gate was open, the Mule was there, but the Scout was gone. I told Thad to take a look around as I went up to the front door and knocked. After a couple of knocks the door cracked open and Mark's wife peered out.

"What do you want, Morgan?"

"Is Mark here?"

"No, he's gone out." She looked back over her shoulder, then back at me.

"Everything all right?"

"Yeah, it's just early. I don't know what he's doing."

Mark's dog, a big black mutt of some kind, was raising hell behind her. The dog rushed the door, knocking it open a few more inches. I was looking down at the dog and saw bags packed and sitting by the door. "Did he take that prisoner with him?"

"I told you I don't know. I've got things to do. Good-bye." She shut the door in my face.

I went to the ATV where Thad was waiting. I asked him if he had seen anything. He hadn't, and told him what had just happened. We headed for Danny's and found Jeff and Danny sitting on the front porch. Danny was drinking a cup of tea and Jeff some coffee. They greeted us by raising their cups.

"Got any more coffee?" Thad asked.

"On the stove in there, cups are over the sink," Danny said.

"Something's going on with Mark," I said. "We have to talk."

Chapter 29

Colonel Fawcet followed Sarge into the barracks they had been assigned to. They had enjoyed a leisurely lunch, and though the menu was far from fine dining, it was certainly better than what most people were eating these days. The old two-story building was probably from the forties but was in decent repair and enjoyed the benefit of heat from the base's central boiler.

From the back of the one large open room they could hear arguing. Sarge headed back toward the latrine with the colonel in tow. Coming around the corner, Sarge found Mike and Ted standing in front of a shower, wrapped in towels.

"I'm next, dammit!" Mike shouted at Ted.

Sarge stopped in the door of the shower room, his hands resting on his hips.

"Fuck you, I called it after Ronnie," Ted fired back.

"You two fucksticks done?" Sarge shouted over the sound of a running shower.

Ted and Mike both spun to see Sarge, then the colonel. As soon as they saw the Colonel they both snapped to attention and saluted, and Ted's towel fell to the floor as he did. Sarge stood there shaking his head. "Mike, you know damn well it's Teddy's turn to sleep on top. You two hurry up and get your makeup on."

Both of them held the salute and Sarge looked over his shoulder to Colonel Fawcet. "You wanna release these two?"

Fawcet offered a slight salute. "As you were, gentlemen," he said, then quickly added, "Strike that, I think 'at ease' would be more appropriate, at least until the First Sergeant and I clear out."

Mike and Ted both dropped their salutes.

"Colonel, you know he's just kidding—" Mike started to say.

Colonel Fawcet raised his hands in mock surrender, shaking his head as he backed out the door.

"Aw, come on, Sarge, tell him yer just bullshittin'!" Mike called out.

"On the bottom, Mikey, on the bottom," Sarge said as he turned to follow Fawcet out the door.

"That's fucked up, Sarge!" Mike shouted.

Fawcet headed for the door, wiping tears from the corners of his eyes. "I needed that. Everyone has been so damn uptight, it's nice to see someone normal enough to mess around with."

"Colonel, I wouldn't call us normal, but those are some good men back there. We'll get to work pretty soon and do the best we can," Sarge replied.

Fawcet paused at the door and turned to Sarge. "Linus, you need anything let me know. Things are kind of limited right now, but I'll do what I can for you." Fawcet stuck his hand out.

Sarge gripped his hand. "You just give me what you promised and we'll come up with the rest." The two men shook and Fawcet headed for the door.

"Good luck, First Sergeant."

Mel and Bobbie had a large pot of oatmeal prepared for breakfast. The girls weren't real happy about that, though. They wanted to know why we couldn't have scrambled eggs or something. Mel explained to them that we needed to start mixing things up a little, and that we couldn't always eat what they wanted.

I took the girls aside to explain things to them. "Listen up, ladies. We've had it pretty good at our house, and lots of people don't have it half so good. And when you make a face at Bobbie's oatmeal, how is she supposed to feel about that? She's gonna feel bad, because Danny and Bobbie don't have enough to share with us. If they had eggs and waffles and ice cream, do you think they wouldn't give you some? I'm not mad, but you need to understand the new polite: if someone offers you food, you say thank you like it's your favorite thing. You get me?"

They looked embarrassed enough and said, "Yes, Daddy," so I let them go eat.

Danny, Thad and Jeff had no issues with oatmeal and were quickly doctoring bowls of the hot goop with honey, raisins and powdered milk. I like a little pinch of salt with mine and quickly made up a bowl of my own.

Little Bit saw me add the salt and climbed up on a stool at the bar beside me, peering over the edge of the bowl. "You wanna bite?" I asked.

She scrunched her face up. "I guess."

I scooped out a spoonful and held it out to her. She blew on it for a second then took a little bite. Her face lit up and I smiled at her. "Want some?" She nodded her head. I slid my bowl over to her and told her to eat it, that I would get another for myself. Lee Ann and Taylor were eating and showed no sign of disappointment.

While we ate, we discussed the events of the previous night, what we needed to get done and trying to come up with a plan. Burying the bodies was the first priority. Getting some gas would be our next priority. We agreed that we would load gas cans on the four wheelers and go down to the Kangaroo to see if we could make a trade. Once breakfast was done, we headed out to get to work.

Danny and Jeff went out to the shop where we had left the two bodies. They were going to drag them out to the woods where we were going to bury them. In the meantime, I went to look for Reggie and his tractor.

I found Reggie at one of the houses that had burned the night before. He was wading through the wreckage of the house, trying to drag one of the three bodies out. There was a small audience gathered watching him. They were leaning on the fence in front of the house, just watching. Meanwhile, Reggie was standing knee-deep in ashes trying to wrench a burned corpse from what remained of the house.

I stopped as I came through the gate, and I was pissed. "Why don't some of you go help him?" I shouted to the gawkers.

With no more effort than a cat uses to look up as someone enters a room, one of them turned his head slightly and said, "They ain't our problem."

"Well, they damn sure aren't his either. He isn't related to anyone here!"

"He's got the tractor. I ain't got a tractor." The gawker turned his attention back to Reggie, resting his chin on his forearms.

Now I was really pissed. I jumped off the ATV, raising

my carbine to my shoulder. "Then get the fuck out of here, you lazy fuckers!"

They didn't even bother raising their heads to my shouts. The round I fired into the ground in front of them did get their attention, though. The four men and boy leaning on the fence jumped back, looking at me. "I said fucking get! Now!" They raised their hands and started to back off.

Reggie had stopped his labors and watched, shielding his eyes with his hand against the eastern sun. Once I was sure the onlookers were going to leave, I climbed back on the ATV and headed for the house. I left the carbine on the ATV and pulled a pair of gloves out of my cargo pocket, putting them on and wading into the ash and soot. Reggie smiled as I walked up to him, sticking a gloved hand out as I approached. "Thanks, brother."

I was still mad. "Fucking people. It's not enough that we defended their goddamn homes last night. Now we gotta clean up the mess too."

"I tried to get those assholes to help me, but they wouldn't. We can't just leave these bodies lying around or we'll all get sick."

"I know, man, there are some serious clingers around here."

Reggie and I worked together to drag the three bodies out. I hadn't known the family, but from the size of the bodies it appeared there were two adults and one teen. We tried to show respect to the bodies as we fought to free them from the house, but bodies burned as badly as these don't always hold together. We placed the bodies, all the pieces, one at a time into the bucket of Reggie's tractor, and he drove them over to the hole he had dug.

We used whatever we could find to wrap the bodies in: old

tarps, pieces of plastic, whatever, to keep them together. We put them in the hole and covered them up without ceremony. I wasn't religious, but it made me think that having a preacher around would be a good thing. There was so much to take care of and so much to worry about, we didn't have the energy to think about how to send the departed off properly.

As soon as we were done we headed for Danny's. We found Danny, Jeff and Thad out behind the house in the wood. They were sitting or leaning on the ATVs, the three bodies lying sprawled on the ground like discarded meat.

Reggie immediately went to work on the spot Danny pointed out, quickly digging a hole four or so feet deep. We didn't handle these bodies nearly as delicately. Thad pushed two of them into the hole with his foot and Jeff pulled the third over to the hole by a leg and simply let it slide in on top of the other two. Reggie filled the hole, running the tractor over the fresh dirt to pack it down.

With this part of the job done, we went to the house for a break. Bobbie brought a pitcher of tea and glasses out to the back porch for us. The five of us sat around on the chaise lounges and chairs scattered around and enjoyed the cool tea. Lee Ann and Taylor came out to sit with us. They asked what we had done with the bodies. We told them we had buried them. They asked where and Danny said they didn't need to worry about it.

Reggie said he would go check the other houses to see if there were any bodies there and take care of them if there were. He asked that we try to get some gas for him and I said that any we got would be for all of us to use. Danny went into the house to get some things to trade. He came out with a couple of bricks of .22 ammo. I told him I would get some things from the house when we got there.

Mel came out and said she wanted to go to the house, she had things she wanted to do. Lee Ann said she wanted to go too, and Taylor and Little Bit wanted to stay with Bobbie. We decided to go and try and trade for gas. We would make sure Mel got home with the Suburban and then the four of us would take the four-wheelers with as many gas cans as we could haul to the store and see what we could get. Jeff wanted to take his bike. He said, "I ain't gonna ride bitch behind Thad."

I looked at him with a grin. "What, you skeered to wrap your arms around him?"

Thad said, "You can sit in front if you want, lil' fella. I can reach around you and still grab the handlebars."

Danny spit tea out of his nose, I started to laugh and, of course, Thad started that deep baritone laugh of his. Jeff shook his head. "Fuck you, assholes, I'm going to get my bike." He headed for the gate with all of us still laughing.

The rest of us climbed onto our machines and I stopped to pick Jeff up. "Come on, I'll take you to the house." He gave me a look then hopped onto the rear rack, facing back.

At my house, I made sure Mel had her pistol. I had to make her put on a holster and wear it. I went to the shop and dropped a couple of canned hams and a couple cans of SPAM in my pack. Almost as an afterthought, I picked up a can of Coleman white gas. Back outside I could hear Jeff's scooter coming down the road. He stopped at the gate and waited for us. The three of us got on our machines and headed out.

As Thad passed through the gate, he slowed to say something to Jeff. I couldn't hear because Jeff was gunning the throttle on the old Harley. He had his hand cupped to his ear and was shouting, "I can't hear you, I can't hear you!" I watched as Thad's huge head rocked back on his shoulders, laughing as he pulled out of the gate. As Danny and I passed him, Jeff gunned the throttle, ensuring nothing was said.

Jeff quickly passed the three of us and as he did I noticed the Mosin was in the scabbard as he went by. Rene's dad John was at the barricade as we passed by. He waved and smiled at me. I was glad to see him out now and I thought things must have been getting better for him. I reminded myself to go check on Rene, and Miss Janice and Howard, for that matter. The four of us pulled out on the road, turning left, heading for the store.

I was surprised to see the number of people on the road. Traveling in ones, twos and what appeared to be family groups, they were all heading toward the forest. This made it even more curious. Why the forest? As we passed, some turned and looked at us as we went by—not for long, but they were certainly checking us out.

I hadn't been to the store in a while. Jeff was in the lead and stopped short of the store. We all stopped as we came to him, seeing the reason. The parking lot was full of people. There was what looked like a line, disorganized, forming at some tables. A couple of guys in uniforms were standing at the entrance off 19 and were looking at us looking at them.

"What do you think?" Jeff asked as we pulled up.

"Don't know, let's go see," Danny replied.

We started toward the store. Danny was in the lead and as he came up to the entrance, the men there held up a hand to stop us. One of them was just dripping in tacticool shit. He couldn't have been more than five foot tall, yet he had to be carrying eighty pounds of crap. He was wearing a tac vest that was stuffed with magazines, a pistol in a drop-leg holster and a massive knife that would have brought out Rambo's O face. The vest was adorned with all sort of morale patches, numbering nearly as many as the gadgets hanging from his AR. We all slowed as the mall ninja walked out. "What can we do for you?"

"We want to trade," Danny said.

The guy looked us over. "Who you guys with?" he asked, looking at me.

I pointed to Thad beside me on his quad. "I'm with them, they're with me."

He wasn't amused. "No, I mean who are guys *with*. We're with the North Lake Militia."

I looked at Danny and shrugged. "We aren't with any militia," Danny said.

While Danny was talking to the guy, another walked up. This one was different. He wasn't as tacticool and was wearing what looked like a real uniform. He wasn't looking at us so much as he was looking at what we were sitting on. He stopped and took a long look at the machines. I watched him. He looked up at me, holding his gaze for just a moment too long.

"Can I help you?" I asked.

Taking another look at the machines, he asked, "Where'd you get these ATVs?"

"What's it matter to you?"

Danny was ignoring the little guy he was talking to. Thad and Jeff were both looking at the newcomer, Thad with far more interest than any of us.

"Where you guys from?" the new guy asked.

"Down the road," I replied.

"Down the road," he repeated with a grin, dropping his head slightly. "What's your name, there, friend?"

Thad caught my eye and shook his head. I looked back to my questioner and said, "Haywood."

"Haywood what?" the questioner asked with a dour look.

"Jablowme," I replied with a smile.

A slight grin cracked his face. He lowered his eyes, scuffing at the sand on the road with the toe of his boot. Raising his eyes back to mine, he said, "Well, Haywood, I'm sure we'll see each other again."

As he was speaking, I looked past him at the crowd. There was a table where it looked like people were turning in firearms. It was stacked with long guns of all sorts and there was a bin on the ground in which handguns were being dropped. A spindly legged woman started toward us with two more of what appeared to be the militiamen following her. She was carrying a can of Vienna Sausages, from which she would extract a tube of meat, suck the jelly off, then push into her mouth. Even from this distance I could see she didn't have any teeth and used her tongue and gums to mash the meat by-product to the point she could swallow it.

"What're 'ese fellers lookin' fer, Billy?" she said as she tossed the can to the ground, adding to the already considerable amount of litter already covering the parking lot.

The militiaman cocked his head slightly toward her. "They say they want to trade for some gas."

The old woman cackled, her lips curling around her bare gums. "I don't need no dayam gas. 'Bout all I got is gas."

"We want to *get* some gas," Danny said.

"Oh, ya need some? Well, what'cha tradin'?" she asked.

Slipping my pack off and opening it, I took out one of the hams. "How about something better than Vienna Sausages?"

Her face broke into the collapsed grin common to toothless people. "Now yer talkin'. I like them!"

"We want to fill all these cans. How about two of these and two cans of SPAM?" I offered.

She looked at the back of the ATVs with all the cans. We had a total of nine five-gallon cans between the three machines. "That's a bunch of gas; what else ya got?"

Pulling the can of white gas from my pack, I set it on the fender. "I don't really want to trade this, but the canned meat and this for all the cans filled."

"Deal. Lyle, you an' Billy bring 'em in an' fill thur cans." She started toward me with her hands out.

"Ah, no offense, ma'am, but I'll give this to you once the cans are full."

She chuckled. "Don' worry, you'll get yer gas. Billy, bring me the goods when yer done."

With that she turned and headed back for the store, her two guards in tow. We pulled the ATVs up to a spot in the parking lot where the fuel trucks usually filled the underground tanks. Another man was there, and he pulled the cap from one of the tanks and dropped a hose in connected to a hand pump. It took him a minute of furious pumping to get it to prime, but once it did he went straight to work filling the cans. While he worked, Thad and Jeff stood watch, watching the crowd gathering at the tables. Danny and I talked with old Billy to see what he knew.

"What's with the lines?" Danny asked Billy pointing toward the tables.

"That's where you sign up for assistance from FEMA. There are camps they can take you to."

"Who was that other guy?" I asked Billy pointing toward the other uniformed man who had been questioning me.

"They're with DHS, providing security for the FEMA folks."

"And what are you and the militia doing? Danny asked.

"We provide security for Sharon there. She was the manager of the store and since things have gone to shit, she's just sort of taken over. She tries to trade for things, keep the store working, sort of, but it's running out of everything."

"DHS doesn't mind you guys being armed? I remember hearing a radio address where they said guns were now illegal," Danny asked.

"We work with 'em, we help 'em out and kind of help with manpower when they need it and they leave us alone."

I glanced at Danny and he frowned. I knew he was thinking the same thing I was: here was a militia that prior to the event I was sure was decidedly antigovernment. Now they were working alongside them to keep some sort of autonomy.

"You guys hear anything about raids going on, groups hitting neighborhoods and burning houses down an' all?" Danny asked.

Billy jerked his head toward the tables. "Why you think all them people is here? It's been going on all over. They say that gangs come in an' raid houses, shoot people, steal anything they can get their hands on and leave. They set fire to any house they can't get into. Some even say they're taking women an' girls."

"Has anyone fought them off?" I asked.

"Not that I heard. They come in at night, sometimes on four-wheelers; sometimes they just walk in and are there before anyone knows it."

"What are you guys doing about it?" Danny asked.

The question caught Billy off guard. "Wha'daya mean?"

"You guys say you're a militia. What are you doing to help people?" Danny asked.

Thad came up and motioned for me to follow him. I

walked over to where Jeff was standing. He was watching a small knot of the DHS security guards watch him.

"What's up?" I asked.

They went on to tell me that the DHS security had been particularly interested in us since we arrived. They had made a couple of passes by the ATVs and Jeff said they were obviously trying to get some info off the machines. Thad said they had been on the radio. They both thought we needed to get the hell out of there before things got sticky. I agreed and went back to where the cans were being filled.

Danny was strapping three of them down when I got back. The man pumping the fuel had one more can to go. I handed the canned goods and the white gas to Billy and quickly started to strap three cans to the back of my Polaris. Danny carried the other two over to Thad's machine and set them on the rear rack. As soon as the last can was full, I took it over to Danny. He set it on the rack and went to strap them all down.

"Well, Billy, thanks for the gas. Tell Sharon there we'll be back sometime for some more."

Billy nodded at me as I climbed on the machine and started it. Somewhere behind me I heard Jeff's scooter roar to life. Without talking about it, we started out in single file for the house.

Chapter 30

"First Sergeant Mitchell?" a voice called from the front of the barracks.

"Back here," Sarge replied, sitting up. He swung his legs off his rack and shoved his feet into his boots. Not taking time to tie them, he headed for the sound of the voice.

Sarge found a sergeant in ACU BDUs waiting by the front door. The man said, "Colonel Fawcet sent me over to take you to the motor pool to pick up your new ride."

"Outstanding." Sarge turned and shouted into the squad bay and yelled, "Come on, you dickheads. We got work to do!"

After a moment Ted, Mike and Doc came walking out. "What's up?" Doc asked.

"We gotta go get some gear," Sarge said.

They went out and climbed into a Humvee waiting out front. The sergeant drove through the base while Sarge and the guys took in the view. As they passed a small stadium, they saw a lot of armed guards. "What's with that?" Ted asked the sergeant as they passed.

"That's where we put all the DHS guys."

Sarge looked out the window. "Why's it always a stadium? You people should read some history."

"What?" the sergeant asked.

Sarge didn't reply. He just looked out the window as one

of the DHS was being led to a waiting Humvee, hands bound behind his back and a hood over his head. The Humvee wheeled into a drive and pulled around behind a large, squat brown brick building. As they passed through a gate at the midpoint of the building, all the equipment parked there came into view. The Humvee stopped at a large roll-up door that was open. There were several small UTV-style vehicles sitting in the open bay.

The sergeant jumped out of the Humvee and called out into the cavernous bay. Sarge and the guys climbed out and stood together in front of the open door. From the bowels of the building came a cursed response. The sergeant said, "Watch yer manners; we got comp'ny."

Shortly, a thickset fireplug of a man appeared from behind a couple of large tool boxes. He had a rag in his hands, wiping grease from them. A cigar-shaped object protruded from his mouth. As he approached, the object swapped sides.

"What the hell you want, Martin?"

"This is First Sergeant Mitchell; he's here to pick up your toys."

The burly man bristled. "I don't know who you are, or what yer up to, but I do know I don't want to give these to you."

Sarge looked him up and down. "Master Sergeant, I assure you I will show your toys as much love and care as you have."

Master Sergeant Antonio Faggione looked the older first sergeant before him up and down. Taking the cigar shape from his mouth, he replied, "Somehow I doubt that."

Sarge smiled. "Is that a cigar you got there, or a piece of cat shit you're chewin' on?" Mike started to snicker, Ted was laughing on the inside, and Doc rolled his eyes in a "here we go again" way.

Sergeant Martin, who was standing beside Sarge, breathed a low "Oh shit."

Faggione looked at the object in his hand, then back to Sarge before putting the Tootsie Roll back in the corner of his mouth. "If I only had a cigar. I gave up cat shit years ago. Just couldn't get the taste outta my mouth."

Sarge smiled, gesturing to the two machines behind the master sergeant he asked, "These beauties mine?"

Faggione smiled. "No, they're mine, but if you're nice I may let you use them."

"Very well, I wanna take one for a spin."

"Not until I check you out on them," Faggione said.

Sarge jutted a thumb over his shoulder. "Check *them* out. I have an errand to run." He stepped up into the smaller of the two machines and started it. Before Faggione could protest, Sarge was pulling out of the bay and racing down the road.

Sarge headed for the barracks, impressed with the speed and feel of the machine he was in. He would have some questions for Faggione when he got back. Pulling up to the front door, Sarge leapt out and ran into the old building, heading straight for the stack of gear they had salvaged from the truck. He started pulling out cases and boxes.

Inside the cardboard box, he found two jars and set them aside, then went back to the cases, looking for one in particular. Finding the small case, he pulled it out of the pile, picked up the jars and headed for the door. Setting the loot in the passenger seat, he climbed in, started the machine and headed for the motor pool, keeping a hand on the stash beside him so it didn't roll out.

When he got to the gate of the motor pool, he stopped for a moment, picking up the small case and opening it. Reaching in, he took out one of the dark silky cigars. Sarge didn't smoke very often, but he liked the occasional cigar. On a trip through North Carolina he had stopped at JR's Cigars and bought a box of Rocky Patel 1990 vintage Robustos. Rolling the oily cigar between his thumb and forefinger, he fished out his Zippo, set it on the seat and went into his pocket for his knife. After cutting the tip, he stuck it in his mouth and lit it, drawing the thick smoke in and blowing out a cloud.

Sarge gripped the cigar with his teeth—he had to because he was grinning so hard—put the machine in gear and headed for the back of the building. When he came up to the open bay door, Faggione had his back to him. Sarge stopped and propped a foot up on the dash of the machine and took a long drag on the cigar. When he finished the point he was making to the guys, Faggione turned around, and just as he did Sarge blew a couple of perfect smoke rings at him.

Faggione stood there looking at Sarge. His eyes were mere slits in the hunk of meat on his shoulders. After a moment the Tootsie Roll hit the ground and he stepped toward Sarge. Sarge took the cigar from his mouth, holding it out as to admire it, then looked at Faggione.

"Nothing better than a quality smoke, huh, Master Sergeant?"

Faggione crossed his arms over his chest. "What'cha got there, a White Owl, or maybe a Dutch Masters? You don't look to me like the kind of guy that can 'preciate a decent smoke."

Sarge tucked the cigar back in his teeth and picked up one

of the jars, spinning the lid off. "Not only do I appreciate a good smoke, I also appreciate a good drink." Plucking the stogie from his mouth, Sarge took a pull from the jar, trying hard not to squint.

"Well, aren't you just full of surprises."

Sarge stuck the cigar back in his mouth and grinned at him, then reached over and picked up the case with the cigars. "Would you care for one?" he asked, holding the box out.

Faggione stepped over and peered into the case. "Patel, nice cigar." He reached in and took one, inspecting the band. "Vintage, even," he said with an approving nod. Faggione reached into his pocket, took out a cutter, clipped the end and quickly produced a lighter, struck it and puffed the cigar to life. Taking in a deep drag, his eyes closed and his head rocked back slightly, gripping it between his fingers he pulled the cigar from his lips, followed by a slow thick cloud of smoke.

"First Sergeant Mitchell, I think you an' me is gonna get along just fine."

Sarge smiled, his cigar clamped in his teeth. He took one of the jars and tossed it to Faggione. Faggione spun the lid off, held it to his nose for moment and sniffed. Then put the jar to his lips and took a long drink, swishing the hard liquor in his mouth and swallowed it with no more consideration than he would a drink of water.

"Mighty fine, mighty fine," Faggione said.

"Hey, what about us?" Ted asked.

"Forget it, you're on duty, dipshit," Sarge replied.

Faggione's cigar was planted in the corner of his mouth. "Come in here and let me introduce you to your newest love," Faggione said as Sarge climbed out of the machine.

Danny pulled up beside me. "We got company!" he shouted, nodding his head over his shoulder.

I looked back to see another ATV behind us. When I looked back, so did the other guys. We slowed down, coming abreast of one another. Thad asked what we thought about the guy. We had no idea what he was up to but decided not to go straight back to the neighborhood. It was Danny's idea to take a trail into the forest. It was just ahead of where we were and wound its way into the back of the neighborhood without having to get back out on the road. Jeff said he'd take the guy for a tour of the area and the three of us turned off as Jeff sped off down the paved road.

As we rode through the forest, we stopped occasionally to see if we were being followed but, never hearing anyone, we eventually found our way back to the neighborhood. The way we came in brought us in beside Miss Janice's house. Seeing her house made me think of the ATV tracks we had seen and the men she said she saw back there. As we came out of the woods, I pulled up to her house and Danny and Thad followed me.

The three of us sat on the ATVs looking at the house. We would have to go in and look, but even from here I knew it wasn't going to be good. The front door was caved in.

"Who lives here?" Thad asked.

"An old lady. We brought her some food not too long ago," Danny said.

"By herself?" Thad asked.

"Yeah, by herself. Danny, you want to come with me to look?" I said.

"Not really, but I guess we need to."

"I'll go around back and make sure no one is out there," Thad said.

Danny and I slowly approached the door with our rifles at low ready. Stopping at the shattered door, we peered in. Miss Janice's feet were sticking out from behind the island in the kitchen. We slowly entered the living room. Danny went to the left and I went to the right. There was a door on my right. I opened it and saw the master bedroom. I did a quick check and found it empty. Quickly crossing the living room, I caught up to Danny as he backed out of the bathroom. Together we cleared the other two bedrooms. The house was empty except for Miss Janice.

She had been strangled. There was deep, dark bruising around her neck. Her eyes were bloodshot and her mouth was open. Looking down at her I could just imagine the ter-rified scream that those hands choked off; even dead she looked scared. We never said anything, Danny and I. He went to one of the bedrooms down the hall, returning with a sheet. We spread the sheet out over her. I knelt down and raised it from her face and closed her eyes, then gently laid the sheet back over her.

Thad was out front when we came out the door. "She dead?"

Danny nodded and we all climbed aboard our machines and headed for Danny's house. Once there we unloaded all the cans of fuel into his shop, throwing an old tarp over them. Danny stepped back, looking at the tarp, and said, "That didn't cost us too much."

"Speak for yourself, there, sport," I said. He looked over, his head cocked to the side. I smiled. "I'd rather not trade ammo if we can avoid it, 'sides, I got more cooked an' canned pig innards."

Thad said, "There's cost and there's *cost*, if you get my meaning. We're on somebody's radar now, I guarantee you that. I don't think we should go back there no more."

"Yeah," I said. "You're probably right about that."

Reggie came down the drive toward us and said, "I slaughtered a hog and have it on the smoker. Tomorrow we'll have some good eats." That broke the suddenly solemn mood.

"Damn, that sounds good!" Thad shouted, rubbing his stomach.

"Well, I had to. I'm running out of feed for 'em, gonna have to start slaughtering 'em all."

"There's got to be something we can feed 'em; I mean, they'll eat anything," Danny said.

"I'm open for ideas," Reggie said, shaking his head.

"Hell, I doubt there's a chicken or pig left around here, 'cept for my birds and your pigs. We need to try and keep 'em around if we can," I said.

We all stood there for a minute thinking about the problem, trying to come up with ideas, after a minute Jeff spoke up. "I got nuthin'. I don't know shit about 'bout pigs 'cept I like bacon." This brought another round of chuckles.

Thad said, "Hell, you can turn 'em out to feed. They'll keep comin' back so long as they know you got feed for 'em. I done it myself."

"Think they'd eat swamp cabbage?" Danny asked him.

"'Course. Damn things are like goats."

It would take some work, but there was plenty of it around—swamp cabbage. Danny and Reggie immediately agreed to head off and see what they could do, how much work it would take to get to a whole heart of one of those palm trees. Danny grabbed an axe and a machete and headed for the gate with Reggie.

Reggie stopped and turned back to the three of us still standing in front of the shop. "How much gas did we get?"

"Filled nine cans. If you need some, it's in here," I replied, pointing to the shop.

Reggie nodded, gave a wave and turned to catch up to Danny. Thad and I talked for a minute about what we needed to get done. We needed to bury the old lady, but we agreed to wait for Reggie to get back and use his tractor. In the meantime we decided to go up to the barricade and see how the foot traffic on the road looked. Just as we were pulling out, Jeff showed up.

"How'd it go?" I asked him.

"Took him on the scenic tour, like I said. Eventually he gave up. He must have known I could have outrun him, and I'm guessing he put that together with the fact that you guys were gone and figured I was just screwing him around."

Thad said, "You did good, but I'm warning you guys: don't think this is over. That guy's gonna have a pretty good idea of where he lost us, and people already been over those trails out back of Miss Janice's house. I'll tell you another thing: you remember the way that guy was looking at you at the market? The guy you said Haywood Jablowme to?"

"Yeah," I said.

"It didn't piss him off none, you notice that?"

"Yeah, he was a pretty cool customer."

"What's that tell you? It means he's probably got bigger fish to fry. But when he gets around to it, I bet you he's got the time and the manpower to find where we're at. And he ain't gonna forget you pissed on his boots."

I hadn't liked the look the guy gave me, but I hadn't taken it as far as Thad had either. I knew he'd been through some bad shit, and I knew this was something I should listen to him on. "I hear you," I said. "I don't know what we can do about it right now, though."

"We can get ready, that's what. I thought I was ready, but I wasn't. I ain't gonna make that mistake again. I mean, shit, you thought you were takin' care of Miss Janice, right?"

That made me kind of mad. "You saying I wasn't?"

"Don't get all pissed, Morg. I'm sayin' you were doin' what you thought you should be doin': takin' her food, checking up on her. But I'm also sayin' that that ain't gonna be enough anymore. We gotta get ready for some bad shit, because it's out there."

That calmed me down some, and he was right. Jeff wanted to know about Miss Janice, and we told him. That left all three of us in a down mood.

The three of us rode down to the roadblock and were pissed to find it unmanned. The gabions we had constructed were still waiting to be filled with dirt, but it wouldn't really matter if they were filled or not if no one was around to keep an eye on the area.

We didn't say anything. Each of us, I'm sure, were running the possibilities through our minds. There had been steady stream of people walking north on Highway 19. It wasn't a mob, but it was growing. We had seen some of them on the way over, and a few were passing as we sat on our machines. The people walking along the road were carrying backpacks and bags of all sorts. I saw more than one grown man wearing a pack for a child, and it reminded me of the shows about the border where the immigrants would be trying to walk from Mexico to the US with a Hello Kitty backpack. A few of them were dragging rolling-style luggage, or maybe a wagon with bundles in it and a child or two.

Our presence didn't go unnoticed. We drew a few looks from some of the passersby. The gaunt faces showed little emotion; they simply shuffled along. Despair, hopelessness and desperation, that's what came to mind looking at them—blank windows into abandoned building. We sat for a while watching the march of the hopeless and helpless. Thad spoke up and said he would stay on the barricade tonight, and Jeff immediately agreed he would stay too.

"This is what I was talking about; we gotta be prepared, gotta get organized. We can't leave this open, not with all these people walking right by the front door," Thad said shaking his head.

"I'll bring dinner up to you guys in a bit. Anything else y'all need?" I asked.

"Coffee," Thad said flatly.

"Lots of it," Jeff added.

"All right, guys, I'll bring it down in a bit. You guys have a flashlight?"

"Naw, I don't," Thad replied, looking at Jeff, who just shook his head.

"I'll bring one down as well. I'll even bring the NVGs. Shit, we shoulda done that earlier. If Lance and them had had NVGs, well, you know what I mean. I don't want to lose you guys too."

Reggie and Danny went back to Reggie's place. There were plenty of cabbage palms on his place and they would check on the smoker. Reggie pulled the ATV to a stop beside the old propane tank he had converted into a smoker. Lifting the top exposed the whole hog lying on the expanded metal cooking surface. Reggie had skinned the pig, cut its head off and cracked its shoulders and pelvis to lay it out flat. In the firebox on the side of the smoker, a pile of cured oak smoldered, and a pan of water sat on the grate beside the pig. Not seeing anything that needed addressed at the moment, he dropped the lid.

Together, the two of them walked out across the pasture toward the rear of Reggie's property. Danny was carrying the axe and machete, his AR slung across his back. Reggie had his head down, looking at the ground as he walked. Without looking up, he said, "Wonder how much we'll get out of one of these."

"Don't know. I've never cut out a whole one before. I like 'em, though," Danny replied.

"Never had it."

Danny looked over. "It's good. Morgan's little one loves the stuff. Every time we go in the woods she keeps us busy pulling up palmetto hearts." A smile spread over his face and over Reggie's too. Danny was one of those good-natured, perpetually upbeat people, and his attitude was infectious.

As they approached the chosen tree, Reggie asked what the plan was. Danny said they had to cut all the fronds off and start cutting the tree open. Reggie stuck his hand out and Danny handed him the machete. Hefting the big blade in his right hand, he lopped the first of the fronds, working his way toward the trunk of the tree. Danny was standing behind him holding the axe as Reggie hacked at the tree.

Reggie grabbed a particularly long frond and chopped it from the base of the tree. "Sumbitch!" he shouted as turned to run from the tree, swinging the big blade in the air around him. "Shit!" Reggie ran from a horde of mahogany wasps that were tearing his ass up. The bad part was he was still holding the frond their nest was attached to.

"Drop it, drop the palm!" Danny was backpedaling, trying to keep some distance between himself and the hoard. Reggie finally dropped the frond and ran toward the barn, where Danny caught up with him.

"Goddamn, they hurt!" Reggie bellowed, rubbing various parts of his head, neck and arms.

Danny was laughing. He was trying not to, but he couldn't help himself. Reggie looked up at him and said, "That shit ain't funny!"

Danny finally broke out into uncontrollable laughter. "You were running from 'em, but draggin' 'em behind you the whole time."

Reggie was pissed and rubbing a particularly painful sting on his cheek under his right eye. "Hey, how's 'is look?"

Danny walked up and looked seriously at Reggie for a second. "Hard to tell."

"What'da mean hard to tell?"

"Hard to tell with all the ugly around it." Danny broke out into laughter again.

"Asshole!" Reggie shouted and reached out to grab Danny, who easily dodged.

"Come on, biggun, let's go get some cabbage for them pigs."

They were far more careful on the subsequent attempts and managed to get the hearts of a couple palms. Reggie wasn't sure if the pigs would eat it. Danny cut a piece off and handed it to him. "Try it."

Reggie sniffed the white succulent flesh, then hesitantly put it to his lips, taking a small bite. After he chewed it for a moment, his eyebrows went up, "Hell, that ain't bad." The pigs did indeed like it, not that they were very particular. As Thad had demonstrated, they'd eat about anything.

Back at the house, Mel packed up a nice supper for the guys. She had made a big pot of spaghetti using venison and some jarred sauce from the pantry. There wasn't much else, but there was a big bowl for each of them. She made a fresh pot of coffee and poured it into two stainless thermoses. While she was pouring the coffee, I filled a half-gallon Igloo jug with tea to add to it. That much caffeine should keep them up all damn night. And that made me think that two guys weren't enough for a real watch. I trusted Thad and Jeff to stay awake, but what about the others who pulled the duty? There was too much to think about, and what Thad had said started to get to me: maybe things were unraveling at the edges but I was too busy putting out fires to see it.

Their dinner was packed into a cooler that I strapped on the back of the Polaris. Little Bit came running out as I tightened the last strap and asked if she could come with me. Since all I was doing was taking them dinner, I said she could.

"I wanna drive, Daddy, I know how!" she cried.

"Okay, you sit in front and drive."

"But you gotta get me through the gate. I can't do that yet, but then I get to drive."

"Go tell your momma you're going with me."

She turned and ran back into the house. I made sure the cooler was secure and climbed onto the ATV. Since she was coming, I slung the AR on my back so it didn't bang against her. I hit the starter as she came back out the door. With the ease only a child possesses, she was up and on the machine in the blink of an eye. She reached out and grabbed the handlebars. "Let's go!"

I maneuvered us through the gate and she took over, steering us down the road. I had to remind her to take it easy on the gas, but she did a good job. Thad and Jeff were leaned over one of the barricades, casually watching the slow but steady procession of people heading north into the forest. Jeff looked back over his shoulder as we approached. Little Bit let off the gas and braked us to a stop. Jeff smiled and looked at her and said, "You let him drive?"

She smiled. "He has to get me through the gate, but I can do it after that."

Thad asked, "What's for dinner?"

"Skapetti!" Little Bit shouted back.

"Sounds good to me," Jeff said, rubbing his hands.

"Well, come on over and get something to eat," I said.

I opened the cooler and handed each of them a bowl. While they ate, Little Bit and I hung out. She stepped up onto one of the logs so she could watch the people go by. Between bites of pasta and swigs of either coffee or tea, we talked about the traffic going by. They said no one had come and stopped to talk to them.

Jeff had sauce all over his face. "Where's the napkins?"

I looked at him like he was stupid. "Use your sleeve."

"I ain't gonna use my sleeve," he said. "You know how hard it is to wash clothes these days? Damn, Morgan."

Thad smiled, his head over the bowl and noodles hanging from his mouth.

"Use *his* sleeve," I said to Jeff, nodding my head at Thad.

Thad slurped the noodles up with a smack. "Ain't using my sleeve either," he said with a smile.

Little Bit brought our attention back to what was going

on out on the road. There was a little girl approaching the barricade. The two were smiling and waving at one another. In and of itself, this wouldn't be a concern, but it caused her mother and father to move our direction as well. The dad was pulling a wagon with a younger child sitting in it wrapped in blanket. Even though it was bundled like the kid from *A Christmas Story*, it was obvious the child was gaunt and malnourished.

I looked at the little girl, who was now just on the other side of the logs from Little Bit. The little girl had long blonde hair, and she too looked too thin. It was kind of hard to see it as she was wearing a coat that was too big for her, but the little leggings that hung from her shouted the fact.

"Amy, come back over here," her mother called.

"Dad, can we give her some skapetti?" Little Bit asked.

The face of the little girl lit up. "I like sketti!"

The woman looked up at me, then back to Thad and Jeff and their dinner sitting on the cooler. She crossed her arms and looked at us, and her husband soon joined her. We should have known this would happen. They weren't eating on the side of the road, but they were close. The man looked at his wife, then at Jeff and Thad, who by now were standing in front of the ATV. He couldn't see the cooler with the bowls on it.

"What's going on?" the man asked.

"They got sketti, Daddy," the little girl replied.

I reached out and grabbed Little Bit by the shoulder and pulled her back, trying to maneuver her behind me. Being a child, she didn't catch on to what was happening and stopped at my side.

"I'm sorry, we don't have any extra food," I said.

The man looked at me, then at Little Bit, then at Jeff and Thad. "Y'all don't look like you been missin' many meals." He paused for a moment and looked at Little Bit, then added, "Neither does she."

This scared her and she moved behind me, holding on to my waist. I reached back and patted her shoulder. Thad and Jeff stepped up behind me, one on either side. The man looked at us with contempt on his face.

"Look at you assholes. You don't look too damn miserable." He pointed at me and said, "Got all them guns, what are you doin', goin' 'round robbin' yer neighbors?"

"No, actually we've been burying them lately," I said. I started to add something about raiders and the need to be armed, but decided at the last moment against it. I made a decision and leaned toward the man. He stepped back in fright. I said, "Look, here's how we're gonna do this. I can't have everyone walking down the road asking for food. We don't have enough; we just don't. You wait till there's no one who can see and then bring your family over here. You stand on this side of the barricade while you eat so no one else comes asking. When you're done, you go. I'm sorry, mister, but that's the way it has to be."

His bitter face fell and suddenly he was crying. "You serious?"

"As a heart attack. You think you can do what I said?"

"Sure, mister."

"And when dinner's done, you got to move on. I wish we had a place for you here, but we don't, okay?"

The man nodded through his tears and went to tell his wife.

"Are we gonna help them, Daddy?" Little Bit asked quietly.

"Yeah, baby. But you understand we can't help everybody, right? We want to, but we can't."

"I understand," she said, but I doubted she really did.

"Take her home, Morg. They can have the rest of our dinner," Thad said.

"No, I'll go get some more. Just make sure no one sees, okay? It has to look like they're with us. I don't want to come back here and find a fucking bread line."

"Yeah, man, we got it," Jeff said.

"All right, come on, baby girl." I reached down and put a hand on her back.

I climbed up on the Polaris and pulled her up, planting her on the seat in front of me. "You gonna drive?" I asked.

She sat there with her hands in her lap and said, "No, you do it."

"Hey, did you bring the goggles?" Thad asked.

"Oh yeah." I took a case off the front of the ATV and handed it to Thad. "Just in case."

Thad smiled at me, that big smile, and took them. "Just in case."

We rode back in silence. I tried to make her laugh, goosing the throttle and rocking the ATV, swerving, just playing, but she sat stoic, not reacting. When we got to the house I set her off and she headed for the house. I followed her in and she went to my room and climbed into the bed, pulling the down comforter up over her head.

Mel asked what was wrong with her. I told her about the little girl, that she was probably sad. Another little girl, just like her, and she knew even though we gave them dinner, they probably wouldn't have breakfast the next day, or lunch, or dinner.

Mel went into our room. I felt bad but I didn't really

know what to do. I put together some more food and ran it out to the barricade. The family was there tucking into the spaghetti. They were grateful and shook my hand, but I was glad I wasn't going to be there when Thad and Jeff had to move them along.

I drove back home and went to the shop. The laptop that Jeff had rigged to my radio was sitting on the bench. Flipping open the screen, I hit the POWER button and watched as the Windows logo appeared. It felt kind of good to see, like it wasn't all gone, like it wasn't all over.

When it booted up and was ready, I opened the program and typed *Where are you, old man? We could use some help.* After turning on the radio and verifying the frequency, I tapped the ENTER key and watched as the little LEDs started to blink. The little box squawked like a fax machine.

Chapter 31

Sarge was stacking gear, sorting out what he wanted to take and what he felt they could do without for now. Mike, Ted and Doc were going through their gear, distributing the extra ammo they had received as well as some of the other trash. They now had two vehicles. One looked sort of like a Raptor UTV, only armored and with seats for four. The second one was larger and could hold seven men. Sarge had decided to use the larger of the two as his. It had some rather interesting goodies onboard and Faggione had taken great delight in demonstrating its capabilities to him.

The buggy had a telescoping mast that held a thermal and conventional camera. There was an LCD display mounted in the cockpit that could be viewed from either of the front seats. Each entry point of the vehicle had a weapon mount, and there was also one on top. The gunner stood on a platform behind the roll cage. It had a cargo area that was being filled with packs, bags and assorted gear. Fuel was going to be the biggest concern. To address this issue, Faggione provided a trailer. The sides of the trailer were armored with a double layer of thin steel. The plates were armor-grade steel and the two layers meant that even if a round penetrated the outer layer, it would just bounce around inside the void. At least that was the theory.

The trailer would be packed with fuel cans and any additional gear that wouldn't fit in the two buggies. Their mission was pretty simple: find places where the feds were in numbers and report back so that appropriate actions could be taken against them. Beyond that, the orders were *real* simple: persecute any target of opportunity.

Sarge had gone to the quartermaster with a list of what he wanted. The colonel had told him that if he needed anything to let him know, and Sarge could have done that, but old habits died hard. Instead, he kept the folks in supply busy trying to find impossible items while the guys cut a fence and went to work. They had driven both buggies straight there from the motor pool and helped themselves to what they needed.

Sarge was berating a corporal when Ted wheeled around to the open bay door of the old Quonset hut. Seeing Ted, Sarge looked at the bewildered corporal and said, "Never mind, you're useless as tits on a boar!" and stomped off to the buggy. Climbing in, he looked over at Ted, who just smiled and started to move forward. Sarge put a boot up on the dash of the machine and said, "Good."

Mike and Doc were already back at the barracks when Ted and Sarge returned. Mike was leaning in the doorway, and as Sarge stepped out he said, "You've got mail."

I sat there absentmindedly watching the little lights blink. Looking over at the door, it was obvious that something would have to be done about it tomorrow, but right now I just really didn't care. I should have felt good about feeding those people, but I didn't, both because it took food out the mouths of my own family and because I knew it wouldn't help in the end. Just like all the people who had gone before them, they were going to end up in the forest and starve. And who knew what horrible things might happen to them before then.

I headed back into the house. Mel was sitting on the couch reading a book to Little Bit. Her sisters were lying on the floor in front of the fireplace reading books as well. I took off my coat and hung it on the hooks by the door. Mel looked up at me and smiled, and Little Bit craned her head around and smiled too. That did a lot to mend my mood.

I flopped down in my chair and put my feet up on the ottoman. It was quiet and the fire was nice. I sat there staring into the fire while Mel finished reading *Where the Sidewalk Ends*. When she was done we all sat in the quiet for a bit. Little Bit fell asleep and Mel motioned for me. I picked her up and carried her to her room. She snuggled against me and I dropped my face into her hair. It smelled like it always did, a scent that is hard to describe but could only be that of a little girl.

I laid her in her bed and pulled the quilt up over her. Back in the living room, Lee Ann and Taylor were talking to Mel. We sat there for little while chatting. Mainly they were telling us about the books they were reading. I sat there looking at them as they talked. They seemed so normal, so out of touch with what was going on. But I was glad—glad they weren't sitting around worrying all the time. For now anyway they could enjoy their youth.

Mel announced it was bedtime and surprisingly the girls didn't complain. Lee Ann rolled over and stretched, yawning. They got up and came over to my chair, where I had planted myself after putting Little Bit to bed. Each of them gave me a hug, then Mel, saying good night. As they headed for their rooms, Lee Ann said, "Dad, can you come say good night?"

"I just did."

"No, I mean in my room?"

I smiled at her and for a brief second wondered how much longer she would do that. "Of course. I always do." I sat for another minute and then went to say good night to the girls.

Mel was in our room getting undressed when I came in. She was leaning over kicking her jeans off and I walked up and slapped her on the butt. She looked over her shoulder at me and smiled. Then I realized my rifle was leaning by the front door.

"I gotta get my rifle," I said as I opened the door.

"Hurry up," I looked back to see Mel patting the bed.

I went out and picked up my rifle and made the rounds to make sure all the doors were locked then headed for the bedroom. The lamp on my side of the bed was still on when I came back in and Mel was peeking out from under the covers at me; all I could see were her eyes. I leaned the rifle against the wall beside the bed and started to undress.

"Take off your utility belt, Batman."

"Batman?"

"Look at all the crap you carry around."

"I got your Batman right here."

I climbed under the comforter and reached over and turned off the light, then rolled over.

"Oh, Batman," Mel said, and I couldn't help it and started to giggle. Mel was soon giggling too.

As had become my custom, I woke up about five thirty in the morning. Pulling on a pair of flannel PJ pants, I picked up the XD and headed for the kitchen to start the coffee.

Once the coffee was brewing on the stove, I looked out the sliding glass door at the shop; it was just like I'd left it. I went out on the front porch. It was cold out, and clear. It was too dark yet to see anything so I just stood there listening. It was just as quiet as it was still.

Back inside I dressed quietly, putting on a tac vest and holster for the pistol, then slinging the AR. By the time I got back to the kitchen, the coffee was bubbling in the pot. I poured it into a stainless steel bottle and wrapped it in a dishtowel then dropped it in a cargo pocket. There was still about a cup left in the pot, so I took an insulated travel mug from the cabinet and poured it in, then added some powdered creamer and sugar in and headed for the door.

The seat on the ATV was cold. Meathead and Little Girl came running up as I started it up. They ran behind me as I went out the gate. Thad and Jeff were standing around the burn barrel trying to keep warm. They looked up as I arrived and that big smile was on Thad's face as I walked up to them.

"Coffee?" I asked as I pulled the bottle out of my pocket.

"Damn straight," Jeff said, snatching the bottle from my hand. He quickly poured himself and Thad a cup.

We stood around the fire drinking our coffee. The road was empty and I asked them how the foot traffic had been overnight. They said it had tapered off around ten and had completely stopped by midnight. There were no more incidents with people walking by and Jeff said he thought the best thing we could do was not to man the barricade, to pull the security farther back and make it appear the place was empty.

"Pull it back to where?" I asked.

"Back there, where you guys put them stocks. It would

cut down on the amount of real estate we're trying to se-cure," Thad replied.

I looked down the road. "That would put my house on this side of it."

They just stood there sipping their coffee for a moment, then Jeff said, "You could move to another house. There are some empty ones back there."

I didn't hesitate. "No way, not yet at least. That would be hard on my family and I'm not ready to do that to them. I mean, I've got power, water, a whole setup. You guys know how busy we've been. When would I find the time to redo all that?"

"It may come to that," Thad said.

"Not yet," I fired back.

When the coffee was finished I suggested that they go get some sleep. Reggie would have that pig ready later in the day, and I knew they would want to be there for that. It wasn't a hard sell; they saddled up and headed down the road. I stayed there for a little while, leaning over the log barricade, thinking about what they'd said. It was still early and there weren't any people out on the road so I decided to ride over to Reggie's and see how the pig was doing. No one else had showed up to stand watch yet, but I didn't have the patience to wait and probably be disappointed. I knew that that kind of "fuck it" attitude was dangerous, but I gave in to it because I knew I'd be back in less than an hour.

Reggie was splitting some wood by the smoker when I pulled up. He tossed a piece of wood in the firebox as I walked up. "How's the pig lookin'?"

Reggie closed the door on the firebox and said, "Ready about any time, really. What time you wanna eat?"

"Let's get everyone together around noon."

Reggie wiped his hands on his pants. "Sounds good to me."

"I just wanted to drop by and see how you were doin'. I'm going to go up to the barricade for a while. Jeff and Thad were out there all night."

"Any trouble?"

"Nah, there's just a lot of people moving by lately. Looks like they have a camp set up out at the range, or maybe folks are still thinking they can make it in the woods."

"No way in hell I'm going to a damn camp."

"Me neither, brother; me neither."

Danny showed up at the barricade about ten. I was sitting on the Polaris watching a group of six people walk by. He parked beside me and we sat there talking about the people. The one thing that really caught our eye was that none of the people we saw go by had any kind of visible weapons. We theorized that they had turned them over to the feds in order to get into the camp, though it seemed cruel to make people walk to a refugee camp without protection. Anything could happen to them, and we knew it probably would.

About half an hour after Danny showed up, we heard a vehicle coming down the road from the north. We sat there listening to it approach, and then a tan Humvee came into view. There was a gunner in the turret, and when he saw us he swung the weapon around and said something to the driver. The truck stopped and sat there for a moment. Neither of us moved, mainly because looking down the business end of the SAW scared the shit out of us. The thought of jumping for cover and giving them the green light to open up on us was another reason. If we didn't act like a threat, maybe they wouldn't treat us like one.

Three men got out of the truck. The driver and gunner

stayed. They looked around the area for minute then walked toward us. Danny leaned over and said, "What do you think they want?"

"Don't know, but we're about to find out."

I raised a hand and waved. "Morning."

The guy in the lead nodded, then stopped and inspected the barricade before speaking.

"You guys live here?"

"Yep," Danny replied.

The man looked around, then back at the logs, putting a hand on the top crossbeam and shaking it. "Looks pretty sturdy."

"Just keepin' honest people honest," I replied.

He looked back at us, from Danny to me, in one of those awkward silences. Danny and I just sat there, and finally he spoke. "Some of the people walking down the road say they are being robbed by men on the road here."

"Not around here; we haven't seen anything like that," Danny said.

"That's not what I heard."

His statement caught us both by surprise. "Heard from who?" Danny asked.

The man looked over his shoulder at someone in the Humvee. We were shocked when we saw who stepped out of it.

Mark approached the barricade, wearing the same uniform as the man before us.

"Morgan, Danny," Mark said with a nod.

We were both speechless for a moment. Before either of said a word, the other man continued. "Mark, you said there was some raiding going on around?"

"Yeah, there were a couple of raids."

The man looked back to us. "So you haven't see anything like that?"

I looked at Mark. "Dude, what the fuck? You went to the camp, took up with these guys?"

"Don't look so surprised. We talked about this; people want to be told what to do, and I simply went along with that line of thought. Now they come to us and we tell 'em what to do."

"You know how fucked that sounds?" Danny asked.

Mark looked at him. "Why? We're just giving them what they want, someone to feed 'em, tell 'em when and where to work."

The other man cut in. "Though they don't really like that part," he said with a grin.

Mark continued, "Like you said many times, things are different now. There's no more free ride; you gotta work for your keep now."

"So, what—people come to the camp and you guys push them around?" I asked.

Mark shifted his feet. He had a look on his face like he smelled shit. "We're not pushing anyone around, but you have to work."

"And what about us?" Danny asked.

"What about you?" The other man said.

"What about those of us who don't want to go along with"—I paused for a moment looking for the proper word—"your program?"

"You will eventually; you can't last forever."

I looked at Mark. "I think you know better than that."

The other man smiled. "You may not like the taste of the medicine, but sometimes you just gotta hold your nose and swallow."

"I've never been much of one for doctors or medicine. We'll just take care of ourselves."

"You have that option for now, but the day is coming. We've got shit to do. I'll be seeing you around," Mark said as he turned to leave.

"Not in your camp," Danny said.

Mark stopped and looked back, and the other man let out a slight laugh, shook his head and headed for the truck. Mark turned and followed him.

We stood there and watched the truck as it drove away. Danny asked if I thought Rick had gone with Mark and we agreed he must have. They had both disappeared the same day. We talked about whether or not the sheriff was in on it too. There was no way to know, but we had to try and find out. From the way those guys had been acting, we had start thinking about bugging out, somewhere they didn't know about. The alternative was to sit there and wait for them to show up, and that damn sure wasn't going to happen. The discussion continued as we headed for Reggie's. We needed to talk this over with everyone.

Reggie had put up a folding table beside the barn and Mel and Bobbie had set the food they made out on that. We had brought a stack of paper plates and plastic spoons and forks for everyone. I asked Reggie if I could invite John, his wife and Rene, and he said that was fine. Rene and the girls were over looking at the pigs in the pen. The women were all fussing over the table while the guys and I were trying to get the pig out of the smoker without dropping it on the ground.

Danny pulled a couple of sawhorses out of Reggie's shop and set them up. Then, with a pair of welding gloves and the help of a prybar, we got the whole grate out of the smoker and set it on the horses. We all brought camp chairs with us and set them up around a fire pit Reggie had dug near the smoker. We sat around the fire eating plates of tender pork, mac 'n' cheese, baked beans and a big pot of green beans. Danny had even made some okra, much to Thad's delight.

I tossed my plate in the fire when I finished and sat sipping on some tea. The girls were all talking and laughing. Rene was looking better but was still thin. They looked like typical girls at the moment. Reggie was telling some kind of BS story to Jeff and Thad, who were both laughing. I stood up and walked over to the smoker. There was still a big stack of wood there and I leaned over and picked up a couple of pieces.

I didn't hear it, or maybe I did, but I was hit in the chest. I heard screams, then the shooting, lots of shooting. I couldn't breathe. I was flat on my back on the ground and I couldn't get any air. I looked over to the fire pit. Little Bit was on the ground, Taylor on top of her. Her eyes were full of tears, her mouth open. Was she screaming? Was it her? Her little eyes locked with mine and she reached out. I couldn't hear her, but I could tell she was screaming, "Daddy."

Looking past her, I saw Mel and Lee Ann on the ground, trying to hide under a damn plastic folding table. She had her hands over her ears, and she was looking at me. I reached out, but they were so far away. Finally a breath, just a wisp of air. God, it hurt. I rolled on my side. I could see Danny firing, I could hear the crack of the bullets, then something louder, not as fast, but steady. I was laying on my AR. I tried to pull it around, but I still couldn't take a full breath.

Like a turtle on its back, I rolled around trying to free the AR. The shouts and screams became louder and I finally managed to pull the rifle out from under me. I saw Danny firing toward the back of Reggie's property into the woods.

Lying on my side, I started to shoot in that direction, shooting under the smoker. I couldn't see anything, didn't see anything, just started throwing lead into the woods. The mag in the rifle ran dry quickly.

I tried to pull a mag from the vest, but it wouldn't budge, so I went to another pocket and pulled one out. In the time it took me to reload, the firing died down. Suddenly Little Bit was at my side, shaking me and screaming.

"Get up, Daddy, get up!"

Taylor was there too. Tears were streaming down her face, leaving little trails of mud. I reached out and pulled them down behind the smoker and croaked out, "Stay here, I'm gonna check on your mom and sister." Taylor wrapped her arms around her little sister. She said, "Are you okay, Dad? Were you shot?"

I cracked a little smile. "I don't know what happened, but I think I'm all right. Are you two okay?"

They nodded back at me. I reached out and smoothed Taylor's hair, then Little Bit's. "Stay here, I'll be right back."

"Don't go! Daddy, stay here!" Little Bit cried.

"We'll be okay, you just stay put," I said, then started to crawl over to where Mel and Lee Ann were. They had managed to move around the side of the barn and were lying on the ground with their backs against the wall. Danny was standing beside them looking around the corner toward the woods. Lee Ann was holding her calf, both hands tightly wrapped around it. My heart sank when I saw the blood that ran between her fingers.

When she saw me crawling toward her she cried out, "Daddy! Help me!"

Mel had a rag and was trying to get her to move her hands so she could wrap it around her leg. When she cried out,

Danny looked back over his shoulder at them. Seeing what was going on, he immediately dropped down to his knees and pulled a dressing out of a pouch on the vest he wore. All I could see was my daughter, but behind me someone was still screaming. I needed to get to Lee Ann.

She was crying and so was Mel. Mel was about to panic. "Oh my god, she's been shot! She's been shot!"

Danny was trying to get a bandage on the wound and calm Mel down at the same time. When I finally made it to them, I tried to calm Mel. I told her to sit beside Lee Ann and hold on to her.

"It's all right, kiddo, you're gonna be okay," I said as I helped Danny slide the leg of her jeans up. In our current situation, cutting up a good pair of pants was out of the question unless it was life-or-death.

"It hurts so bad, am I going to die?"

"You're not going to die; just sit tight," Danny said.

With the pants pulled up we could see the wound. There was an entry and exit on her right calf, behind the bone. It was bleeding, but not profusely. The one dressing was big enough to wrap around her little calf. Danny tied it off and the pressure of the dressing slowed the bleeding. Danny told me to stay with them, and that he was going to check on everyone else.

I pulled myself up so I was sitting beside Lee Ann and wrapped my arms around her. Mel was on the other side of her and laid her head on my arm. I tried to comfort them both, telling them it was going to be all right. They both sat there crying. We sat there for a few minutes, then Danny came back with Taylor and Little Bit. They both sat down against the wall with us, and now there were four of them sitting there crying and scared.

Danny caught my eye and nodded for me to follow him. I told the girls I would be back shortly and followed Danny around the barn. Reggie was sitting in one of the camp chairs, leaning forward with his head down. He had his hands together in front of him. A steady rivulet of blood ran from them, pooling on the ground in front of his boots.

He looked up at us we approached, and through clenched teeth he said, "They shot my fuckin' finger off! The bastards blew it off!"

My eyes went from his eyes to his hands, and he opened them. The ring finger on his left hand was gone, and the pinky looked like it had been skinned. He quickly gripped it in his right, squeezing. I pulled a bandage out of my vest and tore it open. He took it and laid the mangled hand into it, then squeezed it.

Thad was by the table, kneeling down. I looked over and saw a body on the ground in front of him. It was Rene. I walked over just as he was raising her head off the dirt, sliding a folded coat under it, then gently laying it back down. Her eyes were open, glazed a little, but she was awake. I looked her over and didn't see any blood. Thad looked at John and his wife and said, "Just stay with her, keep her awake. I think she's in shock, so don't let her go to sleep." John nodded and held one of her hands as he knelt beside her.

When he stood I asked what had happened to her. He said he didn't know, that he had just found her on the ground unconscious. Knowing how malnourished she was, we guessed she must have gone into shock and passed out. Maybe too much food at one time all of a sudden, then the shooting and adrenaline rush was just too much for her. At least we hoped that was all it was.

"What the hell happened to you?" Thad asked.

I looked down at my chest, patting it with my left hand. "Don't know, guess I was hit."

Danny stepped in front of me. "I guess so," he said and reached out and grabbed one of the mags in my vest and pulled on it. He had to really yank to get it out.

The side of the magazine was caved in and split. He held it up for us to see. He ran his thumb across the dent in it. His thumb fit in it. "That was a big round."

I took the magazine from him and looked at it, "Yeah, must have been a pistol round, maybe a .45. I think a rifle round would have went through it."

"An' through you," Thad said.

Jeff came trotting back up. "They went that way," he said, pointing off to the east. "You wanna go after 'em?"

I looked off to the east. "No, I need to go get the doc for Lee Ann and Reggie."

"I'll go, you stay here with them," Danny said.

"I'll go with you," Thad said.

"Thanks, guys," I said.

Jeff stayed with me. He tried to help Reggie, who really didn't want any. I went and checked on Lee Ann. The bleeding had stopped. There were just the two little holes, one in and one out. Looking at them, I started to think about it. Whatever hit her was low-velocity. If it had been a high-velocity round, the damage would have been much worse. Then I thought about that magazine; it was probably the same kind of round. After making sure Lee Ann was okay, I went over to the smoker and started looking around.

I found the bullet under the woodpile. I had to dig all the way to the bottom of the stack looking for it. It was a full metal jacket nine-millimeter or .38. My guess was 9mm. I rolled the projectile between my fingers looking at it. Jeff came up and said he wanted to go look for the guys. I told him we should wait and we began to discuss the whole situation, who it could have been and why. The possibilities there were numerous.

Jeff said he was going to go out to the tree line and keep an eye out in case anyone came back. He was also going to look for anything they might have left behind. I told him to be careful and went over to check on John and Rene. She was still lying on the ground but looked a lot better now. John was a mess, though; he looked like he was about to fall apart. I pulled him off to the side and asked if he was okay.

"We can't take this anymore, Morgan. I mean, all we were doing was having a cookout and someone starts shooting? Look at my daughter, look at yours."

"I know, but what are you going to do? We just have to learn to be more careful, I guess."

He stood there for a moment, looking off into the distance. "My wife wants us to leave."

I looked at him like he was nuts. "And go where? Where do you think you will be safer?"

He looked back at me, his face blank. "The camp."

"You gotta be shittin' me. You think that will be better?"

"We don't have any food. I have a shotgun, but that's it. Look at all the guns you guys have and people still just attacked you."

"I don't see being herded into a camp as a good thing. I'll take my chances here—hell, anywhere but there."

He said, "That's the decision you have to make for your family. I've made mine. Thanks for what you've done for us; I really appreciate it." He stuck his hand out and I shook it, then he turned and walked away. I watched him walk back to his family. He and his wife helped Rene to her feet and they moved toward home. Rene stopped by Taylor and knelt down beside her. They hugged and there were more tears. Rene stood up, wiped tears from her face and started to walk off, her mom's hand in her left hand and John's in her right. When they got to the gate, she turned and smiled at Taylor and then they were gone. I went back to Lee Ann. She was watching John's family go.

"Where they going, Dad?" Lee Ann asked, still holding her leg.

I was looking out toward the dirt road they had disappeared on. "Not sure, honey." I looked down at her and smiled. "You okay?"

She looked at the ground between her feet and nodded. "It hurts a lot."

"I know, baby. The doctor is coming."

Now that things had calmed down a bit, Mel got up. "What are we going to do? If we aren't safe here, where are we going to go?"

I let out a long breath. "We'll be okay, we just have to start being more careful."

"How can you say we'll be okay? You were shot in the chest. Lee Ann was shot in the leg. Either one of you could have died. What we would we do if you were killed?" She was upset and getting more so.

I stepped up to her and wrapped my arms around her. "Calm down, we'll figure something out."

She just stood there for a minute, her face in my chest. She pushed me away. "It's cold."

"What's cold?"

With her index finger, she poked one of the mags still in my vest. "Where's the doctor? Is she going to be okay?" she asked, looking back at Lee Ann. All three of the girls were lined up, sitting against the wall.

"Keep an eye on them. I'm gonna check on Reggie."

Mel nodded and went and sat down with the girls. Reggie was still sitting in the chair, leaning forward. The blood had stopped running out of his hands, but the dressing was soaked. Looking around the fire pit, I found his .45 and picked it up. Dirt was caked on the blood spattered on the grip and slide. The checkering on the front of the grip had a ding in it where the bullet must have hit. I sat down in the chair beside him. The effort of sitting made my chest burn.

I stuck the barrel of the pistol into the little mesh cup holder. "Didn't know you were a lefty."

Reggie looked up at me, his jaw clenched. "Not anymore."

Trying to take the edge off things, I said, "Yeah, guess this really fucked up your sex life."

He grunted, "You're an asshole, Morgan," then looked up at me. I shot a shit-eatin' grin back at him and he shook his head and smiled.

The sound of a couple of approaching ATVs brought me to my feet, carbine at the ready. Thad and Danny came through the gate and the doc was riding with Danny.

Sarge pushed past Mike into the old barracks and headed for the little table the radio gear was set up on. Sitting down he read the message on the screen: *Where are you, old man? We could use some help.*

"Who the hell's he callin' old?" Sarge shouted.

"If the shoe fits," Mike replied.

"Shut up, dipshit."

Sarge typed a quick reply: *Watch who you're calling old. What's the situation?* and hit ENTER. He looked over at the little box connected to his radio and watched as the LEDs blinked.

"What's the plan, Sarge?" Ted asked.

Spinning around in his chair, he saw all three of the guys were standing there. He looked at each of them and said, "Time to start the dance. Get your dress on, Mikey. We have to meet the riggers at 0100. They're going to sling our rides and insert us."

"Where we going?" Doc asked.

Sarge glanced over his shoulder at the screen, then turned back. "Looks like we're going to Lake County to start with."

What was left of the afternoon was spent in frenzied activity, each of the men packing the gear they wanted in their packs and loading them into the vehicles. Then working together they started to load all the supplies they had "acquired" from the quartermaster earlier. As the work started to wind down, Sarge told the guys to decide who was going to hit the rack and get some sleep. In the meantime, he went to the radios with a thermos of coffee and put his feet up on the table, staring at the screen.

The doc hopped off the ATV and, seeing Reggie's hand, headed for him. Reggie waved him off with his head. "Go take care of her; I ain't going anywhere."

The doc went to Lee Ann. Danny and Thad took up positions to keep an eye on things. I went over and knelt beside Lee Ann. The doc unwrapped the bandage from around her leg, and the fear reappeared on her face. She reached out and grabbed my hand. I told her the doctor was here and she was going to be okay.

After unwrapping her leg, he inspected the wound, gently turning it to inspect the exit wound. He didn't say anything, just adjusted his glasses, dabbed at the wounds with a sponge, then gently laid her leg out on the dressing he removed.

"It looks pretty clean, but there is a risk of infection. There could be some fibers from her jeans in the wound."

"Am I going to need stitches?" Lee Ann asked.

He looked up at her and smiled. "No, honey, these holes are small. They'll heal on their own, but you're going to have to keep it clean, and even though it hurts, you need to walk on it too."

She nodded her head but said nothing.

Chapter 32

Sarge leaned against the fender of the Humvee, watching the riggers. He was always amazed at how these guys could sling a load perfectly. There were six of them at work on his babies. The two buggies and trailer were being connected to straps. The men crawled over the equipment like ants, on top, underneath and around all sides. They shouted and cussed at one another, but the straps were secured one by one. When all was ready, Stalker One, the first of two Black Hawks, came into a hover over the mass of gear. One of the riggers reached up and attached a strap to a hook on the belly of the helo, then ran out from under it, gave the pilot a thumbs-up, and watched as the big bird took the slack.

Sarge could hear the change in pitch as the big helicopter took the weight of the load slung under it. The two buggies and the trailer lifted as one; they jostled around and found their center point, but all of them were almost perfectly level. As soon as soon as Stalker One was clear, Stalker Two taxied out. Sarge looked over his shoulder at the three men standing behind him. Their faces were smeared with camo paint and each of them was hard as iron.

"Let's go! Saddle up, ladies!"

As one, they nodded at him, then ran toward the waiting

helo. Sarge waited till Doc passed him and paused for a moment, watching these incredible warriors as they sprinted toward the waiting Black Hawk, and shook his head. *Damn, I love this shit*, he thought, then ran out to catch up.

We brought Lee Ann and her sisters home. Taylor went to her room and came back with Jeff's iPad and a set of headphones. Little Bit disappeared and returned with a pillow from her bed for her sister to prop her leg up on. Mel asked if there was anything she could do for her. Lee Ann said, "Some mac 'n' cheese would be nice, thanks."

Mel went straight to the kitchen to heat some up. I knelt down beside Lee Ann and asked, "Is there anything I can get for you?"

"Can you start a fire? I'm cold."

I smiled at her and rubbed a hand through her hair. "Sure."

With the supplies I kept by the fireplace, I had one going in no time. Pine needles and lighter wood make it possible for anyone to start a fire. As the fire built, Lee Ann fell asleep. She was out cold when I turned to ask her if it was good enough. I went to her room and pulled the quilt off her bed, returned to the living room and laid it out over her.

Mel walked in with a bowl of mac 'n' cheese. I said, "She's out."

She stood there looking at Lee Ann and asked, "Is she going to be okay?"

"The doc said she would. We just have to make sure she takes the antibiotics and that we clean it every day. He gave us those pain-killers, but I really don't think she'll need 'em. Honestly, I'm more worried about Reggie."

"What are we going to do? I'm scared."

I walked over to her and wrapped my arms around her. "I know, baby. Tomorrow I'm going to talk to the guys and figure out what to do." I stepped back from her and said, "We may have to leave the house."

"I don't care where we are, as long as the girls are safe," she said. She put her hand on my chest. "How do *you* feel?"

I hadn't thought much about it, but I was sore. Every breath hurt. "I'm fine, baby. I was lucky."

"I don't want to rely on luck; you've got to be more careful. I don't know what we would do without you."

I tried to put on the confident face, but inside I wasn't so sure. It had been too close. I still had the bullet in my pocket, the one with my name on it. Maybe as long as I had it, there wouldn't be another one. It was a nice thought, but I knew it was bullshit.

"I promise, babe, I'll try. Besides, someone has to be around here to complain about your cooking." I nudged her.

That little joke didn't even get a smile from her. "I'm tired, I'm going to bed," Mel said.

"Go ahead, I gotta go back out to the shop for a minute."

"Don't be long."

"I won't."

Mel headed for the bedroom and I went out the slider toward the shop. I still hadn't dealt with that damn door. Inside, I tapped the touch pad on the laptop and it came to life. There was a message blinking back at me: *Watch who you're calling old. What's the situation?*

I smiled when I saw it, knowing it chapped his ass. I

typed a reply, telling him what had happened and who I thought was behind it and hit ENTER. The LEDs blinked, and the laptop grunted and groaned.

Thad and Jeff both stayed with Reggie. The doc did what he could, but he was no plastic surgeon. If Reggie survived the inevitable infections, he would have the use of his hand, but it would never be the same.

"That's all I can do." The doc leaned back, letting out a breath.

Reggie, sweat-soaked, looked at the sutures in his hand. The ring finger on his left hand was gone and a patch of raw red skin had been pulled tight over where the knuckle had been and stitched together. The pinky finger had a string of stitches running down the inside of it. It was swollen and sore as hell.

"Thanks, Doc, I appreciate it."

"It's not pretty, but it's the best I can do." He reached into his bag and pulled out two bottles, setting them on the table beside the couch. "This one's an antibiotic; take it three times a day. This one is for pain; take it as needed, but be careful, it's a heavy dose."

Reggie looked at the two bottles, then over at Thad. "You staying here tonight?"

Thad nodded. Reggie reached over and picked up the bottle of pain-killers and spun the top off with one hand, shaking out two of the big pills. He quickly tossed them into his mouth and swallowed them dry.

"I said be careful! That's gonna make you a pile of mush!" the doc shouted.

"Good," Reggie said, then laid his head back on the pillow and closed his eyes.

Mike was sitting by the door, an elbow resting on his knee and his chin in his palm looking out as the blackness passed in a blur. Sarge reached over and punched him in the shoulder, knocking his elbow off his knee. Irritated, he looked back at the old man. Sarge tossed a set of earphones to him and motioned for him to put them on. Mike pulled them over his ears and immediately began to hear radio chatter.

". . . ger that, Stalker One, Bronco Three's bringing up the rear."

Mike looked over and keyed the intercom. "That the same Bronco that saved our ass out in the swamp?"

Sarge nodded his head and keyed his mic. "Doc, Morgan and some of his got wounded. Soon as we get there, you see to them pronto."

Doc nodded as he keyed his intercom. "What sort of wounds?"

"One of his daughters has a gunshot wound to her calf; doesn't sound too bad, but you need to look at it. The other is a little worse. Sounds like one of his boys had a couple of fingers shot off."

Ted was shaking his head. "Why didn't he call for help sooner? If it's that bad he should have been on the horn to us."

"He's just fuckin' thick-headed, I guess," Sarge said.

"What kind of trouble they got?" Mike asked.

"He's not sure. They were raided a couple of days ago and managed to fend those guys off, and yesterday they were ambushed. That's when they suffered the casualties," Sarge said.

"Whoever they are, they're some sorry sons-a-bitches for shootin' a little girl," Ted said.

"Damn straight. Let's go make dead out of 'em," Sarge said.

I closed the door of the shop and stood there looking up at the sky. It was cold out and the stars were brilliant. I remember sitting out by the fire pit on nights like this and watching as the International Space Station passed overhead. It made me wonder if it was still up there, and if it was, how long they could last without support from Earth. Would they run out of food and starve, or run out of oxygen and suffocate first? Either way would be horrible.

I went and checked on Lee Ann. She was sleeping soundly, so I added a log to the fireplace and, after a quick check of all the doors, went to bed. Mel was already sleeping when I got there. I didn't disturb her as I took off all my hardware, leaning the rifle beside the bed and laying the pistol on the table. I climbed under the blankets and quickly went to sleep.

The next morning I slept late. I woke up to an empty bed and light coming in through the blinds. For a moment I just lay there in a haze, much as I would on any other ordinary Sunday. I was absentmindedly watching a beam of light that cut through the blinds and landed on the wall opposite the bed. Little particles of dust floated on the light. Then suddenly I remembered—remembered that things were different. It wasn't an ordinary Sunday. I jumped from the bed and grabbed the XD from the table. The door swung open and

I raised the pistol. Taylor froze in the door, holding a cup of coffee.

I looked at her, then at the pistol and slowly lowered it. "Sorry, baby, I overslept."

She surprised me with her lack of reaction to me pointing a gun at her. "It's okay, Dad. Mom said to let you sleep. You want some coffee?"

"Yeah, thanks, sorry about that."

She smiled and walked toward me, offering the cup, "It's okay. Things are different now. I get it."

I smiled and took the cup from her. I knew she would want to know if I liked it or not, so I took a quick sip. It was really good; she always made a good cup of coffee. "Mmm, that's good. Go on, I'll be out in a minute."

She smiled and said, "There's eggs and biscuits for breakfast."

I took my time dressing. Mel had a plate sitting on the table for me, scrambled eggs and a biscuit. A can of Red Feather butter sat on the table, a rare and precious luxury. Before sitting down to the plate, I went to check on Lee Ann. She was still lying on the couch, playing on the iPad. If she was doing that, I thought she must be all right.

"How you feeling this mornin'?"

She didn't even look up from whatever it was she was doing. "Better."

I rubbed her head and went back to the kitchen to eat. Little Bit was sitting at the table, pushing some eggs around her plate. Her elbow was sitting on the table and she rested her head on her knuckles.

"You okay, rug rat?"

"Yeah."

I reached over and slid her plate out from in front of her.

"If you're not goin' to eat these, I will," I said as I went to scoop some eggs off her plate.

"Hey! Those are mine!" She reached out and pulled the plate back to her far side and making a show of shielding it from me.

"Okay, guess I'll have to eat mine. Hey, you want some butter on your biscuit?"

She perked up a bit. "Sure. I wish we had some jelly."

I looked back at Mel, who was still at the stove. "Are we out of jelly?"

"I haven't gone out to the shed to look."

"Sit tight, I'll go look," I said to Little Bit.

I knew I had a few jars of grape jelly put away. I found it behind the peanut butter. While I was looking, I noticed how thin things were getting on the shelves. There were still many buckets with various contents in them. We would have to start utilizing the stuff in them and get away from the fast and easy canned food.

As I was heading out of the shed I reached over and tapped the mouse pad on the laptop. The screen came to life and I read: *Friendlies inbound, 1200 hours tomorrow.*

I stood there reading those five words over and over. He was coming here? It was 8:37, three and a half hours till he or whoever got here. I went back inside and opened the jelly jar. Little Bit insisted on spreading her own jelly. I sat there eating the eggs without really noticing, thinking about what was going to happen that day. Running the scenarios through my head brought me around. I quickly finished the eggs, smeared some butter and jelly on the biscuit and headed for the bedroom.

Sticking the biscuit in my mouth, I put the vest on, holstered the XD and slung my carbine. A quick check told me it was still chambered. I was eating the biscuit when I walked back into the kitchen.

Mel looked at me as I came in and asked, "Where are you going?"

"I got a message from a friend, sounds like they may be coming here. I need to get up to the roadblock."

"Who's coming?" she asked, and then she looked confused. "How'd you get a message?"

"Tell ya later, I gotta go."

Little Bit looked up from her plate. "Can I come?"

"No, you stay here an' stay inside today, okay?"

That hurt look she does so well came across her face, and she went back to picking at the eggs again.

Chapter 33

Sarge used a red LED to look at his map. It was the same one he had marked up with the route that Thad, Morgan and Jess would take to get home. He had picked out the LZ the day before when he had met with the pilots. It was a small lake, and he remembered Morgan saying it was used as a mud bog. Considering how the weather had been, he knew it would be dry. Baptist Lake wasn't far from Morgan's place, and Sarge wanted to get close.

The lead Apache came on the radio. *"Stalker One, Draco."*

"Stalker One."

"Looks like the LZ is clear. Stay to the west; the center of the LZ looks a little soft."

"Roger that, Draco. Stalker Two will do a bump and go to drop these guys. We'll just cut the sling once the load's on the ground."

"Roger that, Stalker; we'll orbit the LZ."

The pilot's voice came over the intercom. "Ten minutes, guys."

Sarge keyed the intercom. "Roger that, we're ready. If that LZ looks iffy, just get us close and we'll jump out."

"If you're good with it, I am," came the reply.

Sarge looked around the dark cabin. He could just make out the eyes of each of his men through the camo paint. There was no real emotion on their faces; it was just another milk run to them, or at least that's how it looked.

"Two minutes," the intercom cracked.

The helo dropped and when they were about five feet off the ground, Mike shoved his pack out and jumped. The others followed.

Stalker One immediately began to increase power and pull up and was soon moving out across the LZ. They looked up and could see Stalker Two coming into the LZ. Ted reached into a cargo pocket and pulled out two cyalume sticks and cracked them as one. Stepping out into the LZ, he began to give the pilot some directions. Stalker Two came into a hover and began to slowly descend. As soon as the load was on the ground, Ted waved his arm in a cutting motion and the sling dropped from the belly of the Black Hawk.

Ted and Doc immediately went to work disconnecting the web of straps. Mike and Sarge were keeping watch over the operation. Sarge's radio crackled. *"Draco One, Stump Knocker."*

"Go for Stump Knocker."

"Good luck, guys. Call us if you need us to bail your ass out again."

"Thanks, Draco One, we appreciate the help."

"Get up, Av'ry!" Marvin shouted as he slapped the sleeping man in the side of the head.

Avery bolted upright, rubbing the side of his bandaged head. "Shit, Marv, that hurt! Watch ma damn ear!"

"You didn't hear 'em helocoptors?" Marvin asked as he pulled on his tactical vest.

Avery jumped up from the couch he had been sleeping on. "Choppers, wur?" he asked as he started to look for his own gear.

"They was out thur sum'ers," Marvin said, motioning with his chin as he clipped his pistol belt around his waist. "Hurry up an' git yer shit together. I'll git the boys." Marvin hurried out of the room to get the rest of the troops together.

"Wur's my damn gun?" Avery shouted as Marvin closed the door. He stood in the middle of his small room in the trailer—one of several in what the guys called "the compound"—turning in circles and kicking crap out of the way. The floor of the room was buried in everything from empty beer cans and dirty clothes to Quarter Pounder wrappers, even though there hadn't been one of those made in many, many weeks.

Marvin was the head of the North Lake County Militia. Prior to things going to hell, they used to get together a couple of times a month to drink beer, tell lies and shoot shit. They were decidedly antigovernment, and after the bottle had made the rounds of the old fire pit a couple of times, the usual venom about the Zionist government—the ZOG—would start. Even with all the alcohol-fueled hate speech, the only thing they ever killed was a case.

With the collapse, the guys had gotten together quickly, preparing to fight off the impending invasion of federal storm troopers. What happened instead, though, even they wouldn't have believed. After establishing themselves as the security force for the Kangaroo store and the old woman who ran it, they had met the first of the DHS security forces coming in to set up camp at the bombing range. Instead of the fight they had always seen coming, they had entered into a partnership. When they were safely couched in the confines of the compound they would laugh and howl at how they were getting over on the feds.

They agreed they would work with the feds so long as the

weapons, ammo and MREs kept coming. So long as the government was willing to arm the militia, they would take everything they could get. That way, by the time the feds had been whittled down trying to deal with the civilian population, they would have the means to take the feds on and win.

Avery walked out the back door of the house, dragging his web gear behind him as he tried to buckle his forty-four-inch belt around his forty-six-inch waist. To his surprise, there were only two other guys there with Marvin.

"Wur is ever'one?" Avery asked as he hunched his shoulders and strained at the belt.

"Them bastards is all hung over. It's jus' you, Willy, Ned an' me."

Avery got the belt on and let out a long breath. "An' you want fer us to look for them choppers?"

Marvin said, "Of course, you idjit, there ain't no reason fer no helocoptors to be flying out here. It must have crashed, an' if'n we get to it before the feds do, we can git whutever was on it."

"Oh," Avery said, nodding his head.

"Yeah, 'oh,' fatass," Marvin said.

The men climbed onto their four-wheelers and took off with Marvin in the lead. He had heard the ships early that morning when he was pissing off the front porch. Each of the men were armed with a pistol and a primary weapon. As part of their relationship with the feds, they had acquired some H&K MP5 submachine guns. And the best part was, they were fully automatic. With them had come cases of ammo. Their side of the deal was simple: do whatever the feds asked.

Up to this point that had been easy. FEMA and the DHS were trying to get people to leave their homes and go to the camps they were setting up, and some of them needed a little persuasion. That was where the militia came in. Unlike what many people thought, the government didn't show up and drag you away. It was much easier to convince you to beg them to let you in. Until recently, all they had to do was ride in and scare the shit outta folks, throw some Molotov cocktails around, maybe take a piece of ass if it was convenient, and the next day they would be lining up for the camp.

A few days ago they had hit a neighborhood where things didn't go according to plan. Sure, there was always a little shooting, but nothing like what they encountered there. The militia had lost men, a first. Then they were told to hit them again, but no one wanted to go back. So Avery drew the short straw and was sent back to keep up the heat.

When he got back, he was bleeding from the head. Marvin's wife cleaned it up enough to see that his left ear had been shot in two. It was still attached top and bottom, but the middle of it looked as if someone had taken a melon baller to it. But Avery was proud, said he knew he killed one and hit another. He said he saw one of them drop beside a big smoker, told everyone how them sons-a-bitches were smoking a whole pig. He also told them how good it smelled, what the food looked liked. Avery was a big man and, as he liked to tell the others, a big man's gotta eat.

Mike and Sarge were taking the straps off the buggies while Doc and Ted kept watch. Sarge was dropping the last strap into the trailer when his radio cracked, *"Draco Three, Stump Knocker."*

Sarge turned from the buggy to look out across the dried-up pond, keying his mic. "Go for Stump Knocker."

"Looks like you've got some fast movers heading your way from the east. They aren't heading straight at you, but I think you're their destination."

Sarge looked around. "Roger that, Draco Three, thanks for the info."

"You want us to hang out, or to engage them?"

"Negative, I think we can handle 'em."

Sarge walked around the buggy and said, "Hey, Mike, you an' Doc take your ride an' head into the woods there. Stay outta sight, we got some company headin' our way."

"Roger that, Sarge," Mike said as he and Doc ran toward the smaller of the two buggies.

Sarge took a seat in his ride, reached into the breast pocket of his shirt and drew out one of the Rocky Patels he had managed to hide from Faggione.

"Sarge, you think we should be doing something?" Ted asked.

Sarge took a cigar cutter and a lighter from his pocket, clipped the end and lit it. After taking a long drag from the oily cigar, he blew the smoke out and said, "Nope, just relax. Let's see who's comin' for a visit." He leaned his head back and took another long drag on the Rocky.

Sarge tapped his cigar, watching as the thick solid ash cracked then fell to the ground. He looked over the side of the buggy to see it still mostly in one piece, then looked at the expensive cigar and smiled. Not because of the ash, but the thought that there would never be another one made, and there he was, literally burning something that was priceless and irreplaceable. Ted was looking in every direction for the enemy.

"Chill out, Teddy, you're making me nervous," Sarge said.

"I don't like being out in the open like this, just waiting for someone to ride up on me," Ted said.

"Don't worry; it ain't anyone to be worried about," Sarge said. He keyed the mic on his radio. "Mikey, you guys set up?"

"Roger that, Sarge, we got a couple of SAWs set up. I'm at your four o'clock and Doc is around your seven o'clock. We got you covered," Mike said.

Sarge looked at Ted and said, "See, nothing to be worried about."

When they heard the engines, Ted's back stiffened. Sarge rested his elbow on the top of the seat and propped his head up. The four ATVs came into the clearing from Sarge's nine o'clock, not exactly where he'd thought they would, but good enough.

Marvin knew kinda where he had heard the choppers. He lead them in the general direction, hoping he would find it. Avery was bringing up the rear and when they stopped at a branching trail he asked Marv why they weren't seeing any smoke or fire if the choppers crashed. Marv told him, again, just how damn stupid he was, and fat, and so Avery wasn't exactly in the best of moods as he followed along, eating the dirt and dust from the three machines in front of him.

Marvin pulled into the clearing that used to be Baptist Lake. As he passed through the trees, Avery didn't immediately see the buggy and the two men with it, but Marv did. He stopped as soon as he cleared the trees.

Ned and Willy rode up beside him. Willy was smoothing his long goatee, a perpetual unconscious habit. It was about six inches long and had earned him the nickname Goat.

"What'cha think, Marv?" Willy asked, tugging at his beard.

"Fancy-ass buggy. I think I want it."

"They look kinda like soldiers," Ned said.

"Soldiers, my ass. Where the hell soldiers gonna come from? Ned, you stay here with fatass. Goat, come with me."

Marv and Goat slowly rode toward the two men. Marv was watching the one standing up. From the way he stood there, Marv was of the opinion that the man thought he was a real badass. Well, he was about to find out differently. The second man was sitting in the buggy, the buggy that would soon be Marv's. The man raised his hand and waved. Marv didn't wave back.

"There's one still inside the tree line," Mike called over the radio.

Sarge raised his right hand to signal to Mike he'd heard him. Two of the men approached. The third stayed back by the trees and the fourth was still inside the trees. The two men rolled up and stopped twenty feet from him. Sarge sat there, making a show of just how relaxed he was. The men shut down their rides and sat there. Sarge smiled and nodded to them, stuck his cigar between his teeth, stepped out of the buggy and crossed his arms, not in a threatening manner, but in amusement.

The two men sat there looking at him, trying to mean-mug him. Ted just stood there looking back, no expression, no emotion, all business. Ted wouldn't say anything before Sarge did, and Sarge damn sure wouldn't say anything. The other guy would have to break first.

So the four men stood there staring at one another with no one saying anything. Sarge smoked his Rocky and the two men on the four-wheelers sat there looking at one another, then back at Sarge. With his arms still crossed, Sarge pulled the cigar from his mouth, leaned forward a bit and spit a small piece of tobacco out, then took another long drag, squinting one eye as he did. Ted stood there rubbing his thumb on the safety of his carbine. The very tip of his index finger rested on the front edge of the trigger guard. It would happen so fast they wouldn't even be able to react.

Marv sat there watching the old man. That's how he thought of him. He was wearing a camo uniform and had a nice .45 in his holster. He looked just as cocky as the other dude did. The way he was smoking that damn cigar really pissed him off too. Looking at the other man, he could tell he was itching for a fight. Goat glanced nervously at Marv. He wished someone would say something, he didn't like the silence one damn bit. When Marv saw the old man spit, he waited a second before hawking up a loogie and spitting it out between him and the old guy.

The old guy looked down at the phlegm, then back up, and smiled through his clenched teeth. He reached up and took the cigar from his teeth, blowing out a cloud of smoke as he did.

"Who are you guys?" Marv asked. The question actually startled Goat, who jumped a little.

"We're just a couple of guys in the woods," he answered with a smile.

"Well, this mornin' I heard a couple of choppers. Y'all seen any choppers?" Marv asked.

The old one looked over at his younger buddy. "You hear any choppers?"

"No," the young guy answered. His eyes never drifted from the two men.

The guy bugged Marv. "You got a problem, man?"

The guy didn't answer.

"Don't worry 'bout him. He ain't a mornin' person, if ya know what I mean," the old man replied.

Marv sat there looking at the younger one—he thought of him as Junior—for a second.

"An' who might you fellas be?" Old Guy asked.

"Ma name's Marvin, an' I'm the head of the North Lake County Militia."

"Militia? What are you guys doing around here, then?" Old Guy asked.

"We're responsible for the security 'round here, an' since we don't know you fellas, yer gonna need to come with us." Marv watched the old man for any reaction. "An' we need yer guns too."

Old Guy made an exaggerated surprised face. "Oh, so you boys are the law, then?"

"Yep," Marv said.

"Says who?" Old Guy asked.

"Says the DHS—" Goat was saying before Marv cut him off.

"Says me!" Marv snapped.

"An' here I thought we would become friends, but I ain't feelin' the love. You feelin' the love?" Old Guy asked Junior without looking at him.

"Nope."

Marv's hands were still on the handlebars of his ATV, but he'd had enough. It was time these shitheads saw the light. He let go of the handlebars and went to lean back. His rifle was lying in his lap. Before his hands even left the grips, Junior had the safety off his carbine.

"I wouldn't do that, friend. You boys just need to be on your way an' leave us the hell alone," Old Guy said.

Marv was pissed. This was not the way things were supposed to go. "I have more men. You think you're gonna get out of here? I already sent men to fetch the DHS, and your ass'll be sorry when they get here." When Goat heard Marv say he had sent men to get the DHS goons, he showed his hand by looking over at Marv.

"You do have other men, that part is true, but there ain't no one else coming." Old Guy paused for a moment and looked at Goat. "Is there?"

"Keep yer mouth shut, Goat," Marv said.

"Goat!" Old Guy shouted in amusement. "Where's the rest of it? I see the ass on yer chin." He laughed.

Goat didn't say shit. He was scared, these were nothing like the people they usually dealt with. They were hard and he had no doubt they were ready to kill.

"Tell your other men to come on so we can all get to know one another," Old Guy said.

"I got men in the woods, they'll cut you down!" Marv shouted.

Old Guy grinned and keyed his mic. "Round 'em up, Mikey."

Goat was surprised and Marv was furious. He looked back over his shoulder at Ned just as another man walked out of the woods with a damn machine gun pointed at him. He watched as Ned put his hands up, climbed off the ATV and was forced to kneel down.

Avery was sitting in the woods watching. He couldn't

hear anything, but everything looked all right. It looked like they were just talking. Then he saw the other man come out of the woods with that big-ass gun. His heart leapt into his throat, and he fumbled with the key, trying to start his old Honda. His hands were shaking so bad, as bad as the other day when that bullet had sliced his ear.

He didn't hear anything, but he damn sure felt the cold. At the moment it was so cold it was as if it were burning his skin, just below that same ear.

"Hands up," a voice said, almost cheerfully.

Avery yelped with fright and threw his hands up. "Don' kill me!" he pleaded.

"That's up to you. Move slow an' behave, an' you'll be fine," the voice said.

Mike walked a very compliant Avery over to Sarge. Doc already had Ned there by the time they got there. Marv and Goat were kneeling on the ground beside Ned and Mike told Avery to get down with them. He pushed Avery down to a kneeling position and the man obediently put his hands on his head.

Chapter 34

I ran out and jumped on the Polaris, then realized I had left the key inside and had to run back in. All the girls were in the kitchen looking at me. I paused for a moment, flashed a big smile and waved the key at them and turned and ran out the door. Meathead was unfortunate enough to be standing outside the door when I crashed into it and it into him. He jumped off the porch and looked back at me in what could only be the dog version of *sumbitch*. He got over it and was at my side as I started the ATV and put it in gear and took off for the gate.

I was in a good mood despite everything that had happened. The thought of Sarge and crew showing up gave me hope that we could stop all the damn raids. I turned right at the road and raced off down the road toward Reggie's place, Meathead hot on my trail. Thad and Jeff had decided to stay and look after Reggie, since the painkillers had knocked him right out.

As I pulled through the gate, Jeff came around the corner of the house with his Mosin shouldered at low ready.

"Where's Thad?" I asked him as he tried to keep Meathead from licking his face. That damn dog had some reach when he stood up on his hind legs.

Pushing the dog off and wiping his face with the back of his hand, he replied, "He's inside. Stupid-ass mutt."

"What? He likes you," I said with a grin.

Jeff looked at the dog then at me. "I was talking about you," he said with a smile.

"*I* like you too," I said, bouncing my eyebrows.

He let out a laugh and headed for the house. I followed him, but Meathead smelled something and, with nose to the ground, headed around the back of the house. Thad was tending to the fireplace when we came in. There was one of those enameled tin coffeepots, the kind you buy in the camping section of Wally World, sitting on the coals. He looked up and flashed a big smile. Reggie was lying on the couch snoring.

"Hey, man, you need to come with me," I said to him.

His smile faded. "What's up?"

"It's a surprise; I can't tell ya."

Thad's brow furrowed, causing wrinkles almost to the crown of his bald head. "I don't like surprises anymore."

"Come on, get up. It's a good one, promise." Looking over at Jeff, I asked if he would hang out.

He looked at his wrist, then back to me. "Don't be long. I have an appointment with boredom in an hour."

"Don't worry, this surprise will take care of your boredom," I said with a grin.

While he didn't look thrilled with the idea, Thad did finally get up and follow me to the door. He stopped at the door, picked up his trusty old scattergun and put on his coat. I looked around for Meathead and couldn't find him, so I headed around the side of the house to look for him.

I found him out by the old barn where we had had the cookout. He was eating something off the ground, and I went over to see what he was up to. After all the shooting and people running and diving for cover, much of the food was spilled, except for the pig, thankfully, which Thad had taken inside. I was watching him eat mac 'n' cheese when Thad rode around on his four-wheeler. He pulled up beside me and stopped.

He sat there for a minute looking at the dog. "Get that."

I looked over at him. "What?"

"That," he said, then drew the big bowie knife I had given him during our walk home, flipped it so he was holding the blade and threw it. It stuck in the ground and I looked where it landed.

I didn't see anything, but walked over to it. Caked in dirt and dried grass was a finger. I nudged it with the toe of my boot. It was the tip and second knuckle. I reached down and picked it by the tip, looking at it.

"What'da you want to do with it?" I asked, looking back at him.

"Don' know, jus' don't want your dog to eat it."

I walked over to the fence and threw it out into the woods. What else could I do with it, feed it to the pigs?

There really wasn't anything else to do, so I walked around the house and got on my machine. Thad followed me out the gate as I headed for the roadblock. We rode along without talking and when we got there Thad still wasn't talking. He just leaned against the logs and looked at the people walking by. It wasn't a horde or anything, but there was a steady stream of people walking north into the forest.

After a few moments of staring at people walking by, he looked over at me and said, "What's this 'bout?"

"Believe me, it isn't a bad thing," I said, then kinda looked off to the side. "Well, that's debatable."

Thad stared at me for a moment. "All right, I'll play your game. You better hope it ain't debatable."

We silently watched the people pass by for a while. It was the same crop of poor, pathetic-looking souls as before. None of the people we saw going by looked like they had any hope, any fight left in them. It made me reflect on our situation, on how fortunate we were to have what little we did, and that little was getting littler every day. I was absent-mindedly watching the people, lost in thought, when I realized the people had stopped. They were all just standing in the road, looking north. They didn't appear scared or anything, just stopped, almost as one, looking down the road. A couple of them were shading their eyes to get a better look.

With the roadblock set back off the road as it was, we couldn't see down the road to what they were looking at. Thad noticed they had stopped as well and straightened, resting the old coach gun over his shoulder. "Somethin's comin'."

"Looks like it," I replied as I stepped around the barricade. Thad followed me and we walked out to the road. A few of the dozen or so people close to us saw us as we approached. Some of them moved away from us, and others simply looked away, back down the road.

Out on the road we could see something but couldn't make it out. It looked like a large object, long, but not real tall or wide. We could see the walkers step out of the way as whatever it was slowly worked its way past.

"What the hell is that?" Thad asked, more to himself than to me.

I was straining to see when I remembered the binos. I pulled them from the pocket on my vest and took a look. Without knowing I was doing it, a smile spread across my face. Thad must have looked at me and seen it. "What the hell you smilin' at?" He looked back down the road. "Gimme them," he said, reaching out for the binos.

Taking them down from my face, I looked at him and smiled, then handed them over. He took a look after adjusting them so he could see. Thad stood there for a long minute looking down the road.

"What the hell?" Then he dropped them and looked at me. "Is that who I think it is?" Before I could answer, the binos were back at his face. "I'll be damned, it is. You knew he was comin'?"

"I just got the message this morning, said we had friendlies coming. Didn't know for sure it was him, though, and it looks like the guys are all there too."

Thad took another look through the binoculars. "Looks like they got some other people with 'em too," he said, then handed them back to me. "Look."

I took another look down the road. They were closer now and I could occasionally see two or three other people step out from behind the buggy Sarge was riding in. Naturally the old man was in the passenger seat and looked like he had his feet up on the dash.

"Almost looks like they're tied up," I said.

Thad said, "What I thought too."

It didn't take long for the two buggies to make their way to us. Sarge was grinning from ear to ear. Ted was beside him, driving what was beginning to look like one hell of an ATV buggy of some kind. Mike and Doc were behind them and in between them there were four men. Their hands were bound, and they were tethered to some kind of strap. Fortunately for them, the ATV wasn't going too fast.

It rolled to a stop in front of us. The people who had been

standing there looking at their approach stared at them for a moment before continuing on their way, showing little interest at all in what was happening. Sarge sat there with a foot up on the dash and hands resting on his knee. Thad was grinning ear to ear.

"Look at this pair of nuts, Teddy," Sarge said by way of a greeting.

"You boys lost?" Thad asked.

"You know the old man could get lost in a round room," Mike called out.

"Shut up, dickhead," Sarge called out. "Nah, I knew you two would get yer asses in some trouble an I'd have to come bail you out."

"Who're your friends?" I asked.

Sarge looked up at me, jutted a thumb over his shoulder and asked, "You know any of these shitbirds?"

The four men just stood there. One of them looked pissed. At first I didn't realize I'd seen him before. I was looking at the biggest of the bunch, who looked as though he had been crying. Before that realization came to me one of them spoke up.

"I know who *you* are, Haywood."

I looked at him and a thin smile spread across my face. "Oh yeah, I know you. Looks like you boys really screwed the pooch."

"Tell this sumbitch to let us go. You know who we work for."

I got a chuckle out of that. I remembered the exchange we had had at the store. He didn't say enough that day to give me much of an impression of him either way. But here he was, tied up behind Sarge's war wagon, and that was all I needed to know.

"How's your little girl an' the other casualty?" Sarge asked.

"She's doing okay, but I'd like Doc to look at her. Reggie is all right, he's just pissed that he lost the finger," I answered.

The man who had been speaking snorted.

"Anyone else hurt?" Doc asked.

Thad pointed at me. "Him. He took a round to the chest, magazine stopped it."

"Were you hit the same time as they were?" Sarge asked as he stepped out of the wagon. Mike, Ted and Doc also got out and walked up and we all shook hands.

"Yeah, I was standing in front of a big smoker. Lit me right up, I imagine," I said, then reached down and stuck my finger through the hole in the mag pouch.

"Damn, how's your ribs?" Doc asked.

"Still a little sore, but I'm all right. Can you come up to the house and check out my daughter for me?"

"Sounds good. Mike, you an' Ted stay here an' keep an eye on things. We'll take our friends with us," Sarge said as he walked around and climbed in behind the wheel of his war wagon.

Doc got in the other one while Thad and I headed for our ATVs. Sarge looked back over his shoulder at his prisoners. "Y'all keep up, now, ya hear?" and started to pull through the barricade. I sat on my Polaris as they came through. The one in the lead, the one I remembered, had a look of disgust on his face. The next two looked resigned to whatever was in store for them. The last one, the chunky guy, looked me in the eyes as he came past. He looked pained, scared maybe.

Thad raced ahead to show Sarge the way, and I brought up the rear. As we eased along, the old boy looked back at me once. Something was there. I wasn't sure what it was, but it was definitely something.

As we came up to the house, Mel, Taylor and Little Bit came out on the porch. Little Girl was barking at all the activity. When the girls saw the four men, they stepped behind Mel. Mel was looking around, first at Sarge and Doc then at the other guys. Sarge was out of his buggy and untying the men from the tag line. They still had on the flex cuffs that bound their wrists.

"All right, ladies, take a seat and behave. Try anything an' you won't live to see what happens," Sarge said. "Doc, grab yer sack of goodies an' let's have a look at the little girl."

Doc reached in to pull his bag out as Sarge headed for the porch. I met him there to introduce him to Mel and the girls, who were still hiding behind her. I'm sure to them he was quite intimidating: camo uniform, all sorts of gear and weapons hanging off him and his personality took up a lot of room.

As he stepped up to the porch he took off his boonie hat and said, "Ma'am."

"Sarge, this is Mel, my wife, and my daughter Taylor," I said.

Little Bit had stepped over behind me, hiding behind my legs. Mel greeted each of them. Taylor was a little shy, but they were friendly. Little Bit wouldn't come out.

Sarge knelt down. "An' who's this little lady?"

She buried her face in my leg. I reached back and put my hand on her head. "This is Ashley. We call her Little Bit."

Sarge let out a laugh. "Well, if there ever was a Little Bit, she's it," he said with a smile.

She relaxed a bit and came out from behind me. Mel and Taylor relaxed as well. Doc came up with his big pack, and

I introduced him. Sarge asked Thad to stay out and watch the men on the ground. Thad nodded and tilted the old shotty over his shoulder. The rest of us went inside to see Lee Ann, who was still lying on the couch.

She looked up as we came in, a little nervous at first with the new people, but Doc had a great bedside manner and was soon checking her over. She got a little nervous again when he asked her to lie back and started pressing on her belly. His diagnosis was that she was okay, but that the wound looked a little red—not infected yet, but it could be heading that way. He was concerned there could be some foreign debris in the wound, maybe a piece of denim from her pants. As a precaution he was going to give her an intravenous antibiotic that he said he had brought just for this.

Lee Ann wasn't real thrilled with the idea of the needle but she took it like a champ. Doc told her to just rest and let the medicine run in. Then he made himself a hero by pulling three cans of Coke and three Hershey bars out of his pack, distributing them to the girls. They all squealed with delight when he handed them out, each saying thank you before tearing into them.

Thad opened the door and stuck his head in. "Morg, you guys need to come outside." From behind him we could hear shouts and arguing.

The three of us went out the door. Mel started to follow, but I stopped her, asking her to stay in the house. I wasn't sure what the hell was going on and I didn't want her or the girls outside. She nodded and said she would keep the girls in the house. Outside I saw that one of the men was sitting off from the others and the other three were yelling at him, telling him to shut up.

Sarge wasted no time, wading into the three men and

telling them to shut up. They ignored him, so he had to get their attention.

"Shut up, dammit!" Sarge shouted.

"You keep yer mouth shut, fatass!" the one the fat guy called Marvin shouted.

Sarge kicked the man in the chin. He sprawled out onto his back, unconscious. The other two quickly looked away, not wanting the same. Sarge looked back at Thad and said, "What the hell's goin' on?"

"Morg, you need to talk to that one," Thad said, pointing to Avery.

I looked over at the man who was separated from the others. He looked as though he had been crying. He sat on the ground with his bound hands in his lap. I asked Thad what was up.

"Ask him," he answered.

Sarge was still standing amidst the other men and Doc was on the porch leaning on the handrail. I walked over to the old boy and nudged him with my foot. "What's up?"

He looked up at me and his face started to contort. "I didn't mean to shoot the girl. It was an accident, I'm so sorry," he blubbered.

It took a minute for it to sink in. "What?" He looked away from me. "You sayin' you're the one who shot at us the other day?"

"Yes, sir, I was told to come back and try to scare you folks. If you'da just went to the camp, it wouldn't uv happened."

I looked back at Sarge, then over at the other guys, then back to the one on the ground. The man Sarge had kicked was starting to come around. He was moaning a bit and rolling his head.

"Wake up, asshole," Sarge said as he kicked the man in the thigh.

I stood there thinking. These were the men who had attacked us the other day, and probably the same ones who had been in on the previous attack. I was getting pissed. I hadn't noticed that Doc had walked off the porch and was standing beside me. I stepped away with my hands on my head. This guy almost killed Lee Ann.

"I was jus' doing what I was told," the man whined.

I spun around and started toward him. The carbine was across my chest hanging from its sling, but I didn't think about it and instead drew my pistol as I approached. The man still had his head down as I started to bring the pistol up. Doc grabbed my hand. He was shaking his head. "Not now. We need to talk with these guys."

"They almost killed my daughter! There's no talking now!" I shouted at him.

"Don't worry, Morgan; they're going to get what's coming to 'em, but first I need to talk with 'em a bit," Sarge said.

The other two men on the ground were suddenly restless. The third man was finally sitting upright, rubbing his chin and spitting blood. He glared up at Sarge. "You dumb sumbitch, you don' know who yer fuckin' with."

Sarge ignored the comment, instead looking at Thad. "We need a place where we can talk with these guys—not around here, not where's there's any kids."

"Let's take 'em back to Reggie's place. There's a barn there we can use," Thad said.

"I want to move these guys, but I don't want to parade 'em through town. Morg, that Suburban run?" Sarge asked, and I nodded.

"Thad, go up there an' get Mike an' Ted; I'm gonna need

their help," Sarge said. Thad jumped on his ATV and headed for the barricade. "Get 'em on their feet and load 'em into the truck. Morgan, I know this is personal to you, but trust me, they'll get what's coming to them, just let me do what I need to first."

I didn't acknowledge his statement. I just turned and kicked the one man in the ass. "Get up," I said as I holstered my pistol. Sarge told the other men to get to their feet, the man he had kicked wasn't moving fast enough for him, so he kicked his boots. "Hurry up or I'll do it for ya."

While Sarge was wrangling his prisoners, I went over and started the old truck. I hadn't driven it since I had acquired my Polaris, and it took a few cranks to get it started. I let it sit there and idle for bit and went into the house while Doc and Sarge were loading up the men. Mel was sitting on the couch with Lee Ann. The other girls were lounging on the floor in front of the fire, half dozing. Mel looked up as I came in. "What's going on out there?"

"It appears those guys are the ones who shot at us at the cookout."

"They shot Lee Ann? What's going to happen to them?" she asked, anger rising in her voice.

"Sarge wants to interrogate them, then we'll see what happens," I said.

"You better kill them. They tried to kill us; you better not let them get away."

I leaned over and kissed her. "There's no way in hell they are getting away, I can promise you that."

Mike and Ted were standing beside the truck when I came back out. All the guys were loaded into the back of the Suburban and Sarge was talking with Thad. He stopped as I walked up and said, "Let's take 'em down to Reggie's place."

I climbed in and Sarge got in the passenger seat. He looked over and smiled a creepy smile at me, then Mike and Ted got in the back seat. I drove out the gate with Thad and Doc following in the two buggies. Nothing was said as we drove along. In the rearview mirror I could see Mike watching the men in the back. As we approached the corner where the stocks were located, Sarge let out a chuckle.

"What the hell's that, Morgan?" he asked, looking out the window.

"We built them to have something to do with people that broke the law. Shooting everyone for everything wasn't working out."

"I guess not. Good idea, how'd it work out?" Sarge asked.

"We only had one person in there and he probably needed killing."

Sarge looked over but didn't say anything. The rest of the trip was silent. Jeff was at the gate when I pulled through it. Thad pulled around me and waved for me to follow him around the house to the barn. I stopped the truck in front of the door into the small room on Reggie's barn.

As we were getting out, Reggie came out the back door. He stood there for a minute looking at the group as we all emerged from the old Suburban. He walked up to me, looking at Sarge and crew with suspicion.

"Who the hell are they?"

"No worries, man, they're friends," I said, but it didn't do much for his disposition.

I did a quick round of introductions. Reggie shook each of their hands. As he was shaking Sarge's hand, the old man looked down at Reggie's.

"Well, looks like all the fingers are on this one; how's the other one?" Sarge asked.

Reggie held his other hand up, still bandaged up. Sarge looked at it, then called over his shoulder, "Doc, come take a look at his hand, see if he needs anything." He looked back at Reggie and said, "Let him take a look at it. He's a pretty good sawbones."

Reggie nodded and Doc walked over to him. The two of them went into the house. When they walked away, Sarge returned to the truck and opened the back gate. He said, "Okay, ladies, end of the road. Get out," and waited for the men to climb out. He told Mike to keep an eye on them for a minute and went over and opened the door to the small room in the barn.

Sarge went over and whispered to Mike and Ted and then asked me, "Is there a toolshed or anything like that around here?"

"Yeah, back over there," I said, pointing behind the barn. "I'm gonna go get another friend of mine I want y'all to meet and later, and if it isn't too much trouble, I got another guy that Doc needs to look at."

"Fine," Sarge replied with a wave as he headed for Reggie's shop.

I climbed back into the Suburban and drove over to Danny's house. I wanted him to meet Sarge and the crew. When I got to his house, he wasn't there. Bobbie said he was over at Miss Janice's house digging her a grave. *Shit*, I had forgotten all about her. I drove over to her house and found him working on the soft sand in her front yard. He must have known I was coming. He had two shovels there, so I dropped in beside him and started digging.

Chapter 35

Doc was finishing up the redressing of Reggie's hand when Sarge got back from taking a few things from the toolshed. Sarge asked how it looked and Doc told him that it looked really good, that someone did a good job. When Reggie told him it was a vet, Sarge let out a laugh and shook his head.

"Lucky you got a good vet, then. Did he give you your shots when you was there?" he asked with a grin.

"Naw, but when I woke up I had one of them damn lampshades around my neck."

"Oh damn!" Sarge shouted, and Doc laughed.

"I hope he didn't clip your nuts; I ain't checkin' on them," Doc said, and Reggie and Sarge both laughed.

"Hey, Reggie, you got any water?" Sarge asked.

"Yeah, they's a drum out back there. I fill it at Morgan's house—well, he fills it and brings it down here."

Sarge stood there for a moment studying the man. "Ole Morgan's a good man, huh?"

"Yeah, he is. He does a lot to help people. A few of us around here stick together, we look out for each other."

Sarge nodded his head. "I know: people worth a shit seem to be drawn together. I'm gonna get some water."

"Help yourself," Reggie said.

Sarge found the drum. There was a piece of hose sticking

out of the top, and it didn't take long to get water flowing out into an empty bucket that was sitting there. Sarge filled the bucket, carried it over to the door in the barn and set it down.

Inside the small room, there were four men standing on their tiptoes with their hands tied to trusses over their heads. Sarge told Mike to go find something to blindfold them with. Ted had one foot in the seat of the chair and was resting his elbows on his knee. Sarge looked at the men and smiled. He was met with blank stares for the most part.

"You boys sure are quiet," Sarge said.

"We ain't got shit ta say ta you," Marvin told him.

"You will, you will," Sarge said, nodding his head, then looked at Ted. "Help me take him down."

Ted and Sarge took Marvin down from where he was hanging. He tried to struggle once, just as Sarge had hoped. They cut him down, but his hands were still bound. Marv tried to hit Ted, more of a push so he could make a run for the door. When he did, Sarge was waiting. He was holding his Taser in his hand. He had removed the cartridge and was all ready for the contact tase he delivered to Marv's neck. Marv immediately yelped and went rigid. They dragged him over to the chair in the center of the room and without a lot more effort had him seated and tied, hands to the armrests and legs to the chair legs. Sarge then knelt down and cut the laces on his boots, pulled the boots off Marv's feet and then his socks and tossed them aside.

"What the hell are you doin'?" Marv yelled.

Sarge stood up and looked down at him. Reaching out and tousling Marv's hair, he said, "Don't worry, you'll see soon enough."

Mike came back into the room with an old sheet and an old towel. Sarge told him to save the towel and cut up the sheet. Mike and Ted went to work making blindfolds, and the ripping and tearing of fabric unsettled the men a bit. Sarge took one from Mike and hung it on a nail, tossing the towel over his shoulder. Mike and Ted covered the eyes of the other three men. With the blindfolds on, there was a very noticeable change in the breathing of all the men, an obvious increase in the rate and volume of air they were sucking in and blowing out.

Sarge motioned for Ted and Mike to follow him and they stepped out the door.

Marv started fighting against his bonds as soon as they left, rocking the chair and straining with everything he had to try and break free.

"Marv, did they leave?" Goat asked.

"Yeah, see if you guys can get loose. We need to get the hell out of here."

When the door opened again, though, their hopes sank. Without saying anything, Ted and Mike grabbed Marv on either side and tipped him back, laying him on the floor.

"What're you doin'?" Marv shouted.

Sarge was standing over the man, looking down at him. There was no smile this time.

"When I was a boy, I had a dog," Sarge said.

"Who gives a shit?" Marv shouted.

"It was my dog, but I wasn't allowed to feed it. Worst beatin' I ever got was for givin' my dog a hot dog." Sarge paused for moment, then continued, "You know why I wasn't allowed to feed that dog?" He looked down at Marv.

After a moment Marv realized the old man wouldn't continue until he answered. "Why? Like I give a shit what they fuck—" Sarge planted a boot on his chest and pressed the air out of him.

"I wasn't allowed to feed the dog 'cause my old man fed the dog, an' he was a mean sumbitch. He fed the dog 'cause he pissed in the dog's food ever' time." Sarge paused for a moment, looking at Marv. "Know why he did that?"

Marv shook his head. He was relieved when the old man took his boot off his chest. He took a deep breath, and Sarge straddled him.

"He said he did it so the dog would know who the boss was." As Sarge said this, he reached for his fly and started to undo it.

Suddenly Marv had a terrifying realization and started to cuss, but a towel was quickly pulled tight over his face, so tight he couldn't even turn his head, though he continued to scream through the towel.

"You son of a bitch! Don't you even think of it, don't you fucking dare!"

"Right now, you're about to see who's boss." With that, Sarge reached into his pocket, took out a plastic bottle filled with water and unscrewed the top. "So who you think's the dog in this equation?" He began to slowly pour the water onto Marv's towel-covered face.

At first Marv sputtered against the water, then he simply pursed his lips so none of it would get in his mouth. He was still growling through the towel, or maybe it was a choked cry. Marv tried to hold his breath, but the way the towel was holding his head back, it ran into his nose. Even clean spring water on a warm summer day that finds its way into your nose will burn, and that burn just reinforced the idea that this man was pissing on his face.

Sarge looked up to Ted and nodded, then reached back to his fly and pulled his pecker out. Ted quickly pulled the blindfolds down on the other three men so they could see Sarge shake it over a soaked Marv, who was trying to blow water out of his mouth. The other three men hung from their ropes, mouths agape. Ned shook his head slowly from side to side and his eyes were wide with shock. Sarge waved at Mike, and he pulled the wet towel off.

Before Marv could catch his breath and say a word, Sarge opened the door and reached outside for a PVC pipe he had loaded with sand earlier. With the other three men watching, Sarge gripped the pipe and swung like he was batting cleanup in the bottom of the ninth in the World Series. The slap that followed the impact to the sole of Marv's right foot was thunderous, but not nearly as loud as the scream that came immediately from Marv.

Danny and I didn't say a word as we dug the hole. We moved like machines, neither needing direction nor offering any. When the hole was deep enough, we went into the house to get the body, again in silence.

I went into a bedroom and stripped the sheet from the bed and carried it back out to the kitchen. We spread it out on the floor and with Danny grabbing her feet and I her shoulders, we moved the body onto the center of the sheet, wrapped it up and carried it back out to the hole. As is always the case with this sort of work, filling it in went a lot faster than the digging.

Danny was smoothing the small mound that would be the only indication that this was a grave. In a few years even the mound would be gone, leaving no outward sign of what this place was. I was leaning on the handle of my shovel as he smoothed the soft earth over. When he finished, we both stood there for a minute looking at the place. Again, there would be no words, no prayers or clichés. After a short pause, I looked at Danny.

"Hey, man, we need to go to Reggie's. There's some people there I want you to meet."

"Who is it?"

"Remember the old guy I told you about? Sarge? He's here with his crew."

"What are they doing here?"

"I sent him a message. He gave me some gear and told me to stay in touch, but it took me a while to get to it. I told them what's been going on here lately and they showed up."

"Cool, I'll meet you over there."

I headed back to the Suburban and drove back to Reggie's. Jeff was standing at the gate when I pulled up, looking a little disconcerted.

"What's up, dude?" I asked as I rolled to a stop.

Jeff looked back over his shoulder in the direction of the barn behind the house. "What the fuck is going on back there?" he asked, looking back at me.

I looked in the direction of the house for a long moment, then back to him. "I would assume Sarge is having a word with those guys."

At that moment, a long shriek rose from behind the house.

Marv screamed. His back was arched as if he were trying to push himself off the floor. When Marv was at the end his scream, Sarge swung the pipe again, this time at the left foot.

The pipe landed with a sickly slap. Marv's lungs were empty from the first strike. His tongue shot from his mouth, the veins on his neck and forehead stood out and he raised his head from the floor. He took a deep breath and letting out another long wail of pain.

Just seeing what he knew was in store for him was more than Goat could take. He started to scream and thrash against the rope binding his hands over his head. Ned just hung there, jaw slack and his eyes wide in terror. A puddle slowly grew around his boots. Avery simply cried, no struggle, no fight. He wept openly.

Mike moved quickly and delivered a quick butt-stroke to Goat's stomach. He immediately stopped screaming and went limp on the rope, moaning. Marv's scream had trailed off into a cry of sorts. Sarge took the pipe and tapped the man on his chest, causing him to flinch, close his eyes and look away.

"I assume I have your attention now," Sarge said as he leaned the pipe by the door. "You an' me are gonna have a talk now, an' if you got a brain in yer head you'll answer my questions."

Marv was breathing hard, his chest rising and falling as he huffed air. Sarge opened the door, reached out for a five-gallon bucket and brought it back in. After dumping his collection of goodies out of it—hedge clippers, an awl, pliers and other things—on the floor, Sarge turned the bucket over and sat on it, looking down at Marv.

Sarge sat there for a moment resting his elbows on his knees with his hands folded in front of him. He stared intently at Marv, then reached down and picked up the hedge clippers, holding them by the handle and chopping them a couple of times.

"What's going on down the road there?" Sarge asked and chopped the clippers again.

Danny walked up to Jeff and I as we stood there listening to what was going on behind the door in the barn. He looked at each of us curiously. "What's going on?"

"I think Sarge is in there having a talk with the guys who shot up the cookout the other day," I said.

Reggie and Doc came out of the house. Reggie's hand was wrapped in a fresh dressing. We stood in a group, trying not to really pay attention to what was going on behind the door, though for a moment it was quiet.

"How's the hand, Reg?" Danny asked.

He held it up and looked at it. "All right, I guess, for missing a finger. If I ever catch the sumbitch who shot it off, he's gonna pay for it."

Doc looked toward the barn. "Well, he's in there."

"Who?" Reggie asked.

"The guys that ambushed us at the cookout," I said.

"What, they're in there?" Reggie asked, glaring at the barn door. "How'd that happen?"

Doc said, "They greeted us when we landed, but they bit off a little more than they could chew. Once the old man heard them say they were working for the DHS, he scooped them up. We had no idea that they were the ones who ambushed you guys, but that fills in the picture a little. DHS has been trying to scare people into their camps."

Reggie moved toward the door, but Doc reached out and grabbed his arm. "Just wait. Sarge is still working on them."

Reggie shot a glance at him. "*Them?* How many are there?"

"Four," Doc said.

The door swung open and Sarge stepped out with Ted and Mike in tow. For a moment no one said anything. The door was open and we could all see inside, see the men hanging up and one on the floor.

"What's the word?" Doc asked.

Sarge scrunched his eyebrows and looked at the ground then crossed his arms. "Well, these boys—one of them, anyway, is the one who shot at you guys the other day. He hit Reggie there; you, Morg; an' your little girl."

"Why'd they do it? We wasn't botherin' them. Doc said they was workin' for DHS?" Reggie said.

"Yeah. They're being used to push people into going to the camps, the FEMA camps. If an area isn't down with the idea of being relocated, these boys go in and try an' scare 'em. Most of the time it seems to work. Sometimes, like with you guys, it doesn't and they get tougher. That's what the shootin' was about."

"What are you going to do with them?" Danny asked.

"That's up to y'all. I got what I needed from 'em. I ain't gonna do anything with 'em," Sarge said.

"What did you need from 'em?" Reggie asked.

"I needed a little info about the DHS operation and what was going on out there at the old bombing range."

"Right," I said. "Reg, you care if I do it in your barn?"

"Now, hold on," Sarge said. "If you boys are going to shoot 'em, and believe me when I tell you they need shot, use 'em to make a statement. Let the DHS goons know people aren't going to take their shit," Sarge said.

"What do you suggest?" I asked.

"Let's leave 'em where their buddies will find 'em. Oh, an' that reminds me, they have more back at their little trailer park compound who will have to be dealt with," Sarge said.

"Sounds good to me. Morgan, let me have yer pistol," Reggie said.

Sarge put up a hand, "I know you want ta get even, but wait on killin' 'em."

"Why? Let's get it over with," Reggie fired back.

"Simple: it's easier to make 'em walk than it is to drag 'em around. We get 'em to where we want 'em then do it, just less work."

I said, "Makes sense to me. Sarge, this here is Danny; Danny, this Sarge, Ted, Mike and Doc."

Danny went around and shook hands with everyone, and when that was done he said to Sarge, "You said there were more of these guys somewhere. What are we going to do about them? They got to be close by."

"We'll take care of them," Mike said.

"Need any help?" Danny asked.

"We'll work it out, but yeah, we could probably use the help if you want to."

We spent a little time going over what Sarge envisioned for the crew hanging from the rafters in the barn. I asked where they were planning on staying, mentioning there were plenty of empty houses around and they could probably take one of those. He said that it wasn't a good idea for him and the guys to stay there as they would probably draw a bunch of unwanted attention. Which brought him around to our security situation. He was less than impressed.

He liked the log barricades, if we were being attacked by Sherman tanks. He said the gabions were a really good idea, but they didn't have anything in them. He pointed out, in his usual colorful manner, that they were far more effective when they were filled with dirt. His overall opinion was that the area we were in was nearly impossible for us to secure with the number of people we had. He said we either needed to consolidate to the back of the neighborhood or relocate entirely.

None of us were very happy with the idea of having to leave our homes. Sarge made it pretty clear that he wasn't saying to abandon our homes yet, but that it might come to that. He said he and the guys were here for a reason and we weren't it, though they had enough mission latitude to include helping us out. He said that tomorrow he and the guys would start looking for a place to work out of, someplace out of the way and defensible.

I said, "I know a place. Not far from here, about ten miles, there's some cabins on the Alexander Run, coming out of Alexander Springs."

"That's a good idea if they're empty," Danny said.

"You'll have to show us. I'd like to get a look at them soon," Ted said.

"How about tomorrow?" I asked.

"That'll work."

Ted and Mike said they needed to go do something and took Reggie with them. They headed back to my house to get their ride and I got with Doc. I wanted him to go look at old Howard; it had been a while since I checked on him. There was just too damn much to do. Sarge and Danny went to take a look at the neighborhood to see what could be done to improve the security situation. Jeff headed for the barricade to check in on Thad. Doc, Jeff and I hopped into the Suburban and headed for the house.

"You really going to off those guys?" Jeff asked.

Doc looked back over the seat at him. "It's a messy

business, but what else can we do with them? They tried to kill you guys, weren't you there?"

"Yeah, I was there, and at the time I wanted to kill them, but now, after the fact, it seems different."

I said, "I was there too, so was my little girl who took a bullet from one of those sons of bitches. They need to pay, and there isn't much else to do with them. They deserve what they're going to get."

He didn't say anything in reply. I glanced at him in the mirror and he was looking out the window. I knew how the guy felt. Just a few months back, the police would have been called. An arrest would have been made and charges filed. The defense and prosecution would offer deals back and forth and then a compromise would be settled on. But things were different now. There was no law to call, no courts, and now men had to settle things amongst themselves. I understood that before everything fell apart, the "might makes right" argument didn't hold water, but it was different now. It wasn't that might made right these days, but if you didn't have might, you had no chance of ensuring that right—justice—would be done. And there was no one else to do it for you.

I knew Jeff hadn't expected to land in the middle of our troubles when he decided to stay with us and he was kind of playing ethical catch-up. It was more satisfying for me to explain things in terms of vengeance in this case, but I knew that underneath my rage there was a larger moral issue. I told him, "Think about it this way: these guys didn't give it a second thought when the DHS told them to shoot innocent folks and burn down their houses, right?"

Jeff said, "Yeah, I get it: they're bad guys. But still."

"I know. Judge, jury, executioner. I'm not comfortable

with that either. I mean, I know I'm doing the right thing here, but sure, there are plenty of people who are gonna take that too far. But I don't know what we can do about that right now. It's a big issue, and the big stuff is gonna have to wait until we see if we can survive the shit coming at us day by day. But what I do know is this: if we don't take care of these militia assholes, they're gonna do the same thing to someone else's family. So how do we sleep at night if we don't end them and later we find out they shot someone else's little girl? What I mean is that it's not just revenge, we have an obligation to take care of this because we *can*. Yeah, it sucks, but we can't just kick the can down the road. We *have* to finish this. If we don't, good people will die, and like it or not, that'd be on us."

Jeff thought for a second and said, "You should have been a lawyer."

I snorted at that. "Thanks, asshole."

"You know what I mean."

"Yeah, I know."

Chapter 36

Jeff walked up to the barricade from Howard's house while Doc and I went in to check on Howard. His wife met us at the door. She looked frail, gaunt, like it had taken all the effort she could muster just to open the door. She was gracious and kind, offering us coffee, though I doubt she had any. Doc and I both refused politely and asked about Howard. She led us into the living room where we found him sitting in a recliner.

From the looks of the chair and the debris piled around it, it looked as though he had been living in the chair. There were some plates and empty food cans. The most telling, though, which were as much an assault on the eyes as they were the nose, were the bottles of piss and the bucket half full of shit. It was obvious that he could no longer make it to the toilet, not that it probably worked anyway. I looked over at Doc and could see in his face the situation was not good.

Howard's chin was on his chest and it rocked back and forth in response to the old man's breathing. Howard's wife came in behind us, shuffling across the carpet in an old pair of slippers.

"Howard, honey, Morgan's here with a friend," she said as she moved blankets from the sofa. She was obviously sleeping there as well.

The old man roused in his chair, lifting his head. His eyes

looked wet and bleary, and at first he didn't understand. It took a moment for him to come around, but he pushed himself up in the chair and a thin smile spread across this lips. He blinked a couple of times and then his voice croaked, "Morgan, how are you?"

"Good, Howard, how's the leg?" I asked. I introduced Doc to them.

Doc took off his pack and set it on the floor and knelt down to start inspecting the wound. The couple had long since run out of bandages and from the looks of things were not boiling the old ones and reusing them. Paper wrappers from Kotex pads littered the floor, along with used pads stained with blood and discharge. Soiled strips of bed sheets were mixed in with it, adding to the foul mess around the chair.

Phyllis puttered around the room, fussing about the mess and ashamed that she hadn't had a chance to clean up before we came. Once the leg was exposed, it was obvious that it was not good. The leg from the knee down was red, swollen and angry-looking. There were dark red streaks running up the leg past the knee. Doc pulled a large absorbent pad from his pack, unfolded it and gently lifted Howard's leg as he spread it out on the footrest of the chair and laid the leg on it. He then went about cleaning the wound.

I stood off to the side as Doc worked, not saying anything while Phyllis sat silently on the sofa. Howard grimaced and shuddered a couple of times as Doc scrubbed the raw wound with a Betadine-impregnated surgical scrub.

"Howard, does the leg hurt much?" Doc asked.

Howard mashed up his face. "Naw, not really, a little sometimes but not really."

Phyllis looked over at her husband and said, "Now,

Howard. It does, mister, he's just too proud to say it. It hurts him plenty."

"Howard, I'm gonna get a couple of things for you. Just hang tight for me," Doc said as he stood up and motioned for me to follow him.

"Take yer time, Doc, I'm not going anywur."

I followed Doc outside. I shut the door as we went out. "What's up?"

"He's not going to make it. It's just a matter of time. All I can do is try and make him comfortable, sort of," Doc said.

"What do you mean 'sort of'?"

"I don't have enough pain-killers to keep him sedated till he goes. I'm going to leave them enough."

"Enough for what?"

"Morgan, you see how they're living. He hasn't been out of that chair in a long time. When was the last time you were here?"

"It's been a few days, I guess. I just got busy and forgot about him, honestly." I felt bad. I was the one that should have been checking on him, and I knew no one else would.

"It's not your fault, Morg. You're one man and can only do so much. These people are simply waiting for the end to come. That old man is going to die and then she will, one way or another."

"You're going to give them an out, that's what you mean, isn't it?"

"Yeah. If you can take her in, then do it. But if you can't . . . He's not gonna make it, and maybe they'd like to go together."

We went back in the house and Doc talked to Howard and his wife as he took out a small hard box. He took out a small vial of morphine and showed them how to use it. Doc used an alcohol wipe to clean Howard's leg, stabbed the small needle in and squeezed the light amber liquid in. Howard immediately went to sleep. Doc left the small bottle and a couple of syringes with her, stressing to her how much was too much, making sure she understood it.

Doc redressed the wound, using some of the Kotex pads from a box beside the chair. I assumed he didn't want to waste good dressings on the old man. Every decision we made anymore was a kind of triage. Once the leg was wrapped, Doc pulled some MREs out of his pack and left them with her. I asked about her water situation and told her that I would bring some over. We left the house, closing the door behind us. I didn't have much to say and told Doc I would see him later. I wanted to go home. He nodded his head and we parted ways, me going through the hole I had cut in the fence and he out through Howard's gate.

Taylor was sitting on the porch playing on Jeff's iPad as I came up to the porch. She smiled as I stepped up on the porch. I took off my rifle and laid it on the handrail, took off the vest and dropped it on the floor. She was sitting on the bench with her feet up. She sat up a bit and I sat down and she laid her head in my lap. I sat there rubbing her hair while she played some kind of game on the tablet and I looked out across the yard. It looked so normal. After a bit, she asked, "You all right?"

"Yeah, kiddo, I'm good, just wanted to hang out with you for a bit. It feels like I haven't seen you in forever."

"Yeah, you're gone a lot. Is everything okay?"

"So long as we're together, it is, don't you think?"

Mel came out on the porch and smiled when she saw me sitting there with Taylor. "Well, look at you two. You want some lunch?"

"I'd love some, if you two will eat with me."

"Lee Ann and Ashley are at the table," Mel said.

"Well, come on, kiddo, let's eat," I said to Taylor.

We went in and had lunch as a family. Mel had made a black bean soup from some of the freeze-dried stuff we had. Black beans, onion, green pepper, carrots and some spices of some kind—a simple dish, but it was damn good. I talked with the girls, told jokes and tried to pretend that it was any normal day and they had just come home from school. When we finished lunch, the girls cleaned the table off and worked together to wash the dishes. I went into the living room and sat on the couch. Mel brought me a glass of tea and we sat for a while, just sitting.

It didn't last long, though. Meathead started barking and a knock on the door soon followed. Thad was at the door with his big smile when I opened it.

"What smells so good?" he said.

"Black bean soup, you want some?" Mel asked.

Thad smiled and patted his belly. "I don't turn down good groceries, ma'am," he said.

"I don't know how good it is, but I'll get you a bowl."

"Don't let her fool you, it is good," I said as I waved him in.

"Thank you, Miss Mel. Can you put it in a cup so I can take it with? We need to go."

"Sure," she said.

"What's up?" I asked.

"Sarge wants to get this done," Thad said.

Mel walked up with one of those oversized coffee-cup-bowl things and handed it to Thad. "Get what done?"

I told her, "We're gonna take care of the guy who shot Lee Ann. Don't wait up, okay?"

Mel nodded and said, "Good. Just be careful."

I kissed her and followed Thad out.

When we got to Reggie's, he, Danny, Jeff and Sarge's guys were waiting.

"Now that yer all here, let's get down to business," Sarge said. "I know you fellas have had a couple of scrapes up to this point, but things are about to go to a whole new level and if any of you want out, just say the word. No one will think any less of you."

"No disrespect meant, but we don't need the speech," Danny said. I'd known him for a long time, but his determination there showed a different side of him.

"All righty, then. Ted, Mike and Reggie are going to hit the rest of these douche bags at their place and take them out. The rest of us are going to take out this trash, leave them where their DHS buddies are sure to find them," Sarge said.

"How are we going to do that?" I asked.

"I figured we'd take 'em down toward the range and leave 'em in the road. That way their patrols would find 'em," Sarge said.

"How are we going to take 'em out? If we just shoot at 'em, they'll be all over us," Reggie said.

Sarge looked over at Reggie. "That's a good question and shows yer thinkin'. Mike and Ted are going to use suppressed weapons when they hit those guys. You'll be outside to take out any runners."

Reggie stood up from the table. "I can take care of myself. I can go in there with 'em."

"I'm not saying you can't, but this is how this kind of operation is done. Someone has to be outside to take out anyone who gets past the first team. These guys have experience in this business; when was the last time you kicked in a door?"

"Since never. I got you," Reggie said.

"What about us?" I said.

"I'm coming along with you guys. We'll get the prisoners tied up and load 'em into to my buggy. Danny, I want you to drive it. Morgan, you and Thad ride ATVs, one in front and one behind, got it?"

"What about me?" Jeff asked.

Sarge said, "How good are you with that peasant rifle?"

Jeff didn't blink. "This isn't your average peasant rifle."

"I bet it ain't. You're with us," Sarge said as he turned away. "Reggie, we need some rags. You got any?"

Reggie nodded and headed for the house. Sarge went to the door on the barn and opened it. "Thad, Morgan, come in here and help me take these guys down."

We loaded the militia men into the Hyena. Ted was finished with Jeff's instructions and Sarge called for everyone to load up. Reggie got into the rear third seat of the buggy Mike and Ted were talking while Thad and I got on our ATVs. Danny climbed in behind the wheel of the Hyena and Sarge gave a couple of last-minute orders to Mike and Ted. They were to take up a position south of where we were going to drop the four men and wait for us. Mike nodded his head and drove away in the fading light of evening.

We took a trail out the back of the neighborhood with me in the lead. Mike followed along for a while until he got to the point where he would break off and head for their target. Since I was out front I didn't see them break off the trail, but the two clicks in the headset Sarge had given me followed by a one-click reply from Sarge told me they were leaving us. We still had a ways to go to get to the spot we had decided on.

Mike stopped on the thick edge of a swamp. The three of

them took a few minutes to cover the buggy with a camo net before taking a knee and going over the plan one last time. Ted scratched out a rough layout of the little clump of trailers, detailing how he and Mike would enter, go through them one at a time and then exit the area. He stuck a stick in the soft dirt to show where Reggie was to position himself and gave him instructions on who to engage and how to engage them. Women were off the list unless they were armed and posed an immediate threat. Any women he and Mike encountered would not be harmed unless they had to, and they hoped not to find any.

When the instructions were done, Mike handed Reggie a night-vision monocular, helped him get it on and showed him how to use it. Then Mike handed him one of the captured MP5s. He said, "I put an IR laser on this; here's the switch." Mike turned the weapon on its side to show him. "It'll show up nice and bright in the goggle, but no one else will be able to see it. You've got your radio. If you see anyone coming, let us know. If you see anyone running, take them out, got it?"

Reggie nodded and Ted said, "When we're in position we'll let you know. You reply with one key of the mic, then we'll move in. You ready for this?" Reggie nodded his head and turned to move off into the darkness. Mike and Ted were immediately on the move, heading the opposite direction from Reggie's line of travel.

Reggie moved carefully through the woods, like he would if he was deer hunting. He felt like he was moving too slow, but he knew that going quickly and being quiet didn't go together, and he forced himself to take his time. He could hear voices coming from the clump of trailers, and he knew if he made any noise they might hear him too. It was still early, but without electric lights, most people went to bed soon after the sun set. He made it to his assigned position and once there he understood why the guys had chosen it: it was the logical escape route from the trailers, almost a funnel out of the place.

Mike and Ted slipped silently around the edge of the group of trailers. Occasionally they caught glimpses of a fire burning out in the center of the park, but they couldn't tell if anyone was out there. The occasional voice drifted through the trees, but overall it was quiet. They made it to the corner of the first trailer, where they would start the clearing operation, and took up a prone position behind a long-dead pine tree. Ted keyed his mic. "In position, gonna wait a bit." A single click answered him.

Chapter 37

As we approached Highway 445 on the trail, I slowed to see if there was anyone around. Stopping a good fifty yards off the road, I called back to Sarge to tell him we had arrived and I was taking a look. He told me to be careful, and I eased up to the edge of the forest to take a look. I knelt down and listened to the black night, looking both ways, then listened again. Not hearing anything, I called back and told them it was clear and to come up, then climbed back up on the Polaris to wait for them.

It didn't take long for them to show up. Sarge waved me forward and I quickly crossed the road, pushing the Polaris wide open so as not to expose myself for long. The Hyena and Thad both crossed without incident and we were soon heading down an old power line right-of-way.

Ted looked at his watch then up at the sky—it was black as pitch. He tapped Mike on the shoulder and pointed toward the house. Mike nodded and the two men stood up. Ted keyed the mic and said, "Moving." A single click answered him.

Ted stepped up to the first trailer and gripped the knob. Mike nodded at him and he slowly turned it. It wasn't locked and they went in. Ted went left and Mike went right.

Ted moved down a small hall. The first door he came to was a bathroom, and he quickly pushed the door shut as the smell coming out of it assaulted his nose. The second door was a bedroom. There was a small bed there with a body lying under some blankets. From the size of the figure and rest of the room's contents, he concluded it was a child, a little girl. He quietly shut the door and moved to the last room. Ted looked in and saw a form on the bed, a woman. He shut the door and went back to the front door.

They moved on to the next trailer, and this one had lights on inside. Mike gripped the knob, looked back at Ted, got the nod and opened the door with a jerk. The door entered into the living room and the kitchen was visible off to the right. Sitting in a recliner was an older man, hunched over a TV tray, eating something. When the door opened he looked up, but never made a sound; a 230-grain, .45-cal ball from Ted's pistol crashed into his forehead, snapping his head back and splattering gore all over the wall. The suppressor on the pistol made a dull coughing noise and no more. The only other person they found was an old woman still asleep in the back bedroom. They left her as they found her.

After crossing the road we made our way through the thick sand under the power lines. We had to pull off the right-of-way when it turned to the west, crossing over the highway, and the many forest trails became our new route. I had been on many of them during hunting season or just riding around the woods and knew which ones to take to keep heading in our intended direction of travel. We wound our way along for some time, then Sarge called for a halt. I stopped and he pulled up to me. He had a map out lying in his lap. Thad rolled up behind him and walked over to us.

"I don't want to get any closer. We're close enough. They'll find 'em here." Sarge paused and said to Thad, "You an' Morgan ease out to the road and see if anyone's out there. Take a minute and look an' listen. We ain't in a hurry."

We moved off toward the road, making our way through the small sand pines and thick sand. It reminded me of my walk through the forest north of there to get home. The same green gloom filled my goggles as it had then.

We stayed just inside the tree line looking and listening for several minutes, not seeing or hearing anything. Finally Thad made a noise and I looked over in his direction. He jutted a thumb over his shoulder and I stood, half crouched and backed away from the road.

Danny, Jeff and Sarge had the four men out standing in a line.

"See anything?" Sarge asked.

"Nope, looks clear," I said.

"Let's get this done, then," Sarge said, then reached into the passenger floorboard of his buggy, took something large and flat and tucked it under his arm. "All right, ladies, hands on the shoulders of the man in front of you. Give me any shit an' you'll regret it." To emphasize his point, he drew his Taser, pulled the cartridge off the end and hit the trigger. The loud snapping and popping made the men jump, and they immediately raised their arms, groping at the air, looking like zombies in a bad B movie. When they were all lined up, we started out into the brush again.

When the four men felt the road under their feet, they were visibly relieved. Sarge turned and looked at us kind of expectantly. I just looked back at him. Not getting the reaction he was expecting, he held his arm out and waved it at the four men.

"Well? I can't do it. Has to be one of you," Sarge said.

I wanted to ask why. I don't know if it was genuine curiosity or a subconscious stalling tactic on my part, but I didn't get the chance. A loud pop and a flash of light caught me by surprise from my right. I ducked and looked just in time to see Goat fall back onto the pavement. Jeff was standing in front of the falling man, his suppressed Glock in his right hand. The other three men jumped at the shot and Jeff shot Marv next. Avery and Ned started to run blindly down the road into the night. Avery tripped and fell and it took two shots for Ned to go down. Jeff walked toward the fat man as he rolled around trying to get up. Jeff shot him in the top of his head and he fell over. Continuing past him to where Ned lay, he fired a round into his head as well.

Jeff calmly changed the mag in his pistol before reholstering it in the shoulder rig under his coat. Seeing everyone looking at him, he said, "What?" He nodded at me, and I knew my speech earlier had hit home.

Sarge said, "You're a weird little fucker, aren't ya?"

"Yeah, but in a good way," Jeff said.

Sarge smiled and shook his head. "All right, drag 'em all to one spot."

We worked together to drag the bodies together. Sarge wanted them all in a sitting position, leaning on one another with their legs out like an X. Once they were all positioned, Sarge took out what was tucked under his arm. It was a big piece of cardboard. He unfolded it and painted in large letters it read LOOTERS AND MURDERS WORKING FOR THE DHS.

We didn't linger once the job was done; no high fives or shit talking. It was a quiet and somber walk back to our rides.

"Where are all these guys? There were more here earlier," Ted whispered to Mike as he shut the door to the trailer.

"I don't know. Where's that fire we saw on the way in?"

Ted shrugged, then pointed around the corner. Mike nodded and they started around the small trailer. As soon as they rounded the corner, they found the rest of them. They were sitting around the fire pit. One of them was standing and looking in their direction.

Mike raised his pistol and fired at the standing man. Two rounds and he was down. The other three scrambled for their weapons. Mike engaged a second as Ted drew down on the two other targets. After a moment of rapid firing, they changed the magazines in their pistols. There was one trailer left and they quickly searched it. There was nothing inside except a mess; the place was filthy.

The two quickly made their way back to the fire, policed up the fallen weapons and exited out the rear of the little complex. As they moved toward the tree line, Mike keyed his radio. "Coming out," he called to Reggie, who replied with a single click. Reggie fell in behind them and the three made their way toward the trail Sarge and the others would be coming back on. Picking out a spot on the side of the trail, they took up positions and waited.

We rode out of the woods and onto the road, hauled ass down the pavement to the intersection with 445 and made the left onto it for the short distance to the trail. Once we were back on the trail, I heard Sarge call Ted on the radio telling him we were close. They were ready. Through the goggles I saw the UV laser Ted flashed to show their position and soon we were stopped while they loaded up. The rest of the trip was uneventful and we were soon home.

We went back to Reggie's house for quick chat. Sarge and the guys were going to stay there that night, but the next day he wanted me to show him the place I had mentioned. He told all of us that we needed to start thinking about bugging out. He said the neighborhood wasn't defensible, and things were going to get rough soon. Danny wasn't happy with the thought of leaving his house and neither was I, but he had a point.

I went home and found the house quiet. Mel was sitting on the couch staring at the fire that crackled in the fireplace. When I went to sit down with her, she moved her pistol off the cushion.

"You hungry?" she asked.

I shook my head. "No, thanks, though. I'm tired."

"What's wrong?"

I looked at her with a half smile. "What isn't?"

Her reply was to lean over and kiss me, and then she stood up and grabbed my hand. "Come on, let's go to bed. It'll be all right in the morning."

We went to our room and I started pulling off all the gear—vest, holster, the carbine—and deposited it beside the bed, then just fell into it. I really wanted to clean up but didn't feel like taking a cold-ass shower at the moment.

I woke up and bolted upright in the bed, my heart pounding in my ears. If I had been dreaming I didn't remember it, but I was damn sure rattled by something. I sat there in the dark, listening for a minute. Everything seemed fine, but I swung my legs out of the bed and pulled my pants on. After picking up the carbine, I slipped my feet into some Crocs and went out to the living room. Everything was quiet and I went and checked on the girls. After making sure they were okay, I went out the front door and stood on the porch, looking at the blackness and listening to the stillness. There wasn't anything out there, but I still felt weird.

I went back in the house and grabbed my coat, then walked out to the gate. It was quiet and I didn't see anything. About halfway to the gate the dogs came trotting up, yawning and looking sleepy. I figured if they were sleeping and nothing was bothering them I should go back to bed. As I walked back to the house with the dogs in tow, a string of far-off shots broke the silence, five or six full auto rounds ripping into the night. In the old days it was nothing to hear a few rounds popped off, didn't even warrant a second thought, but things were different now, and I wasn't going to go wandering around in the dark looking into it. I went inside, locked the door, checked on the girls and went back to bed.

I slept through the night without any more disturbances and woke up feeling good. Knowing I was going to meet with the guys that morning, I decided to make some breakfast for everyone. I set a bunch of eggs out and lit the old Butterfly then headed out to the shop for a can of the Red Feather cheese. I grabbed one of the last two canned hams I had and headed for the house.

The stove was ready and I set the twelve-inch cast-iron skillet out, then poured in a little oil. After cracking the eggs, chopping the ham and shredding the cheese, I poured the eggs into the skillet and stirred them around until they firmed up then added the cheese and ham. I took the pan from the heat, set it aside and replaced it with our small, flat skillet. Since things had gone south, Mel had been keeping fresh tortillas in the fridge. She made them every couple of days as needed. Taking the stack from the fridge, I heated them one at a time on the skillet and then filled and rolled them.

When I was done I had about a dozen burritos. I thought about making coffee, but knew Sarge would certainly have some ready when I got there. I felt kind of bad about not leaving any of the burritos for Mel and the girls, but there was plenty for them to eat, even if was only oatmeal. I put the burritos in a plastic grocery bag and went to tell Mel good bye.

She was still in bed and she let out a little sound—half groan, half sigh—when I put my arm over her, pushed my face into her back and held her for a minute.

"What are you doing today?" she asked without rolling over.

"We're going to go look at the cabins on the Alexander Run. We might have to move there."

She rolled over now, far more awake. "Move there? Why would we need to move there?"

"Things are going to get a little more dangerous around here. We did something last night that's going to stir up some shit."

"I don't want to leave here. As bad as things are, at least we still have our home. How do you think the girls would take it?"

I rolled away from her, putting my feet on the floor. "We may not have a choice. As bad as things are, they might get a lot worse."

Mel sat up on her left elbow, looking at me. "Well, I don't want to leave unless we have to. And I mean *really* have to."

"I got it. I'll see you later. What are you and the girls going to do today?"

"We're going to rake pine needles from the driveway and use them to replace the hay on the floor of the porch. The chickens have made a mess of it and it needs done," Mel said as she sat up.

"Good idea. I'll be back as soon as I can. Love you."

"Love you too."

After strapping on all my hardware and grabbing my sack of burritos, I headed out for the Polaris. As soon as I came out, the dogs were on me, or at least they were on the bag of breakfast. They followed me to the ATV and sniffed around as I climbed on. They followed me to the gate and I had to lock them in to keep them from following me to Reggie's.

I found all the guys sitting on and around the picnic table behind Reggie's house. Sarge and a couple of others had coffee, though I didn't know how much longer that was going to last. My stock was down to two cans. The burritos really got them excited.

"Hot damn, breakfast! We were just talking about shootin' one of the hogs and dressing it out just to have something to eat," Sarge said, then stuffed the end of a burrito in his mouth.

We had our breakfast and then it was time to get down to business. Sarge wanted to take his two buggies to go recon the cabins. Since there were eight of us, he wanted four of us to go and four to stay. If he had his way, the four who stayed would start packing up and getting ready to move, but Danny and I held our ground about not wanting to bail out of our houses so quick. Sarge let it die for the moment and then went about making assignments. Mike, Ted, he and I were to go on the recon. The rest of the guys were going to hang out and keep an eye on things.

I pointed out the general area of the cabins on Sarge's map.

He said, "Looks like a good spot. Having the creek there behind it helps it with defense, not to mention having water right at the back door."

"Yeah, it's a nice creek too, good clear water and lots of fish."

"Let's go look at the place, then."

We took off toward the back of the neighborhood and picked up the trail out into the forest. Sarge and I led the way. He had his boot up on the dash he looked relaxed with the SAW swinging from the loose grip of his right hand. Our route to the cabins on the creek would take us past a small neighborhood, a collection of houses out in the forest, which made me wonder how those folks were doing. The only real issue they would have was water, the creek was about a mile from them and it would be a long walk to haul water.

I said, "We have to pass some houses up here in a bit, don't know if there's anyone there or not, or how they are going to react at seeing us."

"Is there a way around 'em, or do we need to go through 'em?"

"We'll be on a dirt road that runs past them. We could go through the forest around them if we need to."

"Let's see what it looks like when we get close to 'em. If the road is blocked or looks hinky, we'll go around."

The trip through the forest was uneventful, we didn't see anyone. We picked up the dirt road that would run us past the houses, and I told Sarge to keep his eyes open. He nodded and we kept going. Sarge called Ted on the radio and told him to keep his eyes open too. Mike was driving the second buggy and Ted was on the SAW mounted to the passenger side. It didn't take long to find out if there was anyone around; we came across three of the residents walking down the road.

Sarge and I saw them at the same time. He sat up in the seat and kept an eye on them as we approached. Hearing us close on them, the three turned and stood on the edge of the road looking at us. They were all young guys, midteens from the look of them. Each of them had a rifle of some sort and one of them was holding three or four limb rats by the tail. I slowed as we came abreast of them and they stood there looking at us and at one another nervously.

Sarge leaned back in the seat, putting a boot back up on the dash. Sarge stretched an arm out and rested it on his knee.

"Looks like you boys had some luck," he said. I was sure if he hadn't broken the ice the three of them would have stood there forever.

The one holding the squirrels raised them a little, looking at them. "A little. Three limb rats don't go far, though."

"Y'all live over here?" I asked.

The one that answered had long blond hair sticking out the bottom of a knit watch cap with a skull and crossbones embroidered on it. "Yeah, but most everyone has left. There's only a few of us left now," he replied and wiped his nose on the sleeve of his hoodie.

"Where'd they go?" Sarge asked.

"Some went to stay with family, some went to the camp over there at the range," Snot Nose said.

"Are your folks still around?" Sarge asked.

The one holding the squirrels answered, "Yeah, they're back at the house."

"Can we meet 'em?" Sarge asked.

The same one asked, "You guys with the government?"

Sarge chuckled. "Naw, son, we ain't with the government, I promise you that."

"That's good. Wouldn't be good to meet my old man if you was."

"If y'all want to hop in, we'll give you a lift home and meet your folks," Sarge said.

The boys hesitated for a moment, then with a shrug they got in. The blond-headed one gave directions to their house. It was only one turn off the main dirt road onto a smaller, secondary dirt road. After turning off onto the side road, we started to see people through windows and heads poking through open doors. In front of the kid's house, a big, burly man stepped out of a tidy double-wide sporting a Realtree-camoed shotgun.

He stood there taking in the scene as the boys climbed out of the buggy. His eyes shifted from Sarge and me to Mike and Ted, back and forth. He didn't say anything, just stood there looking with the butt of the turkey gun resting on his hip. The boy that had the squirrels walked onto the porch and spoke quietly to him. What I didn't see was the other men who were coming up the drive. Mike and Ted did and Mike let us know quietly over the radio. Seeing his backup arrive, the big man finally spoke.

"What can I do you for you fellas?"

Sarge stepped out the buggy, leaving the SAW in its mount. The man on the porch shifted the shotgun to a low ready position. Sarge said, "Easy, there, friend, we don't mean no harm. Just saw your boys walking down the road and gave 'em a lift is all."

The man moved his head in a barely perceptible nod. "I 'preciate it. Anything else?"

"No, nothing else. They said a bunch of the folks around here have packed up an' left. Why'd you stay?"

"We can take care of ourselves. We don't need no help from no one. The ones that left needed to go."

He went on to tell his opinion of people who depended on the government for anything, and it wasn't very flattering. Once he was on that train of thought, he seemed to open up a bit and relax. Sarge asked how they were holding up and he said that it wasn't easy but they were getting by. By hunting the woods and making the occasional trip down to the creek for some fishing they were managing to get what they needed. Sarge asked him about how many other people were around, and the man pointed to the five men standing behind us at the edge of his driveway. Aside from them, there were only a couple others.

Sarge asked him about what the feds were up to around the area. The man said that they had come out once about a week ago and offered people to go to the camp. That was when a bunch of folks left and they didn't know what happened to them after that. He knew it was at the old bombing range, but it was too far to walk, unless it was a one-way trip and he wasn't going to do that. He asked what we were doing out in the woods and Sarge told him we were out looking around. It was hard to tell if he believed us or not. Sarge asked him if he was in desperate need of anything.

"We could use a doctor. One of the younguns is sick; bad water, I think," the man said.

"Tell you what, we're gonna go down the road here for a bit then head back. Tomorrow we'll bring a doc by an' he can take a look at your little one."

"We'd appreciate it. I'm gettin' pretty worried 'bout her."

We said good-bye to them and backed out of the drive. The men standing behind us parted, letting us through. We drove the half mile down the road to the intersection with the forest road that headed for the creek. The small road to the cabins had seen better days. From the looks of it, during the rainy season the locals had used it for playing with their four-by-fours. The road was badly rutted, but the good thing about it was that it looked as though no one had been down it. We slowly bounced down the road to the cabins and pulled up to the little gate at the first one.

The gate was made from pipe, a small piece of chain on the end and a padlock secured it to a post. Climbing out, Sarge reached into the bed of the buggy and pulled out a pair of bolt cutters and had the lock off in no time. We walked up to the little cabin. It wasn't very fancy, basically just a plywood shack. The door and all the windows had padlocks securing them as well. Sarge handed the bolt cutters to Mike.

Mike took the big cutters and stepped toward the door, "That last one wear you out? What's wrong, didn't take your fiber this morning?"

Sarge's reply was a swift kick to Mike's ass, to which he responded with a "Hey!" while rubbing his cheek.

"You'll learn to keep yer mouth shut one of these days," Sarge replied.

"No, he won't," Ted said and we all laughed.

Mike cut the lock off, opened the door of the little cabin and stepped in, using his weapon light to illuminate the interior. Ted stood at the door where he could see the buggies

outside while the rest of us went in. There was nothing inside. It was one large room with a counter running along the
full length of the back wall. All the windows had screens
over them with plywood covers over them outside. These
were secured with the padlocks and could be raised and
propped up to allow airflow in the summer, though at the
moment keeping the inside cool was the least of our worries.
Heating these things would be the real issue.

Looking at the place, I was already thinking of how I
could put my wood stove in, and I had two kerosene heaters
as well. Between these, we could heat all of them. The kerosene would run out eventually, but we could get through the
winter with them, *that* winter at least. After looking around
the inside, we went out to look at the creek, the source of
which was the Alexander Spring, about a mile upriver. The
water there would be clean and safe as there were no people
in the area to foul it. The run behind the cabin was also full
of fish and gators. Large schools of freshwater mullet swam
the creek and could easily be netted.

Sarge said, "We need to get some boats."

"We have them," I said.

"What have you got?"

"Between Danny and me we have four kayaks, plus
Danny has a canoe and Reggie has one too."

"Perfect, they'll be real handy. I think this would be a
good place to relocate to for a while. I know you guys don't
want to, but there's a lot more resources here and it'll be safer."

"Yeah, Sarge, it's just like your poacher's cabin on the
river," Mike said.

Sarge just shook his head. "Teddy."

Ted kicked Mike in the ass and Mike spun around. "What
the hell, man?" Ted just shrugged his shoulders.

I said, "There's only three of these things; there's too many of us. I mean, I have five people, and there's Danny and his wife, Reggie, Thad, Jeff and you guys—where's everyone going to stay?"

"You an' your family take one, Danny and his wife can take one. The rest of us will use the third. You gotta remember that we won't all be inside here at the same time. There's gonna be plenty of work and security to pull, so it ain't gonna be too bad," Sarge said.

"I guess we'll make it work if you think we need to move. I know my girls aren't going to be happy about it."

"They may not be happy, but they'll be alive," Sarge replied flatly.

Chapter 38

We returned home the way we came and the whole time I thought about moving. How we would even get everything moved, what we would take. It was a lot to take in; it wasn't like packing a U-Haul in the old days. Trying to move everyone with just the Suburban, some four-wheelers and Sarge's little battle wagons would take a bunch of trips, not to mention fuel, of which there was precious little.

We made it back the neighborhood without seeing anyone, for which I was very thankful. There had been too much killing, too much shit for my taste. I was no soldier, no warrior—just a dad and a husband, and that's all I wanted to be.

We went back to Reggie's house and had a short meeting. Danny, Doc, Jeff, and the rest of us stood around the old picnic table shooting the shit for minute. There was a little talk about the night before, though Mike and Ted did give a quick rundown on their assault on the trailers. I wasn't too interested in the details. The talk finally got around to what was next and Sarge suggested we start the move the next day. Danny was on board with that, and I halfheartedly backed him up. Sarge let the issue drop without saying anything and moved on to his next plan.

"I want to go out and take a look at the camp over at the range and we'll need to do it during the day," Sarge said.

"How you wanna go about it?" Jeff asked.

"We need to be careful with this. I'll leave the operational things up to Ted and Mike. How do y'all want to go about it?" Sarge asked.

Mike and Ted shared a glance, then Ted spoke. "I think we need to take both battle buggies and two four-wheelers as outriders. When we get to the range, we'll need at least two to stay with the machines as backup for those going to take a look. We need to have a SAW on each buggy and those going in need to take Sarge's SPW."

The talk went on around the table for a while until a plan was ironed out. We would go out before daylight tomorrow. We weren't sure where to get a look, as there was a fence all the way around the range and some thick brush between the fence and the actual range. There were two entrances, one on the east side, one on the west. I didn't think we would be welcomed at either one, so we were going to have to find a way in.

Sarge passed out MREs to everyone for dinner. Danny and I both took a pass as I knew there would be something at home. I told Danny to bring Bobbie down and we would talk while we had dinner together. With that, we told Sarge and the guys we would be back in the morning. He wanted us back at 3:30. I rolled my eyes at him and he just shook his head and said, "Pussy." I smiled at him and got on the Polaris and headed home.

Mel had made a shepherd's pie for dinner using ground venison and instant potatoes. Thankfully, the pan was big enough for everyone. Mel came into the living room and gave me a kiss and a hug, then commented on my need for a shower. I hadn't taken one that morning and knew I needed to, so I told her I would go freeze my ass off and get cleaned up. She was happy when I told her Danny and Bobbie were coming down for dinner as she hadn't seen anyone but the girls in days.

The water was cold and made for a quick shower. Getting out, drying off and putting on some clean clothes felt so damn good. After pulling on some clean socks, I walked out to the kitchen to find the girls still at the table.

It was nice to sit with them and talk, a brief moment of normal. The girls were playing a round of tic-tac-toe and I got in on it with them, passing the paper back and forth, laughing at one another as we took turns. The dogs barking outside announced that Danny and Bobbie were there and soon they were knocking at the door. Since the girls had already eaten, we shooed them away from the table so we could sit together. They went into the living room and messed around on Jeff's iPad, and I felt even more respect for him realizing that he had never asked for it back. We ate our dinner and talked amongst ourselves.

The talk finally got around to the move. Danny brought it up when he asked about the cabins. I told him what they were like and the girls were immediately against it. Mel asked about the chickens and what we would do with them, about bathroom facilities and how that would be handled. When I told her we would probably have to use an outhouse of some sort, she was really not happy. Danny and I tried to get across to them that we were not convinced yet that we needed to move, but we might have to and we should start getting ready just in case.

The conversation carried on for a while longer about the whys and why nots of moving until Lee Ann came back into the kitchen with a Scrabble board in her hands, wanting to play. The rest of the evening was spent playing. Little Bit came in and sat in my lap and the two older girls joined in the game. The game took an hour or so and when we finished it was time to head for bed as Danny and I needed to get up early. The girls gave hugs and kisses and Mel and I walked Danny and Bobbie out. Mel carried the pan with the leftovers in it out for the dogs, who were very happy. Once they were headed toward the gate, we went back in and started shutting the house down.

After tucking the girls into bed and making sure all the doors were locked, Mel and I went to bed. I was leaning my carbine beside the bed when Mel pinched my ass. She was wearing only her bra and panties and quickly dropped those and climbed into bed.

"You're clean enough now," she said as she patted the bed.

I smiled at her and turned off the light.

I hadn't told Mel what we were doing, so when I got up at three she was curious. I told her we were going to check something out and I would be back soon. She told me to hurry because the girls wanted to spend some time with me, pointing out that I had been absent a lot recently. I told her I would try and kissed her, collected my gear and headed out.

Danny was already at Reggie's when I got there and the rest of the guys were milling about getting gear ready and loading the machines. Reggie and Jeff volunteered to stay behind and keep an eye on the place. Sarge, Doc and Thad would ride in Sarge's buggy. Mike and Ted would take the other, Danny and I would be the outriders. We performed a radio check using Sarge's radios and headsets and then the old man laid out a map, a surprisingly good map, on the picnic table.

Using the hybrid satellite map, he picked out the area he wanted us to look at. It was on the north side and we were on the south side, so we would have to work our way around the range. With our destination selected, Sarge looked to Danny and I for the route in. What he wanted was a path that wouldn't go anywhere near where we were last night. I told him we could use the route I had walked in on; it would take us to the west of the range and bring us up on the north side. Using my index finger, I traced it out on the map.

Sarge nodded his head as I traced the route. He then picked two rally points out, one for the ride in, one for while we were there, and then pointed out the route to use on the way back. It would take us to the east into the forest before turning south to head home. With the plan laid out and everyone confident in it, we headed for our vehicles.

For this trip Thad was carrying one of the MP5s captured from the raiders. He had his trusty coach gun with him as well. He was riding in the back of Sarge's buggy. The H&K looked ridiculously small in his big hands. Since I knew the route, I once again took the lead. Danny would ride parallel to us, keeping to our east as we moved north. We all had radios and could maintain contact, though it was understood we would keep transmissions to a minimum.

The trip to the north side of the range took a couple of hours. Every road we crossed required security precautions to be taken, slowing things down even more. We didn't see anyone on the way, and that surprised me. As we got closer to the range, I got more nervous, remembering the Humvee I had seen at the barricade and what the hippies had told me about the DHS troopers coming out and making sweeps. I remember the kid with the messed-up teeth saying if you went along with them they wouldn't bother you, but if you crossed the line they'd drop the boot on you. We were almost a mile to the west of the range, moving down small trails that rose and fell when Sarge called me and told me to stop on the next rise for a piss break.

At the crest of the hill I stopped and climbed off the Polaris. The two buggies soon pulled up and shortly after Danny came out of the woods as well. Sarge used the break to give a few last-minute instructions. We would leave the rides on that side of the road that ringed the range and go in on foot. Two men would stay with them and the rest of us would go in. Ted and Doc volunteered to stay behind, and Sarge liked that idea, Doc staying back in case anyone got hurt.

We loaded back up on the rides and headed for the point we would leave them. It didn't take too long, and again Sarge called for a halt. The two buggies each had a SAW mounted on them. Mike picked up Sarge's SPW, the shortened version of the same weapon, and slipped the sling over his head. Little was said as we trotted off toward the range, with Sarge in the lead and Danny and I bringing up the rear. At the road that separated us from the range, Sarge paused, taking a knee and checking the road. After a moment, Sarge waved Mike forward and he sprinted across the road.

After another short pause, Mike gave a thumbs up and one at a time we crossed the road. Once we were on the other side, we immediately set off again. Mike stayed in the lead, working his way toward the fence. Once we were at the fence, a new problem revealed itself. On the inside of the fence and immediately behind it, the ground had been plowed up for about twelve feet and dragged with what was probably a piece of fence weighed down with something. What this did was create a track trap; if anyone walked across it, it would be obvious the ground had been disturbed. This was a problem.

The best solution was to wait out the patrols and time them and see if they were regular or random, and then plan an entry, but we didn't have that kind of time. Instead, Sarge positioned Danny at the fence where he could see down it in either direction for several hundred yards. If he saw an approaching patrol, he was to call it in and we would bug out. Not the best plan, but all we could do at the moment.

Mike cut a small hole in the fence and we quickly moved through it. The final approach was made much slower. Mike set the pace and we slowly made our way through the pine brush. Eventually the trees started to thin and the camp started to come into view. We spread out in a loose line and crawled up on our stomachs, staying just inside the tree line but with a full view of the camp from a small sandy hill. What stretched out before us was impressive and intimidating at the same time.

Rows and rows of tents, the big military style, ran off for what looked like a mile. There were neatly painted signs that I could read through my binos. They were marked with letters and numbers and at intersections there were posts with signs that read MEDICAL, MESS HALL, SHOWERS and LATRINE. The place was not what I had expected; it looked nice. I had been expecting a concentration camp.

I told Sarge that.

He said, "What do you see down there?" looking through his binos.

I scanned the camp again. "Tents, people, chow halls and latrines. Looks like a well-run refugee camp."

"That's what I was thinking," Thad said.

"I see that too, but there's more," Sarge said.

I scanned the camp. "Like what?"

"You see the yellow tape?" Sarge asked.

"Yes."

Yellow caution tape like you'd see on a construction site ran down the two sides we could see, supported intermittently by four-by-four posts.

"See anyone outside the tape?"

I scanned the area, then I saw what Sarge was getting at. There were guard towers at the corners with machine guns mounted in them.

"You see across the camp? See those towers?" Sarge asked.

I looked across the camp. We could only see the tops of several towers, but coming out from behind a row of tents was a part of a cage made from chain-link fence. It even had a top on it. Inside I could see two people in orange jumpsuits. They looked like inmates at the county jail.

"I guess they probably have some bad apples," Thad said.

I grunted.

"All right, do you see that group of people down there working, the ones with shovels?" Sarge asked.

I looked down on the camp and did see a group of people that were filling what looked like sandbags. They worked in twos, one holding a bag, one filling the bag with white sand. Standing around them were several armed men forming a loose ring around them. I still didn't think it was as bad as Sarge was making it out to be. A cloud of dust rose from the front of the camp, and all the people looked toward it, which was what caused me to look that way.

A row of four white buses came rolling to a stop, escorted by Humvees with gunners and machine guns in their turrets. Hearing faint shouts, I looked back to the group that was working. The armed men were shouting at them, pointing and running around. The workers went back to their task, though most of those holding the bags kept an eye on the buses.

A group of armed men gathered around the buses before the doors opened. The doors soon opened and people began to pour out. The group of armed men waiting on them began to drive them toward a fenced area with kicks and shoves. It was obvious the people getting off the bus were disoriented, and that's when I noticed the windows on the buses were blacked out.

"How's that look for friendly?" Sarge asked.

I scanned the camp again, looking back to the group filling bags as shouts drifted across the camp. Two women were working together; an older-looking woman was holding the bag as another filled it. The one filling the bag paused for a moment and looked up toward the woods. She wiped her forehead with the back of her hand, then looked down at her palm and rubbed at it. She turned a bit and I could see her face. I reached over and hit Thad. He looked at me and I pointed.

"Look at those two women," I said.

"Where?" Thad asked, looking at the group.

"On the right side, she's looking this way, see her?"

Thad stared through the binos for a second. "Yeah, I do."

The radio cracked. *"There's a truck on the fence line,"* Danny called.

"Let's go, move, now!" Sarge barked.

We crawled back from the trees and rose to a crouch and began to sprint back to the hole in the fence. Sarge called Danny asking for an update. He told us to hold inside the trees. There was a small hill the truck would start down in a moment and we would be able to cross without being seen.

Mike was kneeling at the edge of the drag, the SPW pointed down the fence.

"Move, move now!" Danny called.

We sprinted across the drag and pulled ourselves through the fence. It seemed to take forever with mag pouches hanging up and other things snagging. As soon as we cleared the fence, we all started moving toward the road in a sprint. Mike hit the road first and took a knee, scanning the road. Once everyone was at the road, Mike sprinted across and I followed him. Just as I cleared the road, Thad started across. He was at a full run in the center of the road when a Humvee rounded the corner fewer than one hundred yards from him.

The truck gunned its engine, and even over the sound of the diesel I heard the gunner yell, "Contact front!" and then his machine gun opened up. The driver drove hard and fast and was between our two groups in a flash. Mike immediately opened up on the truck. We gave them fire from both sides of the road and the driver began to back out as the gunner shouted.

Mike was screaming for us to move, and in the radio I could hear Sarge say he was moving south to cross the road. The firing let up on his side as they started to move. Mike called out, "Reloading!" and suddenly it was real quiet, with only Thad firing. I hadn't even pulled the trigger. The Humvee roared its engine again and the gunner brought his weapon to bear on our side of the road. The amount of lead slapping into the trees around us forced the three of us onto the ground. Leaves, pine needles and debris fell on us like a storm.

The sound of all those bullets cracking over our heads was terrifying. Mike was screaming into his radio and suddenly

Ted appeared, standing over me. He fired the SAW from his shoulder in long bursts and brass spewed from the hot weapon down around me.

He let off the trigger for a second, looked down at me and screamed, "Get up! Get up and fire your goddamn weapon!" Then brass was pouring from the weapon again, a constant flame erupting from the muzzle. Mike had his weapon reloaded and joined in. I pulled myself up and flipped the carbine to fire and began firing at the windshield of the now-retreating truck.

On my radio I heard Sarge call out, *"Let's go, dammit! Get your asses to the buggies!"*

Ted called out, "Reloading!" then looked at me. "Go, go, go, go!"

Thad was just as wide-eyed as I was. The two of us took off at a run toward the machines. We broke out of the trees to find Sarge and Danny already there. Somehow they had crossed the road and made it there before we did. In a flash, Mike and Ted were there as well. Everyone mounted their machines and Sarge called out for us to follow him. He took off wide open to the north, with Danny and me behind him, and Mike and Ted bringing up the rear this time. We ran hard and fast, not knowing if they had a reaction force on the way or not. Any minute I expected to see a helicopter overhead, but we were moving too fast to be too worried about it.

We ran north almost to Highway 40, then turned east, going as fast as we could on open trails. Without slowing or waiting, Sarge crossed over Highway 19 with the rest of us hot on his tail. As I crossed the road, I looked both ways real quick and was relieved beyond words not to see anything. We were on the back side of Grasshopper Lake, a good six miles from where the shootout happened, when Sarge stopped. Ted and Mike pulled up beside him and were talking. I pulled up on the other side of them and stopped beside Thad in the rear.

I looked in at him and said, "Dude, was that Jess?"

Epilogue

Jess grounded the tip of her shovel in the dirt and looked over at the buses that had just arrived. Mary hissed, "Come on! We gotta meet our quota!" She held out the sandbag she and Jess were filling.

One of the DHS goons barked, "It's not break time! Keep working!" and Jess went back to digging. After the raiders had hit her neighborhood and killed her parents, she had been happy to get on the bus to the FEMA camp. There was nothing left at home: no family, no food, no hope. But at the camp, things didn't turn out the way the black-uniformed men had promised. Families were split up, malcontents were beaten or disappeared, and there was no going outside the fence. After a week of denial, Jess understood that she had volunteered for a prison sentence. A week after that, she thought something different. It wasn't a prison; it was a concentration camp.

People she had met who couldn't keep their opinions to themselves—libertarians, old-school liberals, Reagan conservatives—became scarcer and scarcer. And rumor had it that on the other side of the detainment area was a series of trenches dug by bulldozers. People pointed out that the detainees, what the DHS goons called the "resisters," never seemed to increase in numbers. You could see them through the chain-link, but no one was allowed close enough to talk to them.

Mary asked her the question that got her thinking: "We see them arrest people every day and send them to detention. So if there's more people going into detention all the time, how come it's always the same number of people you can see through the fence?" Mary was black, and she followed that question with another one: "You've seen how many black people get off those buses. So where are they? How many black people you know in this place?"

"Just you," Jess said.

"Right, just me. And how many black people do you see in the detention yard? Not so many, right?"

Jess's stomach had done a flip; she knew where this was going, and she suddenly knew she had known it for a week without admitting it to herself. "Yeah, not so many," she said.

Mary said, "I was a math teacher, but anyone can work those numbers."

Jess said, "Maybe they're sending them to different camps."

Mary snorted scornfully. "Sure. Maybe they're putting all the black folk in another camp. What's that sound like to you? But if they're doing that, how come we never see lines of black people being loaded onto buses? I'll tell you why: this place is a DHS roach motel. Blacks check in, but they don't check out. And it ain't just black people; we're just easier to notice. It's the ACLU and Second Amendment people too. Anyone that's doesn't have the sense to toe the line. Anyone that's not going to be a good citizen of the new America."

Jess wondered how it had gotten this bad this quickly.

Wasn't anyone standing up to the government? But she knew the answer, and it was the same answer to the question people had been asking for seventy years: why did the average German go along with Hitler? And the sad thing, Jess thought, was that it was the same stupid answer that every teenager gave when they got caught doing something stupid: "It seemed like a good idea at the time."

She thought about Morgan and Thad and hoped to God they were okay. She knew they'd never agree to take their families into one of the camps, but she knew too that meant they were probably dead.

Turn the page for a sneak peek

BOOK 3 OF THE SURVIVALIST SERIES

ESCAPING HOME

A NOVEL

A. AMERICAN

AUTHOR OF **GOING HOME** AND **SURVIVING HOME**

978-0-14-218129-4

PLUME

Prologue

It took weeks to walk to home, but I made it. The entire time I was focused on just getting there. I never really gave much thought to what would happen afterward. Even my most pessimistic thoughts of how life would be at home didn't come close to the reality. Now our neighborhood is basically empty. Many have simply disappeared. We are down to our small group now: my family, my neighbors Danny and Bobbie, and Sarge and his gang. Fewer people around means more eyes on us, attention we certainly do not want.

In the Before, people used to talk about the FEMA camps and whether or not they would ever choose to go into them. In the Now, with the harsh light of reality shining on the situation, many of those who said they would never be taken to one of these camps were happy to walk in on their own. We've been the target of raiders and of the federal government, both apparently trying to force us into the camps. Now we must decide whether to stay and fight, or find someplace to retreat to. Escape may be our only option.

We have a place—the perfect place for long-term survival, really. But my family, Mel and the girls, may not be ready for it. While the rest of the country may have fallen apart, our preparations are mitigating the effects they feel. With running water, power and abundant stored food—at

1

least for now—they see it as an apocalyptic holiday. But there are forces at play, beyond our control, that may bring about this last desperate move.

Life in the camps isn't what it appears to be. While there is food, water and warmth, the price is near slave labor and virtual imprisonment. In the care and custody of FEMA, backed up by the DHS, those inside the camp have no rights, no freedom and, worse yet, are exposed to the possible brutality of their caretakers. Every barrel has a bad apple, and over time those bad ones start to rot the good ones. Left unchecked this rot can take over the entire barrel. With so much absolute power over so many helpless souls, horrors are bound to be committed. Among those in the camp is our friend Jess, who walked with Thad and me on our long adventure home. We don't know how she's faring, but with the mixed reports about the camp, one thing is certain: surviving in the camp may prove far more difficult than the struggle outside.

Chapter 1

Every day when her work detail was over, Jess would try and visit her brother. It was best to stay busy like that, otherwise the memories would return. It was the thoughts of her mother that were the worst. The image of her mother lying on the cold dirt as the light of the flames consumed what little they had in the world, the dark crimson stain on the ground around her. And her father . . . he'd resisted and was made an example to the others as a result. These images were burned into her mind like an overexposed negative.

Thinking back to the raid made her feel nauseous. Everything had happened so quickly. It was late in the evening when a couple of old trucks sped into their little hamlet of cabins. Before anyone could react, the shooting started. Her dad put up a fight even after he was gunned down. Her mother ran to his side, picked up the pistol and shot one of the raiders, but just after she hit him, she was immediately gunned down. Jess managed to make it into the woods with some of her neighbors, running as fast as her legs could carry her. Waiting as she heard the bloodcurdling screams and shots was agonizing. When she returned back to her home, she found the raiders had stripped the place, taking everything they could physically carry away. And to her shock, she found her brother, Mark, lying unconscious on the ground.

Jess sat on the ground with her brother's head in her lap, shocked. She tied off the wounds on his arm with her flannel and wrapped a blanket that she retrieved from one of the smoldering homes around his stomach, but there was nothing else she could do. She spent the night under the old oak trees, cradling her brother in her arms. Sleep never came as she kept checking his pulse, feeling it grow weaker and weaker with each hour. When the sun rose, she was relieved to see big white trucks show up, American flags painted on the sides and the letters FEMA on the doors.

The FEMA people immediately set about treating Mark, making him comfortable, bandaging his wounds and loading him into one of the trucks. He needed more treatment, and they told her that she could go with him to one of their facilities. She gladly climbed aboard. Once she was in the truck, a man in a uniform clipped a form to her shirt, the label DD 2745 emblazoned across the top of it. As they were pulling away, she could see others loading her mother and father into body bags. She began to cry. At least they would be buried.

Along the way, they stopped at small communities or refugee camps where others joined them on the trucks. Several more wounded were also loaded in beside Mark. All of the stories were horrible, though very similar to Jess's experience. The raiders would come in and take what they wanted: food, guns, tools, tents. The worst stories included people disappearing, women and children mostly.

After a few hours, the truck rumbled through a gate and stopped. When the doors opened Jess shielded her eyes against the midday sun and gazed upon the camp for the first time. Jess climbed down to see rows upon rows of tents filling an area the size of two city blocks. All around her were people in uniforms with guns. While the wounded were carted off to one area of the camp, she and the other healthy refugees were ushered to a large tent. Before entering it, they were subjected to a thorough and invasive search, in which suspect items were tossed on the ground by the guards. Jess's feeling of salvation was fading, being replaced with one of fear.

After everyone was processed, they were given food and a beverage that tasted like Gatorade. It was amazing to be eating meat loaf with mashed potatoes, and Jess savored it. As they ate, names were called out and each person went to a series of tables in the front, where they filled out forms. All sorts of information was collected—the obvious question about name, age, sex and religion, but also more interesting questions, about NRA membership, club memberships, political party affiliation and whether or not they were on any form of government assistance. Jess filled out the questions without a second thought, and it seemed that the others did too. No one was willing to question the process.

The last two stations were the medical station, where they received a very basic physical examination, and a station for a psychological evaluation. Jess answered the questions for the psych evaluation dully, unable to emote the anguish that she felt for her mother and father. Once through the last station, she was free to chat with others in the tent and continue eating her meal, though it was made clear that they were all forbidden to leave. Jess spent her time looking around, observing the disheveled masses that surrounded her. A short time later, a series of names were called and each person was photographed and issued an ID badge. Jess was given a yellow badge. The little plastic card included her picture, name, Social Security number and, once again, the DD 2745 ID number that she was given in the truck.

Once the badges were issued, an announcement was made for everyone to gather under the flags that matched the color of their badges. This was where the first signs of trouble appeared. Families were separated into different color codes, and people began to protest. The agents in the tent assured everyone it was only a temporary situation and would be resolved shortly; the different-colored badges simply meant various kinds of additional steps were needed to secure their status. This satisfied most people and they quietly went off to sit in their assigned housing areas.

Jess sat sipping on her drink, absentmindedly observing the other people that were being processed. A few feet away from her, a middle-aged man sat giving his name and social security number just as everyone else in the room had. His info was entered into a laptop by a woman in a DHS uniform. She asked him to give her the tag on his shirt, which he did. She tapped away, then asked him some questions, which he answered. She looked back to her screen for a moment then looked up to one of the armed guards and waved him over.

Two of them approached, she showed them something on the screen and they exchanged words that Jess couldn't make out. The man was getting nervous. "What's the matter?" he asked.

They ignored his comment, and then one of the guards told him to stand up and put his hands behind his back.

"What for? I didn't do anything. I came here for help."

One of the guards drew a Taser. "I said put your hands behind your back! Do it now!"

The man leapt from the chair. "I didn't do anything! I didn't do anything!" he shouted as he tried to run for the door. There was a pop and the man crashed to the ground in front of Jess, writhing and screaming. She jumped from her seat and gasped, shocked at what she'd just witnessed.

The two guards were instantly on him, pulling his hands back. "Don't resist or you'll get it again!" The man tried to wriggle from the burly officer's grip. "Hit him again!" the guard shouted. Jess could hear the *clack-clack-clack* as the voltage pulsed through the man.

The sudden violence scared a number of people in the tent and they started to get up, trying to get out. Guards wearing gas masks blocked the doors, holding large cans that looked like fire extinguishers under their arm. "Return to your seats or you will be pepper sprayed!"

Jess knelt down in front of her chair. The man being cuffed was a mere four feet from her. She could see his eyes, wide with fear, tears rolling down his cheeks. He was quietly whimpering, "I didn't do anything. I didn't do anything."

Once he was trussed up, the DHS woman who started it all came up and spoke with one of the guards.

"Here's his paperwork."

"Which list is he on?" the man asked, looking the forms over.

"He came up on a couple. He's subversive by nature."

They grabbed the man by his arms and dragged him out of the tent. Jess slowly got back in her chair, thinking, *What have I gotten myself into?*

Once Jess was in her housing unit, a big military-style tent, she listened to the orientation speech given by a red-haired woman in a black uniform who identified herself only as "Singer"—no first name. The speech covered the *security protocols* in great detail. It was stressed that the security rules were for their safety and there was no acceptable excuse for violations. The lecture went on to inform them they would soon be taken to shower (*A hot shower!* Jess thought to herself. *I can't even remember the last time I had one!*) and given a uniform. The guard stressed that it was mandatory to always be in uniform with your ID badge plainly visible on the outside of your clothes. And perhaps most important of all: no one was able to leave the camp without express permission of DHS officials. Even portions of the camp itself were not able to be accessed by civilians—the off-limits areas were identified on a large map of the camp. Some areas of the camp were simply marked as crosshatched areas. Nothing inside these areas was identified. She went on to say that they could use the common area just outside the tent but could not wander freely around the camp—again, for their safety.

Singer told them to each pick a bunk and get settled. As they were bustling around the room, she informed them that the next day they would get their work assignments, which caused a heated exchange as to why they had to work. Some women were up in arms about it, but Jess didn't really care—it was something to do other than sit around and worry about her brother. Singer explained that the shifts for different duties would rotate, and while some were still grumbling, for the most part, the ladies settled down.

Jess approached Singer as she was headed out the door and asked whether she would be able to go to the infirmary and visit her brother. Singer replied that as long as she did her work, she could go. Jess was relieved to hear that; she was sick with worry over Mark. In the truck the medical staff had said they assumed he was bleeding inside his skull, but they had neither the facilities nor the personnel to address such injuries. Time was the only medicine they could offer. She decided that she would head over to visit him as soon as she picked her bunk, eager to leave behind the chattering and noise of her many tent-mates. It would be nice to get a little privacy after today's activities, even if it only meant walking to see her brother.

Jess quickly settled into her new routine at the camp. Each day she and the others were woken up, put in formation and given breakfast before being told their work assignments. Sometimes these jobs lasted a day, sometimes several. All the jobs were mindless and boring. Jess often found herself reminiscing about being in her college classes at FSU—even her most dull ones were more exciting than the tasks she had been assigned so far at the camp. One morning during breakfast, she began to laugh, something she hadn't done in a long time. A young black girl in front of her in line turned around with a puzzled look on her face.

"I'm sorry, but it feels like we're in that movie *Groundhog Day*. We're doing the same thing over and over," said Jess.

The girl laughed and said, "You're so right! Only we don't have Bill Murray here to crack us up. We only have *Singer*," she said, mimicking the DHS leader's strut. Jess giggled and the girl offered her hand. "I'm Mary. I think we're in the same tent."

"Yeah, I thought I recognized you. We came in the same day. And I'm glad that I'm not the only one getting annoyed by our lovely leader," Jess said.

That day Mary switched to the bunk next to Jess. They

became quick friends, relying on each other to listen and for support. They both needed someone to open up to, to share the weight they carried. Unlike many of the women in the tent, Mary also felt as though the safety and security they hoped the camp would provide was beginning to feel more like a sentence than salvation. It was good to have a friend around, Jess thought. It broke up the monotony of their days.

When the shooting started, Jess was on a detail filling sandbags. The sudden long burst of machine gun fire caused everyone to stop and look up. Then several more weapons began to fire in a terrifying fusillade of gunfire. The security detail with the work group screamed for everyone to get on the ground. Three men ran through the group pushing any slow-moving bodies down before falling into the deep sand with their weapons pointed in the direction of what was now obviously a battle of some sort.

Jess covered her head as the gunfire crackled around her, a now all-too-familiar sound that caused her to shake uncontrollably. Mary crawled over to her, hugging the ground.

"What's going on?" Mary asked, fear in her eyes.

All Jess could do was lay there with the side of her head pressed into the sand. She was too scared to even speak.

The security elements' radios were full of shouts and calls. Then the camp siren began its long wail, adding to the din. Just when Jess thought it would never stop, the gunfire ceased. Humvees and ATVs were racing all over the camp as the sound of the siren began to wind down. Shortly after, the security officers jumped to their feet and ordered everyone up. They began herding the work detail back toward the housing area.

The camp was a hornet's nest of activity. Once they were back at their tent, they were ordered to lock down, which consisted of sitting on their bunks in silence. To most of the women in the tent, the idea of sitting in silence after witnessing such violence was a joke. As soon as the door shut, they were all moving around, offering their theories and breaking into their respective cliques.

Jess was sitting on her bunk with her arms wrapped around her knees, her face tucked into them. She was trying to calm down, shaken by the memories of the last time she had heard a firefight. Mary leaned over, smiling.

"Hey, girl, it's okay! We're safe now."

Jess forced a smile in return.

"Hey. I counted twenty-seven today; that's the most yet," Mary whispered to Jess. Mary had been trying to count the number of government personnel working in the camp. It was something to do to pass the time. Until today, she had identified twenty-three.

"I wonder how many people actually work here?" Mary asked, seemingly to the air. Jess knew she was trying to get her to talk, but she just wasn't interested.

Mary continued chatting. "Get this. Apparently the shooting was from people *outside* the camp. Rebels."

Outside of the camp? Jess couldn't believe it, even though her work detail was by the perimeter, and the noise was coming from that direction, the thought of being attacked by outsiders seemed unbelievable. The camp was supposed to be a safe place—and now people were shooting at it? She couldn't take any more. Pulling her wool blanket up, she rolled over and closed her eyes.

Chapter 2

Since I was in the lead, everyone followed me into my driveway. I drove around the house and stopped outside my workshop.

Thad jumped out of the buggy he was in and rushed over to me. "That had to be Jess! It was, wasn't it?"

"Man, it sure looked like her. It had to be."

Sarge was in earshot. "Who, Annie? Was Annie in that camp?"

"It sure looked like her, Sarge," Thad replied.

"Why in the hell are you still calling her that, anyway?" I asked, rolling my eyes at Sarge's nickname for her.

"I'll call her whatever I want!" The old man snorted. "I just wish we could have confirmed whether it was her or not. If them assholes hadn't started shooting we may have been able to."

The guys all gathered around as a lively discussion about Jess began. Jeff interrupted with, "Wait, wait. Who the hell's Jess?" All the guys stopped talking and looked at me expectantly. I gave him the elevator version: how I met her back when all of this chaos started, how she wouldn't leave me alone until I agreed to let her walk with me. Thad chimed in about how she and I met him, and how she took to calling him the black Incredible Hulk. Together we told him about the family we tried to help, and Thad told about the shooting where I was injured. Once Jeff was up to speed, the talk moved back to her being in the camp. Sarge wanted to go get her, but knew it would be foolish to even consider.

"How'd she look?" Sarge asked.

Thad looked at me, and we both gave a little shrug. "Looked okay to me," I said.

"Yeah, she looked all right. She was working, filling sandbags, from what I saw," Thad said.

Sarge nodded his head. "That's good. Anyone hurts that girl, I'll kill 'em deader than shit."

While he was stewing, I ducked into the shop.

"What the hell you doin'?" he called out as I crawled around under the shelves.

Spinning around on my knees, I held up a bottle of whiskey. The old grouch smiled, executed a perfect about-face and stepped out the door. I followed him out, twisting the top off the bottle as I did. I turned the bottle up and took a long pull on it. After what had just happened at the camp, I needed a drink. We stood around by the shop and passed the bottle. It wasn't long before my daughters Little Bit and Taylor came out. They were slightly more at ease around Sarge and his crew now.

Sarge saw Little Bit coming toward us and knelt down, holding the bottle out. "Want a sip?"

She screwed her face up. "Eeww, no, that stuff's gross."

Sarge smiled and looked at me, then back to her. "An' how do you know that?"

"'Cause it's whiskey. I know what that is."

Sarge smiled and patted her head as he stood up. Taylor grabbed my arm, laying her head against my arm. I looked over at her and asked if she was okay. She said she was fine, but I know her too well. Something was eating at her. She eventually got up and went into the shop and started to nose around the shelves of supplies. Sarge watched her as she went in, then jerked his head, indicating we should all walk away from the supplies for a bit.

"You guys know that after what went down today that staying here is a bad idea, right?" Sarge said quietly.

"Maybe, but they don't know it was us," Danny said.

"How many other people around here got wagons like those?" Sarge said, pointing to the buggies sitting in front of the shop. "You can bet yer ass they know who was out there, and they *will* be coming for us."

"What do you think we should do?" Thad asked.

"It's not what I think, it's what's got to be done. We need to un-ass this place. It's time to go," Sarge said flatly.

Danny and I shared a look. It was obvious to everyone that we weren't on board with the idea.

"Look, guys, I agree with him. If we stay here, people are going to die," Mike said.

"I agree," Ted added.

"I personally don't care what we do, as long as it keeps my ass alive," Jeff said.

I looked at my house and property, then back at Danny. "I don't want to leave. As bad as things are right now, at least my family has their home."

"I know you don't. Hell, a lot of people have lost everything recently." Sarge paused and looked at Thad. "If you want to keep them alive, we need to get them out of here."

"You've already got one daughter with a bullet wound, Morg. I know you don't want to see it happen again," Doc said.

"How about this," Danny said. "We start moving some stuff out to the cabins, pre-positioning some supplies, and if things go south we can haul ass out of here with the rest of what we may need."

This would be no small feat. The cabins were seventeen miles away on the Alexander Run. With only the Suburban and the buggies, it would take several trips and quite a bit of time to get done, which added to the urgency. If Sarge was correct and they did make a move on us here, we'd never get out with what we needed if we hesitated. Plus the sooner we started this and had people stationed on the river, the smaller the chance of someone else moving into the cabins. I started to change my mind on the matter.

It was agreed that we should start moving some stuff out as a precaution. Reggie said he wanted to take the pigs, which led to a discussion about how to pen them up. He said he had a solar-powered hot-wire rig. Sarge said we could use that and pen them up against the creek, using it as a natural barrier.

The next issue was how to secure what we took out there. Sarge started going over a head count and how we could split everyone up, but he was forgetting some people.

"Don't forget about Mel and the girls, plus Bobbie," I said.

Sarge paused for a moment. "Can they use weapons?"

"Bobbie can," Danny said.

"Mel, Taylor and Lee Ann can," I said.

"I can too!"

We looked back to see Little Bit standing there. Her comment got a giggle out of everyone.

"I bet you can," Ted said with a smile, shaking his head.

"I can. My daddy taught me."

"So there are thirteen of us, then. All right." Sarge laughed.

The plan we came up with would send Jeff and Mike out to the cabins. With only two of them, it would be tough to maintain a constant watch, but we hoped that being so far out in the woods would cut down on the number of potential intruders. In addition to keeping an eye on things, they would start on some of the projects we would need in place should we have to bug out. Sarge wanted us to do an inventory of everything we had that could be useful to take. With so many people, it was sure to be a substantial pile of supplies.

Sarge said he would take watch down at the barricade, and Thad volunteered to go with him. We all agreed to meet in the morning. Once everyone was gone, I went inside. Mel was just walking out of the bedroom, rubbing the sleep from her face.

"When did you get back?"

"Not long ago. How was your nap?"

"Good. I feel great. You hungry?"

"Of course," I answered as I headed for the living room to check on Lee Ann.

She was still on the couch, as she had been when I left, listening to music on the iPad and drawing. She looked up as I came in and stretched her arms out, the universal sign for a hug. Sitting down on the edge of the couch, I gave her a hug and she pulled the earbuds out. I asked how her leg was, and she said it was feeling better and asked if she could go outside for a while to take a short walk. Danny had come across a crutch from somewhere, and Lee Ann was using it to get around. I told her she could but to be careful and take her sisters with her. She started to hobble toward the back door. With her gone, I went in to talk to Mel about the plan to start moving some supplies out to the cabins. She couldn't remember where the cabins were located, even though we had seen them before when we kayaked down the run.

"What are they like?"

"Primitive."

"How primitive?"

"They're just plywood, really, but they're solid and will make a decent place should we need to go to them."

"Well, I hope we don't have to go to them."

"Me too, but it's better safe than sorry. And after what happened today, we may have to."

"Why? What'd you guys do?"

"I'll tell you later," I said as I headed for the back door. I didn't want to scare her right now. The girls were outside throwing a Frisbee around, with Lee Ann leaning on her crutch, catching the tosses that passed within arm's reach. It was nice to see them hanging out together, actually doing something besides bickering.

I stepped outside and intercepted the Frisbee from Little Bit, then threw it, tousling her hair as I continued to the edge of our property. It'd been a couple of days since I'd seen my neighbor Howard, which was unusual. I decided to go check on him; the last time I saw him he didn't look so good. I headed for his place, nervous about what I was going to find.

There was no answer to my knock so I tried again and waited. It was obvious no one was coming, and I couldn't hear any movement in the house, so I opened the door and called out. There was no reply, only a smell that assaulted my nostrils. Pulling a bandanna from my pocket, I covered my nose and ventured in. I found Howard lying still in his chair, a viscous discharge dripping from the dressing on his leg. His wife was on the couch across from his chair, slumped over with a syringe in her hand. It was just as Doc predicted— they were too proud to ask for help, and now they had reached their end. No wonder he had left them a bottle of morphine. In this new world, sometimes an option that you normally wouldn't entertain was the only way out for folks in dire straits.

The saddest part about standing in Howard's house looking at his bloated body was what I was thinking: I had two more graves to dig. It seemed like this was an almost-daily routine at this point. But it was getting late, and I wasn't about to start digging in the dark. I left the house—one more day certainly wasn't going to make a difference to them.

Once back inside my house, I told Mel I was going to Reggie's house to talk to him for a minute. She asked why and I told her about Howard. While she was certainly sorry to hear, Mel didn't know them very well and so the impact was minimal—just another death. She said she wanted to go to Reggie's too, just to get out of the house, which sounded like a good plan to me. She called the girls inside and told Taylor we'd be back shortly. Taylor asked if she could make popcorn—it was becoming a rare treat, but after witnessing the gruesome events next door, I felt like I wanted to give my girls whatever bit of happiness I could. Lee Ann wanted to watch a movie and Little Bit started going through the DVDs. With the girls settled, we headed out.

Mel climbed on the Polaris, wrapping her arms around me. As I pulled through the gate, I tooted the horn at Thad and Sarge, who both waved.

Jeff was splitting wood by the front door.

"Hey, man, where's Reggie?"

Jeff pulled his gloves off. "Out back, I think. Hi, Mel."

"Hey, Jeff, thanks for splitting some wood for us."

Jeff laughed. "Oh yeah, no problem. You did bring a hot dinner, right?"

I laughed at that one and we started around the house to find Reggie. He was at the barn cutting up a palm heart, throwing the pieces to the pigs.

"Hey, Morg." He nodded his head toward Mel. "Mel, you trust this clown to drive you around?"

"Yeah, I do now. Doesn't happen too often these days," Mel replied.

"I guess not. What's up?"

I told him about Howard and his wife. I didn't even have to tell him we needed to dig graves.

"I'll bring the tractor over in the morning," he said, sighing a bit as he said it.

"Thanks, man; it makes it a lot easier. When are you guys going to start moving stuff?"

"Tomorrow. The old man is making a list of what he wants to take first."

When I asked what kind of stuff was on the list, he laughed and answered, "Weird shit. PVC pipe, the gabions from the barricade, empty buckets, garden tools, fence, rolls of wire." The thing that really topped the list was that Sarge wanted him to go around and check every abandoned house for a water filter, and if there was one he wanted the purple stuff inside it.

"Potassium permanganate has lots of uses," I said.

"Like what?" Mel asked me.

"Water purification for one, explosives for another."

Don't miss any of the riveting installments in the
Survivalist Series

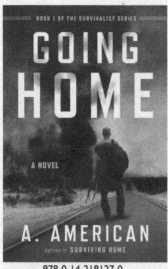
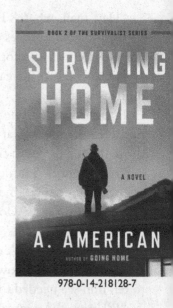
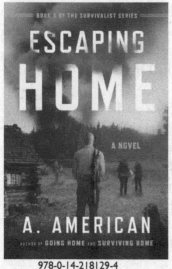